Ann Schlee was born in the United States in 1934. She spent her childhood there and later lived in Egypt, Sudan and Northern Ethiopia. She went to school in England and later to Somerville College, Oxford. She is married with four grown-up children and lives with her husband in South London. She has written several children's books and two other novels, *Rhine Journey* and *The Proprietor*.

Author photograph by Jerry Bauer

Also by Ann Schlee

THE PROPRIETOR

and published by Black Swan

Laing

Ann Schlee

'Certainly he who has made the Koran for thee shall
lead thee back to thy point of departure.'

The Koran.

BLACK SWAN

LAING

A BLACK SWAN BOOK 0 552 99344 1

Originally published in Great Britain
by Macmillan London Limited

PRINTING HISTORY

Macmillan London edition published 1987
Black Swan edition published 1989

This book is set in 10/11 pt Mallard
by Colset Private Limited, Singapore.

Black Swan Books are published by
Transworld Publishers Ltd., 61–63
Uxbridge Road, Ealing, London W5 5SA, in
Australia by Transworld Publishers
(Australia) Pty. Ltd., 15–23 Helles Avenue,
Moorebank, NSW 2170, and in
New Zealand by Transworld Publishers
(N.Z.) Ltd., Cnr. Moselle and Waipareira
Avenues, Henderson, Auckland.

Made and printed in Great Britain by
The Guernsey Press Co. Ltd.,
Guernsey, Channel Islands.

for James Hale

Contents

Prologue – Edinburgh

In the autumn of 1825 Captain Alexander Laing began to compose the story of his life. *The accusation of egotism will be levelled against me*, he wrote, *that I who am distinguished neither by birth, nor as yet by any great achievement, should seek to lay before the world these events and seek to claim for them an individuality* . . .

For reasons of economy he spent his leave at his father's academy in Edinburgh. A further month must be endured before he might return to Africa. He worked during the mornings in his father's drawing room, completing for the printers an account of his recent journey to the hinterland of Sierra Leone. In his oblique regular righthand script he wrote of the moonlit forest near Falaba where he made a final recognition of his destiny; of the old king Assana Yeera, who had said, 'My son, I see your heart is set upon the water, but it is well-known that if you were to leap over the Great River at its source a demon would wrench off your right arm and cut your head from your body.'

In the afternoons, to keep himself in perfect fitness, he walked through the grey streets to the uncanny green of the countryside beyond. Sometimes the black soldier-servant he had brought with him from Freetown walked with him and they were heard to talk like equals in an outlandish tongue, but even when he walked alone the townswomen turned to look after him. He was a tall, well-built man. His youth had hardened in him but not yet wasted. The skin of his face and hands was burnt a deep yellowish brown, quite unlike the ruddy weathering of the country people. His eye, they noticed, was quick and attentive, but focused it seemed at distances beyond their ken. He walked with all the force of an intention long frustrated and long sustained. Four hours later

11

they watched him return with an unwearied stride. When he had dined he retired early from the rigours of his father's table and climbed the stairway to the attic room he had occupied as a boy. There he set out a number of pocket note-books filled with the story of his youthful service in the West India Station and later in West Africa. Night after night in the little attic room he transcribed the tale they told of unremitting effort; for, while the foppish subalterns with whom he served might buy promotion, he must win his by industry or daring. He wrote laboriously in the clear upright script of his left hand to practise it lest any injury to his right hand should prevent his keeping a daily record of his great forthcoming journey.

Then, when the lingering northern light finally faded, he stretched out fully dressed on the bare floor-boards to keep himself in hardiness for his return to Africa.

Part I: Tripoli

At nine o'clock on the morning of May the thirteenth, 1825, a ship was sighted off the port of Tripoli. Immediately a single shot was fired from the palace battlements to advise the town of its arrival. No one paid much heed. The fast of Ramadan was entering its second week; an air of leaden endurance hung about the streets. Only in the palace itself was there a stirring of interest.

In an upstairs room the Bashaw's foreign minister, old Mohammed d'Ghies, heard the reverberations. He recalled that the brig-of-war *Gannet* was a day overdue from Malta. A decision must be reached about the magnitude of salute proper, at the present time, for a British ship of the line. The Bashaw must be roused and informed. Lengthy negotiations could be counted on to follow. At the same time he thought of the report of his informant in Malta that an English traveller had been detained there by fever and would presently arrive in Tripoli on a secret mission to the interior. He had a servant stand by in readiness to ride to Ghadames and alert the Sheikh Babani so soon as the English traveller's arrival was confirmed. He sent a second servant to the French Consulate to inform the Baron Rousseau of these events.

The sound had penetrated to the small darkened room off the first courtyard where the Bet-el-Mel, the keeper of the palace, sat cross-legged on the floor. He too had heard of the English traveller and his mission. The debts of the last such mission were still in part unpaid. Here then was the means to extract the money owing from Colonel Warrington, the British Consul; to incite further debts; to sell at one and the same time his powers to delay and expedite. He too sent to the Baron Rousseau inviting him to call at the palace within the hour. Colonel Warrington must wait his turn.

*   *   *

15

Some wayward gust of wind may even have carried a faint echo of the cannon's thud across the bay to the British Consul's garden outside the town. There, in a room crowded with muslin-tented beds, his three daughters slept. Lately, through the misdemeanour of one of them, they had all been denied permission to attend the evening parties which gave purpose to their lives. Boredom had caused them to retire early and sleep late. The sound did not wake them but perhaps it penetrated their dreams for presently, one after the other, the muslin curtains heaved. Their veiled forms were seen to sit upright. Pale feet and legs appeared over the edges of the beds. They moved about heavy-footed and unconscious of themselves and spoke to one another in sleep-thickened voices. Brilliant light penetrated the room. Soon the shutters must be drawn to protect the house from the savagery of the noonday heat, but for now the air was pleasant. Through the open windows came the soft turbulence of pigeons battering to and fro under the eaves and the cheerful voices of the gardeners splashing water on the flower beds. Another empty day was set upon its course and could not now turn back, but perhaps the cannon's echo lingered somewhere in their cluttered thoughts, for as they fastened up the drawstrings of each other's dresses and combed up their hair their minds were filled with boundless expectation of what the day might bring.

Breakfast at the English Garden was served promptly at ten. The Consul rose early and waited in his room of business until his golden hunter chimed the hour. Then, with his three spaniels Clowder, Bellman, Merriman, running on ahead of him, he strode across the hall. In the dining room his wife and children waited behind their allotted chairs. The spaniels disappeared beneath the table. The Consul took his place at its head. He studied for a moment the table napkins folded in peaks, the clusters of porcelain, the ranks of cutlery, and felt the swift shift of emotion, relief perhaps, that everything was in its proper place, kept by him for one more day from some general disintegration just beyond the compass of his mind.

Four servants stood, backs to the wall; all slaves he had redeemed, Christians, though Papists, who for reasons of their own had chosen not to return to their wretched hovels in Malta or Gibraltar. Little wiry men who always looked ill-shaven. Over them he held absolute sway, as over his wife, whose mild and humourless gaze he was careful to avoid.

Of his children he was less sure. Although they observed the semblances of awe he thought they more or less ignored him. He stood behind his chair, a tall man in the prime of life. A habit of constant activity had kept his body strong and vigorous. His features were well-proportioned and printed so strongly with conviction that no one was ever tempted to attribute to stupidity something fixed and unreceptive in their cast. He spoke the grace and endured the clatter and confusion of their sitting down.

'Well,' he said to them when they were quiet. 'Well, what have you done today of benefit to anyone?'

Once a voice had answered in all honesty, 'Nothing, Papa.'

'Nothing?' he had shouted. 'Nothing will come of nothing.'

Now wisely they kept silent.

'Well?' he repeated. 'Well?' As if there were some answer they deliberately withheld. Yet when they sat there with their heads bowed, their hands beneath the table, he could take pleasure in them; six fine children raised in this God-forsaken place.

He peeled a fig and continued to survey them. Fred, on his mother's right, looked like a Moor, dressed like a Moor, spoke like a Moor. Not, thank God, his heir – two elder sons were serving in Gibraltar. Next to him the youngest girl, Louisa. Then Harry, who might have been himself as a boy, tall and sturdy. Well-featured. A hard goer, like himself. A good boy. On his right the eldest daughter, Jane, his Jenny. There, too, his heart approved. Ossy then, the youngest, undistinguished as yet by any failing other than a tendency to fidget. Then Emma, the middle daughter, who had fallen under his displeasure.

Three days ago the dinner ritual had been disturbed by a most unfortunate occurrence. The grace had been said, the meal begun. The seeded centre of a fig had broken coolly under the pressure of his tongue. 'Just right,' he had called out to Vincenzio, his major-domo. 'They should be picked.' He had dabbed at his lips with his napkin. Then, as he replaced it, stiff and shiny with starch, it had slid from his knee. The servants all were occupied. The Consul himself stooped to

17

retrieve it and found himself staring into an inchoate world just below the decorous surface of the table. He saw a restless jumble of arms and legs, hands gripping one another, whose he could not recognise; dogs being fed, covertly, against his express command; and a note being passed from lap to lap. He had raised his flushed face above the cloth and said, 'Give me that note.' There was a total silence. He had been forced to repeat himself. Then Emma had silently laid the folded paper on the cloth and pushed it towards him. He opened the note and began to read. For an instant the words meant nothing to him. Then he recognised they were in French, a language he declined to learn. Nevertheless no one can reach maturity entirely innocent of its terms. Ma chérie, he was forced to read and, glancing swiftly to the end, Je t'embrasse mille fois, Timoleon. Rousseau's son. He was profoundly shocked. The more so that she sat there looking as innocent as a child with her white dress drawn up like a purse about her neck, her hair cropped short and combed upright with rose water. He had leant and smelt at it with pleasure when he passed, but minutes before. Good God, he thought, it's no time since she was a child, and calculated swiftly that she could be no more than seventeen.

With an admirable restraint, inspired more by respect for the dignity of his table than any consideration for his daughter's feelings, he had controlled himself, pocketed the note, and continued with his fig. Even when the meal was ended he had avoided any distressing scene. Nor had he made contact with the Baron Rousseau. He had merely had his daughters all confined to the precincts of the country house and ordered Vincenzio to hand at once to him any messages delivered at the gate addressed to them.

Still, the incident had left a sour aftertaste which made the atmosphere at table more stiff and silent than it need have been. The Consul would have cajoled them into speaking cheerfully if he could have devised some way of doing so, without appearing to. He could not, and so was all the more relieved when Vincenzio bent to whisper in his ear that a ship had been sighted in the offing and was making its way into the harbour. He thought at once of Captain Laing who had written from Malta of his interesting mission, and of the brig-of-war *Gannet* on which he was due. He rose from the table and strode from the room, shouting for the syce to bring his horse. His spaniels fled before him with lowered heads and upturned eyes.

A quarter of an hour later he was mounted and tapping impatiently on his boot with his riding crop. At last his *chouish*, the Bashaw's man who dogged his every footstep as protector and spy, appeared running from the stable compound, pulling his horse by one hand while with the other he looped his turban hastily about his head. The gates were dragged open and within minutes the Consul was galloping across the dusty plain that lay between him and the gleaming bastions of the town. The *chouish* followed in his dust, struggling to keep up with him.

For the brief duration of the journey the Consul's mind was free to consider this new circumstance. If Laing were aboard, his arrival would be most timely. It was barely four months since the Consul had presided over the triumphant return of Captain Clapperton's mission to the Fezzan. He had celebrated the occasion with a reception of the entire diplomatic corps. Arches of jasmine and orange blossom had decorated the street outside the consulate. The Bashaw himself had attended and taken Mrs Warrington into supper on his arm. Of all wines the Consul had ever found champagne to be the most briskly exhilarating. He had told his servants not to stint its flow.

But only temporarily did the thought of it distract the Consul from the sad decline in his fortunes. The champagne was still to be paid for at a time when his creditors were pressing him severely for larger sums incurred five years ago in the building of his country house. Recent despatches from Whitehall had been remarkably cool on the subject of further public monies borrowed of necessity to facilitate Captain Clapperton's mission. For weeks now the Bashaw, to whom a further sum was owed in connection with that mission, had refused him an audience, although the Consul knew full well from his informants that Rousseau was with him at all hours, jabbering God knows what sedition in the heathen tongue. And now Emma and the odious Timoleon.

It struck the Consul then that if such a man as Rousseau's son felt free to make advances to his daughter, his fortunes must indeed be at their nadir. As he rode steadily on towards the town an abyss of spirit threatened to open for him on the sun-scoured plain; it seemed to Colonel Warrington, as on a number of disastrous occasions in the past, that nothing but a wager on the very highest stakes could hope to restore his affairs to a secure footing.

At once his thoughts returned to Captain Laing, of whom he knew nothing other than that he was a soldier. The better for that. Too often previous expeditions had been manned by sailors, or worse still civilians, who were prone to dying. And the man was not without experience. His letters had made mention of command of native forces in Sierra Leone and against the Ashanti. A colonial regiment, then; the best the poor fellow could manage, no doubt. But the Consul did not hold that against him. He had seen action, was seasoned in the climate. That was what counted. Though there had been something – the too even spacing of the steeply, oblique hand, the ornate signature, the too consciously graceful turn of phrase – that made him doubt Laing was a gentleman entirely. But an educated man. The Consul had respect for that and was ever inclined to optimism.

As he rode he kept his gaze fixed on the point in the palace battlements where at any moment further puffs of smoke would mark the full salute as the ship sailed into the harbour. All still. Some delay, then. At the stable outside the town gates he asked the man who took his horse, 'Whose ship is it?'

'Non so, Eccellenza.' But the Consul was sure it was the *Gannet.* He strode in through the town gate.

The *chouish* took the lead now, laying about him vigorously with his stick to clear the Consul's way through the narrow alleys of the *souk.* His show of zeal was scarcely necessary; owing to the fast the coffee shops were tightly shuttered. Only a few old men sat about on their thresholds, piously hawking their spittle into the road. Even the incessant tapping of the metal workers seemed muted. The Consul thought the place half-dead. Certainly there was no trace of the apprehension the approach of a British warship should occasion. He quickened his stride as he neared the blank white walls of his town consulate.

His Moorish guards leapt from their benches in the entrance hall with much stamping of boots and slapping of muskets. A number of ragged petitioners also rose from the benches and began in wailing tones to ask for this or that in languages he did not understand. One knelt at his feet and grasped around the calf of his dusty boot. 'Not now,' the Consul said impatiently. While the *chouish* beat the fellow about the head and shoulders the Consul stepped free of him into the courtyard and began rapidly to mount the narrow stairway to the roof, two steps at a time.

Once there he made his way between the grain and red peppers spread out to dry on its flat surface, past the flagstaff and the restless shadow of his country's flag, to the corner where his brass telescope stood mounted on a tripod. He swung this instrument until he caught in its lens first the ship and then the little scrap of bunting which proclaimed it to be indeed his King's.

It was for such moments that the Consul lived. His long presence in Tripoli had been a statement, a lonely one at times, that such a ship existed; that others more heavily ordnanced might wait in line just below the horizon; that a word from him might summons them. For twelve years his daily task had been to keep alive the Bashaw's belief in this genie power of his. Lately he had almost come to doubt it himself. Recent manifestations of England's might had seemed distant, arbitrary and altogether unrelated to any scheme of his. Now faith returned. For several seconds he allowed the little flag to fill his eye. Then deftly he swung the tube back towards the land. Flat rooftops, brilliant sky flashed across the lens. The wheeling speck of a kite blackened it entirely. Then it fell with the exactitude of long practice onto the nearby roof of the French Consulate and caught the portly figure of the Baron Rousseau bending and peering just as he had done into that magnified network of spars and rigging in search of his accursed *tricolore*.

It was too hot to linger on the roof. The Consul went below to the cool shuttered room which served him as an office. There he settled at his desk and set about the pleasant task of drafting a despatch for the *Gannet* to take on the first leg of its journey to Whitehall. At the end of the page he left a careful gap in which to record Laing's arrival and the magnitude of the salute when these should be revealed to him. Next he wrote to his wife instructing her to come into the town with her elder children. Emma might accompany them, but not attend the evening's entertainment. The messenger who took the note was to return at once with the Consul's dress uniform.

In his enthusiasm he reached for more paper and wrote one by one to his diplomatic colleagues, inviting them to a reception to greet the new arrival. The de Breughels. Poor old Croutchillo from Naples. Negri, the Sardinian. Dr Dickson and his Molly. The Spaniards who could be counted on not to come. Coxe, the American, who drank too much but had a pretty daughter. Rossini, the Tuscan, and his Maltese signora whose obese charms so fascinated the Bashaw. He had forgotten the Dane, the fool Knutson, worth enduring to reach a hand once more about his wife. And, there was no avoiding it, though out of a sense of decency he penned it last, Rousseau, his wife, that unlovely Greek, and the sickly Timoleon. He remembered then the note and taking it from his pocket scrawled across it. *These ungentlemanly attentions cause distress and embarrassment to my daughter.* He enclosed this with the invitation.

An hour had passed. He went back to the roof. The brig now lay abreast the town and the telescope revealed that it was indeed the *Gannet*. Dinner was served at four. He ordered that an extra place be laid, but when, an hour later, the guns were still silent he dined alone and returned to his lonely vigil at his desk.

Benign thoughts spread now to include his family. Even Emma, pretty Emma, he found he could forgive. For surely she had been his favourite once, when she and Jane were little girls, and she, the livelier of the two, had run about these gloomy rooms prattling and laughing, filling just that portion of the mind's mid-distance which daughters should inhabit. That young Rousseau was infatuated with her he supposed possible. That old Rousseau would take every advantage of the situation he had no doubt. But she might yet be innocent. She was a child. The more he reflected, the more it seemed that love had not come into it at all: that the whole had been a plot of Rousseau's to establish a means of spying upon him through his daughter. The more the simple wickedness of this became apparent, the more he was assured of Emma's innocence. Why, in this very room she had climbed upon his knee when he pretended to sleep and with her little fingers pried open his eyelids, to make him look at her. Could twelve years have passed so swiftly? She was still a little thing. A fragile thing. How could he have allowed his wrath to fall upon her? Sweet thing. Sweet monkey. What could such a creature know of love.

He sat unusually still in the half-darkness of the shuttered room, his fingers pressed together at their tips with a pleasant tingling sensation. Dreams of a wider, vaguer redemption followed and were interrupted only by the boom of cannon from the palace batteries. One, two three. Instantly the Consul dipped his pen and with slow careful strokes began to note down each successive shot.

By the time he had counted up to twenty, the Consul's heartbeat far outpaced the steady thud, thud, thud. Twenty-four. Twenty-five. Twenty-six. The next pause seemed interminable, lengthened intentionally to torment him. Then twenty-seven, twenty-eight, twenty-nine. The full thirty.

The Consul's triumph was complete. The world which had seemed so out of sorts in the morning had righted itself entirely. He went out onto the balcony which overlooked the central courtyard of the house and demanded of a servant whether his uniform had arrived yet from the country. It had. He ordered it brought up directly. He pulled on the trousers and had the servant help him into the coat. This was a handsome garment, scarlet faced with blue and heavily encrusted with gold thread at shoulders, collar and cuffs. His cocked hat was generously decorated with ostrich plumes, purchased locally at half the price he would have paid in London.

Shortly afterwards, resplendent in this uniform which was entirely of his own devising, he left the Consulate with the *chouish* still at his heels and made his way down to the harbour gate.

Laing had stood at dawn on the deck of the *Gannet*, straining to catch a first sight of the town. Already it had been spotted from the rigging and soon he was able to make out a white patch on the low unrevealing coastline of Africa. Two hours later, when the palace's battlement had grown distinct, he watched a puff of smoke detach itself and float upward into the still blue sky. There followed the dull thud of a cannon.

By noon the brig lay at anchor before the dazzling city walls. He ordered his man, Jack, and the two boatwrights he had taken on in Malta to stack all his baggage on the deck, confident that they would be disembarked within the hour, with ample time to seek out the market, purchase native clothing, hire mules and make enquiries about the departure of the caravan. By nightfall he intended to have transported everything through the town and set up camp among a straggling grove of palms visible to the east of the city walls.

These early hopes soon faded. Apparently they could make no move until they were welcomed by the Bashaw's official salute. The sun blazed on the deck. The gunners crouched, sweating and sullen, in what little shade their guns provided. Hour followed hour while the town remained silent and closed to him. Then at last smoke appeared again above the battlements, followed by the opening shot of the salute. Laing retired to his cabin, partly to escape from the din, partly to hide from the ship's officers the violence of his agitation. There, after some debate, he deemed it wise to struggle into the trousers and button up the tunic of his scarlet regimentals. The pomp and publicity of all this gunfire had put him in mind of the British Consul, with whom he had exchanged a number of formal letters from Malta. It occurred to him now that the Consul might see fit to meet him on the quay and that he should dress accordingly. It was not the unobtrusive entry he had wished to make, but the day was now exhausted. There was no hope of setting up camp by nightfall; no alternative but to put himself and his people at the mercy of the Consul's hospitality.

The firing from the shore came to an end and immediately the *Gannet* was shaken by the answering salute. When all was done Laing mounted the companionway in an atmosphere still hazy and reeking with cordite, to find the entire crew lining the rails and manning the rigging. At the sight of him the three young officers flung up their arms and shouted, 'Hip, hip, hip . . .

From the steep triangles of men stacked against the fading sky came a great answering 'Hoorah!' The sound ringing out on the recently silenced air, the generosity of feeling that lay behind it, moved him greatly. Words would not form. He wrung the hands of each of the officers in turn and felt with shame the uncomfortable sensations in his body: the thudding heart, the smarting eyes, the lurch of his sick gut. All must sternly be ignored. He concentrated instead on Mind and felt his spirits borne upward on that magnificent sound, free of the grosser self.

He raised his military cap from his head and waved it slowly to and fro. They cheered again. Their goodwill, their simple acknowledgement of bravery, their love of their homeland racketed about the sky.

A brightly canopied barge was now seen making its way towards the *Gannet*. The first officer identified it as the Bashaw's. It came alongside. One of the oarsmen shouted up for the Capitano Inglese. Immediately Jack and the two boatmen began to hand down the baggage and followed it themselves. Laing shook hands and once more another cheer was raised. He too climbed down onto the barge which, without delay, set out for the shore. The luggage was piled high in the centre. Jack le Bore sat with his bugle case upon his knee. The two boatwrights, Rogers and Harris, sat beside him, all with their shoulders pinched together, their eyes and lips wide and happy, their nostrils flared for the first whiff of Africa. Laing sat opposite, turning his head this way and that and seeing enchantment everywhere.

The Bashaw's men pulled strongly, but the evening breeze had risen and blew against them from the shore so that their progress was almost negligible. It blew from the direction of the palms where he had planned to camp and carried with it a delicious odour of spice and blossom, which Laing in his elated mood took to be the very breath of the place. The town itself, withheld still at this distance, appeared as staunch and gay as Camelot, with its vast fortifications, its minarets and consular flags showing above the battlements. The rest was hidden. He savoured this strangeness which, minute by minute, the eye must erode. The walls and domes flushed with colour as if he watched a sudden resurgence of the day, then as they entered the harbour the quick dusk of the Mediterranean fell on his illusions. Torches had been lit by the harbour gate. They threw an obscure and dramatic light on the quay, where now Laing made out what must be the figure of Colonel Warrington pacing strenuously about among the lounging figures of the Moors.

He had been advised from one quarter in Malta to make no move without the advice of Colonel Warrington; from another, to avoid involvement with him at any cost. Douce, douce, he told himself. There was no escaping him: the last old man to stand between him and the realisation of his scheme.

Colonel Warrington, as the barge drew in, spotted Laing without difficulty by his scarlet coat, and noticed with surprise that his three companions were all as black as the ace of spades.

He too had heard the cheers echo across the water and in the emotion of the moment would have rushed forward had not a native shrewdness held him back. He waited where he was and let Laing climb up upon the quay and approach him, thinking, What have we here? What have they sent us this time? But so poor was the light that he could make out little of this new contendent beyond his respectable height, his soldierly bearing, his air of assurance in speaking to his own people. All this boded exceptionally well. Impulse overcame him. He strode forward, holding out his hand in frank approval, saying with true warmth of feeling, 'My dear sir. Captain Laing.'

Major Laing in the field, but that might wait till morning. For the present they stood with their hands gripped together in a mutual enthusiasm, while Laing's people handed the luggage up the steps.

'I have much to thank you for in advance,' Laing said. 'Your letters. Your encouragement.'

He was a Scot. The moment he spoke it was apparent. No matter. 'They gave poor indication,' the Consul said, 'of how completely I shall devote myself to the success of your mission.'

'England has a true friend in you,' Laing said next.

'A devoted servant only. And a fearless officer in you. No. No. I have been told.'

By whom, Laing thought? Which version of himself? But they had reached a stalemate of goodwill. Both at the same moment directed their attention to the mounting pile of baggage at their feet: the fifty or so bundles of gifts purchased in Malta for the greater and lesser chiefs along his route, the boxes of instruments and medicines, the portfolio.

On the quay the lounging Moors had come alarmingly to life. The air was filled with hectic utterances. They fell upon Laing's goods as if dividing plunder. He had intended to take a careful inventory on the quay, but that was impossible without discourtesy to the Consul, who seemed filled with an admirable zeal to move forward. Laing saw the box of instruments heaved up onto a skull-cap as if it were a sack of corn.

'Mon dieu,' cried Jack, snatching at it.

'French?' hissed the Consul. He made it a dreadful syllable.

'My man,' Laing told him. 'French-speaking. From San Domingo.'

'Good God. Is he loyal?'

'Entirely.'

The Consul took Laing by the elbow now and propelled him forward with all the certainty of one who knows the road ahead. With his free arm he gestured violently to the Moors to follow them through the harbour gate, at the same time leaning towards Laing and saying in a low, triumphant voice, 'Thirty. Did you count them? Only twenty-six last month for a British ship of the line! I told His Bashawness direct. Went straight to the palace. He likes me for that. Thirty guns, I told him, for a British warship. No more. No less. But no chance until today to put it to the test.'

They had passed under a massive gateway. The Moors leaning there, rapt in the monotonous dream of their own lives, watched Laing's entry to their town with only a clouded interest. The chouish, whom Laing supposed to be a servant, went ahead swinging a lantern from side to side. The light slid down a white wall, over the accretion of dust that filled its angle with the road and then danced up again before it showed him the uneven surface. A shadowy dog slipped past them and looked back with lowered head. The light flared in his flat green eye. *The evil eye*, a phrase he'd read and relished as a boy, came back to him.

The Consul, as he strode on ahead, was saying in a loud deep voice, 'There's some say you can only know these fellows if you speak their lingo. But I say none of that. They understand me well enough. Stick to the essentials. Stick to the things you can point your finger at. Don't get drawn into niceties. Don't get drawn into promises. That's always been my way.'

27

In the dark Laing released his little smile. He was fluent in French, Mandingo and Fantee, and during his recent illness in Malta had made a start on Arabic.

'My children all speak it,' the Consul went on. 'Jabber like Moors. Even the girls. I let them go to court. They're in great demand among the women there, in the hareem. Useful, you know. I call them my spies. My pretty spies. They like the sweetmeats, and carry back all sorts of gossip, prattle on about all sorts of things they scarcely understand.'

'As well,' Laing thought grimly in the dark. He had little taste for confidence.

Now the Consul was saying, as people will to strangers, 'I have eight children. All beautiful children. And good, I trust. I've raised them strictly, Captain Laing, as my old father, and I bless him for it, raised me. But it was a different world then, a harder world but a safer one. I'm much perplexed at times as to what to do for them. I'd an education of a sort. My father cared about such things, but they've had none. It is a great anxiety to me.'

As he spoke he turned without warning through an arched entry-way lit with torches. A guard scrambled to attention. 'You'll meet them presently,' the Consul said, 'and all our little circle.'

In the short time it had taken the Consul to collect Laing from the quay the consulate had been transformed. The central courtyard had been covered with a canvas awning, to accommodate the evening's guests, and lit with hanging lanterns. It made a pretty, exotic room with its fountains and its fragrant trees in pots. A number of servants shouted directions at one another as they manhandled a pianoforte into position by the cloister.

'I shan't detain you,' the Consul was saying to Laing. 'The guests will be here soon. You'll want to wash yourself. Hot water for the Reis here,' he said loudly to the servants, twisting his hands vigorously as if none of them understood any language and all must be done in dumb show.

The first of Laing's luggage was carried into the consulate. He followed the porters up the narrow stairs and out onto the central balcony. There he was shown into a room where by now boxes and canvas bundles were being stowed about the walls. Jack le Bore squatted on the tiled floor, head down to his knees in concentration as he unrolled the various strips of cloth which held the tools of his particular mystery: the blacking, the dubbin, the bone, for Laing's boots; the polish, the leather, the sheepskin buffer, the notched metal plate for his buttons; the razor and the strop.

Laing smiled at him and shrugged. More luggage was carried in. He directed it here and there. 'Leave it as it is,' he ordered Jack. 'It's all to be taken down again tomorrow.'

The hot water was handed through the door in jugs. Jack shaved him before it cooled. Then, while Laing washed, the Creole found a clean shirt for him and shook it out and brushed the woollen tunic. Later he helped Laing into it and held up a little square of mirror while Laing ran his wet fingers through his springy reddish hair and plucked at the brighter, coarser whiskers growing on his cheeks.

He was uncertain whether to go down or wait until he was summoned. The room seemed intolerably confined. Its only window looked inward on the courtyard. He went out onto the inner balcony and, leaning on the rail in the still warm night, listened to the excited sounds of preparation of which he himself was the cause. Below light glowed up through the canvas roof. On the floor above a candle flame moved along the gallery, winking through its wooden grille. Overhead in the patch of sky above the courtyard, the large close stars of Africa paled with the rising of the moon.

He made his way to the stairwell and then climbed upward to the next floor and above until he reached the narrow doorway that gave onto the roof. He pushed it open and stood in the open air at last with nothing to impede his view. He could make out nothing of the town beyond a mass of other roofs sloped this way and that, giving no indication of the streets below. Here and there a dome or a minaret rose between them. Moonlight lay over all like an encroachment of sand; no sound, no colour, all life smothered. Far out in the bay white sails moved, but so utter was the silence that it was impossible to believe that any human agency drove them forward.

Awe made it difficult to turn and face the unbroken continent behind him, but presently he did and going to the far parapet stood staring beyond the city to the still luminous distance. He had hoped by nightfall to have taken his first steps into that shining waste.

'Douce, douce,' he told himself, 'what's one more day?'

For he had been five years about this business. In 1820 he had penetrated the hinterland of Sierra Leone to Falaba and the mountains beyond, far enough to have seen through his glass the rocky slopes of Mount Soma where the Niger had its source. With the glass to his eye it had seemed he might reach out and move aside the rock that hid its first shy welling. And still it was denied to him. He had turned back within three days' march of that longed-for sight, mastered by Body's weakness and an old man's dream. It was not the sickness. Had he been dying he would have crawled on until he reached it. He had turned back only because the old King Assana Yeera had come with tears in his eyes and said, 'My son, I have seen your heart is set upon the water, but I have dreamed a dream that you will die once you have seen it.'

That had been the cause of it: that was why he would not allow Laing further passage along the road, but kept him at Falaba until, worn down by want and sickness, he had been forced to make his way back to the coast. You were duped by him, Mind told Laing. The dream was a ruse to keep you with him. And then, more cruelly, The dream was a ruse to extract more gifts from you. Not so. Not so, Laing told himself. He kept me out of love and superstitious fear. I have returned, he told himself. It has begun again.

He stayed a moment longer to let the moonlight still his spirits. So in the exhaustion and the bitter disappointment of the march from Falaba he had lain down to sleep and waked to find the forest filled with moonlight. His fatigue had fallen from him and he had wandered out among the lofty trees and slanting shafts of moonlight in a state of exaltation. He had known then, with mystic certainty, that even if the river's source were denied him, it was he alone who would reveal her greater secret and trace her course to whatever outlet in whatever sea.

Meanwhile he must endure this evening's entertainment as best he might. He tugged down the hem of his tunic, heaved up his ribs and made his way down into the heated confines of the house.

As soon as he entered the courtyard the Consul came forward

to greet him and, gripping him by the arm, drew him closer to the lamplight.

'My dear sir,' he said at once with warm concern. 'You wrote, of course, that you had been unwell.'

Laing said curtly, 'I am quite recovered.'

Now that he had a better look at him, the Consul could see that the reverse was clearly true. 'Nevertheless,' he said, 'you must allow us to detain you for a day or two at least. You will find yourself an object of particular interest here, especially among the ladies.' He gave a high gesture over his shoulder and immediately a servant came forward with glasses of wine on a tray. 'Believe me, my dear sir, you have overcome the worst of your difficulties already, or will have done before you set out from here. From here the way is as open to you as the road from Edinburgh to London.'

'Edinburgh to London.' He raised his glass. This, it appeared, was a toast in which Laing was bound to join. The wine would reach his head before it struck his liver. He might enjoy it for a time.

The Consul raised his glass again and, smiling formally to Laing, said, 'To your safe and swift arrival at Timbuctoo.'

The word had been spoken. 'To Timbuctoo,' Laing said, and drank again.

The tented courtyard had filled with guests. More came crowding in through the vestibule from the street. As Laing followed the Consul in among them, men turned to stare. Women's faces were raised towards him with their vague uncertain smiles: a handsome man, taller than any in the room except the Consul, who propelled him forward from face to face, from hand to hand. He smiled; he bowed.

'Wood,' the Consul was saying. A sallow lively man. Dark hair, eyes like coals. Looked Greek. 'My friend, Tom Wood, late of the Levant Company, who will act as my vice-consul here when its affairs are settled.'

'How do you do?'

'How do you do?'

'And Dickson. Our quack. Our *hakim*. Hack'em, eh, Dickson? Sawbones, eh?' He was very merry, yet how he played the lord among them with his English voice. 'And Mrs Dickson. Ah, my dear.' And the Consul let his handshake fall appreciatively down to her hip. 'This is Captain Laing. She was my children's governess once,' he said to Laing, moving forward, turning back. 'I married them. Well, why not? It's legal enough. They wanted it and might have fretted out a lifetime and she have gone to waste. A pity, eh?' with a glance at Laing to share with him the pleasure to be had from that harmonious swell of lip and cheek and bosom. 'Women age here,' he said over his shoulder to Laing. 'It can't be helped.'

Now there was a little stick of a man with a large nose. 'Signor Croutchillo.'

'Madame Rossini.' Vast.

'Captain Laing.'

'Captain Laing.' They snatched their likenesses of him. The man who went to Timbuctoo.

'Our Dutch Consul. The doyen of our group. Monsieur de Breughel. Madame de Breughel.'

'Good evening.' He need not trouble to retain their names.

'How glad. How very glad . . .'

'I have so wanted . . .'

'Unfortunately,' the Consul told him, 'Rousseau – he's the Frenchman – was unable to attend. A pity, that.'

The Consul shepherded Laing forward until he came upon his wife in the crush. 'The ladies are all agog to meet you,' he assured him. 'Mrs Warrington, reveal him to the ladies, my dear. And to those sweet monkeys,' and raising his glass above the heads of his guests he followed it away.

She seemed an indeterminate woman whose eyes moved at a slight variance with one another. Laing found difficulty in fixing upon the one her mind directed. He made his bow and said his piece: the charm and unexpectedness of this room . . . the company . . . Someone could be heard to strike up on the pianoforte.

'I am bewildered,' he told her charmingly, 'as to where I am,' and made to look about him in bewilderment. But he was very well aware of where he was. Sweat crept inside his heavy tunic and gleamed in the runnels of his hostess's upper lip, whilst hard portions of other people's bodies nudged him unpleasantly in the back. He must stoop to hear her slow deliberate voice say, 'He means my daughters. We shall raise a dance. There are couples enough. Often there are not, and of course Emma is not here, but Frau Knutson will play, which

32

leaves her husband free to dance, and young Rousseau may yet come and there's yourself, and Amy Coxe and Signora Rossini can always be prevailed upon. You wish to dance, I'm sure . . .' but interrupted herself to say, 'This is Mr Wood.'

Laing said, 'We've met.'

'Mr Wood is Colonel Warrington's new vice-consul. He is an indispensable man!' But immediately he was dispensed with, for, now gripping Laing by the elbow, she led him further into the crowded room, all the time addressing him as confidentially as if he were the closest of her gossips, so that he was forced to cup his hand behind his ear to catch any of it. '. . . most concerned about the younger who is receiving the most pressing attentions from young Rousseau. A good family, but, of course – French.'

He made some sound of condolence.

'Jane,' she told him as she moved him forward, 'is generally held the handsomer of the two and is of course the elder, which is why we are so surprised at the course things have taken.'

'Jane,' she called out in a voice that could not hope to carry. 'Have you seen Jane?' she asked a man whom she had caught by the arm.

'But of course,' he said. 'This would be the brave Captain of whom we have heard. Dear sir, you will not have heard of me . . .' Yet he paused for the denial Laing was unable to give: stout, rubicund, foreign.

'He is Herr Knutson,' said Mrs Warrington. 'I shall find Jane.'

'Suffice to say,' Herr Knutson now informed Laing, 'that I am the husband of that angelic being who plays upon the pianoforte.' He held up a silencing finger but all that could be heard was a concluding trill of notes taken over at once by the muffled patter of gloved hands. 'She is an angel,' this gentleman confided, 'an angel to endure this place, but whenever I demonstrate with her it is always the same theme: what I must endure so will she. And there you have the nature of the being. I tell you, an angel.'

Laing said, 'The Consul tells me he has raised his family here.'

'Indeed,' said the foreign gentleman. 'Charming girls. The jewel of our small circle. But they were as good as born here.

33

Their constitutions, as it were, know no better. My wife, now, was reared with the greatest delicacy in Copenhagen . . . Ah, my dear!' for the angel herself, pleasingly substantial beneath her muslin, had joined them. 'I was telling Captain Laing how fortunate the Miss Warringtons are that the harshness of the climate is in their blood.'

'They are angels,' she said to Laing. Then, appealing to her husband, 'Did I not say this evening that I had not known such creatures still existed? So innocent. So fresh. Believe me, Captain Laing, in all the courts of Europe you would not find their like, not in these outrageous times.'

'I have found Jane,' said Mrs Warrington, returning and placing before him a girl of distinct prettiness.

'Is it not as I said?' the angel demanded.

Laing smiled but wordlessness afflicted him.

'What nonsense have you told the Captain, Gerda?' Miss Warrington now said. A little rosy mole moved on her upper lip as she spoke, like a speck of fruit lodged just beyond the tip of her tongue. Then, as if Captain Laing did not exist, 'You are to play. I swear I shall die if I do not dance directly.' And she was gone.

'You must not be responsible for that young woman's death,' Laing told the angel gravely. He mopped his face with his handkerchief and looked about him for the Consul, who was nowhere to be seen. In one corner of the courtyard tables were being set up for cards. No, he told his hostess with a mock regret, he never played.

He stood among a group of men in a room filled with a welter of Moorish lamps, English chairs and gilt Venetian mirrors. They questioned him about his journey with the shamed, wistful air of men who must for pressing reasons stay behind.

The Dutchman said, 'How long will you be with us, Captain Laing?'

'Here: tonight only. I mean to camp outside the town a day or two. No more than a week.'

No one denied him but the dapper Wood sucked in his cheeks, nodded his head, so mimed the part of ignorance being instructed that Laing suspected he knew otherwise. He turned to the doctor, whom he thought a modest sensible man: a former Naval surgeon who had taken up the more congenial posting of physician to the Bashaw's hareem. 'An interesting practice.'

'Aye. They've some remarkable physiques among them.'

'And demanding?' Laing asked him. They looked amusedly at one another's eyes; their faces grave. Two men of a compatible humour. Mostly, the doctor told him, their symptoms were those of chronic boredom. 'The odd accouchement. Fewer now. The Bashaw is not the man he was.'

'Age?' Laing asked.

'Brandy.'

They spoke of the previous mission.

'You knew Clapperton?' Laing asked him.

'Aye. Aye,' the doctor said. 'Both when he set out and when he returned.'

'And Denham, too?'

'It was a bad business. And Oudney, too. Died, poor fellow. You could see it in him from the outset. He was consumptive. You've been ill, I hear,' he said after a pause.

'I am well enough when I am on my way. The fever only strikes when I'm held up against my will.' But he drew back from the lighted supper table as he spoke. They moved towards the doorway and looked down at the dancing couples. The doctor told Laing that his wife was born on the Guinea Coast, the daughter of a trader, at St Elvira, a few miles from the fort Laing had commanded in the Ashanti uprising.

'A bad business that,' he said.

As he was a surgeon Laing told him of McCarthy's head in the Fetish House; how it had stunk abominably but had been so skilfully preserved that it was recognisable and looked as if at any moment it might speak.

'They ate his heart,' Laing told him, 'to get at his courage.'

The sprightly notes of the piano rose up to them. A woman laughed. Enough of that. They began to walk down the steps towards the dancers, into an atmosphere dense with sweat and melted candle-wax.

'Where else have you served?' the doctor said across his shoulder.

'Barbados, Honduras, Freetown,' Laing told him.

'You're a survivor, then.'

It was true. From the arrow that flieth by day. From the

pestilence by night. Ten thousand shall fall beside thee but it shall not come nigh thee. Not Laing.

He said, 'I've had most fevers known to man, but none has killed me yet.

'Amen to that,' the doctor said.

Laing paced about the edges of the courtyard absorbing the graceful movements of the dancing women, the glimmering lamps, the pleasant stirring of the fountain. A dream, he thought, might be as real yet have as little substance in his life. He yawned repeatedly and had to wipe his eyes. The surface of his skin ached with a restless tension. He must exert himself. He danced with the angel. Then with Miss Warrington.

She turned up the corners of her mouth as she came towards him, glanced back as she turned away. They promenaded up the line of dancers. He felt the moist crushed stuff of her dress and let his hand slip down towards the firm swell of buttock. She did not shrink from him but turned a moment later with the same amiable smile. When the dance was done she sank down on a sofa by the fountain and tapped at the place beside her with an ivory fan. Laing sat as he was bidden. She smiled at him and plied the fan so that its cool breath played on both their cheeks. Above its fluttering her eyes assessed him steadily.

'You'll be a famous man when you return from here,' she said. 'Too famous to be spoken to, I think.'

'I'll not return this way,' he told her.

She dropped her fan then and affected to cry, grinding her little fists in dumb show against her cheeks, staring at him all the while with round blue tearless eyes. He thought her very bold, very free. So that he dared to ask in a low insinuating tone, 'Would that be such a sorrow?'

The flush spread charmingly up from her neck to her cheeks. He had touched her then. He warmed. He eased. It was effortless to talk with her. He watched the lovely sheen along her cheekbone, watched the speck of strawberry bob on her lip as she spoke. It scarcely mattered what was said. Some other pleasant interchange went on between them.

'Poor Captain Laing. All that long time with no one of your own kind you may talk to.'

'I'm a solitary creature,' he told her. 'I'm best on my own.'

She was looking at him, the blue eyes very round and solemn. 'I am the same. I often long to be alone.'

At that moment, as if to demonstrate the hopelessness of this, the assiduous Vice-consul stood bowing before her and before she could refuse him had snatched familiarly at her hand and drawn her away to the dance.

The crush of guests had thinned. The older couples had departed or sat in close groups around the card tables. The younger took their turn to dance. Laing had begun to feel the ill effects of wine and drank another glass to alleviate them. Repeatedly he yawned but would not give way to his fatigue. Repeatedly he dug his fingers into his springy hair and dragged back his scalp to force open his eyes. He was aware of a painful acuteness of hearing, as if a violent syringing of his ears had left them too penetrable to sound; so that the thrilling notes of the angel's playing struck individual blows on his very being, while the laughter and excited voices seemed pitched higher and higher until they threatened shrillness and derision.

In a room off the entrance hall, converted to a privy by a cluster of brimming chamber pots, he relieved himself and splashed water from a basin repeatedly onto his face and hair. He remembered the world outside, then; who he was; why he was there; that he would make his purchases early; ride out by noon; be camped by nightfall.

In the courtyard he saw the doctor watching him but would avoid his too solicitous eye and hurried past, saying without pausing, 'I am looking for the Consul.'

'Up there, I think,' the doctor told him, nodding towards the supper room.

The air was fresher there. The shutters that gave upon the street had been flung open. Moonlight gleamed starkly on the white wall opposite.

The candelabra which had blazed so brightly in the early evening had burnt out. Only a few fresh candles had been stuck here and there at slight angles in sockets full of molten candle-wax.

The Consul sat over the debris of the supper table with his stock loosened and his waistcoat unbuttoned. 'Ah, Laing,' he said, raising his glass as if the intervening hours had not been, 'Edinburgh to London.'

The servant moved forward with a glass for Laing, which the Consul himself filled. The toast was drunk.

'Sit down, sit down,' the Consul urged him.

'I mean to make an early start,' Laing told him. 'If I may leave my baggage here till noon?'

'Of course.'

'And if you advise me in what quarter of the town I might seek out the guide Hateeta?'

The Consul drained his glass with a sudden backward toss of the head and said, in the patient voice of a man who reminds his friend of something he already knows, 'Hateeta never comes to Tripoli. He'll wait for you along the way, at Ghadames, perhaps.'

'But I was told, by you yourself. You wrote.' Douce, douce, he told himself, for the Consul's voice for all its geniality of tone had put him in mind of the English voices in Whitehall, chopping at thought, permitting no alternative. 'Was that not the plan?'

'Well, well,' said Colonel Warrington, dabbing with his napkin at his lips. 'It might at one time have been. Come, man,' reaching the decanter towards Laing's glass, which Laing attempted to shield with his hand, 'give way this once. I cannot tell you how eagerly I have awaited this meeting. You are more than half way there.'

'With God's will,' said Laing and drank to that.

'With God's will,' the Consul replied, 'and the Bashaw's.' He smiled across at Laing with an expression of such charm and candour that Laing felt his own lips move like a reflection. 'You must appreciate,' the Consul went on, 'that I have a most difficult game to play.'

With what? With whom? With me? He's no one's fool, Laing thought. There's something here for him he does not mention. Yet a moment later he thought, I credit him with too much guile.

'Set your mind at rest,' the Consul was saying. 'I'll deal with the Bashaw.'

'So you must,' Laing told him simply. 'For I know nothing of these matters.'

'Drink up. Drink up.' The Consul stood and raised his glass. Laing too. 'The King.'

'The King.'

They sat again. Laing watched with gentle absorption as the servant leant forward, held back with one hand the loose white sleeve from the other while he poured more wine. The Consul was saying slowly and distinctly, 'I like you, Laing. I never mistake a man and I like you. You must come out to my garden when we're finished here.'

He toasted: 'Mrs Warrington and her children.'

Again Laing had no choice but to reply.

'Whatever else, we're both soldiers,' the Consul went on. 'But I'm not your run-of-the-mill regimental colonel and you're not the sort of jolly, mindless subaltern they might have sent me. I tell you, Laing, I've half a mind to go along with you.'

'God forbid,' thought Laing behind his smile. At the same time he felt himself drawn into this man's approval as into a void. They had begun to talk to one another like men who had not met for years but had been intimate at one time.

The Consul was telling him of Walter Tyrwhitt, whom he had sent with Clapperton to Murzuk to act as his Vice-consul. They had had no word of him for six months. 'Not that I fear for him,' he said. 'The roads are cut off at present. Besides, he's not one for writing. He's no head for books. An old family, though – all that. He drinks, you know. Only a boy. Can't seem to stop. I thought responsibility might steady him.' He was looking at Laing helplessly across the blaze of candles with tears in his eyes. 'His father was a friend of mine in happier days. A hard man. He cast him off. Poor boy, he was like a son to me.'

It seemed to Laing that there were things that he must say that he had failed to say. His glance fixed on a dish of nuts and seemed too heavy to lift. His mind, too, was oddly tenacious of what had troubled it some time before.

He heard himself say, 'It is necessary, the more so if I am to be without Hateeta, that I set up camp outside the city at once, so that the suspicions of other members of the caravan are allayed, and they become accustomed to me.'

He heard the Consul say thoughtfully 'Nevertheless there is no caravan.'

'No. No,' said Laing. He shook his head as if to disentangle it from annoying restraint. 'Clapperton said . . . not to me, but he has said. They said in London there is but one caravan a year to Timbuctoo.'

'Ah, London,' said Warrington. 'They take these fancies there.'

'But Clapperton himself. I have no reason to suppose he bears me malice . . .' But as that horrid possibility suggested itself he fell abruptly silent.

The Consul allowed this silence to swell about them for a time. Then, leaning across to Laing, he said, 'Have I your confidence?'

'Entirely,' said Laing.

The Consul stabbed about the surface of the table with his forefinger. 'And do you agree that I have lived in this God-forsaken spot these twelve years?' He had pushed his chair back from the table and contemplated Laing a moment longer before adding, 'And that I know the Bashaw as well as any honest Christian is capable of?'

'I believe it entirely.'

'You will take my advice, then?'

'I am fortunate to have it.'

'My dear sir,' said the Consul, 'you have been misinformed as to the nature of things here perhaps, but this is nothing compared to a truth most evident to me: that of all men sent on these missions you are the one most likely to succeed. You are in the prime of life, sir. Oudney was scarcely that. You are experienced in African travel. Denham was scarcely that. You are a man of education. Not one of them, even poor Tyrwhitt, could lay claim to that. You are a gentleman, sir, and Clapperton. Well, Clapperton . . . Do you know that I never sat down to table with him without a dread that something unpleasant would occur?'

Laing said, 'I am entirely in your hands. Only tell me what I should do.'

'Tonight, nothing. Sleep. Rest. Tomorrow we begin at the palace. We'll tackle the Bet-et-Mel. Then in a day or two he'll speak to the Bashaw. Then in another day or two, if we are lucky, and the wind is in the right direction, he'll grant us an audience. Then the bargaining must start. It is the Bashaw who holds the key to your route south and it is I, if I may say so, who holds the key to the Bashaw.'

'To the Bashaw,' Laing gave him.

'To the Bashaw.'

*　　*　　*

He had intended to retire out on the roof. The Consul was loath to part with him; but sleep, rest, it was agreed. Tomorrow they would talk again. Outside, though, on the steps to the courtyard, he found himself remarkably awake, remarkably sober. The tented room was almost empty. Only those most dedicated to the cards or the dance remained. He paused to smile down upon the dancers as they coupled and withdrew: Herr Knutson and his angel; the fair Miss Warrington; the Vice-consul, Wood. Another hour and they would vanish forever from his eye as he from theirs.

He crossed the courtyard.

'Do you retire so soon?' Mrs Warrington called out to him above her hand of cards. 'Surely you would wish to dance again?'

'No,' he told her. 'Thank you but no.'

He made his way along the cloister and climbed the stairs in darkness, bracing his hands against the walls on either side until he found himself again on the balcony, raised up above the heated flicker of lamps and candles into the cool clarity of moonlight.

He began to move along it, passing identical doors, some shut, some opening into darkness. Another and another. This, then? It was ajar and creaked slightly as he pushed it open.

The room inside was entirely dark except where moonlight forced its way through a carved wooden grille on the outside wall. He stood in the open doorway and peered inside. 'Jack?' he called softly. 'Jack?' There was no whisper. No movement towards him, but the hairs on his neck had risen at the presence of another living person and immediately his eye made out, beneath the barred shadow of the grille, the pale form of a woman seated in a chair. Whoever she was she did not wish to be discovered but sat quite still, like an animal who seeks in total immobility its last defence. He withdrew without a word.

Another door. The moonlight that entered with him revealed the heaped shape of luggage around the room and Jack, who had waited for him in the dark, springing to his feet and fumbling to light a candle.

Laing took off his shoes and the uncomfortable tunic. He blew out the candle and lay on the bed. The sound of the piano died away and was succeeded by more raucous shouts and laughter. He heard Jack's steady breathing but knew that he would never sleep in the airless, confining room. When all was quiet he rose, took up his military cloak, broke his new rifle over his arm and climbed the stairway to the roof. There he wrapped the cloak about him and lay down on his side with the rifle along his backbone and his head pillowed on its butt.

I have returned, he thought, but curiously as he fell asleep the image that was in his mind was that of the waiting woman in the moonlit room: the passive curve of her body in the chair; the curious impression that she was weighted down with shadow.

In the month of Ramadan an old man is employed to walk through the town in the hour before sunrise. He shakes a tin box filled with scraps of metal to the slow tempo of his footsteps. The faithful wake at the sound and cook and eat and drink before the call to morning prayers prohibits them.

The servants of the Bet-el-Mel roused themselves from the floor of the great courtyard and hastened to fetch his abstemious meal of dates and water. In his upper chamber Mohammed d'Ghies slept on. He had stayed awake to receive the man he kept to wait at table at the British Consulate. His English was poor but he had not mistaken the words Ghadames and Hateeta. Both men drank, he told d'Ghies; the traveller less than the Consul, but he was the more affected. He was a tall man. His eye was quick. He was a clever man. You could sense it in the way he spoke. And a strict man. He did not smile. Was he a brave man? It was difficult to judge with Europeans, but his eye did not falter. His hands lay still when he was not employed in eating and drinking. Would he turn back? God knew. He did not know. There was that in his eye which made it seem he would not turn back. When he had gone Mohammed d'Ghies dictated a full account of these events to his son Hassuna and despatched it with his messenger to the Sheikh Babani in Ghadames. Then he lay down on his mat to enjoy a few hours' sleep before the inevitable arrival of the British Consul.

In the narrow streets of the town the clanking of metal scraps came through the shuttered window of the British Consulate. In one of the rooms off the caged upper balcony, where as children they had wrapped their pinafores about their heads and played out the servants' tales of love and death, the two sisters lay side by side in their narrow beds.

Only Emma Warrington was wakened by the sound. All night she had slept fitfully. Now she sat upright behind the muslin curtains with her bolster gripped against her narrow breast. Timoleon had not come. There had been footsteps. The door had opened, but it had not been he. Her father had prevented him. They said that he would die of love for her. Perhaps it was his ghost had stood like a shadow and gone so silently away. Warm tears gathered in her eyes, that he should love her so and die. She bit into the linen cover on the bolster, lest the curtains heave, the bed shake with sobs, and her sisters wake and hear her.

She did not know if she had cared for him. Rather she wept with a sense of helplessness and fear of the blank silence that must descend when the clanking of the metal box had passed. For what would happen now? When his letters did not come, when she could not wake and think, Tonight I shall see him at the de Breughels'; tomorrow he will be at the Knutsons'. She thought, Will I die, too? For how might she continue to believe in the existence of the next day and the next if she could not imagine her own existence in them?

The Consul too was roused by the din, but was never one to lie in bed, a prey to morbid fancies. Although he had drunk late the night before, he rose and dressed and went into his office. There he flung open the shutters and by the first light of the day completed his letter to Whitehall. He was happy to express his heartfelt approbation of Captain Laing, whom he found ideally suited to his task, a man of intelligence, a gentleman, though here his pen hovered an instant while he selected 'gentlemanly' as the more precise.

Laing, too, had woken with no idea of where he might be other than that he lay trapped in Body. The dull ache of head and liver was punctuated by the painful pressure of the rifle butt against his cheekbone. He sat upright and recognised the roof of the consulate, the flag-staff, the tripod and the telescope.

He heard the straining cry of cocks and presently the deep sad assertions of the muezzin that there was one God and Mohammed was his prophet, that another day was imminent and would somehow be sustained by these incontrovertible truths.

He dozed. He woke again. The sky was on the turn from grey to blue. Kites already circled overhead keen-eyed for what had died in the night. A moment later the sun sprang above the parapet and instantly he felt his skin coated with sweat. He rose at once and made his way down the cool stairway to the room where he had been intended to sleep.

At ten o'clock a servant knocked at Laing's door and conducted him down through the house to breakfast with the Consul. The courtyard was swept clean. The awning had been taken down. The upper storey stayed silent and deserted. He found the Consul sitting alone, the last night's supper table set for two. His wife and children, he informed Laing, had been despatched to the country in the cool of the morning.

They themselves would set out shortly for the palace and make what settlement was necessary with the Bashaw. In the afternoon, although the Consul made no mention of it, Laing was privately resolved to move his luggage and his people to a camp outside the town.

An hour later they emerged from the consulate and, preceded by the Consul's *chouish*, set out through the narrow streets towards the palace. Laing wore his scarlet tunic, the Consul his splendid uniform. Sunlight sparked on the gold thread of his collar and epaulettes. The ostrich plumes waved. 'Go slow,' he said to Laing, 'or you'll sweat damnably.'

Laing paced beside him. The town was nothing to him. Other men had seen it, other pens had written it down. Still, the eye could not help but take it in, with no defence as yet against the trivial and distasteful. Dogs with haunches sharp enough to break the skin nosed along the edges of the street. A dead cat stretched against the wall; dust had parted its fur and settled on its open eye. It wore a skeletal grin, as if death had it by the scruff of the neck. Children stared at them with gleaming trails of snot cleared in the grime of their upper-lips. Flies clung about their eyes. He felt their insolent wanderings across his own lips too and found his hand had resumed that most African of gestures: the continuous languid motion of the hand before the face that acknowledges there will be no respite between one fly and the next.

Briefly Laing recalled the brave city he had viewed from the barge, the turrets, the flags, the massive walls, which in this uncompromising light he saw to be made of nothing more substantial than crumbling mud and whitewash.

He said to the Consul, 'It's not at all as it appeared to me when I arrived.'

'Oh, the town's a dreadful hole,' the Consul said indifferently. 'I keep out of it when I can.'

They had entered the market. The narrow winding streets were here roofed over with straw matting. They pushed deeper and deeper into alleys that were nearly dark. The air was stifling, with the smell of musk and spices and the underlying sickly odour of rotting fruit. Thicker and still more profound, a universal smell of dirt and excrement was pressed against his nose and mouth like a soiled hand.

They were in the open street again, at the edge of the town. Ahead of them rose the massive gateway and the seeming substantial walls of the palace. They passed through a vaulted entrance-way with its echoing sounds of soldiery, its shadowy recesses where pale-clothed figures leaned and watched. They came out again into a brilliant dusty courtyard thronged with the Bashaw's troops, sitting, standing, playing at dice. A groom led up and down a grey arab who lifted his foreleg proudly to his muzzle, arched his tail and let steaming dung fall onto the confused surface of the ground.

Another passageway. Another courtyard. From an obscure doorway there appeared an elderly official splendidly robed and turbaned in silk. He bowed repeatedly to the Consul and to Laing and pattered out his greeting as if it were a lesson he would hurry through before it were forgotten. Then, with a gracious gesture, he waved them on.

'The Bet-el-Mel,' the Consul said. 'The Cerberus of the place. So far so good.'

A soldier led them up a flight of steps in such a ruinous condition that Laing's boots slipped and grated as he climbed. Then into a dark passage alive with flecks of recollected light. Guards shoved past him in the gloom. Repeatedly he felt the unpleasant sensation of a warm hand thrust against his back. Tonight he would begin his journal: *We entered the palace, I in my dress regimentals, the Consul similarly attired. The*

Barbaric guard stood to attention with much clatter of antique weaponry. They were clad in . . .

Red turbans, gold belts, gigantic pistols . . . too fast, too fast. The mind must flit to take it in. Up more stairs. A dungeon air.

'Well, Laing,' the Consul was saying. 'What do you make of all of this? Light? Airy? I tell you, there's many come along these corridors eager for favour who never come out again.'

Laing might grunt belief. The smell was faded, secretive and old. Shed blood might dominate among all the squandered substances of the body. They turned this way and that, all hope of exit lost. He passed a wooden shutter propped down and, looking down, saw a small square garden, brilliant with sunlight. Instantly he was shoved forward from behind. Another passage and another stair. They filed now along the side of a shuttered balcony and halted by a door. Ten or so Moors had taken up position on either side of it, squatting or leaning as if prepared to wait for an eternity. None moved.

Laing muttered in the Consul's ear, 'I've no knowledge of their protocol.'

'Follow me,' the Consul told him. 'Do what I do.'

They were in a cool dark room scarcely bigger than a cell. An old man sat cross-legged on a dais. As they entered he disentangled his robe from his legs and got nimbly to his feet.

'Mohammed d'Ghies,' the Consul told Laing from the corner of his mouth, 'the Bashaw's foreign minister.' White beard, clear old skin, still wide innocent eyes under eyelids stained with kohl. Laing felt the light dry touch of his hand grope slightly as if it sought out something from the contact. With eyes averted the old man spoke the customary phrases, each with a little sideways motion of the head, as if to say, Yes, this is how it is, with you or with anyone.

A young man, his son, Laing gathered, came forward now to act as interpreter.

'Tell Mohammed d'Ghies,' the Consul said, 'that we wish to see the Bashaw.'

'The Bashaw regrets that he cannot see you.'

'How's this? Ask Mohammed d'Ghies the cause of this.'

'It is the fast,' the young man said after consultation.

'When Abdullah was here the Bashaw agreed to see him during the fast.' He said in a low voice to Laing, 'They called Clapperton Abdullah.'

'It is the fast,' the young man said again. His English was perfect. 'But there is something the Bashaw wishes you to see.' He led the way to a window and, pushing out the shutter, directed his gaze downward. There was the bright sea. Below them on a stretch of sand, a troop of horsemen rode past at a violent and irregular speed, stopped suddenly, wheeled and came careering back in what appeared to Laing to be a disorderly rabble.

The Consul watched this spectacle in attentive silence. Then he said, 'That's capital. I enjoyed that. You can tell the Bashaw that I never saw the like of it. They do him proud. Do they not, Laing?'

Laing, solemn as a judge, agreed.

'Tell the Bashaw,' the Consul went on, 'that I'd not like to lead my old troop against the likes of these. Tell him that with troops like these he need fear nothing from his enemies. Tell him that with troops like these the road to Ghadames is open to his friends. Tell the Bashaw that the *Reis* here has much experience in the training of soldiers and that he is much impressed by what he's seen today. Are you not, Laing? And that he is all the more anxious to meet in person the ruler who commands such troops.'

The old man appeared very pleased with this speech when it was relayed to him. It prompted him again to perform the gestures of greeting, touching the rim of his turban, touching his heart, offering, it seemed, his soul and body. It was apparent, then, through the slight misdirection of this goodwill, that the old man's eyes were less innocent than blind.

'Sit,' he was saying, with both hands trailing their long sleeves, gesturing them towards a row of cushions placed in the angle of the floor and wall.

The consul said, 'Tell Mohammed d'Ghies that I wish to present the *Reis* who, like myself, is a close friend of the King of England, to the Bashaw.'

The young man translated this.

'Sit. Sit,' the old man continued to say. There was a gentle determination in his voice. The gesture, graceful still, resembled shovelling.

'Oh, very well,' the Consul said. They all sat down upon the floor. The old man clapped his hands. Coffee, pipes, and little cups of sherbet were set hospitably on a low table for the

Christians. No one spoke. The cups clinked familiarly. Metal bangles clattered on the servants' arms. The doorway was filled now with silent watchers, raising their chins above one another's shoulders to see into the room.

Through the interpreter the young man questioned Laing about his journey. Was his destination Timbuctoo?

There seemed no purpose in denying it.

And what was his motive in making so arduous a journey?

Laing assured him that he was not lured there by tales of the city's golden wealth, but by his desire to bring the advantages of European trade along the mighty waterway of the Niger into the very heart of Africa.

The old man listened attentively. Then, with a gentle smile he said, 'I think your true purpose is to put an end to the trade in slaves.'

'To replace it,' Laing said hastily. 'To replace with legitimate trade the cruel traffic in human flesh.'

'Ah, my friend,' the old man said. 'I, too who have imbibed many of the ideas of Europe, think slavery to be an unnatural institution, but you will meet many people here who will tell you otherwise. They will tell you that slavery is the natural state of man: that we are all the slaves of custom, of the passions, of disease and death.' He paused to let Laing take this in. Then he added, 'Even the Bashaw signs his *teskeras, From the slave of God.'*

'The reason we have come,' the Consul said, 'is to ask the Bashaw to grant a *teskera* to this *Reis* so that he may enjoy His Highness' protection on his journey.'

The message was conveyed. The old man spoke now with a deprecatory lift of his hands. The Bashaw would not receive them until the fast was over.

Two weeks away. The Consul said, 'The *Reis* must leave before then.'

The old man said nothing. Laing sipped his coffee. He was irritated by the clatter of spoons against the cups. His headache of the morning had never left him and now the skin of his scalp contracted with other familiar sensations. His hearing was unnaturally acute. He could locate the buzzing of flies in a high window ledge in the corner of the room. The little spoonfuls of sherbet melted on his tongue too rapidly to assuage his thirst. He was forced to yawn and felt his eyes water with it.

48

The old man was saying, 'The Bashaw is presently at war. The route to Ghadames is closed. The *Reis* must take the road through Beni Ulid.'

Clapperton's route. Twenty miles out of his way to the west. 'No,' Laing said more loudly than he had intended.

The Consul said in an undertone, 'He's perpetually at war. It was so when Clapperton was here. It's a ruse. They often try it. Come, come,' he said aloud, tapping the floor in front of him with his stick. 'My government's policy is ever one of candour and . . .' He paused as if a word evaded him. The watchers at the door went still. The very flies grew patient. '. . . and liberality,' said the Consul.

The old man bowed when he was told this and immediately rose to his feet and left the room. Laing, supposing that the interview was at an end, made to rise as well but the Consul held him down.

'My God,' he was saying in a violent whisper, 'I can see the print of the cloven hoof in this. He'll not see me. He's been put up to this. Rousseau will have put him up to this for his own ends. Paid him to keep you back. You'll see.'

They waited in silence after that. The young man, Hassuna, had stayed with them in the room, preventing speech. Laing leant his throbbing head against the wall. His high serge collar chafed against his sweating neck. They waited. After some time the old man returned. They rose. Everyone bowed. Their host settled himself, and more coffee was served. Finally he spoke at some length, with a dignity which the interpreter was at pains to imitate.

'His Majesty cannot think of accepting money from the *Reis*. It would ill become his scruples. Besides, what service he chooses to render the King of England is rendered out of love and not from any desire for pecuniary gain . . .'

'Excellent. Excellent,' the Consul said with relish. 'You may tell the Bashaw that I respect his scruples and am delighted that nothing now stands in the way of the *Reis*'s departure, other than the awaited pleasure of an audience with His Highness. Our purpose here today is to ask His Highness to fix the date of the *Reis*'s departure so that I may inform my government forthwith.'

In the interval of translation the old man passed his fine pale hand across his face, as if to brush aside some irritating

49

fly of the mind. When he spoke, the interpreter translated: 'I agree with you, Excellency, that it is folly in His Highness not to make his wishes entirely clear.'

There was a long pause then.

'What are his wishes?' asked the Consul.

The old man spoke at some length. The interpreter began, 'And in consequence of his wishes not being clear . . .'

As the whole was rendered into English, the old man leant back against his cushions. Idly, it seemed, he raised his hand and rubbed his thumb to and fro across his fingers. His eyes were fixed upon the Consul's as if by a blind chance.

'It becomes difficult,' the interpreter went on, 'as these wishes are not entirely clear, for the *Reis* to comply with them. Therefore his departure is in danger of being delayed and the aims of your country of being defeated.'

'Two thousand dollars,' the Consul said.

How much? How much? What had he said? On what authority? Laing looked about him askance. Pain clutched upward from the base of his skull. The old man's dyed lids had fluttered down over his eyes. There was every indication of his having sustained the gravest of insults. He had risen to his feet again and was murmuring farewells as hastily as if he would be rid of them, but again the Consul held Laing back.

'What have you offered him?' Laing muttered sternly when the minister had left the room.

'Two thousand dollars.'

'In sterling, man. I cannot grasp the exchange.'

'Five hundred pounds. A trifle more.'

Laing, like a man who has rashly gripped the handle of a heated spoon, sucked in his breath and shook the fingers of his hand until they clacked together.

'It is a terrible sum,' he said. 'I was told nothing of this. It's as much as I have with me altogether.'

'I'll draw out a bill and send it off to Malta,' the Consul was saying. 'Today. On my own guarantee. On yours, perhaps.'

'It is not in my nature to be indebted,' Laing told him.

'There's no escaping it,' the Consul said, too low for the interpreter to hear. 'He tries me, you see. It's all show with them. He'll have nothing but contempt for us if I offer less.'

'But where is it to come from?' Laing said in a grim whisper. 'I have told you. I'm not your man of independent means.' The

50

long injustice of this fact, the years when he had dragged himself from his bed to teach in the freezing foetid classrooms of his father's school. The soiled bed he had lain in during his illness in Honduras. The weary months toiling as a clerk, before notice and favour had won him a commission, the great risks he must repeatedly endure to win promotion, this sorry hotch-potch, too congested for words, seemed massed at the base of his throat. He was nauseated by the pain in his head. The sweat chilled on him.

'Government will pay,' the Consul said serenely. 'They'll not be pleased at Whitehall, but in the end they'll see the sense of it.'

Aye, thought Laing. It's Laing they'll not be pleased with: Am I to believe you, Captain Laing? You'll get yourself from here to Timbuctoo on six hundred pounds. Chop, chop. The English voices. And oh, aye, your Lordships. You can give me your word on that? Oh, aye, I give my word. And nothing in it for me, my lords, but my fit-out of clothing and my watch. I may have a watch to tell the time with? And a guinea a day for my services? You are too generous. You condescend. And thank you, thank you, thank you.

'No,' he said to Colonel Warrington. 'They'll not be pleased.'

The Consul said in a low voice of scandalised compassion, 'Oudney died of want, you know. Not that life ran strongly in him at the best of times. Still, when a cup of goat's milk might have saved him, it was denied him for the price of it. And the contempt to government, Laing. I cannot forget the contempt in that. We'll not have that for you.'

'For me?' Laing said bitterly. 'I do not think their Lordships care for me.'

'Not a straw,' said the Consul cheerfully. 'What is it to them *who* gets there as long as some one does? But the point is this: if you do not, someone else will.'

'No doubt,' Laing said. 'No doubt.'

'But *who*?' went on the Consul. 'If we could be sure that it was Clapperton when he returns, all well and good . . .'

Oh, aye, Clapperton would do as well as Laing any day.

'But to lose our courage now,' the Consul continued, 'to let the French take it. They'd not thank us for it. If you went skulking back to London saying, 'Please, my Lord, I've lost

51

you Timbuctoo, but here are the five hundred pounds intact. And old Hanmer Warrington's lost his nerve and stood aside, cap in hand, and let the French take all.' '

'I gave my word,' Laing said sullenly. 'In submitting my estimates I gave my word.'

Before the Consul might reply to this they heard, outside the room, the bustle of importance. The old man was returning; the crowd outside the door parted to let him through. He came briskly into the room, his humour quite restored. He smiled about him, once he was settled on his cushion, and urged more coffee on them so affably that it was impossible to refuse. Then he spoke. The interpreter translated. It was by the greatest good fortune that the Bashaw had learned of a Sheikh of Ghadames who was shortly expected to arrive in Tripoli. This man, whose name was Babani, had travelled many times to Timbuctoo and was well connected there. As soon as the fast was ended, the Bashaw would grant an audience to the *Reis* at which he hoped to introduce him to Babani and send them both on their way together with his *teskera*. In addition he would provide a troop of cavalry; that very troop the *Reis* had so admired not an hour ago. They must travel by the road to Beni Ulid. They might leave a week after the ending of the fast. Or two weeks. The exact date was known to God.

'Where is the Sheikh Babani now?' Laing asked through the interpreter. 'How near to Tripoli?'

'It is the business of God,' the old man told him. 'You are impatient to set out, *Reis*?'

'Indeed I am,' Laing said. But even as he spoke his mind fretted and grieved over the cost. So that, seeing him frown perhaps, the old man asked him, 'And anxious as to whether you reach your destination?'

'I have no fears on that account,' said Laing.

As if to protect him from his own presumption, minister and interpreter said in rapid succession, 'Fate is irrevocable and to oppose destiny is sacrilege.'

Then, leaning a little forward and continuing to smile courteously at Laing throughout the translation, the old man said, 'You will see this journey as a great exertion of your powers, *Reis*, a test of which the outcome lies undecided. But in truth it is already written whether you reach Timbuctoo or perish on the way. Nothing you can do will alter that. It is history already.'

The Consul, it appeared, had pressing business in the country and must return at once. He urged Laing to accompany him. But Laing, who shivered in the burning heat of the street, had recognised too well the premonitory symptoms of his recurring fever. If he were to be ill he would be so in private.

He begged therefore to be allowed to return to the consulate and remain there for a day or two, making his excuse that his luggage and equipment must be checked.

As soon as he reached his room in the consulate Laing took out his chest of medicine, had Jack send for water, measured out the dose of arsenic and drank it down. The Creole stood watching him with his head a little to one side and clacked his tongue in sympathy.

'Two more days,' Laing told him. Jack shrugged. Laing wrapped his cloak about him and sat on the bed with his back braced against the wall. He had the Creole open one by one the packages of gifts bought in Malta. He put on his spectacles to check off each on a list written in his pocket book. *To be shared out among the greater personages, the Sheikh at Timbuctoo and Mohammed Bello, the Sultan of Sokoto: one double-barrelled gun, one handsome sabre, one silver-headed cane, one lock tie and twin screw, two magazines each of eight pounds of powder, twenty-eight pounds of assorted shot, one common watch, an additional sword intended for the guide Hateeta.* For the lesser chiefs along the Niger there were guns, swords, pistols, gunpowder, clasp-knives, scissors, spyglasses, twenty kaleidoscopes, assorted beads of coral and amber and twenty yards of gold lace. Nothing was missing or damaged.

Next, he had Jack lay his instruments one by one beside him on the bed. He unwrapped each one from its square of oiled canvas and inspected it carefully, holding it close to the lens of his spectacles, blowing occasionally at a minute tuft of dust, then rubbing gently with the corner of his handkerchief. He warmed the little bulbs of mercury in his hands and moved the arm of the quadrant until the line of the artificial horizon ran exactly on its image.

Lastly he took up the prize of this collection, the silver

plated chronometer he had purchased in London. He had intended to check its performance at noon by a meridian altitude from the consulate roof, but his hand was shaking so that he could not have hoped for any accuracy. He had Jack set it by the bed, where presently he stretched out, drew the cloak over his head and lay shivering, waiting for the full onslaught of the fever.

For twelve days he never left the room. At times an animal misery precluded thought and he lay on the bed in a stupor, watching the light make passage across the wall as the day progressed, listening to the indifferent bangings and shoutings of the distant household. At other times his mind picked obsessively over the obstructions and complications that had beset him since his arrival. These, as if seen through the lucid uncertainties of water, were magnified and distorted, overlaid at times by shifting images of the past. So that, waking in the dark, he cried out in the hut at Falaba, and saw again the guttering candle reflected in the ring of eyes that watched in awe for the white man's spirit to leave him. Or saw his father standing at the bed's foot, saying as if to himself, 'My poor Alexander. He must bitterly regret the suffering he has caused his mother. Poor soul, I think she must succumb to it.' Once he woke shaking in terror at a sound which, when his mind had cleared, he recognised to be the braying of a donkey. He was constantly anxious that he might fall into a delirium for so long that the chronometer would lapse from its steady rate; for winding it was the one task he could not entrust to Jack. He had the Creole rouse him each day at noon and steady his hand while he fitted and turned the key. Then he would sink back again.

Repeatedly, it seemed, he groped along the confused darkened passages of the palace with an unbearable sense of haste and premonition.

On the first day of this illness the Consul returned from the country and sent at once for Dr Dickson, whom Laing determinedly refused to see. Nor would he allow the Consul himself to be admitted to his sick-room. Warrington, although the house was his, could only concede. Before returning to the country he delivered through Jack a letter suggesting, in terms of the warmest concern, that even if Laing should be unwilling to have medical attention now, a physician should be sent for at once from Malta to accompany him on his journey.

The imputation this seemed to cast on Laing's ability, the threat imposed of a further timeless delay (for where was such a man to be found? who was to select him?), worst of all the thought of this unknown white man's babble and persistent presence, was intolerable. He managed to scrawl on a piece of paper, *No doctor.* in a hand so shaky that it belied its message. Then he was delivered up again to the dark labyrinth of the palace.

Despite the curtness of this note and Jack's refusal to admit him to Laing's bedside, the Consul continued to ride in daily to inquire after his health. On each of these visits he left messages informing his guest of his progress with the Bashaw, which Laing in his more lucid moments managed to read. With a tireless optimism they assured the sufferer that everything was being done to further his cause.

There was no sign of Hateeta. Had not the Consul known as much? He had been right, too, about Rousseau, who was undoubtedly bribing the Bashaw to delay Laing's departure. Of the Sheikh Babani he had also made inquiries and found, as he had feared, that the Sheikh was very thick with old d'Ghies, who was a close crony of Rousseau's and probably in his pay. The rebellion in the Garian mountains, he reported on another day, had intensified. Three heads of alleged rebels had been stuck up on the palace wall to frighten the populace, a sure sign that the Bashaw was powerless to quell it. The Consul added that he had attended frequently at the palace, applying himself particularly to the Bet-el-Mel. A little money in that quarter, he thought, would be well spent.

'Not more, not more,' Laing cried out. When Jack came running at the sound of his voice he asked for his writing things, but a moment later when the Creole held them out to him he no longer cared enough to rouse himself.

He dreamt that for his crimes his head was severed from his body. He saw this with the eye of a bystander in some old picture of a martyrdom: the two corresponding segments of pipe stuffed with their dried red rags of blood and the empty space between. Then, in the dream, it seemed that all of him crouched unharmed within his head and sang for very joy at his release and his power of deception over his executioners. He crouched in the gap under the base of the stairwell in the house in Edinburgh, until the angry footsteps quieted, the angry voice ceased. His heart pounded against his gripped knees. He pressed his eyes against his cold bony kneecaps. Smaller, smaller, smaller, lest they find him out. He smelt the metallic odour of his own frightened unwashed skin.

He made his way along the dark breathless passages. He was late. He must hurry. And this passage met another. Left? Right? To the right. In a circle, then. First left. Then right. He was late. Somewhere the old man waited in his room, but the way was continually blocked by hurrying and obscure figures pushing against him in the gloom. Had he gone wrong? Should he turn and fall in behind them? He lifted each leg with an infinite weariness. But when he tried to move forward, which he did now with an increasing urgency, for he was very late, shrouded figures pushed towards him. The soft stuff of their garments wiped across his face and clung like cobwebs to his mouth. He could see no end to this passage but groped along it with a hand on either wall, searching for a door. The old man waited in anger on the farther side.

'Ah,' he cried out, 'it is no fault of mine. I gave my figures in good faith. I did not know how it was. I was not told.' And beat now with his hands along the damp stone. Ahead of him a leopard coughed. On the banks of the Rokelle they lay out the heat of the day deep in the cool lush grass. Brindled and spotted with shadows among the reed beds, they concealed their rage. Might it be stretched on a ledge above his head or crouch at the turn of the passage? He sweated with terror.

Yet he knew it was Jack who raised his head on his arm and gave him water. He managed each day to lay his ear against the chronometer to reassure himself that it had not stopped ticking, and wind it then to last another day. And cried out at the nameless things that pursued him in their fury down the obscure passages.

McCarthy's head spoke to him in the Fetish House, through its putrid lips: 'You are a man of no good sense, Alexander. You have given your word and now you break it.'

He woke and lay still. The watchman rattled his box of nails in the road. He heard it quite distinctly. All his senses seemed rinsed clear by the passage of the fever. Close to his ear he heard the steady ticking of the chronometer. Presently light penetrated the shutters. The door opened and Jack moved soundlessly across the room and leant over him.

'I am better,' Laing said.

'Praise God.'

'How many days?' Laing asked.

'Six of the bad dreams.'

'Quite better,' he said again.

'Praise God.'

'And before that? How many days ill?'

'Ten days together.'

He tried to calculate but was confused. 'Bring me the almanac,' he said to Jack.

He worked back through its list of days to his arrival, to the visit to the palace, then the days of his illness brought him to the eve of the new moon and the conclusion of the fast. Time squandered. Half way to Ghadames in Mind while warder Body had kept him chained to this bed.

The grateful sense of peace with which he had woken deserted him. By noon a mood of intolerable irritation had taken its place. He dressed and had Jack shave him, not caring to trust to the steadiness of his own hand. He was weak beyond belief. Contempt for his own weakness goaded him on. He would not take Jack's arm nor hold the railing on the balcony, but forced himself to walk upright, down the stairs to the room where the Consul had first entertained him. The supper table and the English chairs had been dragged into a corner and half hidden with a screen. Opposite the doorway a wooden divan was built into the three sides of the alcove. It was shuttered but unglazed, so that any breeze there was might be drawn into the shadowy room.

Laing sat there on the hard cushions, stiff and alone, listening for the Consul's arrival, while outside the longest and most wearisome day of the fast wore itself out. Its tired voice washed up to him from under the slanting shutter and as the afternoon passed he thought he could detect a quickening of expectation in its formless murmur.

Jack brought him food which he forced himself to eat. Still the Consul did not come, and now he tormented himself that his refusal to admit him to his sick-room had given offence, and that the Consul had washed his hands of him. If so, what was he to do? And yet, he thought, ten days ago, before I knew him, the way seemed clear enough. As another hour passed he allowed himself the surly conviction that the mission had been delayed not by his illness but by the Consul's machinations at the palace, from which he had been excluded.

The bars of light were fading on the shutters when he heard the Consul's voice in the courtyard below. Within minutes the door was flung open. A plank of sunlight fell into the darkening room. Over it strode the Consul, dust on his boots, sweat on his face: an emissary from a vigorous outer world.

'You've been delayed,' Laing said without any sort of greeting. 'Is anything wrong?'

But the Consul had begun on quite a different tack. 'You are better,' he was saying. 'I spoke to Jack. He tells me you are better.'

'Quite better,' Laing told him grimly.

The Consul had not seen Laing in other than the tight upholding uniform in which he had arrived. It was the loose travelling clothes, he would believe, that exaggerated the languor of his rising. But they could not account for the change in his appearance. The cheeks were sunken as if sucked in and held clamped between his teeth, the eyes seemed magnified and fearful. What have we here? the Consul thought. What have we here? He reached out and gripped Laing by the hand as if he would snatch him from some peril, saying, 'My dear fellow, it distresses me to see you so low.'

The words fell like a reproach.

Laing said all at once, 'I have been wretchedly anxious over this business. Were I but clear of this place and assured of Whitehall's approval of this debt, my health would be restored to me.' Then, seeing the dashed expression on the Consul's face, he heard like an echo the peevish accusing tone in which he had spoken. He saw, too, that the Consul had brought with him a little open basket containing fresh figs settled in a white napkin. While Laing was speaking he had laid it with a clumsy care on the brass table at the centre of the alcove. His awkward inability to present the gift in the face of such churlishness touched Laing with quick remorse. He stood staring helplessly down at the fruit and said as abruptly as before, 'Forgive me. You can have no idea how

58

these setbacks affect the spirits. Mine less than most men's. Yet I am not so unaffected as I could wish.'

The Consul accepted this with the compression of eyes and lips that served him as a smile.

'Of course,' he was saying. 'Of course.'

He had begun a restless circuit of the room, divesting himself of hat, gloves and stick, and adjusting the shutter to let in more air, going to the door to call for wine in his loud pleasant voice.

Laing told himself, I am his guest. Yet he felt bound to say, 'Won't you sit down?' For what with his weakness and the release of his pent up anxieties he found himself unable to continue standing.

'I've something for you,' the Consul said, parting his coat-tails and sitting on the divan opposite to Laing. 'The bag has come from London.' He reached into his pocket and tossed a small packet of letters across to him. With a sick man's slow absorption Laing took out his pocket knife and began to saw through the string that held them. He recognised his friend Bandinel's hand and one from Edward Sabine, who had taught him his astronomy. He fingered them for a moment; then set them aside.

'Well?' he said to the Consul. 'What news?'

'Good news,' the Consul said determinedly. 'Good news all around.'

'What then? Tell me, man.'

The Consul leant back against the hard bolster and hooked his dusty boot across his knee before he said, 'The Bashaw has agreed to see us.'

'When?' Laing said.

'The fast ends tonight. Did you know?'

'Yes.'

'They'll feast for three days.'

'Yes, yes,' Laing said. 'I know.'

'He'll see us on the fourth.'

'You're sure of that?'

'Of course.' Now that he had achieved it, he would have it appear as nothing. 'It's all been show, this business of the fast,' he told Laing. 'I know him well. He makes it seem impossible. Then, when he has you thinking that it is, he waves his hand, hey presto, and we're supposed to be the more beholden to him.'

'This is indeed excellent,' Laing said. His vexation seemed lifted from him like the fever. He leant back against the cushions and smiled at the Consul across the darkening alcove. He thought to send for lights, but hesitated, feeling that it was his host's place to do so, liking the seclusion the dusk gave him from the other's scrutiny.

'There's better news than that,' the Consul was saying. His expression too was obscure. 'You will not be alone.'

'How's that?' Laing said. He was filled instantly with sour suspicion. 'I said no doctor.'

'No, no, no,' the Consul said hastily. 'Better than that, a companion in the field.'

No. Laing's mind quicker than words, it was his, not to be shared. He said, 'How so?' with no pretence of joy.

'My dear fellow, they write to say that Clapperton . . .'

Of all men. No. Would cheat him of it. No. He said, 'But he's in England,' and stood up, for the rigid seat held them too close to one another. Turned away to hide his face. Rang angrily at the bell rope beside the door. Signalled the servant to bring lights. Must alter this. Make it untrue. For Clapperton had tried and failed, had been three days' march from the Niger at Youri and had turned back as Laing would not have done. Had had his chance. Had opportunities denied to Laing. Was unworthy.

'He has arrived in London,' the Consul told him, 'and will set out shortly by sea for Benin. Then up river. Then, if he fetches up at Youri, he'll know he's on the lower reaches of the Niger.' He paused. Caution had perhaps beset him. Still he went on. 'At Youri he'll go east. Overland to Sokoto. He'll have Tyrwhitt's replacement with him. Then he'll make his pact with the Sultan and head back for Youri. If you're not there, then on to Timbuctoo. It makes your delay seem almost propitious.' He paused then, to gauge the silence. Went on. 'There's every hope that you'll meet somewhere along the Niger. He'll scarcely be a month behind you.'

'Not if he has a reception like mine,' Laing said ungraciously. 'Well, he may do as he sees fit. I'll not demean the enterprise by making it a running race with Clapperton.'

The Consul stared at him for a moment, then, shifting round with his back to Laing, said, 'I hardly thought you'd take it so.'

Laing said passionately, 'I do not think for all your words

you trust me to complete this mission without assistance of some sort.' And, when the Consul's silence continued to deprive him, went on in the same wild tone, 'No doubt it's what I am you do not care for.'

'I know nothing of that,' the Consul said with some distaste. 'I had supposed your sole concern, as mine has been, was that England should win this honour . . .'

Park, Oudney, Clapperton, all Scots. And he.

'. . . and that it is immaterial which of her servants should achieve this goal.'

'But must be worthy,' Laing said, turning back only to demand justice, 'worthy of so great . . .' and saw then the Consul's back held rigid, as if he must exert all his effort to conceal his rage. I have offended him, Laing thought, and fumbled on, caught between wretchedness and the need to justify.

'It was Clapperton's reckless bribes inspired greed and I the victim. He would not write to me, even when requested,' he said to the Consul's angry back. 'He refused . . . Good God, the man was accused . . .' But he realised then the servant had entered the room carrying a lamp, and shrank back appalled from the sound of his own words. They were both silent. The servant had gone but the lamp remained on the table, shedding a cruel light on their predicament.

'Would not see me,' said Laing like an echo, for the silence was intolerable. 'Would not give me the benefit of his advice . . . for what it might be worth . . . what sort of a companion?'

The Consul's voice, stiff with offence, said, 'I am sorry that your reception here has not been to your liking. Every effort has been made on my part.'

'Come, man,' said Laing, 'I said none of that.' But he was confused as to what he might have thought and what spoken.

'Then I mistook you,' the Consul said coldly, but he had at last turned.

'Forgive me, then,' Laing cried. 'It was the thought of Clapperton provoked me and the burden of anxiety I find myself placed under. I had intended to be gone from here by now.'

'I should have thought that it was I,' said the Consul, 'and I alone, who was placed in an unpleasant position.'

'You?' Laing said incredulously. 'You?' For what could such a man know of the long struggle without money, without influence? Of the favour he must carry? 'Yes, my Lord. No, my Lord. The memorialist begs to draw his Lordship's attention.' Of the dangers he must undergo? How it was he who volunteered to go after the captured sergeant at Komassie and rallied the demoralised emancipists at the fort of Annamboie? Yet still they denied him his majority, when any idle coward who had the purchase price might buy it as he would his horse. And Timbuctoo the only prize accessible to him that might redress the wrongs of privilege.

From behind the pale area of lamplight which neither dared approach, the Consul said quietly, 'I've staked my all on you. If you get there I've won. If not, my standing here isn't worth a straw.'

The sudden desolation of his tone defeated Laing. All the anger had gone out of him. His eye chanced on the basket of figs just below the lamp. He said again, 'You must forgive me,' and came quickly to sit down again. 'You have been good to me. I am wretchedly ungrateful.'

The Consul said, 'I had supposed the news of Clapperton would have cheered you.'

'Of course. Of course,' Laing said, to end the matter.

The Consul had risen and was patting the surface of the divan in search of his gloves.

'Will the Bashaw approve me?' Laing asked, for he could not go immediately. Neither was yet released from the other. Something more must be found to say. 'Will it be a formality, the audience?'

The Consul said, 'There are one or two things we must discuss. I had hoped to, but perhaps this is not the time.'

'What things?' Laing said.

'I think you are tired by your illness.'

'Please,' Laing said, refusing to rise, 'what things?'

'Well,' the Consul said. He had sat down again but held to his gloves and stick, as if prepared to leave on the instant. 'You'll need two thousand pounds more.'

'What have you said?' Laing asked him in a voice like a whisper.

The Consul said, 'Two thousand pounds sterling more than we have already offered him. With your consent I'll write to Malta for it.'

'Then it's hopeless,' Laing said. 'The whole thing's lost.' But having said it he could not believe it so – that so much effort against so many odds could be dashed by the careless naming of a figure.

In the ensuing silence some outpost of the mind registered the thud of cannon that reported the sighting of the new moon, but neither of them gave heed to the sound.

The Consul said, 'How so?' Then, quietly, 'Unless you wish it so. Unless you're running out on me.'

The sounds of the fast's relief could be heard moving with great rapidity through the streets below, like a flame spluttering along a trail of powder, but neither turned towards the window. Their faces hovered like masks on the edge of the limited light. Laing said, 'You cannot know me if you say that.'

'I think I know you very well,' the Consul told him quietly. 'I think you are like me. I think you'd sell your soul to get to Timbuctoo. I like you for it. I think you'll go, whatever happens.'

Laing said, 'It's true. I think it's so. I'm destined for it.'

'Well then,' the Consul said. 'There's your answer.' He spoke with a particular charm and intimacy of tone, leaning forward now to tap the table with his finger, saying, 'I tell you, Laing, it's a simple thing to me. It's a matter of time till someone gets there. There's no problem if a fellow like this Sheikh Babani's been there twenty times. Edinburgh to London, nothing more. The question is who gets there first, and the answer is either us or the French. And put it to Bathurst thus – "Do you want Laing to get there, or do you want the French?" – he'd not hesitate. But there's no time for that. There's never time. You learn to think for yourself in a place like this. You learn that anything's forgiven you if you bring it off. And you will, Laing. I've never been more sure of anything in my life. I've never placed a bet where the odds were surer.'

Laing said, 'I've grown as fatalistic as the Moors, it seems. I know I'm to go there. If you tell me this is the only way I've no choice but to take it.'

An accepting silence fell between them in which the sounds of rejoicing, cries, the rattle of haphazard musketry, the running of feet in the street below, now had their part. Pretence between them was gone. They felt relief at its departure. Laing rose and threw open the shutter. There, as if it attended

63

upon him, was the thread of moon, the cause of all the hubbub.

'They'll not have seen it yet in London,' he said. The thought pleased him that Mind's swift decision might happen now while they were powerless to know of it until his letter came. Four weeks. Five weeks. The same again before the packet might bring a reply. It hovered in his mind like a sword fight in a dream. He would lift his sword . . . four weeks for his blow to fall. Four weeks more, while his adversary heaved up his reprimand and brought it down on poor Laing's head. By then he would be gone. All the interval was his. He felt the sudden lifting of the body's weight, the flight of mind as if he had leapt over the edge of the known world and was no longer accountable to it. He said to the Consul, 'If they're displeased with me, let them seek me out in Timbuctoo and tell me to my face.'

The audience was granted four days later. Once again Laing penetrated the palace, under the gate where the rebel heads were stuck at angles like lumps of tar, across the crowded courtyard, up the confusing stairways, along shuttered galleries. Again he glanced into deserted rooms and down through spy-holes into brilliant cloistered gardens. This time they followed a different thread to the hall where the Bashaw sat enthroned.

That night he wrote on the first sheet of paper in his folio:

All along the brightly tiled walls of the audience chamber the Bashaw's guard stand shoulder to shoulder, like so many basalt obelisks, their antique blunderbusses upright. His Bashawness sits elevated on a dais resplendent in a pair of pink silk stockings. The tassel of his burnous falls absurdly over one eye. Pale, stout, fifty. What manner of creature, with eyes so shadowed with kohl that they appear to turn inwards only, on what lurid scene! Behind the throne a gilded canopy and hanging from it the model of a great silver hand, each finger terminating in a ruby. Apt enough; for Colonel Warrington informs me that he stabbed his brother at his mother's feet as she attempted to bless and reconcile them both. And all to be raised this paltry two inches from the floor amidst such tinpot panoply. And yet he's little faith in his ju-ju. For look, the horrid fear of the tyrant. Here, as in no European court, his guards stand armed. One beside him holds a silken cushion with pistols on it and protruding from beneath the cushion he sits upon behold the diamond handle of a scimitar.

He broke off here. Dusk had fallen outside the room. He would not strain his eyes by lamplight. In the course of a single day everything had been arranged. A sum which the Consul had been careful not to name had been sent for to Malta. Two thousand dollars would be paid on its arrival to the Bashaw, to cover the expenses of a troop of cavalry which would escort Laing through the territory presently at war. Beyond that the Sheikh Babani would take full responsibility for his welfare. An agreement of terms would be signed in the Bashaw's presence as soon as the Sheikh reached the town. Within a day or two of his arrival, which was surely imminent, the expedition might set out.

Before he set his writing things aside Laing slid his hand deep into the pile of foolscap and felt the smooth surface of the unseen page. On it his own writing would emerge to tell of events which waited for him in the unformed time and space ahead.

The time between, Laing had agreed to spend with the Consul in the English Garden, to take a series of observations that would establish its exact position on the world's map.

Accordingly, at five o'clock on the following evening, the Consul rode in to meet him at the town gate with horses for himself and Jack, and a pack mule for his tent and box of instruments. The other luggage was left locked and guarded in the consulate. The boatwrights, Rogers and Harris, he had left in lodgings in some unseemly quarter of the town where he might trace them when the time came to depart.

They rode out across a sandy tract where Nomads had erected dark oblong tents. Their evening fires were already lit; the sedentary forms of men and the stooping outlines of women were grouped about low orange mounds of flame. Dogs barked. Children came running towards him and stood irresolute between their tents and the road, their hands raised in solemn salute, which Laing returned. He was moved by the simplicity of these scenes. His quick glance gave him the entire lifetime of these people, while he passed among them with the boldness of a comet whose course they could only guess at.

It was the very hour of his arrival. He rode towards the line of palms where he had resolved to pitch his tents on that first evening. The simplicity of that plan mocked him now. His route was changed. Hateeta was despaired of, as was the caravan. He was indebted for an amount five times the sum of his original budget. Nevertheless, as he rode forward he was filled with a profound peace, as if the city itself had created these complexities and the one could be cast off with the other. He turned in his saddle and saw it already at a distance, simplified behind its whitewashed walls. He looked upward at the sky. The hard blue of midday had faded and taken on a premonition of change, but of a quality so inevitable that he felt himself caught up in the great calm acceptance that surrounded him.

He and the Consul rode on ahead. Jack, the *chouish* and the man who led the mule followed at some distance to avoid their dust. The sound of horses' hooves was muffled by the sand. The genial clinking of the harness rang clear.

Beyond Ghadames, the Consul told him, he would find a horse more trouble than it was worth. Clapperton had said that; that two camels were necessary to carry the water to keep one horse alive. More than ever he had told Laing.

The Consul calculated the number of waterskins Laing must buy in the town before he set out. Each of the riding camels could carry three. The others six. Ten or eleven camels. Say fifty. Best play safe and say sixty.

They rode towards the east. The sun sank behind them. The limewashed walls of the village they approached grew pink in the still intense light of the evening. They passed a mosque and saw the muezzin climb up into its low square tower to call out the dismissal of the day. Now their horses ambled along sandy lanes pitted with hoof prints and walled in by high hedges of fig. Behind them groves of orange and pomegranate heaved up their sighs of resignation and rustled back in place again. The same sweet odours which had reached him in the Bashaw's barge came in gusts. From the secluded gardens he heard the sound of water running and single voices calling. Everything was awed and stilled by ebbing light.

He heard the Consul say, 'There were dreadful scenes, Laing.' He spoke with distaste, as if of something he had been forced to witness at a distance.

'Oh, I can tell you, there were tears and I don't know what

not. My own child like a mad thing. I tell you I feared for her sanity, Laing. My own child. All for some infatuation for a sickly boy she'd scarcely spoken to. You mightn't credit it, but Rousseau asked me for her for his son. Just now when you were laid up in the town. The younger, mind, not the elder. I told him he might go to Hell first. More diplomatically of course, but that was the gist of it.' He was silent for a time, dwelling on the insult. Then turning slightly in his saddle, he said, 'I must warn you, Laing, we live a life of rusticity here. There's little polish on them, but then there's no deceit. They're open in their manners, Laing, as English gentle-women were when I was young. And might fear nothing of it then. God, when I think of it. Boys and girls together and no thought of harm. But here in the company we are bound to keep . . .'

He had reined in his horse and turned abruptly through an open gateway to his left. Laing's horse followed of its own accord. Grooms ran forward to help them dismount. Laing found himself being ushered by the Consul between low sta-ble buildings into a newly planted orchard. Ahead of them was set a low whitewashed villa of the kind he had glimpsed through winter woods on his way to embark at Falmouth. It made him smile. It had the startled look of any misplaced thing.

The chouish left them with a bow, to wait with others of his kind, perched on their hunkers on the verandah steps. More servants ushered them inside, along a hallway, out onto a screened verandah which overlooked an open stretch of dusty earth. There, arranged like figures in a panorama, were the members of the Consul's family, seated stark and incongruous on wooden chairs, waiting for a miracle of foli-age to rise out of the bare ground and unite them to this place. The mother, in a white cap, read aloud from a book. The three daughters sat bolt upright, their needlework held high. One son lay stretched out at his mother's feet, à la turque, propped on one elbow with one knee raised. The other leant over the back of his mother's chair. Away among the rows of sapling fruit trees a child, a boy, crouched motionless, watching some scuttling creature. The evening breeze, cool and heavy with moisture, had come suddenly. Laing felt it through the open screen and saw it lift light portions of the women's dresses.

67

The swollen orange sun was close to the rim of their protecting wall and would fall suddenly behind it. He saw the mother lift her book and turn it to catch the last of the light. The daughters let their needlework lie still. Laing watched them, charmed. He stood aside so that a servant might place a lamp upon a table, and as if it were a signal they all rose together and walked slowly towards the house.

Part II: The English Garden

For the next few days Laing, with Jack's assistance, set about his series of observations. At the lower boundary of the Consul's garden, where a high stone wall protected it from the encroachments of the desert, they erected a small canvas canopy to shelter the instruments from the heat, and made a table from the packing cases where Laing could work at his journal and correspondence and write up his calculations. At night they slept there, one on either side of it.

In the chill hour before dawn he would wake to find Jack kneeling with one cheek on the dusty ground, lips pursed to blow up the embers of the fire. The flame sprang up. His quick hand thrust on sticks, one, two, three. There was no sound at all other than the snapping of the burning brush and the cry of cocks in the village beyond the walls. Overhead the sky had quickened with a colourless glow. Walls, trees, leaves stood out against it as flat grey shapes made all of one substance. Bats criss-crossed above his head in hectic, irrational flight.

Laing rose, pulled on his trousers, sat hunched, wrapped in his cloak, watching for that precise moment when everything became distinct and sucked into itself the heightened colours of the dawn. The branches of the trees glowed pink. Their leaves shone. The bats vanished. Invisible birds filled the air with a multitude of short cries.

Each morning he watched with joy this swift creation. A moment later the intensity of it had passed. Laing saw only the world stored and docketed in Mind. Wood was brown again. Leaves hung upon it and were green. Birds flew here and there and were pigeons or otherwise. The sky was blue and would remain so.

A transformation had occurred inside him, too. He could not remember so great a sense of physical wellbeing as

71

during these stagnant days, when in the normal course of things he would have fretted intolerably. Body floated at ease and made only the briefest and most habitual demands on him. He woke with the strings of his faculties pleasurably taut. He heard, saw, tasted with a new acuteness. He moved about the morning ritual with an anticipation he could not account for of that moment later in the day when he would walk up through the plantation to the house.

On his improvised table he wrote to Bandinel:

The father has made it plain that his daughters are beyond my reach. So be it. I have no desire to add a wife to my impedimenta – though the young ladies in question – at least the eldest – seem pretty and amiable enough. And Master Ossy has already declared himself ready and willing to come with me to Timbuctoo, and to the edges of the earth if need be . . .

On the first morning this youngest child had come to stand shyly a little way from the fire. When the two men did not tell him to go away he came and knelt down between them with his hands clasped between his knees, watching the clear bright flames.

Jack said gravely, 'Good morning, Mr Osman Warrington.' Laing said nothing, but he had smiled at the child.

After that he came each morning and was absorbed into the rituals of the camp. He was allowed to fetch Laing's boots, one in each hand, leaning forward with the weight of them, forced to run across the trampled ground by the fire to keep his balance. Jack spat on a boot, a great white gob. 'You too,' he said. Ossy spat, little, clear, frothy, nothing like. 'Good' Jack said and worked both in with his bone.

Jack told him how, when he was a boy, he'd squatted by the little fires in the hills and sharpened his stick the way they taught him. How he had gone to be a soldier then to fight for Buonaparte. They gave him his bugle and a uniform with gold on it and a hat with feathers, and shoes because he was a free man.

Jack let him hold his bugle, He let him rub it with his cloth. Held it up. Let Ossy see his twisted face reflected in it. Laughed.

Jack told him how he went to France on a great ship. Night and day and the waves above his head. And everybody sick,

72

black man, white man, all the same. Only Jack was not sick. Then the little English ship came. Boom, boom. He puffed out his cheeks and was the cannon. He sprang to his feet in front of Ossy and fought them with the razor, Jack alone against all the English sailors, until they said, 'Put up your sword, Jack. We take care of you.' He went to England and the people stared, not at feathers or the gold or the shoes, but at his black skin. He laughed at their simplicity.

But the child studied the Creole's blackness with awe. The palms of his hands as he wielded the boot-brushes revealed it as an impermanent thing. They had been scrubbed pink again, though blackness lingered in the creases of the skin. Once, in the early morning, when Ossy came up behind him, Jack turned and grinned at him through a beard of white soap Then he raised the blade delicately with his little finger outstretched and scraped away a strip of foam. The blackness shone through undisturbed. Still, the evidence of the palms made it a transitory, mysterious thing.

Laing let him wind his watch. No one but Laing might touch the chronometer, but he might wind the watch if Laing held it. Ten winds. No more. Everything was very precise and important. He was filled with the size and strangeness of what they were about.

And Emma Warrington, leaning in the early morning from the bedroom window, looked out across the haze of little trees to the thin column of smoke rising from the camp; the only thing that moved in all that static landscape. Later she walked down through the trees until she could make out the brief decisive movements of the two men through the haze of dust they raised about the camp, and catch their curt familiar exchanges. All the time she was afraid they would look up, see her standing foolishly there and call out for her to go away. Then, when they remained absorbed in what they did, she felt rebuffed, as if it were they who had summoned her out in the heat and then dismissed her. She would not go again, but the next day she told herself that Ossy should not run about at midday and hurried down towards the camp.

To get complete accuracy, and so that he and le Bore might have more practice in the reading of the chronometer, Laing took an observation at noon on each of the appropriate days.

Le Bore stooped under the canvas with his eyes intent on the twitching hands. Laing waited at a little distance, watch, notebook and pencil at the ready. It was the fourth day, the sun hotter and more brilliant with each observation. Ossy squatted at his feet, shaded his eyes with both hands, squinted upwards and memorised Laing's every move. 'Stop', he cried out to Jack and pressed the stopwatch. He went back to the canopy with Ossy trotting heavily beside him.

'I've to do my sums now,' he told Ossy. 'You're to be quiet, mind, or I'll do them wrong.' He hooked his spectacles about his ears. The child leant against Laing's shoulder and breathed intently close to his ear. Laing took out his tables and began to trace with his finger down the long columns of figures. He said in a slow abstracted voice, 'Now do you know where you are?'

'I know where I am, Laing.'

'Where's that?'

'I'm here.'

'Where's here?'

'It's here where I am.'

It was nearly noon. Laing left off his calculations and wound the chronometer. Ossy must not touch it. It told what the time was in England. If it should stop Laing would not know where he was. Ossy said, 'You could wind it up again.' But Laing told him he would not know where to put the hands. 'You could look at your watch.' But that would only tell him the time where he was, which was not the same. He peered into the chronometer. The very air of England with its separate time lay trapped there under the glass.

Ossy came and sat by Laing. 'If I opened the lid, would it stop?' he asked him in a whisper.

'Yes,' Laing told him curtly, lest he tamper with it.

The child went outside into the sun. The bare ground shook with light. The little trees, robbed of their shadows, seemed insubstantial. He did not understand about the different times. He came under the canopy again and sat by Laing cross-legged, just as he sat, leaning his slight weight against Laing's shoulder. Laing went on writing. Finally the child said, 'Which time is better? Our time or England's time?'

74

Laing looked over his spectacles and said, 'Our time. They haven't had it yet.'

'We're ahead?' Ossy asked him.

'Yes.'

'Won't they catch us up?'

'They can't,' Laing said, writing again.

'In an hour,' the boy said, 'won't they catch us up?'

'No,' Laing said. 'Not ever.'

'In a day?' the boy persisted. When Laing did not answer he sat puzzling over it. 'If it stopped, would they catch us?'

'Very likely,' Laing said without looking up. 'Very likely.'

The child sat frowning, his elbows on his knees, his cheeks pinched up between the heels of his hands. After a minute he said in his loud breathy whisper, 'If it stopped, would you die?'

'Aye. I might that,' said Laing with a laugh like a cough.

'You'd die?' the child said again. 'If someone opened the lid and it stopped?'

'Ach, what nonsense is this, Ossy?' he said irritably. 'I'd not die because it stopped. I'd be lost, as I said. I might just die because I was lost.'

After a while the child said, 'I won't touch it, Laing.'

'Good' Laing said.

'I won't tell anyone about it.'

'That's right.'

One of the Miss Warringtons was calling, 'Ossy, Ossy.' Laing could see her from under the flap of the canopy moving between the shoulder-high trees, a straw hat on her head, something white around it tied under her chin. The second sister, Emma, of whom the consul had spoken.

'What?' Ossy shouted in a loud uninquiring voice. He did not move from Laing's side. She came on through the wavering light. Laing continued writing in his neat hand.

'Ossy,' called the girl again. She had come up to them but held a little away and said now, in a fierce penetrating whisper, 'Come away. You bother him.'

'I don't,' Ossy said, and leant his head against Laing's shoulder as he looked at her. She darted suddenly under the canopy, snatching at her brother's hand, but the child shook her off with a rough indignant gesture that jogged Laing's arm. He put the notebook into his pocket, rose, lifted Ossy by his tightly bent elbows and set him to one side. Then, ignoring them both, he took out the key to his chronometer. The girl stood watching him, her expression as artless as a child's, but she stood too close.

'Don't touch that,' Ossy told her jealously. 'It's not allowed to be touched.'

'I wasn't,' she said, and to Laing, 'You'll be going soon, I suppose.'

'Aye, Miss Warrington, soon now.' He was counting inwardly the number of turns.

She said in her shrill hurried voice, 'Papa says you are to ride with us to the ruined palace. To show it you. For you to camp there. Will you like that? It's haunted, you know. At night it is.'

'Oh?' he said as he put the key back into his pocket.

Ossy said, 'You'll like it, Laing. There's hundreds of people dead there. They were asked to dinner and when they came, one by one . . .' His voice slowed dreadfully. He reached his hands around his own throat and gave a dreadful rasping noise.

'Don't, Ossy,' the girl cried out affectedly, but did not move away.

'You told me,' Ossy said. 'She used to tell me in bed,' he told Laing, as if he boasted braving horrors.

'We took Walter Tyrwhitt there,' the girl said. 'Papa sent him to Murzuk, you know. We all cried so when he left.'

'I dare say,' said Laing at his driest. At the same time, with a clarity that shocked him, he had felt the pressure of that hard thin body with its film of sweat, the warm breath, the incessant whispering of horrors. He said sternly, 'Be off with you now,' as if he spoke only to Ossy.

'Oh why, Laing?'

'Because I can take no more of you,' he said.

He watched her after that. Her eyes were very dark, as was her hair. Her skin was without a trace of colour, though her lips were puffed and suffused with blood as if she nibbled at them. He never heard her speak at table, but thought there was something bold and plaguing in her silences; that he recognised a soundless bitter dialogue between the girl and her father.

It was mid-afternoon. The Consul had stepped out into the wavering light and walked off towards the stables, towering

76

over his little trees, shouting for his syce and his elder sons. Laing had chosen to stay behind. He had pleaded his need to confine his reading and writing to the daylight hours. In truth he found himself unaccountably drawn to the tense lassitude of the party which remained on the verandah: the elder sisters with their sketching books, Mrs Warrington with her needlework. Inside the house Louisa practised the pianoforte. Ossy came and went about his own affairs.

The neglected journal lay open in front of him on a table, but he made no attempt to write. Instead he stretched back in his chair and watched the two young women from under the brim of his hat. They had arranged themselves at the farther end of the verandah, consciously apart, the one drawing, the other, the younger, posing.

She sat motionless on her stiff wooden chair. Jasmine grew thickly on the trellis-work that screened them from the sun. Its scent came in sudden gusts into the shadowy area where they sat. The outer light, sifting through its leaves, cast floating lozenges of green over her white dress, her narrow throat and breast. Now that she kept still and did not speak she no longer seemed entirely young. He thought the daze of innocence had passed before experience might fill the void. She had, like all of them, an air of indefinite waiting.

Her mother was saying in a bewildered voice, as if this truth had come upon her suddenly, 'This is a poor place to bring up girls. I do not know who will marry them. Indeed I do not, for there is no one here. Tyrwhitt would have done,' she told him presently, 'were he not half-way to being a drunkard, and penniless since his father cast him off.' Then, after a silence, 'And Timoleon Rousseau is well-born in part, but is of little use, being French. He's a sickly boy, in any case. The Consul does not care for him.'

All the time she spoke she never ceased her sewing. It seemed to have set the rhythms of her speech, with the methodical stab of her needle and the occasional break for the severing of the wool, which she effected with an odd savagery by using her teeth.

Laing felt no obligation to answer. These thoughts he recognised as her familiars. She troubled to voice them only because of his presence. With a slow luxurious movement he pulled the journal towards him and began to write.

77

'And for that matter, the boys,' she mentioned presently, 'for who is to employ them?'

When next he glanced at her she had fallen asleep. The confused reverse of her needlework lay uppermost on her knee. Her cap was a little awry. One bare puckered arm was tossed over the side of her chair, as if she had abandoned it. This was one of many, many afternoons.

His Highness's manner towards me, Laing wrote, *seemed a touch cold. Nevertheless he spoke with a gratifying respect for His Majesty and has promised me the protection of a troop of cavalry as far as Beni Ulid, and by good fortune the company of one Babani (a much respected sheikh of Ghadames and Timbuctoo itself) whose imminent arrival in Tripoli I now impatiently await.*

The words came easily, as though poised and ordered on the brink of Mind. He watched them move across the paper in his well-formed hand, but recognised them as not being entirely true. Some urgency had left him. It pleased him obscurely to be accepted by the Consul's family, whom by the nature of his journey he would never see again, who could be nothing to him, nor he to them.

Presently the artist cleared her throat and asked demurely if she might draw him. He laid down his pen and slowly unhooked his spectacles from behind his ears. 'Would you have me face you?' he asked her. She had come up close to him and settled herself with her book propped up on her knee.

'You would quite put me off,' she told him. 'Over there, that I may catch the nose.'

In obliging he found that he had drawn into his vision the sister's pale defiant face. He had been curt with her and would make his peace before he went. He said stiffly, taking care not to move his head, 'How do you fill your days, Miss Warrington?'

Her sister said, 'Oh, I am forever sketching, or playing, or doing something.'

Laing said gravely, 'I can see that. So I especially asked your sister.'

'I am Miss Warrington,' the elder said, glancing at him pertly over the top of her sketching book.

'Who is she, then?'

'Oh, Miss Emma, I suppose. People so seldom address her when I am in the room.'

'Oh, Miss Emma, then,' he went on doggedly. 'I asked you how you spend your days.'

She turned to stare at him a little blankly but having taken his stand he would persist. 'Miss Warrington here sketches with her pencil any poor creature who will promise to keep still. I wondered if you had any similar pursuit.'

'She writes with her pencil,' Miss Jenny said, drawing all the while, but she had lowered her voice and he saw them both glance swiftly at the sleeping mother. He thought them very secretive, very sly; their conspiracy quite as deep as their hostility towards one another.

'She writes to her frog prince,' the elder went on in her little mocking voice. 'He must stand on a stool to whisper his replies. It is most affecting. Do you not find it so, Captain Laing? Mama will be sure to know if he kisses her, for she will break out in warts directly.'

Good God, Laing thought, how little they must make of me. He felt the burden of courtesy lifted off him. In another moment he said rather coldly, 'Will you excuse me? I am bound to continue with my writing. I must put on my spectacles and quite spoil your drawing.'

Which he resolutely did, for the afternoon was wasted by them. A moment later he heard the eldest Miss Warrington snap shut her book and depart into the house. How gauche I am with them, he thought, not even to rise. But he continued steadily to write. To Sabine now:

I am indebted to you for your advice on the best method for taking soundings. By all accounts that I can gather here, the river at Youri is little more than a trickle in the driest month, scarcely sufficient to float a canoe in, and now with these delays I am losing hope of reaching there before it ceases to be navigable. If this is true I am very sorry, for it puts paid to any hopes for a steady riverine commerce with the interior. Nevertheless near its outlet it will be fed by rain swept in from the Bight and whatever outlet it finds will be as swollen and muddy as any on the coast.

It was very quiet. Occasionally he heard a distant voice. Mrs Warrington's wicker chair creaked as she stirred in her sleep. The shadows of the leaves, the shapes of light enclosed between them, shifted constantly on his page. The other girl had stayed where she was. Annoyingly now her extreme silliness began to fret at his attention. His flow of talk with Edward Sabine was disturbed by the need to devise some new remark sufficiently foolish to trick her into speech. But to his surprise it was she who moved suddenly to the chair her sister had vacated and said in a low aggrieved voice, 'Mama promised me that I should go to England when I was eighteen. All the time she talked of it. "When you are eighteen, Emma, you will go to England." But she says nothing of it now.'

When she fell silent he must speak, but was confused as to what she expected of him. She sat so close that he might at any moment have reached out to touch her hand, her cheek, her breast. He had lost all sense of the sleeping woman, of the verandah itself, in the effort to understand what it was she wished him to know of her, and had to say something so that she would speak again. 'Do you remember England?' he asked her.

Which tasted of coal smoke. Where the milk came to the door in a cart with a horse. There was a blue painted stool for her to sit on in the kitchen. The big sweating maid. That's no way to hold the cat, bless you. Laughing. That's not the way.

'No,' she said, lest he ask her questions she had no answer to.

'Not at all?'

She shook her head. She would not lie twice. 'We went to Grandpa Price's house in the boat,' she told Laing suddenly. The looking-glass had had blotches eaten into the mercury by the sea air. She had thought that they grew on her face and had cried, 'It's the sea. Look! The sea.' Laughing. Big women, forcing happiness upon her. In the wind their skirts had whipped about their legs and slapped at her face.

'It was very empty by the sea,' she told Laing, out of that one poor sensation of misery. All the words she could not speak stayed massed painfully at the base of her throat. She could not breathe. She rose awkwardly and went into the house. Tears came to her eyes that she had spoken so clumsily. She thought, He will not speak to me again.

And how was she to give account of herself? She was who she was. She did not trouble to set a pattern on things. From the window in the morning you could see a bright strip of vegetation and beyond that a blue strip of sea. Days came.

They went. Other people had the ordering of them. Only sometimes there would come a quickening and thickening of event: when Walter Tyrwhitt had stayed, when Timoleon had written his letters. Then she might tell herself stories: how he had come to the house . . . and the next day he had said . . . and the next day . . . and then . . .

There was a woman: she was a slave and very beautiful. It was a true story. The maid had told her. Her voice went on and on inside her head as if she told it, for her own gratification, to a listener in the dark she could not see. A rich man had a passion for her and kept her in a palace. And his enemy was jealous and told the man she had another lover. And the rich man said to kill her. So his enemy went at night and hid in the garden. And she came out alone to walk in the moonlight.

She told herself this story again and again, until she dispensed with the words and could see the woman, who was small like a child, walk fearlessly out into the moonlit garden, so used to being alone that even when the leaves rattled she never looked around. But Emma, who knew, saw him there creep closer and closer, and would cry out to her although nothing could prevent it happening because it had happened.

She was very indifferent, very bored, very restless. Laing watched her move about the salon in the evenings when the lamps were lit and the tea brought in on a brass tray. She trailed her arm behind her, touching at things as she passed for no other reason than to see if anybody watched her. When the tea things were cleared away, the card tables were set out. The Dicksons sat at whist with the Consul and his wife. Louisa stitched her sampler. The elder brothers lounged in the open doorway and presently removed themselves. Ossy kept himself from sight behind Laing's chair, to prolong the gap before the inevitable bedtime. Laing sat with Tom Wood watching the elder Miss Warrington make much of a spaniel, murmuring over it and pulling back its ears until its eyes bulged horribly. Knutson wandered restlessly about the room bestowing his approval now upon his wife, now upon the card game, now upon the younger people.

Wood said across to Laing, 'You're staying here, I gather.'

'For a night or two. And you?'

'I do from time to time. I live in the town. They take pity on me.'

Silence fell between them of Laing's choosing. Then he said, 'Tyrwhitt came here too, I'm told. Before he went to Murzuk.'

'Oh yes,' Wood said with his quick enthusiasm of speech. 'He lived here with them. He was a great favourite.'

'I gather,' Laing said. 'Like a son. And Clapperton?'

'Oh no,' Wood said. 'I don't recollect Clapperton being here. In town, yes. But not here. But with Tyrwhitt there were great games. Great romps. Do you know,' he said, lifting up his voice to draw in the two young women, 'that when I laugh the skin behind my ears becomes extremely painful. I know of no one else who suffers that. Of course,' he added, 'I laugh now far less than I did.'

'Poor, poor Wood,' Miss Jenny said. 'You suffer so.'

'I do,' he agreed and, dropping his voice, said out of the corner of his mouth to her, 'and all on account of you.'

'That's not true,' she said to Laing and added, 'He's a very wicked man, you know.'

'You have no proof of that,' Wood said. 'You see, Laing, how they make use of me. They use me to demonstrate their playfulness. To you, I think.' He leant forward, speaking, it seemed, to Laing alone. 'Young women frighten me. They become whatever happens to them. God knows what will cross their path or what they must become in order to devour it when it does. For they will, of course. Like that monster. Good God, what was it called?' He slapped his hand flat upon his brow. It astonished him that he had forgot. The others had all gone silent with the gentle greed of such people for any entertainment. Knutson came and leant over the back of Laing's chair. 'What was it called?' Wood said up to him. 'That monster that changed all the time?'

'Proteus,' Laing told him.

'Capital, capital,' Wood cried out, quickening at the memory of it. 'Listen to this, young Ossy.'

Ossy had come out from behind the chair and stood there, staring fearlessly.

'He was a monster,' Wood told him. 'What did he look like? You are going to ask me, but that's just it, Ossy, he looked like whatever he met. You see how your sister Emma has not

82

smiled once since Captain Laing came into the room. She's grown as grave as he is. So Proteus. He was a lion, Ossy. Someone threw a net over him – so what did he become?'

'A mouse,' Ossy said. He knew that story. 'A rat.' He was child enough still to name the bigger animal in a bigger voice.

'Right,' cried Wood. 'Now, listen to this. Proteus was now a rat and he met a cat. What then?'

'A dog,' cried Ossy. 'He turned into a dog.'

But Wood at that moment had called out, 'There, I have caught you.' For the younger sister had forgot herself and watched him open-mouthed, her small features gathered up into a look of wild sly amusement.

'Ah,' cried Knutson, moving swiftly forwards, 'but that is Emma. We have seen her now.' He reached out and caught at her narrow chin, saying, 'Like that. When will I draw you like that?'

She turned her head as sharply as if it had been struck away.

Wood said, 'Herr Knutson is the artist of our little circle.'

'Is she not cruel to me?' the artist cried. 'Are you not cruel, Emma, to your old friend who has wanted for all these years to capture that look? Are they not cruel, Laing, to poor Wood and myself?'

But she ignored Laing, met no one's eye, said nothing, kept her head at that unnatural angle as if she would advertise a wrong. He thought her different from the others; the only one of them resistant to her fate, with her fragile anger, her restless longing to be gone.

She sat on the verandah. It was afternoon. The vine stirred but she could feel no breeze. Her mother dozed and shifted in the creaking wicker chair. Tom Wood held his book at an angle before his face. She did not think he read it. From the house Jenny's tune began and halted, began again and on the same note halted. She could hear Ossy's shrill voice from the direction of the camp and later, she thought, the black man's laugh. They hunted the frogs by the well.

'He should not go there,' she said. 'He bothers them.'

Tom Wood said nothing. He had lowered his book, though. The green shifting light reflected on his face. He watched her with his clever eyes and said, 'I saw Timoleon on Wednesday.

He spoke to me especially, knowing I would see you. He has not given up hope, Emma. He is devoted to you. Only he is unsure, he says, of your feelings for him.'

She said, 'Oh, what is the use of it?'

'He does his best to keep his spirits up. Only, as you cannot write to him now – some assurance from you? He's not well, you know, Emma. Poor Timoleon. Some word from you I could pass on would give him heart.'

He had a plump face without any serious expression; he was unable to meet her eye. She thought it came awkwardly to deliver this other man's message. 'Oh, tell him what you will,' she said.

'I'll tell him that you care for him?'

'Tell him I think of him sometimes when I'm very idle.'

'That's always.' He never smiled when he made mock of her.

'No. Not always.'

'Of someone else, then?' he said quickly.

'No.' She was very careless. 'Of Walter Tyrwhitt, sometimes.'

'Ah,' he said, as if she disappointed him.

The paint on the rail of the kiosk had blistered in the sun. She broke the thin crisp domes with her thumbnail. 'He must know it is impossible.'

'He will wait,' Tom Wood said.

'Oh' she said 'wait, wait, wait,' and after a moment, 'Papa says he has heard nothing all this time.'

'Heard nothing? Oh, from Tyrwhitt.'

'Is that true?' she said, looking quickly at him. 'There's been nothing?'

'Oh, I dare say he's not found time to write. That's ridiculous, of course. Poor fellow. There's time enough. Perhaps there is simply nothing to write about.'

'But he would tell me? He would not keep it from us, if he did write? He would not keep it from whoever the letter was for that it had come?'

'Of course he would not.'

'You would tell me?' she said. 'You would know and you would tell me.'

'I would tell you.' He made her ill at ease when he was silent. It was unlike him. She sat touching the salt sweat on

84

her lip repeatedly with the tip of her tongue. His silences were always more significant than anything he said. He stared at her but she would not look up to catch him at it.

Presently he said, 'What shall I tell Timoleon?'

'Oh, tell him . . . tell him . . . I will think what to tell him.' It was too airless. She stood up awkwardly. Laing was coming up between the trees with Ossy riding on his shoulders. With his hands he clutched Laing's hair and looked about him from his vantage point, turning his head imperiously from side to side.

She went inside the house. She would not look at him again. She would not speak to him unless he first spoke to her. His hair was red and stood out wildly from his head. Through the half-open door she watched him comb it roughly backward with his fingers. His wrists, she had noticed, were thick and square as if there were a plank of wood inside them, and covered with coarse red hair. Now, when he threw back his head when he reached up to comb back his hair, his shirt-sleeve fell back from the brown skin of his hand and wrist and bared the dead white hidden arm.

She stood in the hall. From behind the closed door she heard the gruff interchange of talk. Papa's voice. The other voice. On and on. Turn by turn. She leant her forehead against the wall and turned her head from side to side. She was giddy with the heat. Inside the room a chair-leg grated on the tiles. She started upright and hurried back to the verandah, where she sat and fanned herself with a tight angry motion that gave her no relief.

It had grown dark. Inside the salon the lamps were lit. Her sister played on the piano an air that Laing had taught her. She strained to hear his voice among the voices in the room. Even on the verandah it was airless. She stood up suddenly and went inside.

He sang, in a loud tenor voice, outlandish words she could not understand. Jenny played. He leant over her. He stretched his hand across her shoulder to turn the page so swiftly that his voice never altered, nor did she falter in her playing. Now he urged her to sing with him. Some of the songs, he said, came better in a woman's voice. How she tucked in her chin, pretended to be shy, said she had no voice; said she liked a man's voice; said it made her shiver. She shook her shoulders as she said the word. She was laughing, with her head thrown back and her arms extended to the keys. Almost her head had touched his arm.

'Do you not sing?' he said to Emma in an altered voice. He was being kind because he had surprised her looking at him.

'No,' she said, as if she cared nothing for it. She neither played nor sang.

She remembered suddenly his face as it had been when he first came. It had been different then. How long ago? She could not count the days. His beard had grown, begun to curl, and fill out the hollows of his sunken cheeks. His mouth was startling in it when he sang; moist and pink.

She would not sit with the others. If she sat with the others and he should cross the room and sit by her, there would be no significance in it. She sat alone by an open window, holding up her book to the dim light of the lamp, but unable through distraction to make out a word of it. Clowder came towards her. His claws rattled on the marble floor. He laid his long jaw across her knee and stared at her as if his heart might break. She pulled back his ears until his face had a skinned and frightened look. 'I love him. I love him,' she whispered at the dog, though who it was she spoke of she scarcely knew.

On the next day at mid-morning Ossy came up through the plantation. She knelt quickly on the floor of the verandah and took him by the shoulders to make him attend to her. 'What are they doing?' she asked him. She felt the sweat start out on her face and prick beneath her arms. He was staring at her and began to twist his shoulders under her hands and she to shake him slightly, saying, 'You've been there, haven't you?' Then she held him to her impulsively and kissed the damp edge of his hair again and again while he struggled and suddenly jerked free of her and ran off into the house.

The Dicksons dined with them. Mrs Dickson said, 'How pale Emma is. Is it the heat? Is she not pale? Emma, you have not eaten. Is she feverish?' But she had twisted her head aside and went to the window and took up her book and never turned the page.

The doctor had brought his fiddle. When the tea things were cleared away, he played the quick airs and tapped his foot and spun around and smiled at Laing, who smiled and nodded and hummed over the tunes as he played.

'Come, man,' he called over the bow to Laing, 'you surely know it.'

Fred and Harry rolled away the carpet. The doctor tucked the fiddle underneath his chin and struck up the tune again. Then Laing began with total absorption the lone and intricate dance. At first she could not bring herself to look at him; a grown man dancing with his arms flung above his head like a savage. Everyone went silent. She watched the rapt attention on his face. He did not look about him for their approbation but downwards at the rapid exact placing of his feet. Still, it was a wild dance in its way. The sweat flew from his lip. He performed it with a fierce perfection; an isolated joy. It hurt her to watch him. The loneliness and introversion of the dance, its intolerance of error, caused a swollen sensation to press outwards against her ribs. When it was over they noticed that two bright red spots stood out upon her cheeks, as if it had been she who danced. She covered them quickly with her hands. She felt breathless, altered and alarmed.

They had ridden in procession to the ruined palace where Laing would camp, so that he might inspect the water in the well: Laing and Papa, Wood and Jane, herself and Louisa, Ossy and Harry, Fred and the *chouish*. They had dismounted at the gates. The others had run forward as if hastening towards some assignation in the empty garden. She could hear them ahead of her, trampling and shouting in the wild game that Walter Tyrwhitt had taught them a year ago.

Emma followed slowly along the path that once had been the fatal entrance to the palace; where even now the ghosts of murdered men must wait for darkness; where Walter Tyrwhitt had jumped out at her and gripped his hands around her throat. She had been too frightened to cry out. He had let her go and then, while his face was close to hers, had laughed privately and not unpleasantly, and turned and run away. And she immediately had hurried after him and run up and down the paths in her light and indifferent body, shouting as they had done. She was startled by the recollection of such happiness.

Beyond the yellow piles of rubble was the palm grove where she could see pale figures darting backward and forward over the dried palm fronds that littered the neglected paths. She walked past them, down the edge of the grove, listening to the discontented sighs and movements of the palms high overhead. She began to pluck roughly at the overgrown jasmine vines that grew at the edge of the grove. They would not snap until she twisted them. They cut painfully into the inside joint of her finger and released a bitter odour. As she walked along she bound the blossom into a tight bunch.

There, at the edge of the grove, were the tree trunks that Fred and Walter Tyrwhitt had shifted into the shade. Nothing had been disturbed since she had been here last. Beyond the trees the sun beat glaringly on the bare expanse of ground. Only by the well had the vegetation kept its vivid green. Everything had withered with neglect or grown unchecked, with all its tangled blooming wasted. She sat on the log, holding the bunch of jasmine against her face.

Behind her in the grove the shouts had died away. Presently she heard them come crashing over the dead leaves towards her. The game had failed. Nothing was, after all, as it had been on that other day. They were hot and irritable and perched on the logs, looking about them for some other diversion. Before she saw the movement of her hand Jane had snatched the flowers from her and held them tormentingly above her head, saying to Tom Wood, 'Look at the flowers Emma has picked for you.' Now she leant over, tucking them into the swath of veiling in the brim of his hat, saying, 'It's only a poor little jasmine posy but she picked it for you. Aren't you pleased, Wood? Aren't you pleased that she did that for you?'

Tom Wood sat on the log with his legs stretched out before him, smiling slightly under these attentions, with his eyes so narrowed that it was impossible to tell at whom he looked.

She was saying in a tone of mocking passion, 'I know it is me that you love most, but say you love her too, just a little.'

Papa had come. They all stood up and would follow him through the trees. The day would be over and nothing come of it. 'I'll fetch Ossy,' she said.

She began to walk away from them towards the well in a careless distracted way, as if she went about some business that was of no concern to her. Beyond the shade of the grove, everything was parched and brittle. Entire plants had died where they stood, their blossoms held upright on their rigid stalks and clenched like shrunken fists. Heat pressed down on her head. The rasping voice of the cicadas, like demented echoes of an original single sound, multiplied endlessly.

She heard Ossy shout excitedly and Laing's loud rough laugh. She heard them stumbling and scuffling in the bushes beyond the well.

Frogs crouched there, she could remember, on dry grey leaves shaped like scimitars. They were blotched brown and grey like the leaves. She had hidden there, crouched down between her knees, playing the game they played with Walter Tyrwhitt. She had made herself keep as still as the frogs so that he would not hear her. There had been a red dragonfly and a bright green plant growing in the wall about the well. She had heard his feet come crashing over the dead leaves. He had seen her but he had not called out as he should. His face had had a foolish swollen look, although he had not been drunk. He had kissed her then with a mouth like a hole and stood away looking at her with a loose meaning smile, but never said a word. He was sent away after that. Papa sent him to Murzuk.

There was a cistern beside the well. She leant over the wall of it and stared at the reflection of her face pulled this way and that in the water. Two frogs hung suspended in it with hands and arms outspread like dancers. She heard Ossy cry out and turned and ran towards the sound, as if it were a signal she had expected. Her anger against Laing was formed already complete in her head.

He was kneeling on the ground among the bushes, holding the boy against him and repeating wretchedly, 'Don't cry. Don't cry.'

Ossy's dazed face stared at her over Laing's shoulder. He wasn't crying at all.

'I was too wild with you,' Laing was saying. 'Ossy, Ossy, there, I never meant it. What have I done?'

'I fell over,' Ossy said across his shoulder. Laing turned then. He had been unaware of her.

'You're too rough with him,' she said shrilly. 'You might have hurt him. I'm bound to tell Papa.' But it was she who trembled and felt warm tears gather in her eyes.

Around her the heat vibrated. The cicadas kept up their incessant pulse of sound. Douce, douce, he told himself, she's too young to know what she's about. There were tears in her eyes.

He too was trembling, ashamed that he had spoken so. He stayed there kneeling on the ground and spread his hands out helplessly towards her. But she had gathered up her skirt in tight handfuls, turned away and hurried from him towards the house, with her narrow shoulder-blades pinched together under her flimsy dress, and her little teetering walk.

That evening, when he had sung his air, he crossed the salon to the corner where every evening he had noticed Emma Warrington sit alone. He thought she might rise and walk away and leave him standing there foolishly. He sat down quickly and said in a low voice, 'I have made my peace with Ossy. Will not you forgive me, too?' The words, which he had carefully prepared, sounded ungracious and peremptory. She stared at him without a word. Then she lowered her eyes and smiled.

After a pause he began again. 'Do you really wish to go to England? I can picture you in no other place than this.'

She said, 'Of course I do,' scornfully, as if she had caught him out in some insincerity. 'Don't you? Want to go home?'

'I've had little to do with any home since I was younger still than you,' he told her.

She was watching him awkwardly. 'Papa says you are ill.'

To speak aloud of himself was perilous and strange. 'Ach well,' he said, 'the sickness is no part of me. I give it little heed.'

Something in his voice had wakened a queer show of pity in her. He said, 'Don't look at me like that.'

He thought she would go then, but lacked the grace to do so. Silence fell between them for a time. They sat there side by side by the open window. The night here kept up its intercourse with the lighted room. He could hear the tiny relentless tick of insects hurling themselves against the lamp. The lingering warmth, the starlight reflected from the close crowded sky, suggested hollow areas around the house which might be penetrated. He had begun without effort to talk.

He told her of his trip to Falaba. How Jack le Bore had not known him. How Jack had tamed an ox so that it followed him like a dog and kept a monkey as a pet. How the old king Assana Yeera had said, 'Now I have seen three marvels, a tame ox, a tame monkey, and a white man. I am content to die.'

She was very young, too blank to set up any resistance to him. He found it pleasing to watch her as he spoke, touching that she turned now and sat a little forward, her eyes fixed with listening, her lower lip a little fallen, her small uneven teeth revealed, uncertain as to whether she should smile. On the next evening he came again to sit by her; and on the next, and on the next.

While he spoke she kept her eyes lowered, a half-smile stayed on her lips as if every word carried an equal weight of pleasure. Then suddenly her eyes would lift delightfully and she would stare without caution until, startled by her own boldness, she would lower them again. Then he would pitch his voice more softly and shift his chair closer to hers.

The words came effortlessly; memories obscured for years returned to him, anything that would entice the sweet upward movement of her glance. He told her of the inn in the Highlands where he had stayed the night as a boy. Where the sky stayed light until eleven o'clock at night, and the deer came pacing cautiously out of the woods. Where an old piper had marched to and fro outside the open window, playing with a mournful beauty, and the barefoot maid had fetched water from the burn and poured it from a jug, so cold it almost hurt the throat to swallow.

She marvelled at it. Were the days really so long? How could that be? How could the water be so cold and plentiful in summer? Did he mock her because she knew no better than to believe him? How big was a deer? As big as a horse? When he laughed she pressed her finger to her lip and looked about her anxiously.

On Sunday the Protestant community assembled for Matins in the salon: the sofas and chairs were arranged in rows. Laing was shown to a favoured place by Mrs Warrington's side. The de Breughels and the Knutsons filled up the first rank; Wood, the Coxes and the Dicksons the second. Then came the Consul's children and, at the rear, Jack and the Consul's emancipated slaves who, though Papists, he assured Laing could come to little harm as they understood not one word of the service.

The Consul stood behind a little table on which the Bible and the Prayer Book were laid open side by side. His voice as he read the service was strong and clear, as free from the mumble of indifference as from the dangerous throb of enthusiasm. He kept the dignity of the service as best he might. The sudden intrusion of his dogs, distant shouting, both heathen and domestic, caused him to pause terribly until order was restored. Miss Jenny took up her seat at the piano, biting her lip demurely, smoothing her skirt beneath her. They all exerted themselves to sing the robust hymns. But even with Laing's strong voice added to theirs the sound had a touching reedy quality, rising from so small a congregation so far removed from any other. He strained, now, without daring to look over his shoulder, to distinguish Emma's voice from amongst the others.

Three of these Sundays had come and gone. At the start he had climbed daily to the roof of the villa and, first with his naked eye, then with his glass, scanned the area through which Babani's caravan must approach the southern gate of the town. Beyond the garden there stretched an unvarying landscape of sand and small black rounded bushes. Behind each of these the prevailing wind had heaped half-cones of whiter sand like pale shadows, which in the distance might persuade the eye it saw the dark forms of laden camels with their pale dust rising behind them. Any distant thing, he had discovered, if stared at long enough in that hope, will appear to move. But when he raised his glass either there would be nothing but sand and bushes, or, if indeed there were a troop of men and camels stretched out like a crooked pencil-line across the sand, it would be indistinguishable from any other and they must wait for news of it from the town. It came by evening: the Sheikh Babani was expected soon and might arrive tomorrow. Whether he would was known to God.

At first Laing would have received the news with bitter disappointment. Now, three weeks later, he felt with each delay a sense of reprieve. He told himself more time was needed to perfect his preparations.

On the Consul's recommendation he rode twice a week into Tripoli to take lessons in Arabic from a melancholy Jew who had accompanied Clapperton to Murzuk as his interpreter.

The Consul also recommended to him the services of one Bagoola, who had acted as steward to the former mission.

The man had a sullen overbearing manner. He produced from an inner pocket a fulsome letter written by Clapperton, which did nothing to make Laing like him more. Nevertheless the Consul was insistent that he must enlarge his train, and assured him that the difficulties of provisioning in so empty a terrain had best be left to someone of experience.

Now in the evenings he recited to Emma the little phrases of Arabic the Jew had taught him. She laughed and pursed up her lips in mimicry of his pronunciation, then raised her chin to make the guttural sounds he could not master. He feigned a frown of concentration as he studied her throat and lips.

Early one morning he and the Consul, together with Fred and the chouish, rode three hours into the desert to the camp of one Yahia Mohammed, who they had heard might be willing to act as Laing's camel master.

By mid-morning they had arrived at a small settlement: two long low tents, a rough palm shelter with a camel tethered in front of it, a scattering of sheep and goats amongst the arid bushes.

A man rose to greet them from the tent's shade. His name, they told Laing was Yahia Mohammed. He nodded to one side and rapidly touched each of their extended hands without interrupting his flow of greeting. He was a small wiry man, not young. His skin was lined, the whites of his eyes yellowed with jaundice. He gestured them to the shade of his tent. A young girl came shyly to hand Laing a wooden bowl of camel's milk. She kept her headcloth gripped between her teeth so that her face was hidden by it. The milk was warm and rich and fatty. He sipped at it cautiously over the thick rough brim of the bowl. The camelman made little encouraging sounds as he drank and smiled at him.

When they had refreshed themselves he had Fred question him about the route. How many days to Beni Ulid? To Ghadames? To Timbuctoo? How many camels would they need? Yahia Mohammed told him he would need four camels for riding, another seven to carry the baggage and the water. Eleven camels. To handle so many camels, he told Laing, he would need two other men, whom he would undertake to find.

The journey had become a thing of simple certainties, but even as Laing's heart gladdened at it his eye took in the alteration of the light. The dinner hour at the Garden would have passed. The evening would have worn itself out before their return; another day be gone out of the dwindling supply that remained to him.

'Eleven camels. Three men,' Laing repeated. He spoke in Arabic. The man was delighted and clapped his hands. They discussed the terms of his hire: so much to be paid to him at Ghadames, so much at Timbuctoo, the promise of a new camel purchased there for his return. The camelman leant forward, marking the amounts in the sand, looking up to engage Laing's eye, anxious from the start that there should be no misunderstanding between them. Laing thought he was a man that he could trust.

The Consul was expecting daily the lesser sum of five hundred pounds for which he had first applied to the treasury at Malta. It was agreed that as soon as it arrived Fred would ride out to Yahia Mohammed's camp with the necessary money for the camels. When they were purchased he should come with them to the English Garden in readiness to depart for Timbuctoo. It seemed a little thing for him to undertake. Outside the tent the goats strayed, their shapes flattened into shadows by the swirling dust. Two little girls with tangled matted hair ran among them and stopped to stare as they mounted and rode away.

Already it was dusk. Three hours' riding lay ahead of them. Now Emma would rise from her chair, gather up her sewing and move slowly towards the house. He rode ahead with the Consul. Fred and the *chouish* followed at a distance. For a time they talked of the afternoon's achievements. Then they fell silent, thinking their own thoughts.

Now she would take up her accustomed place by the open window to listen for their return. They were later, surely, than was usual. When they returned the windows might be dark, the salon empty.

Darkness fell. For the first time since Laing's arrival the night sky was overcast. They could see nothing of the Menchia as they approached it, but at last heard the dogs barking with the feckless braggadocio of early night. Later the tone would grow toneless and incessant. A donkey brayed as they rode beneath the first of the shadowy trees, birds twittered and fell silent. The Consul said suddenly, 'If you

94

were staying on here, Laing, I'd ask you to take them in hand. Teach them something, Ossy and the girls. It's too late for poor Fred, and Harry would never have the patience for it. But they'd take it from you. Oh yes,' he said at some modest sound from Laing, 'I've seen you with them. They'd take it from you.'

What's this? Laing thought. What is it that he wants of me?

He sensed by the Consul's voice that he had turned in the saddle to watch him as he said, 'It's Emma I fear for. She's frail, Laing, very frail.'

His heart had begun to beat so insistently that he thought it must affect his voice. 'Is it her health?' he asked.

'She's not ill,' the Consul said with the same slow deliberation. 'Only there's a delicacy in the constitution that the others are spared. I'm bound to fear for her; to wonder what may become of her.'

'Why, she'll marry,' Laing said. 'She'll regain her strength and marry.' Even as he said it he thought how intolerable it was that she must marry into the limited society of the place, breed sickly children, have the bright rebellious thing worn out of her, grow prematurely old and die.

'Oh, she'll not marry,' the Consul told him. They had turned into the garden gates. 'That's one thing certain, she'll never marry. She'd not sustain it. Too delicate in mind and body.'

They had dismounted and walked together towards the house. Lamp-light still glowed in the lower windows. The pale forms of women could be seen to move indistinctly within the room. Beside him in the dark the Consul said, 'Perhaps you could have steadied her, who knows? Found her a book to read. Something practical. Nothing that would trouble her.'

He was in the room. Nothing had changed. Wood and Harry played at cards. The spaniels lay with their heads on their outstretched paws; their eyes rolled upwards. They knew him now; their tails rapped briefly on the floor. The mother sewed. Miss Jenny played, Louisa stood by her. Their faces turned towards him, their arrested expressions merged into smiles, and yet he scarcely saw them. Quicker than thought itself his eye made out the still tense form of Emma, seated by her window.

He did not go to her at once, but sat by Mrs Warrington.

Behind him he heard Fred and the Consul enter loudly the subdued room.

'Jenny remembers England,' she was saying to him. He had not attended to what had gone before. He was in a state of violent agitation. For surely the Consul had directed his attention most specifically towards Emma. Yet had he not at the very same moment warned him from her?

'Do you not, Jenny?' Mrs Warrington called out at a pause in the music. 'And the dancing lessons, and the fine dinner afterwards, and that little swansdown bonnet. Where can that be, now?'

He had risen and crossed hastily to where Emma sat. Immediately his agitation stilled. He began at once to talk to her, as if they had been speaking just before and only momentarily distracted. At something she said – he scarcely knew what it was; it was the sly quick way she looked at him when he said it – he threw back his head and laughed.

'Hush, you must not,' she said, and pressed her hand across her own mouth. 'He will see us. He will not care for it.'

'Not care for what?' Then, quickly, 'You wrong him, you know. He wishes me to talk to you. He spoke of it just now. He wants me to instruct you. Though why, I can't imagine. I'm sure you know everything you wish or need to know.' The blur of lamplight prevented him from seeing her clearly. He pushed it impatiently to one side. He said very quietly to her, 'You must know how sad it makes me that I cannot. You know that I am going?'

'When?'

'It cannot be long. A week at most before I set up camp.' But he could force no sense of time, no feeling of sorrow into the words. He could feel that he was smiling. She, too, was smiling. A great simplicity seemed to have fallen about him. All mistrust had gone from her. He thought, She has forgotten what I am.

Someone called out that it was raining. He heard chairs creak and grate and footsteps hurry out onto the verandah, but did not trouble to look round. He must speak to make her speak again, but scarcely could remember what it was they had been speaking of. Yet he spoke and she spoke. Their voices in the empty room sounded subdued and odd. All the time he was staring at her across the little table. She was

96

saying, 'He reads my letters. He makes the servants take them to him.'

He watched the edges of her teeth bite on her lower lip; the tip of her tongue slip swiftly across her lips.

'It's very wrong of him.'

'He's concerned for you,' Laing said. He could feel the blurred foolishness of his smile. He was laughing so slightly that it scarcely intruded on his words. He saw that she was disconcerted by him, but would not look away. She said, 'I will go away from here.'

Wood's voice called through the open door. 'Emma, Emma, you must see the rain. You must not deprive the Captain of the rain.'

She stood as if he had jerked her up and began to walk rapidly and mechanically towards the door. Laing followed close behind, snatched suddenly at her hand, and pressed it hard in his against the damp warm back of her dress.

They stood on the verandah. Wood leant over the railing and reached up his hand to the sky, calling out gaily, 'It raineth on the just, you see.'

The smell of rain on dust clung at the back of Laing's throat. He was saying to Emma, past Wood who seemed to stand between them, 'I must say good night.' He thought, She does not want me to go. His eye printed the thought on the dark pattern of leaves and trellis-work; on Mrs Warrington's placid stare as he bent over her hand and assured her that he would return tomorrow evening. He had walked past Tom Wood and Jenny. 'Good night. Good night,' and down the steps and out among the trees.

The odd rain had ceased almost immediately, but the stars and moon were still invisible. The wind had risen and stirred ominously in the branches of the little fruit trees. The dim light from the house was lost immediately, only the regular planting of the trees enabled him to find his way down to the camp. Jack le Bore lay sleeping with his head pillowed on his bugle case. The embers of the fire had been extinguished and made pungent by the rain. Laing too stretched out on the ground. The fatigue of the long day's ride came suddenly over him and he slept almost at once.

*   *   *

97

He was wakened before dawn by the violent flapping of the canvas awning. He heard the sound and recognised it, but lay where he was with terror pressed down upon his breastbone. His throat smarted with a degree of thirst unknown to him. It was in the sense that it was simultaneously stiffening and contracting that the terror lay.

He forced himself to sit upright and found his blanket weighted down with dust. When he rubbed his eyes his fists and cheeks were gritty with it. It coated his teeth so that they dragged against his inner lip. His tongue clung to the roof of his mouth.

An hour later, when dawn broke, the wind dropped as suddenly as it had risen, but still the daylight was obscured by a drab biting dust. It had gathered everywhere, in the folds of his clothes and in the creases of his knuckles. It formed a scum on the surface of his tea. It was an alien substance, redder than that he scuffed underfoot around the fire and rode over in the alleyways of the Menchia. He knew the desert had reached in and laid its hand on him.

There was not a breath of air. He sat by the smouldering fire in a confused state, half bemused, half alert, like a man who wakes suddenly and finds the thoughts most vividly in mind pertain to some dream already fading, while one by one the items of his waking life return freshly and intolerably. For what business had he lingering here, forming attachments he could never hope to honour?

It was three weeks since he had left the town; left the bulk of his luggage unprotected by his own people; left the two boatwrights to their own devices. The temperate months of April and May had been lost to him through illness. Now he let June slip past him while each day's delay forced him closer to the savage heats of summer. He had incurred a dishonourable debt. He had given his word in Whitehall and broken it. The money he would take with him was as good as stolen. Now the fear suppressed throughout these weeks sprang out at him, that before the money ever arrived from Malta despatches would come from Whitehall, cancelling his credit, cancelling the mission, demanding his immediate return. He thought, I have been beguiled by this place. I must be gone from here.

By noon the air had cleared, although the dust still made a

dazzling haze among the trees of the plantation. The verandah was deserted. He went around the side of the house not over-looked by the salon and knocked on the shuttered door of the Consul's room of business. The Consul was seated at his desk. Wood was perched carelessly on the corner of it, swinging his leg.

'Ah, Laing. One moment,' the Consul said and turned again to Wood.

Laing went back onto the verandah. He gripped the rail and stared at the placid figures of two gardeners hoeing at the scarcely settled dust with no perceptible progress. The limping tune of his air came from the salon. He went back into the Consul's office and said abruptly, 'I have been thinking that I have presumed too long upon your hospitality. I'll not wait until Babani comes. I'll set up camp at once in the Menchia and wait for him there.' He broke off. The surface of the desk was littered with open and unopened letters. The packet had arrived from Malta with the London mail. He asked sharply, 'Do they know yet of the debt? What have they said?'

'No,' the Consul said. 'No. It's far too soon for that.' He pushed across a paper which Laing perceived to be a draft for five hundred pounds, the first instalment of the loan. Already he had turned back to Wood and was discussing some other matter.

Laing chose to feel excluded from this talk. He paced rest-lessly to and fro in the crowded room, feeling annoyed and slighted. Finally he interrupted them to say, 'How do I obtain the money from this? There are several purchases I wish to make in the town. I presume I may.'

The Consul raised his eyes slowly from his letter. Laing noticed that he placed his finger on the word at which he had been interrupted. Yet he smiled pleasantly at Laing and said, 'I'll take a hundred to pay off the Bet-el-Mel. You can do what you please with the rest.'

'What's that?' Laing asked. 'I know nothing of that.' He could hear in his own voice the poor man's panicky mistrust of money and guess at the Consul's contempt of it.

Warrington said in the same agreeable tone, 'I wrote to you of it when you were ill.'

'That you advised it.' They had not spoken of it since. 'You never said that you had promised it.'

'It's a small thing,' the Consul said carelessly. 'It's expected. I'd have thought you'd know. Nothing gets done without it. You do agree?'

Why ask him now? But it was clear why. Wood's presence was being used to shame him into acquiescence. Resentment at the position he was in came bitterly to life. He said, 'Is there anything else I have given my consent to that I should know about?'

The Consul ignored this and turned back to Wood. Across his shoulder he told Laing carelessly that he had arranged to ride at once into the town to exchange the bond. Laing insisted that he ride with him.

They set out in silence. Laing could not speak for fear he would betray the anger of which he was already half ashamed. The Consul rode ahead with Fred, rising in his saddle with a perfect grace, head held high. Once he turned back to smile at Laing, ignoring his silence as before he had ignored his rudeness. Presently he reined in his horse, leaving Fred to ride on ahead and Laing no choice but to come alongside of him. His face was expressionless, but he spoke with a great kindliness of tone. 'I think you are cast down. Really, you should not be.'

Laing answered in a rush, 'It is the reprimand from Whitehall that oppresses me. It is constantly on my mind. It is bound to come.'

'I'd not have thought you would care for a thing like that,' the Consul told him. When Laing was silent he said, 'What is it but words?'

'I know myself,' Laing told him. 'I know myself too well. I cannot abide a slight. It's the resentment I am bound to feel that troubles me, more than the thing itself.'

They had come up to the gates of the town. The Consul did not answer him.

That afternoon one Giovanelli, a Jew from Naples, called at the consulate and exchanged the bond for five hundred silver dollars. Early on the following morning Laing took three hundred of these and rode with Fred back to Yahia Mohammed's encampment in the desert, to instruct him to purchase the camels and return with them to the English Garden by the end of the week. At noon, in spite of the glaring heat, they set out again for the town where Laing must set about assembling his people and his baggage.

If he had supposed all this activity and the sojourn in the town would free him of thoughts of Emma Warrington, he was mistaken. The minutes spent with her in the salon returned to him in the midst of tasks that would once have absorbed his attention. With the clarity of a vision he saw each of her slow movements towards him and away; the enchanting raising and lowering of her eyes. He remembered the intensity of his happiness and cursed himself that he had so wilfully forgone the last few days he might have spent with her.

At that hour of the day, when he had made his way up through the plantation to the house, he found himself especially restless. He must collect his thoughts and write to Bandinel.

Should I succeed, my position in the world may be much advanced, he wrote. *More and more I am convinced – for reasons not entirely scientific – that whether I leave by ship from Benin or retrace my steps across the desert, I should be well advised to return to Tripoli. I must tell you I am interested – more than interested – in what I find here, and begin to hope that whatever the outcome of my journey, I might expect a cordial welcome here, in one amiable quarter at least.*

On the morning of the thirteenth of June Laing rode slowly out of Tripoli at the head of a small troop. Behind him came the two boatwrights, mounted on horses lent them by the Consul. The baggage followed on hired mules. Each had a driver trotting at its side, hitting puffs of dust from its flank with a stick. Two additional servants, whom he had hired at the Consul's insistence, brought up the rear and tugged along two sheep on lengths of rope. He was in a state of intense excitement which the tedious pace of their advance could only exacerbate.

When finally he arrived at the English Garden he found a group of camels kneeling in the shade of the giant fig tree outside its gates. Their owners squatted in the dust beside them and sprang up when he dismounted. The eldest of them he recognised as Yahia Mohammed.

'Are you ready to go?' Laing asked him.

'Yes, *Reis*, I am ready.'

He had brought his brother and his nephew to assist him. Everything they needed for the journey was hung in a few leather bags from their saddles. Each carried a flintlock, which Laing's experienced eye could see to be lovingly maintained but of such ancient design as to be little more than a badge of status. He shook each of them gravely by the hand and murmured the words of greeting in Arabic.

Jack le Bore appeared from inside the gates. The bivouac had been struck; the instruments and equipment packed and ready to be added to the loads already carried by the mules. Now the family came through the gates to wave him off. Ossy ran up fearlessly and butted his head against Laing's riding boot. Fred and the Consul greeted the camelmen. The three girls, dressed in white and veiled against the dust, stood together by the gatepost. With what sure knowledge his eye distinguished Emma from among them. He had supposed there would have been time to speak to her; to touch her hand again; to reassure her that he would return. But one of the mules had slipped its load. It must be readjusted. A loud dissension broke out between the servants and the mule drivers. A sheep broke its lead and ran back down the road in a hopeless bid for escape.

When order was restored he mounted quickly and raised his arm in the signal to depart. The mule drivers shouted and beat at their charges. The sheep bleated with shrill premonition. The camels lurched upright. The whole party jolted forward so suddenly that Emma, to whom his eyes turned at the last, was half-obscured from him by a great cloud of dust.

That evening Laing sat by his fire in the new encampment, with his journal open on his knee. The tents were pitched near the well. The mule drivers had watered their beasts and headed back to town. The two boatwrights had earlier been prone to apprehension, even to sulkiness. Now Laing was relieved to hear them chattering to one another as excitedly as children. Throughout the afternoon they had crawled in and out of each other's tents, arranged and rearranged their few belongings, volunteered eagerly and simultaneously for every task. The camelmen had built themselves a separate fire and sat apart. The hired servants from the town kept to theirs. Jack moved jauntily among them all, whistling his oddly rhythmed version of the Ça ira.

It was the moment he had longed for. He was at last his own master, with his own people around him; the corruptions of the civilised world put from him; the first step taken of the journey into that pure void where he might seize his destiny and shape it how he would. Yet at the very moment when he should have felt profound contentment he found his thoughts turned back to painful partially-severed things.

As the day cooled the garden let off its wild fragrance. Presently the hubbub among the servants and the sudden silencing of the sheep told him that the hour of their execution had come. Shortly afterwards the odour of roasting mutton came drifting from the servants' fire.

How vain are human conjectures, he noted in his journal, *how short human foresight, how transitory human happiness. How often the very granting of a man's desire must deprive him of a deeper want, which he had not perceived until it was too late.*

Four days had passed since Laing's departure for the garden of the ruined palace. For all that time Emma had moved from room to room, eaten her meals, worked at her stitching, with a strange enlarged attention to what she was doing, though she cared nothing for it. She could retain nothing of Laing in her mind but what she had last seen of him, riding his horse in the swirling dust, shouting his orders. His face had turned in her direction, but his expression had been hidden from her. He had seemed to be not at all the man who had spoken so feelingly to her; who had stared with still, demanding eyes when she had found the words to answer him. He had pressed her hand. She could not gauge the significance of that.

I am in love with him, she had discovered, but the words seemed meaningless with no one to confirm them.

It was four o'clock. The dinner bell had rung. Tom Wood was to take ship for Leghorn in the morning to see to his affairs there. They would not see him for a month or so. He had come to say goodbye. She sat in the bedroom looking in the glass she shared with her sisters. She dragged her splayed fingers down over her eyes, over her cheeks, and peered oddly at herself. She must go down. What should she say to them? The old language of commonplace had deserted her. Jenny was in the passage, saying, 'Where have you been?

The Knutsons are here.' Then she turned without another word and went before her down the stairs. Emma followed. At the foot of the stairs, in the passage, was a box of medicines that the doctor had brought as a farewell gift for Laing. She stooped to touch it as she passed, so swiftly that if anyone had seen her they would think nothing of it.

She was in the salon. All around her there were voices that seemed to speak at a distance, as if she overheard them from some other room.

'Ah, here is Emma. Emma, my angel, where have you been? Is she not charming, Theo? Look, look at Emma.'

'I have sent Ossy to the garden and Jane upstairs and I called and called but we could not think what had become of you. I said to Gerda, to Frau Knutson – did I not, Gerda – "Where can Emma be?" '?

She must kiss Frau Knutson, and stand quickly behind the chair rather than be made to kiss Herr Knutson, whose lips were wet and clinging and crept from her cheek to the corner of her mouth. She stood behind the chair with her hands gripped into the carving, staring at them all.

'And I will draw you,' Herr Knutson was saying, 'in just that pose you took when Wood told you that story. Come now, we'll practise it. Jenny, too. Come, Jenny, here on the sofa, come, come. I am an old friend, eh? As old as your father. You must permit. We are all old friends, are we not? Dear old friends. Emma, Emma. Here, here. Now so. On the sofa, Emma. Now so. You must permit me. The head so. Perhaps so, against Jenny's shoulder. How is that to you, my angel? Ah, charming, charming. But Emma's little chin is lost. Her little chin. Ah, no. Permit me to turn your head. No, no. You must relax. Do them separately? Do them as a pair? He is right. Tom Wood is always right. How dull we shall be without him. Is he not right, my angel? The two. Jenny so, and Emma turned so in profile, so that the chin is so. What do you say, Colonel?'

And Gerda Knutson was saying to her mother, 'Oh how I envy Tom Wood! Italy! To think! Indeed if it were not for you, and of course Herr Knutson, I should leave this place tomorrow. And Emma, too, I think. Would you not, Emma? I feel it in you. The desire to be gone.''

But she with her chin poised so, on Herr Knutson's scented finger, need find no answer. And lamb and rice and do not reach out your hand to the glass when the plates are changed, lest you touch the servant's hand. Clowder had his head across her knee. She stole a piece of lamb from her plate and fed it to him. And do not feed the dog.

'Sheikh Babani has not come.''

'Laing will not go, then?'

'Not for another week.'

Joy like a blow struck at her while she sat there. It was a wealth of time. 'Poor Laing,' she heard her father say. 'He's weary with the waiting.'

'Poor Laing.'

'A fine man.'

'A brave man.'

'Do you not think so, Emma?' Tom Wood, dropping his napkin as if by chance, touching her ankle as he lifted it again. 'Do you not think he is a fine brave man?'

'Oh he is very fine,' Jane said for her. 'And very stiff, I think.'

'Hah! We'll order up the next contestant then. Something a little less stiff for you; a little less tall and splendid for me. But he's a brave man, though. Good luck to him.'

And Laing, Laing, Laing, like blows now that had been withheld, for it seemed some last prohibition had been lifted when they spoke his name. The enormity of what had happened to her was beyond her grasp. He would come to dine with them tomorrow. She could not think beyond that.

She sat on the sofa while Herr Knutson drew her likeness. He stared at her with such a fierce detached concentration that Emma did not feel present at this act. She must keep her face still. She must not speak.

She saw the woman on the wall. She saw her walk out into the garden. She was so used to being alone that she was fearless when the leaves stirred. But Emma saw. Could not but see. Shut her eyes. Still saw the man. Stood behind the man. Saw the woman. As in a nightmare was the woman, who did not see him creep closer and closer from bush to bush. Emma saw him. She would cry out. Could not. Could not hear herself cry out. Laing. And ran in terror on the wall. Saw her feet fitted on the wall, tangled in the cloth she wore. Would fall and ran. Ran so as not to lose her balance and fall. Had no choice but to turn at the corner and run again, so that she must run towards him now with the ground sliding past below. Terror in her throat. All exposed in that light and he crouched below. She saw him. Saw his eye glint. Saw him raise his pistol slowly. Saw her with no choice but to run towards him. Saw him raise the pistol. Ran faster and faster. All around the lighted desert stayed empty and still. Laing. He raised the pistol. Fired it. She ran. She felt the pain. Far away she fell; a little thing. She could not move. She could not speak, caught in a knowledge she could put no words to.

He had come to the house. He stood quite close to her. The doctor had brought him a case of medicines as a farewell gift. He was saying to her father, 'There could be no better gift.' He sounded glad, as if he thought of nothing but the medicines, as if he wanted to be gone. He spoke her name. She could not answer him. There was no certain voice in which to speak. She could not look at him. She let her look fall short. When Jenny played; when he stood behind her at the piano and stared across at Emma, she knelt down by the box of medicines and pretended to examine them, lifting out the bottles, frowning over the cramped writing on the labels. As if a pendulum were swung and a clock set ticking, she was aware of each minute's erosion of the stock of time remaining.

He would go now. He would come again, he said. He was looking at her. He would not say goodbye. In a day or two, before he left, he would come again. It was intolerable. It could not be. She was running over the moonlit shadows of the trees with the stony ground pressing into the thin soles of her shoes. She stood half-hidden in the shadow of the stables, waiting for him to come, but at the first glimpse of movement turned away abruptly as if she would deny all part in what she did.

'Will you take my hand again?' he said. He had come up very close behind her, so that when she turned her shoulder jarred against him and they both let out a small sound. He had her hand pressed harshly to the stuff of his jacket.

She was involved now in his breathing. His hand was very dry. She could not look at him. He was saying in a voice not used, 'We need not say goodbye yet.'

'No.'

'Emma, Emma,' he was saying.

He was smiling at her foolishly, holding out his arms in an odd ashamed gesture. She had gathered up the lapels of his jacket in her fists. She was shaking them in and out, saying 'You must not go,' repeating in an appalled whisper this urgent message from a source unknown to her. He had taken hold of her wrists to set her from him. She shut her eyes and held up her face with her lips very stiff and still and presently felt his warm mouth press upon them. His lips were open. She seemed to see his mouth a warm black void which would engulf her.

He was saying repeatedly, with his mouth against her hair, 'I'll come back.'

'You said that you would not.'

'That was before this.'

'How? How?'

'It doesn't matter. Whatever happens. However long it takes. I'll fetch up here again.'

She could not see him now with a face that was not his, smiling foolishly, laughing, not listening to what she told him. 'How many days? How many days?'

He said distinctly, as if to a child, 'I'll be away for ninety days to Timbuctoo.'

'And ninety days till you come back?'

'Yes.' He was touching her face with his finger so that she pulled away, saying impatiently, 'Ninety days, ninety days.' The words meant nothing to her. She had no means of adding them together. 'I'll wait,' she told him. 'I'll wait.' Her hard swift unpractised kisses pressed again and again against his mouth.

'Eh, eh,' he was saying with the same deep mindless laugh. 'What would your father think of us now?'

'He mustn't know.'

'What mustn't he know, then?'

He held up her chin with his finger, as if he must see the words form on her lips.

She said in a whisper but without hesitation, 'That I love you.'

'And I love you,' he told her.

It was confirmed. The words were said. Inside herself she permitted a great release of happiness. 'I must go now,' she told him. For this seemed sufficient to her; that he had kissed her, that he had said he loved her, that tomorrow evening he would come again. She went away from him and ran into the house.

At dawn on the twenty-second of June a single shot from the palace battlements once more alerted the town of an approaching ship. By ten o'clock word had reached Colonel Warrington that the Tuscan brig *Guerrieco* was in the offing. Knowing it to be out of Malta, he rode directly to the town.

Just before noon a small but interesting procession was seen to make its way from the quay to the town consulate. Four crewmen from the brig carried a stout iron-bound box suspended from oars across their shoulders. They were accompanied by a special courier, the ship's captain and four men-at-arms. Long before they reached the consulate, speculation on the box's contents was diffused into the farthermost alleys of the town and might be seen to act upon the place as a sip of brandy on a dying man. It was said that a gift of gold bars had been sent from the King of England; that the Consul, who was, by some accounts, the close friend of that king, and by others his natural son by a concubine, would shortly present the entire sum to the Bashaw to finance his war against the rebels. The box would shortly be opened and the magic stuff released. A force as powerful as life itself would then be set in motion. Minuter and minuter sums would be released for the repayments of old debts and the simultaneous incurring of new and larger ones.

The rumours reached the small dark room of the great courtyard where the Bet-el-Mel sat cross-legged on the floor and told his beads as rapidly as if he used his abacus. When a request came from Colonel Warrington for an audience with the Bashaw he granted it immediately.

Word of this reached Mohammed d'Ghies in his upstairs room in the palace. He sent directly for his most trusted messenger, whom he ordered to set out at once across the Garian mountains to Ghadames. There he was to instruct the Sheikh Babani that the time at last was right. He might now set out for Tripoli.

All day the Consul's every move had been watched with an attention he had failed to inspire for many months. When, shortly after noon, he set out for the palace, it was noticed that his *chouish* walked with a greater arrogance and a more ferocious use of his stick, and that the Consul strode along with renewed vigour. Two guards followed in his wake, carrying a smaller box between them. The Bashaw greeted his old friend cordially. They talked of many things, but were careful to avoid any mention of money. Only as he left the palace did the Consul enter the Bet-el-Mel's room near the gate and hand over to him the first thousand dollars in part payment for the hire of the cavalry. Then, with his eyes politely averted, he dispensed the further three hundred promised to the Bet-el-Mel himself.

Word had already been sent to Laing's camp, advising him to ride at once to the town to make his final preparations. He and the Consul spent the next few days at the consulate. They purchased two mules and a riding camel for Laing. A small sum was given to the unwanted Bagoola, so that he might equip himself. Thirty dollars were despatched with the Consul's private courier, Sala, as an inducement for the guide Hateeta to make his way to Ghadames and wait there for Laing's arrival. On the advice of Mohammed d'Ghies more presents were purchased from a merchant he especially recommended: one Giovanelli, he who had cashed the bond. The balance of the sum was kept under guard at the consulate, except for two thousand dollars handed over to Laing to cover his travelling expenses.

From Giovanelli Laing also purchased four brace of pistols, two of them silver-mounted, an additional sword, ten gilt-mounted stilettos, five hundred pistol flints and several elaborate garments. These, being intended as gifts of government, he charged to the mission's account. From his travelling money he purchased the sixty waterskins and paid for them to be softened and oiled. On the Consul's advice he bought two sheepskins to place under his riding saddle. Finally it occurred to him that he had no tackle for the boat that Rogers and Harris would build for their voyage down the Niger from Timbuctoo. He purchased this in the market, along with the sounding lines with which he would plumb that river's depths. The lead weights lay mysteriously in his hand, invested with their purpose.

A month ago these purchases, and the time spent in the

Consul's company discussing the journey, would have been a source of delight. Now he was distracted by thoughts of Emma. He watched the Consul for any sign that she had revealed to him the contents of her heart. For surely, when they lived in such close proximity, and were so sly and watchful with one another, it must by now be known. How then might he interpret the Consul's silence on the subject other than as unwillingness to accept him as a suitor?

Douce, douce, he told himself, he knows nothing of it. It is not the time. But the thought persisted that it was his duty to tell the Consul of his change of route before he went, and discuss with him the feasibility of returning by the desert, trading on the good will established during the outward journey. He began a hundred conversations in his mind, but each one foundered on the need to explain to the Consul the motive for his return. At the same time he was filled with a reckless impulse to declare his passion; and test by his reaction the Consul's true opinion of his worth.

But the moment for doing so had passed. The Consul returned that afternoon to the Garden. On the following morning Laing rode directly to his camp with the silver dollars locked in a box and the key on a leather thong around his neck. He allowed himself one brief glance only through the garden gates.

Two evenings later he rode back to the Menchia to spend the evening with the Consul's family. The reins lay loosely in his hands. He let the mare pick over the uneven road at her own pace. He had come to the village before the Garden; already night had settled on it. Only a few wrapped figures moved along the side of the road and turned dark featureless faces towards him as he passed. The shadowed forms of beasts were tethered by the doors of the houses, a sheep, a donkey, a camel. A dog ran beside him, leaping and snapping at his stirrup. Through open doorways he had glimpses of fires and the women who tended them. Then he saw the white walls of the Garden, the shifting mass of the great fig tree, the open gate.

The syce took his horse. He walked towards the house. Only when he had climbed the steps to the verandah did he notice the silence and the absence of light in the downstairs windows. A sharp misgiving made him ask the servant at the door, 'Are they here? Do they expect me?' The man bowed and, turning without a word, led Laing down the hall, past the Consul's study, past the empty silent drawing room, to the door of the dining room. There, by the light of a single candle, he made out the figure of the Consul seated heavily back in his chair at the head of an empty table.

He had come quite close to him before the Consul looked up and said simply, 'Tyrwhitt's dead.'

'Dead?' Laing repeated. 'How dead?'

'Of fever. In Murzuk. The letter came yesterday evening.'

'I'm very sorry to hear it,' Laing said. 'Poor fellow.'

The Consul had leant forward, propping his elbows on the table and allowing his head to fall heavily between his hands. He was unshaven. Laing had never seen him so. He said quietly, 'I'll go.'

'Don't,' the Consul said. 'Sit. Sit awhile.' He handed Laing a paper.

Praise be to God, he read, *and blessings and peace be unto the apostle of God.* It was a letter rendered into English. *You are well aware that the omnipotent God hath ordained to every man a certain age which can neither be increased or decreased, and hath destined to him a grave in which he can neither enter before his time, nor from which he can fly when his time comes. Thus, when you know this, it may be an alleviation to your sorrow and grief when we acquaint you that your son Tyrwhitt ended his life and his days and his hours, terminated by his death on Monday the end of Soffar 1240.*

It was signed by the Sultan of Murzuk, who designated himself the Slave of God.

'He's been dead six months,' the Consul said.

'Good God, why weren't you told?'

The Consul shrugged. 'It often happens.'

'He died alone?' Laing asked him.

'Oh, quite.' He beckoned behind him. A servant moved forward out of the unlit corner of the room and filled his glass and one for Laing. The Consul drank his down silently and steadily. Then he said, 'Mrs Warrington and the girls would send their apologies. They cannot see you, Laing. They are quite stricken with it. It's like a death in the family, you see.

111

You were to come tonight. I had forgotten. Have you eaten?'

He had not, but had no taste for food. Their grief, its apparent power to wipe him from their minds, had struck him to the heart. He heard the Consul say, 'Mrs Warrington had wanted him for Emma. Well, it would never have done.'

'Poor Emma, then,' Laing said.

But the Consul went on, 'I sent him there, Laing. I cannot free my mind of it. He cried when he went away from here. They all did. Mrs Warrington and the girls. They were all most affected by it. He didn't shirk, mind. He saw it as his duty not to be a burden on me. To do what he might for his country.'

'It does him credit,' Laing said.

'I must write to his father. All day I've delayed doing so. Poor man. What he will feel? He'd cut him off, you know. Wanted no more of him. A hard man, Laing. Sent me out his boy because I owed him money. He knew I'd nothing. I suppose he saw it as the one way of getting something back from me. Poor boy. It wasn't his fault. He felt it very keenly that I must have the cost of him. He wanted to go with Clapperton and Oudney, as would any boy his age with any spirit. To set up in Murzuk. I could pay him then, you see, a little, as Vice-consul. Oh, he jumped at the chance, Laing. Anything to make his way. And he might have done. There's nothing to say he might not have done.'

'Others have,' Laing said.

'Indeed, indeed. Poor boy. This is for you, Laing.' He pushed a key across the table. 'They've sent his things to Ghadames. There's a locked box. They think it may have money in it. I doubt that, but there might be something of comfort in it for his mother.'

Laing took it up and, untying the thong about his neck, slid the small key onto it.

'You should sleep,' Laing said, pushing back the chair and standing. He took his bundle of letters from inside his jacket and laid them on the table. 'I'll come again before I go.'

'Yes. Yes,' the Consul said, but Laing thought he had scarcely heard him. The servant ran ahead of him to usher him into the hall. Then he closed the door to the dining room behind him and, laying his finger to his lips, pointed urgently to the verandah. When Laing hesitated he touched him on the arm and urged him silently again past the empty stairway to the open door of the verandah. Laing went as he directed and heard the door close behind him. Already he had made out in the indistinct light Emma's pale dress against the dark vine.

She ran against him crying, gripping at his arms.

'Emma, Emma,' he was saying. 'What's this? What's this?'

But she was unable to answer. She held herself tight and hard against him, with her arms locked like wire about his neck and kissed him repeatedly, butting her hot wet face against his. Still she wept. He licked her salt from her lips. 'Poor Tyrwhitt,' he whispered against her ear. 'Did you not love him a little? These tears are for him, I think.'

'No. No. He was nothing.'

'Who are they for, then?'

'For you.' But she was rigid in his arms.

'For me? When I am alive? When I'm with you and never happier in my life? Ach, Emma, Emma, what's this now? There now, there. Surely that makes it better. And there now. Now, now, is that not better, Emma? You're overset by this. No wonder. Ach, stop now, poor Emma. None of that. Your poor generous heart, Emma, there, Emma. He was nothing but a boy. A poor green boy. I'm not that, Emma.' He put her from him saying, 'Emma, we must not. I am bound to tell your father.'

'No,' she said. 'No.'

'It's nothing I'm ashamed of.'

She had begun to cry again. She said, 'He'd send you off. You will die.'

'Emma, Emma, what wild talk is this? I do not go because he sends me. I go because I wish to go. I've promised to come back to you. I'm sure as any man is able to be sure. My destiny's with you, Emma.'

'No,' she said again. 'No.'

'What is it you want?' he said to her. 'Is this what you want?' But a moment later he turned into the dark, ashamed, saying, 'Is this some game you are playing with me, for if it is I cannot take it. I had not thought it of you.' He could hear the small sharp intake of her breath. 'What do you want of me?' he said wearily.

'I love you,' she told him, speaking these odd words against his back so that he was bound to turn to her and say, 'You don't know what that means.' But he said it very close to her,

113

letting the breath of the words play upon her face, touching her wet cheeks in a kind of wonder at what had come about. He was suddenly and powerfully moved by her. 'That's enough,' he said. He was rocking her stiffly to and fro in his arms, saying, 'That's enough.' He kissed her once more, swiftly, and ran down the steps and up through the garden past the darkened house.

An hour later he lay stretched out by his camp fire in the same mood of heady exaltation he had felt on his arrival two months ago. Then the cheers of the sailors had seemed to carry him aloft to a vantage point from which his destiny lay clear before him. While all the time what had he been but a fool rowed along in a boat, ignorant of the greater destiny that lay in wait on the dark and fragrant shore?

'I saw you,' he would say to her, 'alone in a room. It was you. I had mistaken the room, but it was more than chance that I should open that door.' And all the subsequent delays, so irksome to him then, what were they but the necessary gifts of time in which Emma might be revealed to him for what she was; a being almost of his own devising, an emanation of all that was reckless and aspiring in himself?

Now with mathematical delight this final part fell exactly into place, so that the entire mechanism of his former life was justified and given meaning. He calculated that Emma's birth had fallen in his fourteenth year, at the very time when he, a schoolboy still in Edinburgh, had felt the first formless intimations of greatness. He thought with wonder how, at every moment of his life since, she had been alive somewhere else, withholding in her parallel existence that single element that would make him whole.

He lay on his back, seeming still to feel the hard insistent pressure of her body on his own. Above, the close confusion of stars enclosed with their wide dome both him and her and the vast distance he must travel before he might attain her. His great route had doubled and must circle back to its beginnings, for what now was Timbuctoo without the hope of Emma? And what hope was there of Emma unless he first laid claim to Timbuctoo? He was convinced suddenly of the compelling need to win the Consul's consent before he set out.

In the morning, by the first light, he wrote to her:

Emma, my dear, I have not slept all night for the matter that has arisen between us, and at this time when I expect hourly news of my departure. How eagerly I once awaited it, my dear, and now it seems a sentence of death, when all these newly awakened affections demand that I stay at your side. How can I leave you now, Emma? How can I come to you in any sort of honour (which you must know is very dear to me) until I have spoken to your father. For I would marry you, Emma, but cannot trust myself to see you again until he knows of this; until I have pledged what little Laing has. Indeed, my dear, that is nothing beyond a loving heart and a conviction long felt that I am set apart for greatness. I think you love me, Emma. I think you have as little sense as I. My mind is in turmoil. I pledge you a thousand kisses, dearest Emma, which one by one I shall redeem from you – if all goes well. If not it is farewell to poor Laing and I set out a dead man.

While it was still early he rode with it himself to the gates of the Garden and delivered it to the servant there with a generous bribe and strict instructions that it should be given into Emma's hand; not to the Consul, not to Vincenzio. At the same time he handed over a brief note to the Consul asking if he might speak to him privately on a matter close to his heart, supposing that the very mention of this organ must alert the Consul to his purpose.

That evening he rode again to the Garden. The same servant saluted him at the gate. The syce ran forward to take his horse. He avoided the front entrance to the house and made his way instead around to the side, where the Consul's room of business opened out onto the verandah. The door was thrown open into the warm night. The Consul sat at his desk, his brows arched, his mouth a little open, writing, by the light of a single candle, a steady vigorous flow of words upon the page; so preoccupied that Laing climbed the two steps of the porch and came up to the door without disturbing him.

He hesitated in the dark, wanting to give this moment its due, which the sudden ordinariness of the room and something in the Consul's solid presence seemed to threaten. From the open windows of the salon came the sharp inconsequential notes of the piano. He was aware of Emma's presence in the house like a pressure on his very being. Still he hesitated, for it seemed that as long as he withheld himself

115

nothing would alter, while at his slightest move the Consul must calmly raise his eyes to something that had been surely apparent all along. And then Laing's whole existence gathered up, directed this way or that way, all in a moment that he was powerless to control. Douce, douce, he told himself, for it lay not in the Consul's power either. It was the hand of destiny that ruled them both, and of his destined love of Emma he had an absolute conviction.

'Who's there?' the Consul asked, peering beyond his candle. He spoke without alarm, as if there were comings and going to this window at all hours. 'Oh, Laing.' Directly he lowered his eyes to his writing, saying, 'Sit down. Sit down.'

Laing walked over to the desk and sat. What had he expected? The Consul to rise with some spontaneous gesture of acceptance? 'I shan't be a moment,' he was saying.

In fact, although he had expected him, Laing's appearance at that moment had very slightly disconcerted the Consul. He was engaged in writing to Lord Bathurst at the Colonial Office a letter on the mission's departure.

Now, my Lord, he had just written, *permit me to say better arrangements could not have been made, and a fairer prospect of success could not present itself. Supported by the Enthusiastic Spirit of Major Laing, I feel as Sanguine as it is possible for Man to do, in the uncertainty of all Human Affairs.* True enough. Yet instinctively, as Laing sat opposite, he shielded the paper with his hand, for he had concluded, *I have endeavoured to plant in the mind of Major Laing the cheering prospect of meeting Clapperton at Sokoto.* He had done no such thing and shrank from the task, for he was well aware of Laing's resentment of the man. With these months of effort so nearly at completion he found he had a nervous dread of some little unforeseen difference spoiling it all at the last. Quickly he concluded and signed the letter.

Laing watched him sand and fold it. The silver sander, the heavy gold ring on the Consul's finger, the precise dramatic movement of his hands all laid claim to an importance running counter to his own. He realised that he had made no preparation as to what to say.

'This is for you,' the Consul told him, pushing two other letters towards him. 'To introduce you.' He glanced up then.

'Stating my interest. I think you'll find that counts in the interior more than you suppose.'

He saw Laing stare at him, but it seemed with little attention as to what had just been said. Laing's note, with its odd formality, came back to him. He said with a slight frown, 'You wrote. Has something come up?'

Laing said rapidly and at random, 'I was thinking as I rode along how little we have spoken of what I should do when I reach Benin.'

'Why, get yourself out of there as soon as maybe. I've a horror of the place. I'll write at once to Malta and tell them to have a frigate wait for you.'

'And then?'

'Why, home to England,' the Consul said. 'Reap your rewards.' He leant back in his chair and looked with attention at Laing.

'Not come back here?'

'If you wish,' the Consul said cautiously. 'No one would be happier than I . . . But why here? All your interest surely lies in England.'

'Not all,' Laing said. Then, when the Consul turned on him the disconcerting stare of one who does not wish to be surprised, 'May I speak to you?'

The Consul, to whom he was already speaking, kept silent.

'I wish to speak to you about Emma.' He had risen and moved a few paces away. Now without turning around he said, 'You instructed me to speak to her, to urge her to read.'

'Well?'

'Well, I have done so and something has arisen.' He must struggle to keep his voice free of the delight of his discovery. Yet when he turned back the Consul's face was as grim and uncomprehending as the very rock. 'We love one another,' Laing said, as if he expressed some simple, widely-held truth. When the Consul continued to say nothing he went on with a quickening of his voice, 'Does this mean nothing to you, what I am saying? I only tell you of something that has happened. You cannot dismiss it. Don't you see, the more unlikely it may seem to you the more that proves it was intended so. It is not something that can be dismissed. Else anyone might fall in love with anyone and out again as easily.'

'I think you are mistaken,' the Consul said coldly.

'No,' Laing said, with a little laugh. 'There's no mistaking it.'

'Your own feelings, perhaps. Of hers you can know nothing.'

'My God,' Laing said, 'why will you not listen to me?'

'I have been forced to listen.'

'Nothing has been done dishonourably. You can see that I am speaking to you now to declare my intention to marry her on my return.'

'Your intention!' the Consul said unpleasantly. 'Who are you to have intentions?' His stick stood propped against his chair. As he rose he snatched it up and brought it down an inch or so before Laing's face to strike the surface of the desk. He watched Laing's eyes and at their slightest shift of fear would, without compunction, have struck him too. But Laing, stood rigid and unblinking, like a man in a trance.

At last he said, 'What have you done? Why did you not leave me to make my own way in the first place? I think I'm not the man you wanted for this mission. I think you wanted it for Tyrwhitt. Or Clapperton. I think all along you have dealt falsely with me. Professed support. Friendship, even. I thought I was your friend. Directed my attention to her. Twice. Until I could not ignore it. It was you. Why? If all along you despised me for what I am.'

'Get out,' the Consul shouted. 'Get out.'

Laing said, 'If I go, I'll not come back.'

'That's your affair,' the Consul shouted and found himself standing in an empty room clutching the stick, which he now hurled through the open door where Laing in a matter of minutes had come and gone. A vivid dislike of the man rose up in him at the same time that his former sense of Laing, like a friend in a relentless crowd, seemed swept past him. He heard the piano falter and fall silent; the dogs claw and whimper at the door. If he sat down again his eye would fall on the letter he had been writing. Its fulsome phrases sprang into his head. He could not stay a moment longer in this room with the self of half an hour past, lest he be forced to ask himself intolerably, What have I done? Instead he flung out into the passage and the waiting house where the sounds of his rage had preceded him.

'Emma,' he shouted, 'Emma!' and flung open the door of the

salon. The other people in the room he saw only as vague alarmed movements around the thin rigid form of his child. 'What is this, Miss?' he was shouting at her. 'What have you done?'

And she was shouting at him in the same wild tone, 'Where is he? I know he is here.'

She ran at the door with her hands held up before her face so that when he caught at her it was by her wrists. He felt them thin and bony, bunched up in his hands. At the thought that they might snap, that she might beguile him into harming her, his rage became intolerable to him, but might not be abandoned now. He was shouting at her, 'What have you done? What have you meddled in?' He had her two wrists in one of his hands and with the other reached to shut the door behind his back. Then he dragged her to him until he could lean his weight against the door before he let her free. They were sweating in the sudden vehemence of movement. She was breathing quickly and loudly, turning her head this way and that like a wild thing that would escape the room at any cost. 'It's no use,' he shouted at her. 'He's gone. Your Scotsman's gone.'

The others stood where they were, risen out of their chairs, too fearful of passing close to him to attempt to leave the room. Only Ossy now ran suddenly at the door and began to twist his fingers savagely among the Consul's to pry them from the handle.

'Get out,' the Consul shouted and jerked the door suddenly open so that the child was thrown back before he was released. 'Get out,' he shouted to them all, holding the door for Jane and Louisa, who squeezed past him, clinging to one another.

Outside Ossy's voice could be heard calling Laing's name piteously and repeatedly. 'He's gone, damn you,' the Consul shouted through the door. 'He's gone. She's led him to make addresses to her,' he said accusingly to his wife, who had moved towards him like a woman in a trance, less to protect her child than to draw his rage onto its natural recipient. She stood there supplicating with her hand. For what? For a blow? he would deny her that.

She asked in a bewildered voice, 'What has happened?'

'He's asked to marry her. That's what's happened and she,

119

it appears, has given him every reason to believe that he will be an acceptable husband to her. Well? Have you, Miss? Answer me?'

'I will marry him,' she said, as if she must remind herself.

'You will not.'

'I will,' she kept repeating. 'I will.'

'But he is going away,' said Mrs Warrington. 'Surely he is going away and not coming back?'

'Where has he gone?' Emma cried out. 'Where has he gone?'

'He's gone from here,' the Consul said, 'that's all that need concern you. He can go to hell for all I care. He can do as he pleases but he doesn't come back here again. He doesn't clap eyes on you again, Miss.'

The growing conviction of his words propelled him up and down the room. It rid him too of the sight of his daughter, who stood staring at him now with a face made thin and plain by passion.

'The man's head is turned,' he said. The words rang out like orders righting the world. When her expression did not alter, when she made no effort to deny him, he felt with a sensation of panic that his anger must desert him soon and leave him at the mercy of the thing that he had done. He turned suddenly and shouted at her, 'Get out! Get out of my sight!'

She was in the passage. Her mind was cleared of everything but an absolute conviction that this must not be; that nothing else existed; that her life could not extend into a void where Laing did not exist. She had taken up the little bottle out of the medicine chest without hesitation, as if, when she had first glanced at it, her eye had marked out its exact whereabouts in knowledge of this moment. She was on the stairs, aware only of the vast blankness into which she ran, and the sense of something irretrievable that moment by moment dissolved from her grasp. She knew nothing of the operation of the poison; only that once it was drunk the decision would be made and she would have no more to do but wait in the warm safety of her bed. She spilled a little into the palm of her hand and lapped at it greedily with her tongue. She would wake or she would not wake. The simplicity and rightness of it made it seem unreal even when the metallic taste of it clung in her mouth.

If it were true that her destiny lay with Laing, she must wake.

If not they would lose nothing that had not already been taken from them, and sleep were best then. She hid the little bottle behind her bolster, removed her dress, pulled on her night-shift and lay down on the bed. The house had grown quiet. Presently she heard her sisters come into the room. She heard breathing. The edge of her mattress was nudged. One of them peered at her through the muslin. 'Emma?' She lay still and made no answer. They too lay in their beds and whispered words she could not hear. It surprised her when, some time later, she felt the first exploratory wandering of pain and then a moment later a violent cramp that caused her to cry out.

Despite the darkness of the night and the treacherous surface of the road, Laing had ridden along it at a reckless pace. When he reached his camp he found one of the camelmen hunched over the embers of the evening fire. The others slept inside their tents or stretched out on the ground where they had sat. He too lay down under the crowded heavy sky in which a waning moon was just appearing. His mind was feverishly alert. Scheme after scheme appeared to him with the odd clarity of certain dreams. In the morning he would strike camp and ride back to Tripoli. He would take passage around the coast and rejoin his regiment in Freetown. He would get word secretly to Emma and flee with her to Malta. Shapes moved briefly in rooms, on the half-remembered decks of ships, but could not be retained. He had no hope of sleeping. The barking of dogs, the shirring of cicadas bore incessantly in upon him like some tormenting echo of the sounds within his head. In the closer stillness the champing and shuffling of the horses on their pickets seemed magnified and sinister.

He rose and, telling the watchman he would be gone till morning, saddled a fresh horse. Leading it up through the trees to the road, he mounted and rode back towards the Garden. At the outskirts of the village he tethered the horse to a tree and made his way by foot, keeping to the shadowed side of the road out of the moonlight. The gates stood open. He stood in shadow under the fig tree with his head tilted back against its trunk, staring fixedly at the upstairs windows. Although it was well past midnight they still glowed with light and from time to time he saw the agitated movement of a candle behind the glass. At any moment it seemed she might come running out. He stood with his head against the tree, repeating her name again and again. Emma. Emma. At the first hint of dawn he forced himself to leave, knowing that a part of him was trapped there; that no distance he might travel could free him or restore him to himself.

He rode back to the camp. Exhaustion had cleared his mind. His position was plain enough. He was ruined for the army. He had applied for this mission without his commanding officer's approval. He had not kept to the terms of his contract. The debt had been incurred, the letter sent, his reputation for resource and honesty lost. No redress. No choice but to go on and lose himself in that great void before they might recall him to his shame. He led the horse down through the date grove and, when he had seen to it, continued to pace up and down between the trees, holding from him the chaos of his loss. For he must take up again the line of his journey which the harsh containment of his anger against the Consul made to appear again the simple thing it once had been. All was Laing now. All would emanate from him or not exist. All thought of Emma must be kept rigorously excised from Mind although, as he forced himself to walk up and down, a grieving sense of her pursued him and would not be ignored.

At dawn he gave orders to strike camp. Amid the activity he wrote a final note to Colonel Warrington:

Sir, I consider myself attached to your daughter by a bond from which only she has the power to release me. Rather than pain her by my near presence, I am removing at dawn to Tajura two miles east of here and will there await the arrival of Babani as arranged. I shall set out then for the interior forthwith without returning to the town.

An hour later, when all was packed and ready, he gave the order to depart.

By ten o'clock the Menchia lay behind them. By noon they made their way between the mud walls and hedges of Indian fig that penned in the gardens of Tajura. He ordered the new camp set up beyond the village, within sight of a gleaming salt lake and easy reach of a well which proved sweet and plentiful. He had the tents set at a distance from the road where they might not be troubled by the constant toing and froing of beasts and people. Nearby there stood a group of three date palms. The sand had heaped itself between their trunks to a height where the road could be overlooked some way before it entered the village. Here he kept a man posted as look-out for a messenger with the news of Babani's arrival or even for the Sheikh himself.

Throughout that day he was buoyed up by his bitter sense of grievance against Warrington. He took a precise care in each matter that he dealt with. He had the second sheep slaughtered and the flesh cut into narrow strips and hung to dry on lines strung between the tents. The fat they salted and boiled down over the fire, so that all day the nauseating odour of mutton-fat hung over the camp. He sent Jack and one of the camelmen to town to purchase dates, which later they stoned and kneaded together and packed into a skin. He had each of the skins tested to see if they were watertight. The smallest carelessness would have been intolerable. To achieve perfection in every slightest thing seemed in some way to exact a vengeance for the great injustice that had been done to him. For he had been encouraged, but must not think of that.

Towards evening he walked out with Jack to the lake. He carried the new percussion rifle, Jack his reconditioned old one. Neither had had the chance to try them out in earnest. Now they shot four red-legged snipe and took them back for their supper. It was Friday. If, in a week, no word had come from Babani he resolved to move forward on his own to Beni Ulid. There he would hire a guide and take his chances on the road to Ghadames. He talked of this at night to Jack quietly, out of the hearing of the others. What had they to fear? Far less, it seemed to him, than in the company of laden merchants escorted by a troop of horse demanding food at every starving village they passed through. At Ghadames they would trace Hateeta and with him attach themselves to a caravan, as Laing had first intended. They talked late, when the others had retired. At last physical exhaustion and the soul's powerful longing to relinquish thought overcame him. He slept instantly, like a man who has fallen senseless.

He woke to find the sun already risen and the dark form of a man standing staring down at him from the open doorway of his tent. A second later he recognised the Consul. He sat upright, feeling the hollow racing of his heart, the irrational longing to escape. He said brusquely, 'Leave me for a moment. I've just woken.'

The Consul withdrew from the opening without a word. Laing watched him settle himself on the camel saddle in the scant shade of the tent's canopy. He pulled on his trousers, let himself out the back of his tent and walked a little way away to relieve himself. He heard the Consul call out to Jack for water. He thought, He's heard from Whitehall. They've cancelled the mission. He's come to tell me. He walked around to the front of the tent and propped himself against the packing case on which he wrote, a few feet from the Consul. Neither spoke nor extended his hand. Laing stared out at the brilliant surface of the lake. At the edge of his vision he saw Jack tip the waterskin and pour water in a cup. It was tepid and foul-tasting from the freshly oiled skin. The Consul spat it out and said irritably, 'I wonder you're not camped closer to the well.'

'Get him fresh water,' Laing said. He took the cup and handed it out to the Creole.

'It doesn't matter,' the Consul said. 'Send him away, will you?'

Laing signalled sideways with his hand. The Consul, a florid sweating man whom he hated, sat with his shoulders slumped forward. On the glittering edges of the lake snipe scuttled to and fro. A herd of goats trotted towards the well. A child with hair the colour of dust ran in among them shouting and waving a stick. He let her cross the path of his vision without turning his head. He heard the Consul say, 'It cannot be like this between us. We are too bound up with one another.'

'I think not,' Laing said. 'I think that's past.' He had begun to shake and quickly pressed his hands between his knees to hide the fact.

The Consul said, 'I've come to ask you to ride back with me.'

'No,' Laing told him. 'On no account. I ride on from here. If Whitehall casts me off I go alone.'

'Think of her, man,' the Consul said. 'She's half out of her mind over you. It's on her behalf I've come.' He dragged his fingers down over his face like a man who longs for sleep.

Laing said, 'What good will seeing me do? How could either of us bear it? I could not. I go on from here.'

'I've had the devil of a time, Laing,' the Consul told him, 'the very devil of a time. She's taken poison.'

'Oh no,' Laing said. Some minutes had passed, perhaps. He was standing away from the tent in the heat, seeing with a particular intensity the jiggling motion made by the straight dark backs of the goats, one against the other. He turned back to the Consul and said in the same tone of wondering pity, 'Oh no. She isn't dead? She could not be dead?'

'Oh no, no, no,' the Consul said. 'She came damned near it, though. I'm devilish tired, Laing. I don't know when I've been so tired.' He began to talk on and on. Laing, who could scarcely grasp what he said, kept repeating aloud or within his head, How could she? How could she do that? The sense of Emma, which he had so cruelly withheld, overwhelmed him now. 'For pity's sake,' he said, 'what will become of her?'

The Consul was talking about Dickson. How he had left the box of medicines in the hall and they of course had thought nothing of it. She had taken the arsenic. Instantly Laing saw her there, kneeling down, lifting out the little bottles. 'Good God,' he' said. 'What can have possessed her?'

But the Consul was saying how he had fallen asleep in his office and no one had woken him. In their distraction they had not thought to. And Fred had gone for the doctor on Beatrice. 'Oh God, Laing,' he said. 'She was sick as a dog. I tried not to but I could hear it all. I'm wretchedly thirsty.'

'I'll get some water,' Laing told him. He walked away, calling to Jack to bring the cup. Jack came running, gesturing with it towards the well. 'No, I'll go,' Laing told him.

He walked across the sand to the well and stood there waiting while the goatherd lowered her leather bucket and dragged at the rope. The goats nudged and butted at his legs. It confused him that they were the same goats he had watched pass minutes before, when in the interval he had lived out his great pitying sense of Emma's suffering and the swift undertow of distaste that she had done so rash and violent a thing for love of him.

It bound him to her helplessly. He felt the sun burn at a single point between his shoulder-blades. He saw the child's hair about her face like hanks of felted wool, the fly on her lip, the yellow incrustation at the corner of her eyes. She tipped the bucket towards him and he held out his cup. He felt the warmish water spill over his hand.

He walked back again and handed the cup to the Consul, who drank at it greedily. Laing said simply, as he drank, 'I'll come back with you. I'll give it up if need be. You of all men know what it would cost me, but I'll give it up like that if it would help her.'

'No, no,' the Consul said, looking up. 'That can't be.'

'What is it you want of me, then?'

'Why, to marry her.' And yet it seemed to Laing he set no value on the words.

'You'd consent to that?'

'I have no choice. I was forced to give my word.'

'I cannot take it in,' Laing said. 'What's to be done? What am I to do?'

'Come back,' he said. 'Marry her. I thought that would please you.'

'It does,' Laing said. 'Of course it does. Only I cannot take it in.' He said a moment later, 'What happens then?'

'Then?'

'Do I go or stay?' He laughed his harsh unpractised laugh. 'I am quite overset by this. I cannot seem to take it in.'

'You go on as planned,' the Consul said.

'To Timbuctoo?' He spoke the childish word like a man in a dream. 'And Emma? What will become of Emma while I am gone?' He was staring now at the Consul, who seemed to be the man that he had always been, to watch Laing shrewdly and to speak with all his old command and vigour:

'She stays as she always has done, under my protection at the Garden. It will all be as before. Until your return, that is.'

'And will you marry us? Before I go within a day or two?'

'I have no choice in that.'

'I could wish you had,' Laing said quickly. 'I could wish you had wanted it.'

'I've given my word on that,' he said. 'Only you're to come back here. Do you understand me, Laing? You're not to be a husband to her in anything but name until I've had confirmation from Whitehall that the marriage is legal.'

'Why should it not be?'

'I do not know exactly what my powers are. It's never been

made plain to me.' He no longer looked at Laing, but trailed his hand behind him, turning slightly, feeling for his cap.

'You married Dickson,' Laing said.

'Well, well,' he said, retrieving the cap and hanging it on his knee. 'They were in great haste.'

'Surely you made inquiries then?'

'The whole thing's different.'

'I fail to see how.'

'Good God, man, be thankful for what you are getting. She's too ill and weak in any case. Think of her, man.'

'Can't you see,' Laing said, 'I cannot think of her and still go on. Why raise her expectations so, to dash them down? Has she agreed to this?'

'She doesn't know, Laing. She knows nothing of such things unless her mother tells her, which she'll not do. She's a child in such things. She only wants the name of wife to hold to while you're gone.'

'And then?' Laing said. 'When I come back? What's my standing then? Surely I have the right to ask?'

'I'll know where I stand by then. If they tell me it's not legal, we'll get a priest from Malta to see to it all.'

Laing said softly, 'And if I do not come back there's no harm done. I do not think I'm the man you want for a son-in-law. I think that lies at the heart of it.'

As if he had not spoken the Consul said agreeably, 'You'll come back, then?' He stood as he spoke, butting his head against the sagging canopy, and walked out into the sun.

'Not now,' Laing said. 'I need the time alone. I'll follow you tomorrow.'

As he mounted the Consul said to him, 'We mustn't quarrel. We've set our private matters above the mission. That's where it's all gone wrong. If that should fail we're both lost, Laing.'

'We'll talk more of this when I come,' Laing told him.

'Then or at Beni Ulid. With all this past and no one pressing round us.'

'Till Beni Ulid,' Laing called after him.

He climbed the sand dune and watched the Consul ride away until he was nothing more than the dark core to a glistening cloud of dust indistinguishable from all such men whom he had loved, who in return had thwarted and ill-used

127

him. Then he went back to his camp to prepare to follow after him.

And Emma? She scarcely knew what she had done. She was alive. It was true that she was destined for him. That he must return. That she, Emma, had secured his life. The day after next was to be her wedding day. It confused her that they had given way to her. She seemed hemmed in by quietness. Her voice could not extend beyond it to explain that she had done nothing for herself. Only to save him. After the wedding he was going away. It surprised her that he was. Had she supposed that if he married her he would not go? She scarcely knew. She was very tired still. She could not remember what she had thought. Her throat ached still from the voiding of the poison. It had not been like thinking. It had been a certainty that if she woke a future was assured for both of them. She did not feel it now. She wondered that she had ever dared to put the world so violently at risk. It awed her that she had wielded such power, that they had consented, that everything was as she had wanted it to be except that he was going away. Immediately then she felt inside her head the pacing of her dread. For might not the contract she had struck extend no further than the marriage? Might she, by insisting on the marriage, have secured nothing but the marriage and sent him out into that gleaming hostile space all undefended? So that for ninety days and ninety nights she alone, by the strength of her love, must bear up the burden of his life?

The wedding day had been fixed for Friday the fourteenth of July. Some good, the Consul reflected, might be wrung from this business. Each year on that day Rousseau invited him to attend, with his wife and family, the impious festivities at the French Consulate. Each year he was obliged to find some excuse which would not impugn his reputation for the strictest honesty. Now, with rare satisfaction, he penned a note to the effect that he would not be able to attend the Bastille Day celebrations owing to a previous commitment to marry his daughter.

At midday on the Thursday, Laing called briefly at the English Garden on his way into the town. The sight of Emma moved him deeply. She was seated on the sofa in the drawing room from which they forbade her to rise. She was very pale. The skin was so tightly drawn across her face that the bone shone white down the ridge of her nose. Her eyes were large and looked at him with an intensity that frightened him. He had supposed they might be allowed a little time alone together, but realised soon that the Consul and his wife had no intention of leaving the room. He moved his chair close to the sofa and took up her hand, almost fearful of touching her. Her fingers clung to his in a dry tight grip. If only they would go, he thought, he would lay his hand against her cheek and smooth away that terrible rigidity. Still, as they all talked around her, he was touched to see that the simple preparations for the wedding seemed to please her.

The Consul was to marry them in this very room. Her sisters were to be bridesmaids. They had thought of asking Amy Coxe to make a third, but then they had thought not. She made a little grimace at the thought of Amy Coxe and then for the first time smiled. There was no time for new dresses, but Madame de Breughel's maid was skilful with her needle and was upstairs now trimming their best muslins afresh. They would wear jasmine in their hair and almond blossom. They would twist little wreaths of it in the morning. Emma was the cleverest at that. She would do all three. There would be time. The ceremony was not until four. It would be as well for her to have something to occupy her mind before she dressed.

As chance would have it, Mrs Warrington had discovered a length of lace that would serve as a veil. Her own wedding lace, she told him, was preserved somewhere in England. 'Never did I imagine,' she told Laing, 'that I should still be here to see the girls marry – one of whom was not born at the time – else I should have thought to bring it with me.' Nevertheless in searching out a set of napkins a month or so ago she had come across this other, of less good quality, it was true, but adequate. She had set it to one side. What good fortune, when at the time of doing so she could never have imagined that within weeks – 'weeks', she repeated, looking in astonishment from one to the other – her own child would be wearing it.

They told him then, for there was no way of keeping it from him, of the Knutsons' wedding present. Herr Knutson had begun, quite in ignorance of this, a little sketch of Emma.

129

Then, when the wedding was announced, Gerda, Frau Knutson, had brought out two pendants rimmed with gold, very fine, a pair, surmounted with a pair of tiny eagles, who stretched their wings around the link the chain was slotted through. She had very fine things, Mrs Warrington assured him, family things. And this was the scheme, that Herr Knutson should break off his sketch of Emma, which he had been obliged to do in any case – first because of Walter Tyrwhitt's death and then because of their other trouble – and devote the following day to capturing a likeness of Laing which he could work on after his departure. As soon as Laing had gone he would turn his talents to perfecting the little portrait of Emma, which promised to be charming. If it were not complete before he left Tajura – indeed how could it be? – it could be taken on to him at Beni Ulid.

'Will you like that?' Emma asked him. At last her hand stirred in his. A little colour, he thought, had come into her cheeks.

Shortly afterwards he took his leave of them and rode into Tripoli, where it had been arranged that he should spend the night at the house of the good doctor. The following day, which seemed the most tedious of his entire life, he sat hour after hour for the foolish Knutson. Mrs Dickson had ridden out to the Garden so that she might be there to assist her former charges on the following morning. The doctor stayed in town to keep him company, but by joint consent they made a sober evening of it and retired early. Laing scarcely slept at all. He spent the morning writing letters. He wrote formally to his parents, informing them of his marriage and his imminent departure. To Bandinel he wrote, *She is the most amiable of creatures and is possessed of as little good sense as I am. I knew on first seeing her that we were destined for one another*, for so it now seemed that he had. Of the events of the past week he made no mention in either letter. Shortly before three he dressed in his uniform and rode out with the doctor to the English Garden.

It seemed a little ceremony. Nothing could spell out its significance. It was bound to seem so, with the room and the faces too familiar for the occasion. Fred in his outlandish costume stood up beside him as his groomsman and handed him a ring.

The Consul stood before them, stern-faced and shaken. Emma herself was hidden from him by her lace. Standing, she seemed smaller than he remembered her. She questioned everything. 'Is this where? Do I stand here? Is this right?' All with a little tittering laugh that ended in a cough.

The words were spoken in the Consul's fine commanding voice. Nevertheless the fear contracted in Laing that this was all a mockery. He held her hand in his and slipped the ring too easily onto her finger. 'It's too large,' the Consul said in an aside. 'We'll have it made to fit.' She held her hand tightly around it so as not to lose it.

And when it was done, what should they do? They stood there hand in hand. The veil was lifted clear of Emma's face. She looked at him now, smiling, happy, without thought. It was complete. Thank God, he thought, that it is so for her. He stooped and kissed her on the cheek like a stranger. Jenny came between them then, sobbing noisily, repeating words they could not understand, kissing Emma, kissing him. Everyone began to speak cautiously, as if trying out their normal voices. They shook Laing by the hand and looked at him earnestly, as if for confirmation of what they had just seen. There was no way to flesh out the event other than by an enactment of happiness. And so by eating and drinking, by Emma standing on a chair and tossing her flowers to Jenny, by bride and bridesmaids sitting in turn on Herr Knutson's knee, by Mrs Warrington struggling with her disbelief, by Frau Knutson bursting into tears and crying out with open arms, 'Everyone must come and kiss me. I am growing old,' by the doctor making a speech about hers and Emma's, indeed all the ladies', beauty, the ceremony was performed.

Towards evening the servant appeared at the door of the room with a letter on a tray. It was from Mohammed d'Ghies, informing the Consul that the Sheikh Babani had arrived in Tripoli, and that he and Laing were expected at the palace in the morning to agree to the contract of the Sheikh's employment. Coming on any other day, the news would surely have raised a cheer or at the very least caused Laing's heart to quicken. As it was, it fell quietly upon the room. Emma looked pale and shocked and Laing, who had waited so long for this very moment, could think of nothing when it came but that he must part from her at the very moment that they had pretended she was his.

And so shortly afterwards they were separated, she to the shrouded bed between her sisters', Laing to set out on the hour's ride to his camp at Tajura.

The events of these few days seemed like those in certain dreams, related to reality but of some other substance. So long had he waited in expectation of Babani, so vividly had the event occurred in Mind, that when he once more climbed the crumbling stairways of the palace and stood in the brightly-tiled audience chamber before the Bashaw, he must assure himself that this was happening now before his very eyes, and that the figure that came forward from beside the throne was indeed Babani and did not merely represent him. He was a tall man, well-built, older than Laing by as much as twenty years. He bore himself with quiet dignity, was well-featured, dark of skin, with an expression of benign serenity that could only inspire trust.

The contract was cast.

The Bashaw's cavalry would accompany them as far as Beni Ulid. Laing was to make over to Babani at once the sum of one thousand dollars, to cover the cost of any custom dues or presents required by the various local dignitaries to keep the road open and safe. In these instances, it was suggested, Babani would be in a better position than Laing to drive a satisfactory bargain. 'Yet should not the final say be mine?' he asked the Consul in an undertone.

'Of course. Of course,' he said. 'But it's best to be seen to come from him.'

All this was taken down by a scribe. A contract would be drawn up and submitted for their signatures before Laing set out. For the Consul was adamant that Laing should not be subjected to any further delay, but should set out as planned and wait for Babani at Beni Ulid.

'In how many days will the Sheikh be ready to depart?' Laing asked.

'In ten days.'

'Six,' the Bashaw told him.

'Six,' Babani agreed with the slightest inclination of his head.

'Can we be sure of this?' Laing said aside to the Consul. 'Should I not stay at least until the contract's signed?'

'I'll stay,' the Consul told him from the corner of his mouth. 'It would be folly for us both to leave. I'll keep at his elbow and see to things – ride out with him. We'll both be there within the week.'

How quickly and easily it was arranged. The audience was at an end. Agreement was complete. Laing shook Babani by the hand. He had learnt that little enough can be gauged of a man when the touch is always light and swift and the eyes out of modesty averted. Still, he was certain he might place his confidence in Babani's placid open features.

He returned immediately to Tajura to make his final preparations. There he found Clapperton's man, the sullen Bagoola, had joined their party. Laing had supposed him a servant. Now it appeared he was a man of substance, for he travelled with two camels, a wife and a servant of his own, a downcast boy whom Laing suspected was a slave.

On the following day the Bashaw's man of business arrived in the camp to collect the one thousand dollars for Babani. Laing thought he knew his face; had seen him, perhaps, among the Bashaw's flunkeys at the palace. He would have preferred to give the money to the Sheikh direct at Beni Ulid, but fearing some further delay he took the key from his neck, unlocked the box and counted out the money. Only when the man signed the receipt *Giuseppe Giovanelli* did he recognise him as the merchant from whom, at d'Ghies' advice, he had bought additional gifts. When taxed, the man said imperturbably that he transacted all matters of finance for the Bashaw. 'This is for Babani,' Laing told him. 'It is silver for Babani to carry with him.' The factor assured him he would take it to the Sheikh Babani directly.

He spent the afternoon writing up his journal.

At last, he wrote, as if at some other man's dictation, *I am on my way. The Sheikh Babani arrived Tripoli on the fourteenth July – dies mirabilis. He is a man in whom I am inclined to place an absolute trust.*

The light had slackened. Presently he heard the palms rustle in the incoming sea breeze and felt its cool pressure on his cheek. He had no gift for her. Now he took out some of his supply of writing paper and a dozen pens. On the topmost sheet he wrote:

133

Write to me each day at sunset, my dearest Emma, and I at that same hour shall write to you. In that way our two souls may be together even if all else is denied us.

He wrapped all in a large sheet of paper and set out to spend a final evening at the English Garden.

It was a family party. He was glad for that, at least. Though during the evening the good doctor came alone into the room and pressed his hand and went away again. Emma sat beside him and held his hand in a tight and frightened grip. The Consul kept repeating to her that he would carry Laing's letters back to her when he returned from Beni Ulid. He gave her his gift of paper. 'And when your father comes,' Laing said to her, 'he will bring your letters to me and the portrait, if Herr Knutson has finished it by then.' He spoke to her as they did, as if she were a child and might not fully comprehend.

At midnight he took his leave of them. They all clustered around Emma. 'Kiss him now, Emma.' 'Say goodbye now.' 'There, there, do not cry.' He thought he would never rid his mind of her face as it was then, stricken, pale to death, with tears welling in her eyes. 'There now, give him one smile.' He took her poor face between his hands, smearing the tears across her cheeks, trying with his thumbs to press up the corners of her mouth in the semblance of a smile. 'I will come back,' he told her. 'I will come back.'

He left her then. The Consul had him by the arm and steered him along the hall, out of the door, towards the stables. His wedding gift to Laing, a fine bay mare, was brought out to them. Already the separation had taken place, but he could not bring himself to mount. He must be given time.

'What will become of her?' Laing said. 'If I return here, what is my position with her then? Am I not to know? Oh, how am I to bear this?'

'At Beni Ulid,' the Consul said. 'My heart's too full for now.' His voice was shaken with emotion. Tears filled his eyes. He clapped his hand upon Laing's arm in the rough semblance of an embrace and Laing, himself close to tears, bent down his head until it touched the Consul's shoulder.

When he was mounted he said again, 'You will bring the portrait. Urge him to finish it.'

'Indeed. Indeed.'

'Till Beni Ulid,' he said as the horse moved forward.

'Till Beni Ulid,' the Consul called after him.

It was nearly two o'clock before he reached the camp and stretched himself out inside his tent. Sleep, as always on the eve of a departure, eluded him. He was up before dawn and dressed for the first time entirely in his Moorish clothes. As soon as there was any light he had the camels brought in from their grazing and ordered the loading begun. It was a lengthy business. Before it was completed the Bashaw's cavalry had appeared in a great cloud of dust and wheeled and turned several times excitedly on the plain. At last everything was ready and the koffle assembled in some sort of order. A rifle shot was fired. Jack blew the advance with a flourish and the entire troop began to move, unobserved by anyone but a few fishermen and the seabirds on the lake.

Laing took the lead, mounted on the Consul's bay, which he found he must rein in constantly lest it outstrip the rest. Jack and the two boatwrights rode behind on mules, these latter still too uncertain of their mounts not to be grateful to proceed at an amble. The camelmen walked ahead of their towering charges, dragging the lead ropes over their shoulders. The cavalry rode haphazardly in the rear. The pace settled. The excited chatter of departure died away. Only occasionally the Bashaw's men, in sudden uncontrollable elation, rode wildly past, shouting unintelligibly and hoisting their rifles above their heads. By noon even they were subdued. There was no sound now but the clatter of accoutrements, the melancholy soughing of the wind, and occasionally, more melancholy still, the sudden formless singing of the soldiers. Ahead stretched an expanse of undulating dust. Nothing interrupted it but the receding skyline. For the first time the enormity of the journey he had set himself bore down upon him. Mind, which had held to the abstract, could not now encompass it. The slow funereal pace extended distance beyond its grasp so that he felt, at the very moment of release, like the fleer in a dream who strives with superhuman efforts only to find his feet are weighted to the ground.

Part III: The Road to Ghadames

Throughout that long day's journey nothing before Laing's eyes could divert him from the scenes he had left behind him. The sky was overcast; the air sultry. Nothing occurred to shake from him his mood of despondency. In the late afternoon the captain of the koffle, without consulting Laing, called the halt at a dried-up river bed, the Wadi Rimmel. Laing would have kept up the march for another hour at the least, but taking into account the newness of the venture and the wide disparities between his followers he was disinclined to argue. With a despatch and order which surprised and pleased him the baggage was unloaded, the camels hobbled and turned loose to graze, the mules and horses watered and fed at their picket lines. Parties of men were sent out to gather brushwood. The clouds had lifted. A serene yellow light poured in over this scene of activity from just above the crest of a distant range of hills. The first day's journey was completed without mishap.

As night approached he wrote to Emma. She too would write at that very hour. He seemed to see her at the table in the drawing room, bent over her pen with her little neck exposed, toiling to write the words which in a week or so he would hold in his hand.

I promise on my sacred word, he wrote to her, *that once I return, I shall never leave your side again. I promise that.*

The servant brought him a plate of rice and mutton. Bagoola himself appeared to ask if Laing were satisfied. He replied austerely that he was. When he was done he made a brief tour of his portion of the camp. His people ate separately, Jack and the boatmen by one fire, the camelmen by another. Bagoola and his entourage had settled around a third.

Laing himself was gratefully fatigued by the day's exertions. He slept profoundly and was shaken awake by Jack in darkness. Already the fires were lit. Some order had been issued unbeknownst to him, or the koffle by its own spontaneous volition was preparing to depart. The camels had been rounded up, the slow task of loading them begun. He breakfasted hastily on coffee and the last of the white rolls packed for him at the English Garden. A rifle was fired. The men stood where they were, holding their hands to the heavens, repeating the prayer of morning and departure:

'Praise be to God, the Lord of all creatures; the most merciful, the king of the day of judgement. Thee do we worship, and of thee do we beg assistance. Direct us in the right way, in the way of those to whom thou hast been gracious; not of those against whom thou art incensed, nor those who go astray.'

Minutes later they had mounted and jolted forward in the dark. He shivered with cold and craved the first touch of the sun, which presently he felt. As the light increased a great plain was seen to extend around them, covered in a faded green. The odour of crushed thyme rose deliciously from under the horses' hoofs. Herds of goats grazed by the roadside, and sheep the same ochre as the stony grounds. They rode past a number of wells where shepherds, amidst much shouting and bleating, sluiced water into wooden troughs. Gradually the tranquillity of the scene sank into Laing's spirits. Mind slowed to the pace of Body. He began to look about him with pleasure, forming in his mind the words by which he would describe it to Emma.

That evening they had camped near a cluster of rude huts constructed of branches and palms and roofed with straw matting. He wrote to her:

I have often wondered how the patriarchs of old found contentment in their simple lives when they were men of such consuming vision. Tonight, watching this scene, thinking, my dear Emma, of our future life together, I think that I, the most restless of beings, might be taught by you to find just such contentment.

As night fell and the herdsmen's tasks were done, they came to stand at a distance from his fire and stare fixedly at him while he wrote. Bagoola appeared shouting officiously to drive them away, but Laing dismissed him and signalled the

140

men to stay. An old man came boldly forward and squatting on his heels beside the fire gave out a peremptory greeting. Laing answered him. The others came now and settled themselves on the far side of the fire. How quickly the night had fallen and the world shrunk down to this ring of wondering faces watching Laing intently as Jack brewed his coffee. A group of women stood further into the shadows, tittering and peering from behind their shawls. He held out his cup to the old man, who sipped and spat the coffee violently onto the fire, crying out, 'Oh, Prophet of God.' The younger men laughed rowdily at him, but when Laing offered each of them the cup in turn none dared taste it.

'What is your country?' the old man asked him. 'Is it the land of the Franks?'

He told them it was England. They looked at one another and shook their heads dismissively. So quickly had the word lost any meaning.

'It is an island' he told them, 'away to the north of this place.'

'Your king must be very poor,' said a young man shrewdly. 'He can have very few sheep on an island, very few camels.'

'It is true,' the old man said excitedly. 'I have heard it said that God has given the Christian many things but he has denied him the camel.'

'He is a liar,' another said. 'If he lives over the edge of the sea his island must stand on its end and all the sheep would fall off it.' Their harsh voices wondered or derided, but he was fearless among them as seldom among his own kind. When they laughed, he laughed too, although perhaps they mocked him. The flaring theatrical light played over their faces as they watched him expectantly for some new wonder. He felt for the lodestone in his coat pocket and fitted it invisibly into the palm of his hand. He waved his other hand before their eyes and smoothed a place in the sand beside the fire. They all leant forward. He laid his pocket knife in the centre of the space.

'Come here,' he called softly to the knife. He stretched out his hand with the lodestone hidden in it until the knife began to move slowly towards him. The old man let out an astonished shout of laughter and slapped the back of his hand against his forehead crying, 'Allah, Allah, Allah!' They crowded around him in a tight ring, jostling one another, boisterous with excitement. He had to perform the trick again and again, as he had done by the camp fires of Falaba. Even when he showed them the stone and let them handle it, they seemed no less astonished. In the end, to quiet them and send them on their way, he gave the old man the lodestone, saying that he was the bravest of them all to have tasted the coffee.

They moved on at dawn. By noon the road had entered a bleak range of hills. As they climbed it came briefly into sight again. Then suddenly and finally it was shut from sight as they descended to the plain beyond. They rode without halting until nightfall.

On the following day they set out at dawn along a dry river bed, but the camels laboured with such difficulty over its stony surface that the captain of the koffle called the halt at noon. Laing was consumed with impatience but told himself that he knew nothing of these matters.

On the fifth day, an hour after setting out at dawn, they entered a wide green plain stretched between low ranges of hills. Scarcely an hour later the halt was called again by a cluster of tents.

'Why?' Laing asked angrily. 'Why so soon?'

'We must wait here,' the captain of the koffle told him. 'The Sheikh of Terhoona will bring more soldiers to come with us to Beni Ulid.'

'Surely there are enough soldiers?'

'There is a band of robbers in these hills,' the man told him gravely. 'They know of you. Perhaps they wait for you along the road. We must wait here until the Sheikh of Terhoona comes to join us.'

Laing did not believe that there were robbers in those silent hills, but there was little to be gained by saying so. He gave orders for his tents to be pitched again and, rather than sit passive under this new delay, had his men check over their equipment and make some slight rearrangement of the luggage that would more exactly balance the loads.

At noon he took the opportunity to check the rate of his chronometer. This he did quite openly, curious to see if it would provoke any show of suspicion or resentment from the Bashaw's men, but although some of them watched him they

142

contented themselves with calling out, 'Are you looking to see the people in your own country, *Reis*? Can you see them?'

'I am looking at the sun,' he told them. They laughed and pointed. 'There it is.'

By evening small troops of mounted men and foot soldiers could be seen filing down from the dusty hills onto the plain. It astonished Laing that such a barren place could yield up so many armed men. By dusk, with the fires lit, the koffle looked like a small army bivouacked.

My adored Emma, he wrote, *We have not progressed more than five miles today. How vexatious to my spirits are these delays. A whole day, it seems has been added to the time that I must spend apart from you, every minute of which I most heartily grudge.*

A moment later his pen jerked on the page at the sound of rifle fire from the hills and an answering salvo from the camp. He set the letter hastily aside and grasped his rifle, but at that moment a man ran past, calling out that the Sheikh of Terhoona had arrived. His men had fired from the hills to warn of their approach. The Bashaw's men had fired back in greeting.

In the morning Laing called upon the Sheikh, whom he found to be a little wizened brigand of a man weighted down with bandoliers and weapons. Together they sipped at minute cupfuls of sweetened tea at the threshold of the Sheikh's tent. Out of sight inside his tent his wives and children tittered. Laing could see their eyes glitter like jet beads in the dark fabric of its sides.

'We are here,' the Jelleman's wives had sung at Falaba. 'But we fear the white man's skin; we fear his gree-grees will kill us if we dare to look upon him. None but the men can behold him.' But even as they sang the words they had filed boldly from the hut, their teeth shining, their pink nails flashing on their little drums, their breasts alive under their knotted cloths.

Here was a different sullen race. The women stayed hidden. The Sheikh stared out moodily over his domain. Silence fell finally between them and Laing felt free to take his leave.

At two in the afternoon the enlarged force set out. The

143

ground was even, the pace brisker than before. They moved with a new urgency. When night fell the moon was already in the sky and strong enough in its first quarter for them to keep up the same brisk pace until it set again at ten. No camp was made. The horses were watered hastily from the waterskins. They would set out again at dawn and in the six hours allowed to them slept on mats unrolled onto the ground.

If it had been fear of an attack that had caused this haste, the morning light dispelled it. A brief shower of rain fell at dawn. They set out again across a wide green plain covered with a pale green herbage which, in the brief hour before the sun had dried it, shone and glistened with all the colours of the rainbow. The horsemen rode full tilt across the plain, singing and shouting and firing from the saddle into the air above. Laing too, for the first time, gave rein to the Consul's bay and in the glory of the morning and the relief of unrestricted speed felt at last that exaltation of the spirit that normally attends the outset of a venture. Perhaps happiness like fear must always be suppressed among the events which give rise to it and only later, in solitude, may be felt with full intensity. Now, as the horse's pace eased, the first great joy of his love rose up in him untouched by recent sorrows and frustrations, and the shining plain and the clear depths of the sky seemed to hold the promise of a boundless and propitious future.

The Bashaw's men wheeled deftly and charged back again. But the hills were at too great a distance to provide cover for attackers and Laing kept steadily on. No human form intruded between himself and the skyline. The horse moved slowly under the mounting heat. By noon a sultry east wind had risen and blew without remission.

He looked back repeatedly to see if the koffle had halted, but it continued to straggle wearily in his wake. The horse had begun to pick its way over rising ground covered with fragments of loose mica slate. The hills were closer. He was reluctant to venture into them alone. Ahead, by the roadside, a solitary acacia cast a thin shadow. He dismounted and let his horse graze while he sat leaning against its trunk. He slept perhaps with his head against the tree for when next he looked out across the plain at the disorderly troop of horsemen and camels he found the sight quite inexplicable, as if he watched some dislocation of the dust which Mind could not interpret. In that instant when the mind wakes, but the body still retains the helplessness of sleep, he thought, What am I doing? Then, as it returned to him, What have they done to me?

They had sent him on this wide detour quite contrary to his wishes, for reasons of their own. They had kept Emma from him on pretence. And he, like a man under an enchantment, had acquiesced. He has abused me, he thought. He does not intend me to return. Then immediately all was reversed. The Consul stood in Mind smiling with his steady benignity. In the morning he would set out in his shining uniform from the English Garden to meet Laing and confirm his acceptance when he returned from Timbuctoo.

All that afternoon they toiled up and down the dusty ridges of the hills, leading the horses and camels now, both men and beasts tormented by the same parching wind. Despite Laing's hat and beard the sun burnt against his right cheek as if focused through a glass. His vision narrowed down to the horse's heaving flank and the stony ground beneath its hoofs. He fell back in the ranks. At dusk he was stumbling up a further rise when a shout went up ahead and, coming to the crest of the incline, he saw the olive thickets of Beni Ulid. He thought he had never seen so beautiful a sight. Their shadows were cast far out over the dust by the setting sun. The slow languorous movement of the palms moved him with a sharp delight.

By six they had unloaded their luggage in a ruinous stone fort where it might be more easily protected. The tents were ranged around it. The Sheikh of Terhoona's men had returned to the hills. Bundles of dried palm fronds had been gathered and the small brilliant evening fires lit. He was too weary to write. Already his promise to her was broken; her face and voice already lost to memory. Yet his mind, as he lay down to sleep, was filled with the sense of Emma's presence. In a week's time this torment would be over. He would read the words that she had written. Her voice would be restored. He would hold in his hand the little portrait. He slept the sleep of exhaustion then, and woke to the sound of birdsong and the first shouted prayer from the low tower of the mosque.

It was Monday the twenty-sixth of July.

* * *

145

On the morning of the day that Laing rode into Beni Ulid, the Bet-el-Mel entertained the Consul and Wood. Over coffee and tobacco he spoke at length to his visitors about the detention of a Maltese slave in the *bagnio* who claimed to be a British subject. Wood translated. The Consul listened with his patient gravity. Only after an hour of this did he produce Laing's contract and request an audience so that the Bashaw's signature might be added to his own.

The Bet-el-Mel inclined his head, smiled slightly, and said, 'That will be unnecessary, *Eccellenza*.'

'How so?'

'His Highness' authority is sufficient to secure the *Reis*' safety. He has given his *teskera*. There is no need for the contract.'

'Does he refuse to sign it?' the Consul said, and struggled to keep down the alarm in his voice.

'It is unnecessary. As for your part, it is well known that the Englishman's word is bond enough.'

'Why will he not sign?'

'He cannot sign it, Eccellenza. The contract says that if the *Reis* does not return alive, the merchant must forfeit his goods. No just man would sign such a document. Why should the merchant suffer if, by some act of God, the *Reis* is killed? What fault would it be of his? There would be no justice to it.'

The Consul rose and beckoning angrily to Wood left the room with the scantest of courtesies. An hour later he rode out to the Garden.

A wind had risen since morning. The Consul chose the shore route as being the less dusty. Always he did his best thinking in the saddle. He rode full tilt. The horse's hooves threw out clods of damp sand in all directions. Wood had stayed in town. He was glad of it. If for one moment the knowledge that Laing should be recalled entered his mind, he did not care to see it mirrored in another's eyes. No one knew of this but Wood, and he was too indebted for his livelihood ever to reproach him.

It's a damned shame, he thought. Poor Laing. He deserves better.

He knew he would not recall Laing. He did not care to examine why he knew it would be impossible to do so. He knew, even while he considered at what hour he should be woken in the morning, that he would not go to Beni Ulid, nor could he shake him by the hand, nor could he look him in the eye as he wished him Godspeed. He did not blame himself for having such sensibilities. Nor would he succumb to them. A man given to introspection and self-blame becomes burdensome to those around him. Laing knew what he was about as well as any man. After all, the Consul might reflect that when Laing had first come among them, he had made none of the provisions for his own safety which the Consul had sought to procure for him. He was no worse off now than he had been then and, being on the whole a reasonable man, would be quick to appreciate that.

He dismounted by the stables and walked towards the house. In his absence, his tents and boxes of provisions had been stacked on the verandah. The mules hired for the journey were tethered at the side of the house, their heads bowed patiently under the stinging dust. He strode past them and let himself into his office by the outer door.

My dear Laing, he wrote, *For the last twenty-four hours I have had such an argument with myself whether I am to mount my horse tomorrow morning, and accompany Babani to Beni Ulid. Inclination is a strong advocate for such a measure, because I should have the consideration of taking you by the hand, and enjoying a few days of your conversation. On the other hand ought I to be the means of detaining you, having already been so much longer than you expected, and as the animals are all fresh you would most certainly wish to be off? There is another point on which nature betrays a weakness, and let the journey or a friend be far or near the farewell shake of the hand is always most unpleasant and I always endeavour to avoid it . . .*

As he wrote, the sound of the piano from the drawing room irritated him intolerably. He called for Vincenzio and sent him to ask his daughter kindly to desist from playing.

Throughout these comings and goings Emma had sat as she was told by an open window in the salon, while Herr Knutson drew her portrait. Frau Knutson and Mama had moved their chairs to a little distance behind the easel and sat there whispering quietly to one another, like watchers at a ceremony. The muslin curtains were slowly lifted into the room by gusts

147

of hot air. She saw the fringes of the carpet run before it like a wave and felt its hot breath on her ankles. Then they fell back again. The lead weights, sewn into the hem, clattered to the floor, one after the other, as if they had been spilled over the edge of a hand. Then all together they were dragged back over the tiles. The sound repeated itself again and again.

He had been gone six days, but still his form as he had sat by her side at the dinner table stayed in her mind, like a black shape cut out of the surface of the things. Upon it lay the image of his hand, with the blue veins standing out like cords, the edge of his shoe, the gaping of his tunic where a fragment of linen shirt showed between the buttons. Already she had lost his face and soon must lose all sense of him.

Every morning of that week Herr Knutson had come, wearing a loose Arab smock pulled over his shirt and trousers and a large silk bow tied about his neck. Each day he had told her again how she should sit, touched her hair, propped up her chin, arranged her hands in her lap with a little pressure of his own, stood back to squint at her with calculating eyes. There was something in this touch and look that made her feel that it was not she, Emma, who sat there, but someone better known to him. At first she had been very curious to see how he had drawn her, for it was herself, her gift to Laing, and must be pleasing to him. But Herr Knutson insisted that she should not see it until it was complete.

The others were allowed to stand behind him, exclaiming at the likeness. They peered at her, past the easel, as if they willed the face they saw to be as Herr Knutson described it. He had the eyes. Oh, how clever to suggest the curls with so few lines, and the positioning of the chin. Just like. Of such she was composed. She had sat still, as if her very being depended on it as if, by so exerting her will to hold her body motionless, she might imprint the pleasing likeness on the page in time for her father to take it to Beni Ulid. Now she saw he would not finish it in time. He was constantly destroying his work, the better to perfect it. The one thing he dreaded, he informed the awed women in the room, was that beauty should be diminished at his hand. 'It is the curse of the artist,' he cried out, tearing the paper from the easel, 'that it is always so; that God's creation must always so exceed our own poor efforts.'

She hated him then. The finished drawing must yet be

transferred onto ivory. There was no hope that he might have it completed in time. The pain of Laing's disappointment fell like a blow on her own heart. For already it seemed that she had failed him. Might he think that she had been restless and distracted by the other people in the room, and so delayed Herr Knutson? Was it possible that she could have willed herself to more total stillness? Had her thoughts strayed for one moment from Laing so that her expression had in some way changed? She thought not. His absence had lifted all restraints upon her love, which was enormous now, a swollen painful thing there was no place for.

As she sat she might see him ride on his horse, the sea to his left hand, the hills to his right. She wanted to cry out to warn him of the disappointment that must lie in store for him. But he rode heedlessly on, his mind fixed upon the moment when he would hold her portrait in his hand. Tears would start from her eyes when she thought of it. A harsh sound of pain and surprise seemed lodged in her throat, unable to be uttered. But she must not cry. He drew the eyes again. It must not be spoilt. She must turn her head to where Herr Knutson held out his hand and then turn back her eyes to meet his bright obliterating stare.

In one corner of the walled domain the Bashaw had granted to the Consul was a small burial ground. It had been completely overgrown, but the hired workmen, set to clear the ground, had come upon the grave markers, dragged out of position but still bearing traces of whitewash and carved to resemble turbans of such amplitude as to indicate the dead were persons of importance. Seeing the agitation of the gardeners, the Consul had immediately cancelled his orders and left that plot of land uncultivated. A little wooden kiosk, which could not have been torn down without causing further disturbance, he ordered to be left to crumble of its own accord. Here every evening Emma came immediately the light began to fail and she was free of Herr Knutson. A jasmine vine had grown up over the roof. She divided it with her hands to get inside. It caught at her hair and clothes and emitted a bitter dusty odour that pierced through the pervading sweetness. Inside it was dim and cool as a cave. Here she kept the writing things that Laing had given her hidden under a loose floor-board. She could not write to him with other people's eyes upon her. Only when the vine had fallen back in place could she allow the words that she would speak to him to come into her mind:

My beloved Laing. He will not have finished it. How can I bear it that the thing that has been promised to you will be denied and that more weeks must pass before you have what consolation my poor face can give you? Until it is done he will not begin upon your portrait or let me see the sketches. So we are doubly denied. Why is it, Laing, that they should wish to make us suffer? Is it through jealousy of the great joy that must be ours? Is it not enough that they must deny us the sweet company that is ours by right? Oh, Laing, I shall not breathe a happy breath again until you return to release me from this bondage.

She seemed to write at the prompting of an unknown voice. When it fell silent she put the pen away and neatly tore the message from the sheet of paper with her penknife, and folded it and put it in the box.

Another day had been gained out of the ninety that were owing. Madame de Breughel had come, as she did each month, to read aloud to them from the French newspapers: what the Countess of so and so had worn at such and such a ball. She translated as she read, stumbling for the words, while they questioned her intently. Did she mean feathers or swansdown? Beads, yes, but of what kind? It was important to know exactly. Usually there would be a month in which to discuss these matters in detail, but they had all agreed to sacrifice their own interests so that the papers could be despatched to Laing in the morning.

Emma must keep her eyes fixed away from them, but the room, which in the past days had come to seem unreal to her, like the memory of a place she had already left, was at the same time so familiar that she might interpret every sound in it. She heard the avid murmur of the women's voices, heard the rattle of dogs' claws on the uncarpeted portions of the floor, heard the curtains rise and fall and the particular ringing of the little shells that weighted down the edges of the fly-net as her mother lifted it from the water jug.

But her thoughts were fixed beyond these things. She strained to listen beyond them for her father's restless presence in the adjoining rooms, and any sound of the preparations made for his departure in the morning. She heard him ride away. Just as they had finished dinner he returned. She heard his voice in the hall, but the words were obliterated by the clatter of his boots on the tiles. She sat with a predator's stillness, willing herself to comprehend the slightest sound, the opening and shutting of the doors, the slipshod movements of the servants.

In the kiosk she had written, *Tomorrow morning Papa will ride out to you at Beni Ulid. His boxes are ready waiting on the verandah. There is not one of them, my beloved Laing, has not felt the touch of my hand, knowing that at some later date your hand may rest by chance upon the very same spot . . .* When she had done she had gathered all the folded notes together out of the box and wrapped them in a single sheet of paper. On it she wrote, *To my husband, Alexander Gordon Laing.*

Already it was evening. Jenny played. Fred read aloud to Mama. She would avoid them. She was perhaps a little feverish. The thought of being among them produced a flinching along the surface of her skin. The notes of the piano, their voices, seemed pitched too loud and were altered, as if they sounded in an empty room. She did not think they saw her pass.

She knocked softly on the door of her father's office.

'Come,' he said. Then, when he saw that it was she, 'What is it you want?' She had the packet of letters in her hand and held it forward, but did not relinquish it.

He said, 'Angelo Heri will take the letters for you.' He was shifting the letters on his desk as if he searched for something. 'It is impossible for me to go.'

She, the letters, were diminished then. She could not have said how. She laid them mistrustfully on the corner of his desk. She was saying, in a low anxious voice, 'I had thought that you were going. I had thought you would want to go.'

'Well, well,' he said irritably, as if she kept him from some more important matter, 'there's nothing more that I can do for him. He's in no danger. There's nothing I need say to him that cannot be said as well by letter.' Then, as if she had accused him, 'What would you have me say to him?'

She did not know what they would say to one another, but had supposed a store of words existed. 'About me,' she said.

'What about you?'

'When he comes back.' She could scarcely bring herself to speak the words.

'When he comes back there's time enough for that.'

Beloved Laing, I write in such agitation that I can scarcely hold my pen or compose my thoughts. He is not to go as he has promised to – to afford you some comfort in your lonely state. You would have embraced him, whom I should have embraced before he left, and I, on his return, might have imagined that I felt the pressure of your arms about me. Laing, Laing, how will your Emma endure so many nights and days before she may enfold you in her arms? A week and a day have passed – I cannot say how slowly. Today I was forced to watch them ride forth, knowing their arrival can only afflict you with further disappointment and suffering –

She broke off, aware of the silence into which she spoke. Early in the morning she had stood by the gate to watch Angelo Heri and the Sheikh Babani ride out. They rode on horseback. Behind them had come the loaded mules and the slow swaying camels with their long legs cutting through the cloud of dust they raised about them. No further mail might reach him till he came to Ghadames. This last letter must be folded and put away till then.

On the morning after his arrival in Beni Ulid, Laing woke with a sensation of joy which he traced at once to the knowledge that the Consul and Sheikh Babani would that morning, at this very hour, be setting out from the English Garden.

It was Sunday. He had Jack bring warm water, and when he had washed himself, dressed in his European clothes. At ten, with Jack, Rogers, and Harris lined up outside the tent in their clean shirts and trousers, he read Matins from the Church of Scotland Prayer Book. A few of the Bashaw's men watched this proceeding with a look of vacant insolence, but made no attempt to intervene. They loitered when the service was concluded, to see if some other diversion followed. When none did they dispersed. On each of the following days at noon he took his observation and retired inside the tent to work at his figures. On the fifth day he averaged his findings of the latitude which proved Ghadames to the west of their present position. He neatly corrected Lyon's figures in the Admiralty charts.

It was quiet. The air was sultry and heavy with other men's sleep. Then, half-way through the afternoon, a sudden din of shouts and a cry of pain came from the direction of Bagoola's tents. Laing sent for him at once. The disturbance ceased immediately and presently Bagoola appeared before him with his sullen unrevealing stare.

'I will not have fighting,' Laing told him, 'among my own people.'

'No one is fighting.'

'What was that noise, then?'

'My servant is a bad servant. Therefore I beat him.'

'And I tell you that while you travel with me you do not.'

'He is my slave,' Bagoola said. 'I do with him what I want.'

'You do as I tell you,' Laing said.

He was agitated, more than he cared to be by so trivial an incident. He walked again to the edge of the town and looked across the barren plain. He told himself that the Consul might already ride over the harsh terrain of their last day's journey. But though he moved his glass minutely across the surface of the plain, he could detect no movement and returned to the airless tent and his journal.

What greater evidence is needed, he wrote, *of the iniquity of this accursed system that enables one man to call another his slave and treat him like a beast of burden? All Captain Clapperton's generosity and kindness to this man have achieved is to enable him to become a slave-owner.*

By nightfall, when the Consul had still not come, he wrote to Emma by the first light of the moon:

You can imagine my feelings on knowing that another weary day must pass before I press the hand that has held yours and may feast my eyes on your dear letters and your precious portrait.

He was shivering. He wrapped his blanket around him and crouched closer to the fire as he wrote.

Bagoola, for whose company he cared little at any time, came and sat on the far side of the flames. Laing greeted him and called into the dark for coffee. Presently Jack appeared and made some in a small tin pot.

'Bring sugar,' Bagoola told him. Jack did not move.

Laing said stiffly, 'He is not a servant. He is a soldier like myself. He takes orders from me as a soldier. From no one else.'

The man shrugged. Laing poured out the coffee and handed a cup to Jack before he handed one to Bagoola. He did not think the slight had gone unnoticed. Now Bagoola said sullenly, 'I need money to buy grain for the camels.'

'Then you must apply to the Sheikh when he comes,' Laing told him.

'I need money now, *Reis*.'

It was the name they had given him. At first he thought they used it as a form of address, that something more familiar like Abdullah would follow it. But no. It was to be his name. He told himself he liked the severity of it. 'The camels are grazing now,' he said. 'They are resting. Why do they need grain?'

'The grazing is poor here.'

'Yahia Mohammed has said nothing.'

'Yahia Mohammed is an ignorant man. Besides, he does not know this road. Once we leave Beni Ulid there is no grazing. There is nowhere where we can buy sufficient grain.'

'Yahia Mohammed is in charge of the camels,' Laing told him evenly.

Bagoola said, 'When I was with Abdullah I was in charge of purchasing all the food for the men and for the camels. The Consul said that I was to do for you what I did for Abdullah.'

Laing sent for Yahia Mohammed and explained to him that in future, although he would remain in charge of the camels, he was to apply to Bagoola for any extra grain he might need for them. The camelman's face remained impassive.

That night the town was once again brilliantly illuminated by the full moon. He slept hardly at all. The shivering intensified. All along his skin he felt the parched and painful sensations of fever.

The next day and the day following he kept to his tent. The fever came and went but even at noon, when he was most free of it, his hand was too unsteady to take his observations, nor did he dare to write to Emma lest his pen reveal his weakness and alarm her. He could find no rest. The camp was in a constant state of agitation. Twice the Bashaw's cavalry mounted and went charging noisily out along the road to Ghadames in pursuit of real or imagined attackers.

On Sunday, buoyed up by expectation of the Consul's arrival, Laing washed and dressed carefully in his European clothes. He delayed holding the service until noon, convinced that the Consul would wish to join him in thanksgiving for his safe arrival. Then he delayed again until, at dusk, he read Evensong with scant attention, so eagerly did he strain his ears for any warning of the koffle's approach.

The agitation of waiting brought on a fresh attack of fever. Throughout the Monday he was torn between impatience for their arrival and the fear of being discovered in so sickly a condition. Although the fever broke at noon he could concentrate on nothing. By evening it had returned but he forced himself to sit upright by his fire, staring in the direction of the hills to the point where he judged his own party had emerged. At last, shortly after ten, he saw the flash of musketry in the dark. There was a shout, then an answering burst of fire from the camp. By moonlight, from his vantage point at the edge of the town, Laing could just make out the slow movement of the koffle across the colourless illuminated plain. They moved forward in a cloud of dust which might in that strange light have been composed of some stifling volcanic ash. Through it he could just discern the tall swaying shapes of the camels, but no minute speck of colour that might indicate the Consul.

At midnight impatience overcame him and he set out on foot to meet them. The moon was on the point of setting, its light fast fading when he came up to them. Babani dismounted, but throughout his lengthy greetings Laing glanced repeatedly past him and asked, as soon as he might, 'Where is the Consul?'

'Not here,' Babani told him, heaving up his open palms as if to comment on some quirk of fate for which there was no explanation.

'Why?' Laing asked him. 'Does he follow you?'

The Sheikh reached inside an inner pocket and extracted a letter which he handed to Laing. The moon was down. There was no light by which to read it. The koffle had begun to move forward and overtake them, but he continued to believe that he had misunderstood what had been told him, and to look about him in confusion among the dusty men and beasts, who in the sudden darkness and their exhausted state moved past like creatures in a dream. He thought he recognised Angelo Heri, the Consul's factor, who smiled and bowed to him but passed by in silence. The Sheikh had courteously declined to mount again and walked beside him, so that Laing, whose mind was in a turmoil of anxiety, must conjure up polite enquiries about his journey.

'And the Consul?' he asked again. 'He was well when you left him?'

'Very well.'

'And his family? My wife?' The word came awkwardly.

'Very well. Very well,' the Sheikh assured him, but Laing was convinced that only Emma's illness or acute distress could have detained her father.

When they arrived at the camp Heri brought him a bag of letters. Laing groped about among his saddlebags until he found a candle. This he quickly lit in the last embers of the fire and, setting it in the sandy ground inside his tent, hastily cut through the string and sealing wax and emptied the contents of the bag onto the ground. He was shaking wretchedly again. The candle dazzled his eyes. He began to fumble through the clutch of letters that Heri had given him, feeling each in turn for the oval shape of the miniature. It was not there. He found among the more familiar hands his name written in one unformed and round, which he hastily ripped open. There was her name, Emma Maria Gordon Laing. One after the other he read the little notes. She had traced out her endearments, her sentiments of love and fear, in touching, stilted phrases as if she tried out a language new to her. He thought of her forming the unfamiliar words, the letters of her new untried name, with a sweet childlike deliberation and was overcome with pity and with longing for her. He blew out the candle, pushed the letters quickly inside his shirt, and pulling the blanket over him lay and shivered on the ground in utter desolation.

All night the incessant barking of the dogs found demented echoes in his mind. Finally, in the brief period of respite when the dogs finally slept and the first cock had not yet wakened, he fell into a feverish sleep. Two hours later, in the dawn of the day he had planned to spend in pleasant conversation with the Consul, he sat by his fire reading through the letters, unable to believe they could provide no further explanation of his absence.

Babani, the Consul had written, *is a fine fellow with a generous and disinterested countenance but recollect he is an Arab or a Moor, therefore trickery, low cunning and a*

disposition to cheat you in every way you must expect. And let
this be your guiding principle: that if at any moment during the
journey you are worth more to them dead than alive – be it by
a single sequin – they will not hesitate to kill you. God bless
and protect you and that success may attend you is ever the
wish of George Hanmer Warrington.

He read this missive with so feverishly acute an ear that the
unfamiliar agitation in the Consul's words seemed to override
his ambiguity. I am ill, he thought, I read too much into this.
He read the words again. They had grown toneless now and
careless: a dismissal thrown across the shoulder of a man
who turns his back and walks away.

The sun had risen and begun to warm him. He folded up the
blanket and drank a little of the tea that Jack had brought him.
He sent a message to Sheikh Babani requesting his atten-
dance in half an hour's time. When he did not come Laing sent
to him again. After another delay the Sheikh at last appeared
and stood respectfully before him. Immediately Laing's misgivings on reading the Consul's letter vanished. The man had
a levelness of gaze rare among these people. They spoke of
the journey ahead. When presently the Sheikh asked humbly
for a loan of four hundred dollars to pay back a debt he had
incurred in Tripoli, Laing reckoned quickly that goodwill
incurred at the start would be amply recompensed. He
unlocked the box and counted the money.

'We shall set out tomorrow,' Laing told him, as he left.

'Not tomorrow, *Reis*. The day after.'

'How is that?' Laing asked him sharply.

'Tomorrow we arrange the loads. The next day we travel.'

By evening the fever had returned. He withdrew inside his
tent and dosed himself with arsenic diluted in the vile-tasting
water from the skin. Then he lay down in his blanket, hopeless
of sleep, to live out another brilliant noisy night as best he
could.

Occasionally he dozed, waking suddenly with Mind
unguarded against the thoughts that rankled there. So that
the words, 'How could he not come?' spoke themselves, and
'Emma, Emma,' piteously, so that he feared he had cried out,
but Jack, whose sleeping form moonlight imprinted against
the hem of the tent, never stirred. There was much he had
wished to settle: the whole delicate question of the terms on

157

which he might return to Tripoli. It had been promised him. And the debt. Were they to order him by the next packet to return? 'You are a man of no good sense, Alexander,' a voice from the bed's foot: sad and implacable. And the Consul's then, an English voice: 'There is nothing so private between us that it cannot be put in writing.' Yet he had ridden out with Clapperton, who was nothing to him, as far as Beni Ulid, a big man in a scarlet coat who had cast Laing off. It was a dream. He had slept again and wakened without defence against such thoughts: that it was all a ruse, the marriage a pitiful deception of the Consul's to rid himself of Laing.

He sat up, taking his fevered head between his hands and shaking it to and fro to rid it of these evil fancies. For such they were: the product of the distempered body which Mind presently dispelled. Towards dawn the fever broke. He lay wrapped in the blanket, sweating profusely, with Mind goaded now to a wild activity. He would write to their indifferent lordships a memorial: Mind's journey already taken. Laing the true discoverer already while Body toiled to follow, footstep after painful footstep. The arguments aligned themselves with complete lucidity.

Dawn found him sitting by his fire with his portfolio open on his knee, the ink-well half buried in the sand, writing in his neat clerk's hand Cursory Remarks on the Termination of the Niger, pointing out that as Clapperton had failed to encircle Lake Chad, he could establish only that no river flowed from it to the east beneath thirteenth parallel. The rest was hearsay, received at the second hand from Sultan Bello. It was noon before he set this work aside. The afternoon lay ahead in which to write his letters.

Jack had reached inside his tent and was dragging out his bedding. 'What are you doing?' he asked him irritably. In answer le Bore lifted up the side of the tent. Through it Laing could see all confused activity of the camp being struck. The camels had been assembled and were already half loaded. 'Get him to me,' he told Jack angrily. 'Get Babani here to me.'

When the Sheikh came he said, 'Why was I not told of this?'

'My servant sent word to your servant.'

'Why was I not consulted?'

'One has come from further along the road to say that there

158

are robbers who plan to waylay us by the well of Wadi Echmed. If we leave now, before they expect us to, we may pass by without encountering them.'

Laing said, 'Why was I not told?'

'We must travel to Wadi Echmed quickly, *Reis*. The road is very dangerous. The moon will allow us to travel for three more nights.'

He spoke with a sober animation, as if he shared with Laing some interesting tale. His steady countenance reflected nothing of Laing's own anger and alarm.

Laing felt chastened by him. He began hastily to pack up his instruments. Then, when everything except the tent itself was ready to be loaded onto the camels, took up his pen again.

To the Consul he wrote, *I wish much, I indeed wish much that you had come.*

There was no time to choose the words. He wrote out of his full heart and must reproach his friend that the reasons he gave for his absence were insufficient. All the time he was listening for the warning shot that would announce the koffle's departure, when he must seal the letter up and hand it to Angelo Heri. He feared he might be obliged to break off with only the harsh words consigned to the paper when in his heart he forgave him.

My dear Consul, he wrote, for had he come this would have been the moment of farewell. He would have taken him by the hand and spoken just these words. *I will say no more to you on this subject when we meet six months hence, and when it will give us both more pleasure to shake each other by the hand than it would have done at Beni Ulid.* The Consul's genial face, expressive of a mild concern, beamed down on him. He consigned to him his dearest, his most adored Emma, and would have signed the letter when a sudden outbreak of clatter and firing drew him to the door of his tent.

He was in time to see the entire cavalry set off down the dusty road at the gallop. 'The tent,' he shouted to Jack, but then saw the camels patiently folded in the dust, loaded and waiting. He sent Jack to enquire of the Sheikh and presently the Creole returned with the report that an old man and a child had come into the camp, saying that when they had stopped at the well of Wadi Echmed a band of armed men had ridden up and driven them away. The Bashaw's men in a final

159

show of zeal had ridden off to clear the road.

The camels were partially unloaded. Everyone settled down to wait. Laing recommenced his letter but the intensity of his feeling had been dissipated in the excitement. Later, when the moon had risen, he wrote to Bandinel, *A regimental Majority is my right, and I should have got it: if they refuse me at the Horse Guards (which I know they will) let them give me the Brevet Major now, and the local rank of Lt Colonel when I reach Timbuctoo. I shall be very dissatisfied indeed if this be not done, not that I care so much about the rank, but because I shall not otherwise be able to divest myself of the feeling of being ill used.*

Shortly after midnight the cavalry returned. At the well they had seen the prints of many horses but their riders had made off to the west and must lie in wait for them somewhere along the road to Ghadames. The captain of the koffle told Laing that his task was done. He and his men must return tomorrow to Tripoli, all but three who begged permission to travel on with him to Ghadames. Laing was glad enough to have them with him. The reduced koffle consisted, besides his own people, of Bagoola and his entourage, the Sheikh and his servants. Of this motley troop only Jack le Bore was well armed and to be counted on under fire. They were all assembled now. The order was given for the final loading of the camels.

By one o'clock at last the koffle moved out of Beni Ulid and continued slowly across a stony desert.

They rode all night without halting and through the mounting heat of the next day. Even prayer did not delay them. In ones and twos at the appointed hours his companions broke away to kneel swiftly by the roadside, facing back eastwards the way that they had come, then they ran after the koffle and mounted with dust still smeared across their foreheads. At noon they rested in the brittle shade of some acacia trees. At four, when the heat of the day had abated, they pressed on again. More than an hour later they arrived at the well of Wadi Echmed. It was deserted but the Bashaw's men pointed eagerly to the heavy trampling of the sand.

Immediately the toil of drawing water was begun, but he noticed how quietly they set about the task on this occasion.

The water was brackish when they drew it to the surface. Nevertheless the horses drank it greedily. He too, when his turn came, swallowed repeatedly though the taste was nauseating. When night fell he slept briefly. At eleven the moon rose. They moved forward at the same urgent pace. At dawn they found themselves on a wide stony plain. By eight the heat was so intense that they were obliged to rest again in a cluster of sparse trees. The horses were tethered to the trunks and hung their heads with exhaustion, while the men poured the brackish water for them from the skins.

Laing sat in the scant shadow and felt the pressure of the heat; each breath he drew seemed weighted with it. The naked surface of the plain glared under the sun. In the spring spear grass and thyme had grown in the neat circle of fragile shadow each tree described, but had been entirely desiccated by the summer's heat. When he crushed them in his hand they disintegrated, letting out a little crackling like the sound of flame, as if in an instant the whole scene and he in it might ignite in one vast conflagration. Blood pounded against the inside of his skull. He longed to sleep but could not. They stayed there until the heat slackened at four. Then they pressed on until darkness compelled them to stop. The camels were hobbled, the mules and horses watered. A single fire was lit and tea made. Laing distributed dates and bread brought from Beni Ulid, but they were all too tired and plagued by the purgative effects of the water to feel hunger. Again he found himself too numbed with weariness to write to Emma. He slept where he was, beside the fire.

But she sat in the rustling kiosk with the writing desk balanced on her knee, writing in her rapid hand the words she had not spoken during the day: *Beloved Laing, you should return to me by ship. Then, while it is still in harbour, we may embark upon it and no one detain us. Only when the walls of Tripoli are fading in the distance will I feel truly yours. Only then will we be known as what we truly are – husband and wife by destiny. The poison has proved it. Then we can be together, Laing, with no one to deny us what by right is ours . . .*

At midnight Jack roused him. A shrunken moon had risen. By its scant light they made their way along the gravelly bed of a dried river. When dawn broke they were following its course

161

in the shadow of a range of sandstone hills. He was chilled to the bone. Through gaps in the rock he could see sun flooding the adjacent valley. Body craved the touch of it. Shortly after eight, they rounded the base of a hill and felt warmth envelop them. Laing's shivering ceased. A minute later he felt sweat crawl under his arms and down the channel of his spine. A wide valley opened up before him. Flocks of sheep and goats and a small herd of camels grazed on the arid land. The low black tents of nomads stood scattered among them. The Bashaw's men told him that they had reached the valley of Bir Serked. He called the halt and ordered Rogers and Harris to set up his tent.

By afternoon he found the heat too oppressive to allow him to write. When his watch told him that it was four, he went outside to wait for the first alleviating breeze, but the air seemed still more sultry than it had been. When at last the evening breeze came it brought no relief but carried with it a stifling, biting dust. There was shouting then. Men ran past him to cover the horses' heads with blankets. They pointed as they ran. He turned to see a thick red cloud of dust come rolling up the valley. All light was suddenly absorbed. Dust filled his mouth. He could neither speak nor swallow. Jack had him by the arm and dragged him roughly back to his tent, forcing down his head to guide him into it.

He lay with his cloak wrapped over his head, sweating in the dark, his eyes and mouth clenched shut. Even so he could feel the dust sift inside his clothes and rasp against his skin. His mouth was parched. The dust was gritty on the surface of his teeth. He could feel it hot and painful, dragged by necessity into his very lungs. Hour after hour he lay feeling the mounting dust weigh on the surface of the cloak and the pressure of Jack's body against his; hearing nothing but the howling of the wind and the helpless flapping of his tent.

Only at dawn did it abate. The whole camp lay under a pall of dust, so thick that men and beasts seemed rescued from interment, and roused and shook themselves like creatures from the dead. The fire Jack had prepared on the evening before was buried entirely. The luggage had become meaningless mounds of dust. His head ached. His eyes were swollen and painful. It hurt him to breathe. Yet he had withstood it.

In the afternoon he and Jack unpacked the instruments. He found that the ether in the hydrometers had entirely evaporated. His watch still ticked, though he could see that dust had found its way under the glass and had no doubt penetrated the mechanism. He opened the glass and blew it carefully away, but dared not open it further lest a sudden puff of wind should increase the damage. The chronometer, to his heartfelt relief, appeared unharmed. But at noon on the following day he found by his meridian reading that its rate had altered to a degree, which made him mistrust his calculations.

Only then did he recall today was Sunday. He and his people were dressed in the clothes they had worn ever since they left Beni Ulid. To find their European clothes and change into them seemed, at the moment, excessive. He called them to him, and standing simply as they were, read Matins.

And Emma at that very hour wrote to him, *What were my feelings, Laing, when in watching Angelo Heri and the Sheikh set out I asked who is that woman? and was told that it was Bagoola's wife who had been indisposed. Why, if it were safe for her, might not Laing's wife travel too? All the time I think how I might ride with you and take instruction from you about the things we see as we pass. At night Jack le Bore would set out a table for us under the stars and we should sit across from one another, by candlelight or moonlight, and talk about all that we had seen that day, or plan together our future when I travel at your side to Europe. Then, my adored Laing, we might enjoy the sweet comforts of the night undisturbed, before in the morning we ride forth again. Oh, if it were so neither of us would feel the tedium that we suffer now, nor care if ever we reached Timbuctoo in this month or the next.*

Two nights later they camped in view of a low line of hills. Sheikh Babani informed Laing that the well of Malhrail lay in a defile between them. Beyond lay a five-day desert. If there were to be an ambush Laing judged this the most likely place for it.

In the morning he sent out one of the Bashaw's men to scout out the defile and listened keenly after him for any sound of firing. Within the hour he had returned to say that there was no sign of men in the hills, nor had the well been recently visited. They moved forward and at the entrance to the narrow valley found the well. Laing gave orders that they should remain here until dawn, resting and filling every available waterskin for the desert crossing.

Once more the camels were unloaded, hobbled and turned loose to browse. The men, shouting and jostling for position, began to lower their leather buckets into the well. The water came up stinking and thick with the reddish earth they had dragged it from. Thirsty as the horses were, they jerked their heads away. Then, after more shouting and cuffing, they drank reluctantly. Laing, too, though he little relished the inevitable effects, forced himself to swallow it down and had Jack fill the waterskin he kept for his own drinking before the water sank lower in the well and became muddier still.

He sat in his tent with the sun focusing its bright spot through the canvas, writing to the Consul: *Two roads lead from here to Ghadames: the one due west, the other longer by five days at least. Babani favours this last, but I think only of the speed with which I can arrive at Ghadames where by now your letters and the portrait must wait already.*

Babani and Bagoola came stooping and crowding into his tent. They all three sat cramped together with the sloping canvas grating against their necks and shoulders, arguing about the route they should take. If any one of them shifted his position the stifling air was filled with dust.

Babani said they must take the longer route south. He drew in the sand a southward loop that turned back on itself and climbed north again to Ghadames.

'How long?' Laing asked him.

'Six days.' He wiped away his former mark with the palm of his hand and drew six strokes, counting and looking up sideways at Laing to make sure he understood.

Bagoola kept on in a low complaining voice, 'This road is very hard. There is no water. We shall not reach Ghadames for many days. We should take the shorter road.'

Babani said, 'The robbers will wait on the shorter road. We have no soldiers now.'

'We have three,' Laing said, 'and my people.' He thought how little likely it would be that Rogers and Harris would

164

stand up under fire, and of the antiquated muskets of Yahia Mohammed and his relatives. His head ached. He longed to be alone to write his letters.

The arguments repeated themselves again and again. At last Laing said, 'We'll take the longer route. We'll fill the waterskins here.'

Bagoola said, 'The water here is bad.'

Later he found the Bashaw's three men squatting patiently on the sand. They stood side by side, speaking in a confused unison, not looking directly at Laing, so that he found it impossible to understand them. 'What is it they want?' he asked Babani.

The Sheikh said, 'They have come to say goodbye, *Reis.*'

'Why is that?' Laing asked him sharply.

'They do not say, *Reis.* They are ill.' This last he said with so little conviction that Laing supposed him to have invented it on the spot.

Bagoola said, 'One of the men is from these parts. He knows the road. He says there is no water on it. No man who might choose to travel would choose to travel on this road.'

'Very well then,' Laing said. He felt hurt and betrayed by the men; any deeper misgivings about their motives for deserting him he repressed. 'Tell them not to leave,' he said, 'until I give them letters.'

It was cooler now. He brought his writing materials outside. He must bid them farewell again.

God bless you, my dear Consul, he wrote. *May God bless and prosper you, and may you ever enjoy that mental happiness which your upright and open disposition so justly entitles you to.*

He wrote then his few nightly lines to Emma: *Are you well? Does my Emma keep happy and not fearful for her Laing? For to be so would only damage her precious health. I myself am in perfect health, impatient only that these delays and detours cause the time to increase rather than diminish until I can hold my precious Emma in my arms once more.*

In the morning he took the letters to the Bashaw's men himself. He shook each by the hand and thanked him. He had Bagoola measure out for each of them a portion of sugar. Then he watched them mount and ride away.

All morning the camelmen and the Sheikh's servants toiled

at drawing up the foul-smelling water to fill every available skin. With the loss of the extra hands the work went on till noon. It was decided to rest until the heat had passed.

In the late afternoon they moved out of Bir Serked on the start of their wide circuit to the south. It was Saturday the thirteenth of August. Tomorrow, a month exactly would have passed since his wedding day. *In five days*, he had written to the Consul, *I hope to arrive at Shati at the nadir of our loop, and shall then be as far from Ghadames as I was this day last month.*

At much the same time as the Bashaw's men rode from Bir Serked with these letters in their saddle-bags, Angelo Heri arrived at the English Garden with the packet of letters that Laing had despatched from Beni Ulid. He arrived at the house in the morning, but it was not until the family were gathered at the dinner table that the Consul handed his daughter the bundle of short notes wrapped and sealed as one and addressed to her.

She had not seen her married name written before. Throughout the meal she kept looking down to where it lay on her lap. As soon as the meal was over Emma hurried to the kiosk. In its shade she read the letters one by one, haphazardly at first, scarcely taking in the words in her delight that he had written them; that all was, after all, as she had believed it to be. Then she arranged them carefully in the order of their dates and read them again and again, hunting now for words that were not there: for any sign of diminution of his love between one letter and the next, for any hint of misfortune that he had sought to hide from her. She kissed them repeatedly, thinking how his hand had lain upon the page. She gathered them together and held them against her heart, as if in that way they might yield up some further secret to her.

In the evening, when the family were settled in the drawing room, she said to the servant, 'Where is Angelo Heri?'

'In the stable, Signora. Shall I send for him?'

'No, no,' she said. She slipped quietly out of the front door and hurried along the path between the trees. A fire was lit in the centre of the stable yard. The syces and some of the house servants squatted around it. The factor sat elevated on a bale of straw to tell the tale of his travels. He rose at once when he saw her, embarrassed at her presence, and ushered her out again into the garden.

'You saw him,' she said without any sort of a preamble. 'Was he well? Tell me how he looked.' He was disconcerted by her. She was dishevelled, perhaps. She herself scarcely understood the haste and secrecy with which she had sought him out. It seemed to draw them together in some conspiracy that was repugnant to her, but she must speak to him who had spoken to Laing. She said again, 'How was he?'

'He was well, Signora.'

'Are you sure?'

'A little fever,' he said, tipping his hand from side to side. 'Only a little. Nothing more.

'What fever?' she said. 'Was he ill?'

'Not ill. Only a little fever on the day that I arrived. The next day, too.'

'And when he left? Had he the fever still?'

'No. No. He was quite well when he left.' But she did not believe him now. She turned abruptly and went into the house.

Not until the next day might she write, *Laing, Laing, Angelo Heri tells me you are ill with fever and, Laing, my heart is cut in two that you lie ill with no Emma to bathe your head. I seem to hold you in my arms and feel your poor head burn against my breast. I have lost count already of the days.*

In the morning it was thought that she was feverish. She could not have said whether she was well or ill. Mama and Jenny in turn felt her hands and her forehead and declared them very warm and she herself, as she had come slowly down the stairs, felt the heavy awareness of her body, the slight pain of its displacement in its own surroundings that fever brings. Her throat still ached from the violence done to it by the ridding of the poison.

The doctor was sent for and sat by her bedside with his fingers on her wrist and his watch in his hand. He asked her quietly and pleasantly about Laing. No one had spoken his name directly to her since he had left. What news had she had?

'He was feverish,' she said, catching at his hand. 'Angelo Heri told me he had fever.'

'You're not to fret over that. I doubt there's a fever left could kill him.' He said it in so brisk and unsmiling a way that she believed him at once and was comforted. 'You must eat,' he said, exhibiting her narrow wrist before her face. 'You are too thin. You must eat more.' It was true. Her hands were thinner. The wedding ring was very loose and she worried constantly that in a moment of distraction it would slip from her finger and be lost. She was loth to remind them of the promise to make it fit; if they took it from her, they might not return it. Or they might substitute it for another that Laing's hand had never touched, saying, 'Look, it is the same. What difference can it make?'

She took silk from her sewing basket and, sitting on her bed with her knees apart so that her skirt might catch it if it fell, pulled the ring carefully from her finger. So to reverse the action of his hand filled her with a kind of dread. Only the fear that she might lose it altogether made it possible to do. She pushed the strands of silk through and through the ring until it formed a band sufficiently thick to hold it more securely in place. Then she replaced it, turning it carefully so that the thread was hidden in the palm of her hand. Still, for an hour or two she was oppressed by a superstitious dread that she had interfered with something so frail that any, alteration might dangerously threaten it. By the following evening the fever had left her as quickly as it had come.

Herr Knutson had finished with her. When she was taken ill he had assured her that it was no matter. He could transfer the drawing onto the ivory in his own home and finish it the better without the distraction of Emma's presence. Even the limited action of sitting was denied her now. 'I am not ill,' she told her mother, but even as she said it she knew she was reluctant to forgo this one recognition that she was in some way altered.

A week passed before she was sufficiently recovered to make her way down to the kiosk and write to Laing. It seemed, although she knew it was not so, that she had failed him, and that he must have immediately felt her neglect. She felt weak and strange as she walked, and was a little faint by the time she reached the kiosk. The steps as she climbed them seemed to have lost their resilience and to give beneath her weight. She sat a while before taking out the box.

Then she wrote hurriedly: . . . *They tell me I am ill myself. I am ill with longing for you. I think our fever is the same and when it rages in me I am happy to think it may slacken in you . . .*

She sat on the sofa. In the afternoons she moved onto the verandah and sat with her feet raised on a footstool. At night she slept in the narrow tented bed between her sisters. At table she sat in her old place, although they all knew very well that, as a married woman, she should take precedence over Jane. She read and reread Laing's letters until the words became meaningless to her.

Herr Knutson and Frau Knutson had come to dine at the Garden. 'It is the great day,' he cried out gaily as he came into the room. 'No, no, no,' he said and lifted the small portfolio in which he kept the portrait teasingly above her head. She was expected to reach up for it but would not.

After dinner they watched him progress from one window to the next, peering at the portrait to see what light would show it to its best advantage. He must be given his due. The thing was still his. 'Ah, here after all where I drew her, the light is best,' and then the servant must be got to move the table, and some other cloth was required. He suggested a simple black.

It came quite suddenly to Mrs Warrington that there was an old black cloak hanging on a hook in the upstairs passage. Minutes later the servant could be seen through the window shaking the dust from it over the edge of the verandah. It was spread over the table and a pile of books slipped under it for the portrait to be propped against.

'There.'

They had taken up position around the table while he darted to and fro before their eyes. Now they all leant forward to see the little thing on its oval disc of ivory. They all exclaimed at it. How well he had captured Emma! What a pretty thing! She was unsure of it and turned away, hiding her face in her hands. 'You don't know,' Frau Knutson told her fondly. 'You do not know how you look.' But the face was pretty, she thought. She was shyly pleased with it.

'Wait,' cried Herr Knutson, for now that they had seen it they were making the first uncertain movements away from the table. 'I must beg advice from each of you as to how it is to be mounted. Gerda, my angel, have you the ivory? Have you the paper? Look now. See the difference.'

He placed the ivory behind the thin paper of the miniature,

stood back as if amazed, then with a flourish like a conjuror's exchanged it for a sheet of heavy white paper. 'Can you see the difference? Look; come close. One at a time. So and then so. Can you not see it? Consul? Mrs Warrington? Jenny? Stand here. See how it changes the whole appearance of the thing.'

It was as he said. They all agreed. The ivory gave it a warm living tone, but the paper was the favoured one. They all exclaimed in turn when he slid it into place.

'Ah,' cried Herr Knutson, 'you are agreed. Did we not say so to one another, my angel, with the same thought, the same breath, that on the ivory this might be the likeness of any beautiful young woman, but that on the paper it was Emma? The delicacy, the refinement the spirituality, that indefinable thing I struggled so to capture with my pencil, and after all it was the blank white paper that created it between my lines.'

They all agreed with him. Emma could not say. The likeness, the detachment of their concern over it confused her. She thought it might be completed more quickly if the mount were cut from paper and chose that. In any case it must be taken away again. Another week would pass before he returned with it framed in its locket.

Again they crowded round, taking it from hand to hand, admiring how the eyes stood out from the delicate pallor of the portrait and how the whole was enhanced by the plain gold band surrounding all.

Later, in the kiosk, she wrote, *Today, my dearest Laing, my poor portrait was at last complete and everyone was very pleased with it and says it is an excellent likeness. For myself I cannot. No wish is stronger in my heart than that it pleases you and gives you solace in your lonely state. I have wrapped it in a little silk cut from the lining of my wedding dress. It will await you at Ghadames where they say you cannot have arrived or Sala would have come. Why, Laing, when so many days and weeks are past? Is it fever? Are you ill? I am sick myself with fear for you.*

For the first time, as the koffle left Malhrail, Laing and everyone who rode were mounted on camels. The horses, with their prodigal consumption of water, must be taxed as little as was possible. Laing took the lead with Jack at his side. Behind, the two boatwrights chose to go on foot. Then came Bagoola and his wife, with the slave boy guiding her; then the horses, the mules and the pack camels with the camelmen and servants trotting in disorderly files on either side. Behind them, in what Laing now realised was the accepted position of command, Babani and the guide brought up the rear. The danger of attack was past. Other factors forced urgency upon their march: the distance to the next well, the number of skins each camel might carry, the rate of consumption necessary to keep the beasts moving, the diminishing speed at which they travelled as their exhaustion increased. All formed a complex and highly speculative equation well beyond Laing's ken.

All that night they kept on without benefit of moon. At seven the next morning they halted and rested out the heat of the day. In the afternoon they moved on again and made what progress they could through another darkened night. At dawn they continued forward until at noon heat and exhaustion forced them to stop. They had arrived in a valley of sandstone set between hills of such even contours that they might have formed some ancient battery thrown up by man, had it not been inconceivable that anyone should wish to hold so forsaken a place. Ahead of them in the distance stretched a range of black gloomy mountains.

'Tamsawa,' Babani said, raising his arm with its dangling hand. 'The water is there, Reis.'

'How many days?'

'Two? Three?' He had asked a pointless question. They could see the hills. There was no other source of water. Only God knew when they would reach it.

By the time the horses and mules had been watered he counted twenty waterskins lying flat and empty on the sand.

'Is someone stealing it?' he asked Babani.

'It goes in the heat.'

'Will it hold out until Tamsawa?' Another foolish question; when that was the business of God. Nevertheless an hour later Babani came to Laing's tent to say that he was despatching two of his servants to ride ahead to Tamsawa on the two swiftest maherries. There they would fill twelve empty skins with fresh sweet water and return to meet the koffle as it advanced.

'When?' Laing asked him.

'Perhaps tomorrow.

An hour after the maherries left, they set out again. The camels moved more slowly now, fatigued by their long marches. Laing walked to rest his and found he might easily keep pace with it over the slightly rising ground.

When, late in the afternoon, they descended into a spacious valley of fine sand and gravel, his own fatigue forced him to mount. The valley was surrounded by a sandstone escarpment marked at half its height and with a perfect regularity by a single layer of darker stone. He was tormented now by thirst. He could not free his mind of the fancy that the entire landscape had recently been flooded with water; that the eroded columns of rock scattered over its surface had shown only as islets surrounded by swirling currents, the hollows in the cliff sides eaten out by persistent frothing tides whose highest point that black line marked, before its sudden ebb had left this arid mould.

As darkness fell the ground became steep and irregular. He was forced to dismount and drag his poor beast along as best he could. At midnight they halted.

At earliest dawn they pressed forward again, but an hour later could go no further and camped where they were to await the water's arrival. Here they emptied the last two skins of the stinking Malhrail water. Laing's portion merely nauseated him and did nothing to relieve his thirst. He lay in his tent unable to swallow, so dry that he must repeatedly peel away his tongue from the roof of his mouth. The lining of his throat seemed swollen to the point where it must seal off breath itself. He could think of nothing but water. He seemed to hear its rush and clatter in the low persistent wind, the rattle of the canvas.

He stood by the burn at Aviemore, where the water ran fast and deep between the stepping stones. 'Jump now, jump. Would you have your father think you a coward, Alexander?' He felt the cold breath of the water on his face and heard its relentless racket in his ears.

He lay with his head buried in his arms. Hours had gone past. The men would be coming with the water. He would roll over and find that the sky above the roof of the tent had darkened.

He would go outside and see the men riding towards the camp, with the swollen gleaming skins jolting at the camel's side. But the light had not altered. He had been misled. He looked at his watch. It had stopped. He held it to his ear and heard its arid ticking. He thought how, when he died, its indifferent mechanism would outlive him by a day. He wound it quickly then, staring at the hands as if they might spring forward to state some truer time. By the time it is dark, he told himself, the water will be here. But it seemed some new force had come into being with power to delay the passage of the sun through the sky and that in the future he must always contend with this. He was unable to write.

Jack came and sat near to him, bowing his head in misery between his knees.

'They'll come,' Laing told him. He reached out and laid his hand against Jack's back. 'They'll come by dark.'

But the words proved powerless. At the moment that the sun disappeared behind the hills it seemed a final dispensation had been missed and there could be no hope at all till morning. Nevertheless Jack roused himself to make a fire and presently others blazed outside the tents. No one attempted to sleep. By common consent they all kept watch, hour after hour, feeding the little fires that marked out their whereabouts in the dark.

At midnight they heard rifle fire and saw the distant flash of muskets. They fired back and heaped up the remaining fuel into a single blaze. It flared up so brilliantly that the riders were invisible to them until they halted by the camp. There was shouting and pushing as they hauled down the camels. Babani said, 'Let the Reis drink first. He is unused to thirst.' He felt the cold slime of the skin's surface between his hands. His throat like a muscle convulsed without his willing it. He pressed his face against the tight swollen skin and drank deeply out of the aperture. Even when he must relinquish it to the next man he rubbed his damp hands repeatedly behind his neck and across his face, smelling on them still the odour of the wetted skins.

For two hours they worked to water the mules and horses. Then, exhausted as they were, they moved on again. Only two of the replenished skins remained full. They calculated, by the time the two men had taken to return with the water, that at their own slow pace another day and then another night must pass in continuous marching before they reached the wells at Tamsawa.

At seven in the morning they came across a withered stretch of herbage on which the camels began eagerly to browse. Though they had set out resolutely determined not to halt, they knew they would get no further that day. They were all more or less sick from the water at Malhrail and the animals were sorely overtaxed. There would be no moon that night. They made no attempt to move on until the following dawn. By ten in the morning they were forced to rest again and drank the last of their water. At four, when the sun relented, they set out again, knowing that there could be no further halt until they reached the well at Tamsawa.

Again there was only faint starlight to see by. Everyone walked. The thirst had returned. Laing thought of nothing but the need to swallow. For very weariness he leant his weight against the camel's woolly flank. When it stumbled he forced himself to go ahead and drag it forward with the rope across his shoulder. Each step seemed levered by a separate act of will. The first indications of dawn brought no revival of his spirits. The light, as he had supposed it would, revealed further emptiness.

No one had spoken for many hours. Once, looking up, Laing saw a black shape on the horizon, but could not force his eyes to focus on it. When he looked again it was still there. He stood where he was until one of the camelmen passed him. Then he pointed silently.

'Tamsawa,' the man said. His voice was so hoarse as to be nearly inaudible. Still, Laing heard the joy in it. 'This is my country, *Reis*. This is my country, where I could live for ever and ever on dates and water.'

They walked towards it through the rising light. The dark mass could be distinguished now as the tops of date trees, and presently he could make out their trunks. He walked over the pitted tracks of sheep and goats. A flight of little birds swept overhead, turned, and swooped back. They were sparrows. He feared then that he was dreaming, but the trees were distinct now. He could see the beautiful free motion of their tethered branches and at their base the moving forms of men. The camels moved more quickly, scenting water, but would stop suddenly to snatch at patches of grass that grew along their track. He waited for his camel out of pity for its suffering and let the others pass him by.

By nine o'clock they were filing along a beaten path between newly planted date gardens. Men worked with mattocks opening low baulks of earth, so that water from the irrigation channels might flow from one plot to another. They called pleasantly to them as they passed, standing ankle deep in the reddish mud with their loose shifts gathered up between their legs. Children played at the edge of the track, slapping handfuls of mud about their feet. Everywhere he heard the prodigal trickle of water.

Now boys ran ahead, and ran back again, jumping where they stood, holding their heads entirely to one side to stare. They cried out, 'Kaffir, Kaffir,' and pulled mockingly at imaginary beards, so that he must remind himself, I am a strange thing: a white man with a red beard. He would have smiled at them but could feel his face stiff and unresponsive with the dust. They kept on. The servants reached out occasionally to clasp the hands that were reached out to them, but they never stopped nor slackened their grim pace towards the well.

In an open space where two paths intersected water fell from a sluice into a wide trough. As they approached a woman snatched from it a gleaming boy child who wept with rage. The sweet fresh odour of the water rose up to them. The camels shoved and jostled. They extended their necks into the trough and sucked up the water noisily while their keepers beat great clouds of dust from their flanks to force them to make room for others.

And Jack le Bore ran in among them laughing and lowering the cup between their hairy sucking lips, and ran with it guarded in his hands to Laing, although he had not drunk himself. He drank it down and laughed out of his strange stiff face. Good Jack. Faithful Jack. Drops of water stood out on the dusty frizz of his hair and the dust had been dragged from his face by his wet fingers to show the gleaming black beneath. Laing handed him the cup. 'Ça va?' he said.

'Ça va.'

Some men had brought bundles of fodder and squatted with them near the wells. Laing shouted to Bagoola to purchase what was needed and, when his camel had drunk its fill, led it himself over to the scattered pile of green stuff. Beside him

Yahia Mohammed said in a low exultant voice, 'Ah, *Reis*, it does my heart good to see the camels eat. For what am I without my camels?' He might love them all, then, men and beasts without discrimination.

They were all filthy and verminous. Laing had Jack heat water and unpack the canvas bath. Then, in the privacy of his tent, he scrubbed himself in muddy tepid water with a lump of soap coated in sand, and with a razor scraped what hair he could from his body. The flesh in those few days had fallen from him. He must eat. He shouted out to Bagoola to purchase fresh meat and fruit for all of them. He would regain his strength. He rubbed at his wasted body with awe at what it had endured. He found that a thick band of suppurating bites encircled his waist. He dried them carefully and smeared zinc ointment on them. He flung his filthy clothes outside the tent for Jack to boil and shouted for his European clothes. They were strange to him, loose at the waist and tight in the leg. He walked stiffly in them.

He sat outside the tent while Jack shaved his head and beard. A crowd collected and watched with interest. He went inside his tent again, took out his portfolio and began to write up his public version of the journey from Beni Ulid to be forwarded to the Colonial Office. The exact times, the names of places they had passed through, the observations taken at Malhrail and Bir Serked he copied carefully from his notebook. Of his own sufferings, and his fever at Beni Ulid, he made no mention at all.

When it became difficult to see inside the tent he gathered up his writing things and went outside. A crowd of people still squatted patiently at a little distance. There was a low murmur among them at his appearance. One or two voices called out to him. The dialect was unfamiliar. He sent for Bagoola to ask them what they wanted.

'They are sick, *Reis*,' the steward told him. 'They say that you will make them well.'

'Tell them that it is too late now. Tell them to come back tomorrow.' But although they withdrew and later the bright flames of his fire screened them from his sight, he continued to hear the low sound of their voices and knew they waited still and watched him from the dark.

All my life, he wrote to Emma by the shifting firelight, *I have longed for someone to whom I could confide my thoughts and the interesting occurrences I meet with, without being thought egotistical, knowing that my most trivial thought or circumstance would be of consuming interest to that one being . . .*

But to her no more than to his sponsors could he confide his sufferings and misgivings. He praised her letters to him. He told her he was well. He counted out the days till they could be reunited. It was Friday the nineteenth of August. He was as far from Ghadames as he had ever been.

And she on that same evening wrote to him:

Laing, Laing today at last I was given your portrait. My hand shook so as I undid the wrapping. I was clumsy, thinking how, in another minute, I should see your face again after this long time. And there for a moment I thought I looked into your eyes, and then a moment later what was it but a scrap of paper? Ah, you are so grown in my heart, how could it compensate me for what I am denied? And yet, Laing, how many many kisses have I pressed, how many many tears have I shed that all my lips might touch was the cold glass?

In the morning the same crowd was waiting. 'Tell them to go away,' he said to Bagoola. 'Tell them to come back an hour before it is dark and I will see them.'

His bowels were still loosened, the more so from their feast of fresh fruit. Frequently he was forced to leave the tent to defecate. Each time the crowd of watchers made eagerly to follow.

'Send them away,' he shouted to Bagoola, who ran among them battering at them with his stick. He would not look at them. 'Later,' he called to Bagoola. 'Tell them later.' There were too many. He wrote steadily on as the patient plaintive murmur of their talk lapped continuously against the sides of his tent. He heard shouting, too, the clamour of accusation, Bagoola and Yahia Mohammed. He opened the flap of the tent and shouted angrily, 'Be quiet, damn you,' in English. Silence then.

At noon he left the tent again to take his meridian observation. Jack stood beside him. They were surrounded at once by clamouring faces.

'Stand back,' he said in Arabic, 'I cannot do it if you crowd me.' They shuffled back a little way, watching him intently.

'Are you looking for your country?' they called out as they had at Wadi Rimmel.

'At the sun,' he said, pointing, smiling, nodding.

'Aie, aie,' an old man cried out, 'he is writing the sun in his book. He has come to take it from us.' But they only laughed and aimed mock blows at the old man's head.

In his own tent Laing would have slept when he had done his calculations, but must return to his writing. He yawned repeatedly. His eyes watered until the words blurred on the page. Yet he dared not close his eyes, even for a minute, lest he sleep out the rest of the day and fail in the completion of his task. Nevertheless, though there was more to do at five o'clock he set the writing aside and called for Jack. Together they dragged the medicine chest outside his tent. He ordered Jack to mix up a solution of silver nitrate for the ophthalmia that seemed to afflict most of them.

A little girl hid her face in the soft recesses of her mother's breasts. He coaxed her onto his knee and felt her pleasant weight against him. He moistened the edge of his handkerchief in the solution and passed it gently over the poor suppurating lids. 'So,' he said to the mother, 'and so.'

A man asked him for a love philtre. Laing smiled and shook his head but the man persisted: it was well known that white men held the secret of aphrodisiacs. Laing mixed him a mild purgative and wished him well.

An old woman fumbled with the cloth across her mouth, then let it fall and spoke with shrill urgency. Her voice was weak. He could see well enough by a shrinking of her lower face and the fierce enlargement of her eyes that she was dying. 'What is it?' he said to her. 'What is it that you want?' He leant forward, putting his ear close to her lips.

She was saying, 'Give me a child, *Reis*. Make me the medicine that will give me a child.'

He gave her some sugar and water. It was too dark to see clearly. He stood up and dismissed them. 'Tomorrow,' he told them. 'Tomorrow at the same time.'

On the following evening he brought out his box of medicines an hour earlier than he had the day before and, sitting on the ground beside it, had Jack bring them to him. He noticed one man sitting with his back against a tree, his legs stretched out in front of him in an attitude of perfect resignation, and had Jack call him over. He squatted down opposite Laing and began to unwind his dusty turban, looping his arm rapidly over and over his head. The inner folds were caked with brown dried blood and, though the man tugged at them, Laing could see that the soiled cloth was sealed to some invisible wound. He felt himself shrink at it. His nostrils and throat seemed coated with the sweet repellent odour of corruption. He had Jack bring warm water and gently soaked it free. The man never flinched. Across the surface of his skull was a deep infected gash.

'How was this done?' Laing asked him.

'With a sword,' the man said simply. He held the man's head against him to steady it. He felt no disgust now, but bathed the wound with a careful absorption until every trace of blood and pus was removed and he could see the white line of the skull between the wound's inflamed and swollen lips. He covered it with a clean bandage which he wound neatly and fastened with a pin. The man nodded and grinned and raised his hand repeatedly to the new bandage in a grateful salute.

In the morning they struck camp and for the next week travelled by short and easy stages along the vale of Shati. Each day, as he took his meridian altitude, he found the latitude diminished. They were travelling northward, cancelling out the progress they had made so far. The heat was intense, the worst he expected to endure. By the time he reached these latitudes again, travelling beyond Ghadames, the summer would have passed.

By day they travelled through landscapes that seemed shaped by ancient cataclysm and abandoned since by God and man. But every evening they would see ahead the beautiful towering dates and camp by welling ponds of sweet water. The moon was in its final quarter; the nights brilliant and noisy with the sounds of living creatures.

On the evening of his first halt he discovered that his fame as a healer had spread before him. Again his tent was surrounded by people begging for his medicines. Among them

Laing recognised the man with the wounded head.

'Why are you here?' he asked him. 'Is this your home?'

'No, *Reis*, my home is in Tamsawa.' The man had followed him.

'How did you travel?'

'I walked, *Reis*.'

'You should rest,' Laing told him. 'You should not have walked so far.'

The man said, 'You will heal me *Reis*.'

With the same serious pleasure Laing uncovered the wound. It had filled again with pus but was less inflamed. Again he bathed it and felt the unflinching weight of the man's head on his hands. He spoke to him constantly as he worked, 'There. There now. That's better now,' quietly in English. When he had covered it with a clean dressing, he said in Arabic, 'You should rest. It will get better.' But he could not bring himself to order the man directly back to Tamsawa.

In the morning, turning his horse to one side, he let the koffle move past him until he caught sight of the man trotting towards the rear amongst the servants, keeping up well with the brisk pace of the rested animals. In the evening he dressed the wound again and ordered Bagoola to give the man dates.

By the last light of the day he wrote to Emma, *We move northward now. Each day brings me closer to Ghadames where your face and voice at least will be restored to me.*

And she at the same hour in the kiosk wrote to him:

My adored husband, last night the moon was full enough for me to take your portrait to the window and gaze upon it ere I slept. And then my small desire was granted that I should dream of you. I dreamt we lay together on a bed – in what place I could not tell – whether it were cold or warm or day or night. Only a sense of joy and ease so great that when I felt myself waking I wept with longing to be there again.

At Berged they halted for two days while arrangements were made to hire more camels to carry their water across the stretch of desert that lay between them and Ghadames. Three days, five days, maybe more, the guide told him. There would be no water until they reached the town. The heat at mid-day was oppressive. Inside Laing's tent his thermometer gave a reading of 107°. He placed his thumb over the bulb and immediately the mercury shrank downwards. He sat in his tent made stupid by heat, performing this trick again and again with the same sense of wonder he had felt as a child when, by the same means, he had enticed the mercury upwards.

All the time voices quarrelled from the direction of Bagoola's tent. He lacked the energy to intervene but sat complaining in his mind that this man, who had been foisted onto him by Clapperton, was useless and abusive, and had caused him nothing but trouble. Later Bagoola came to him, sullen at the prospect of the desert crossing and complaining in his turn that they had not sufficient food and water.

'That's your concern,' Laing told him. 'If there is not enough, ask the Sheikh for money to purchase more.'

He sent for Yahia Mohammed and said, 'Bagoola tells me there is not enough corn for the camels.'

Yahia Mohammed said angrily, 'If there is not enough it is because Sidi Mohammed Bagoola takes it for his own camels. I had brought enough. There was enough before he took over the feeding of the camels from me at Beni Ulid. Sidi Mohammed Bagoola takes your grain to feed his camels.'

Laing said, 'Why have you not told me this?'

The man shrugged. He had supposed Laing knew. He had supposed that if Laing entrusted Bagoola with the corn he would expect him to steal in moderation from him.

'I'll speak to him,' Laing said, but he did not trust himself to see Bagoola until the heat had lessened and his first anger had abated.

By evening, when his food was cooked, Bagoola came unsummoned and lowered himself beside Laing's fire, begging by his very presence a fistful of the freshly cooked bazeen. Laing watched him eat, resenting the nicety with which he gathered up the food in his fingers and the delicate duck of his head as he poked it between his greasy lips; Laing's food taken as if he had a right to it. When he was done he put his fingers one by one into his mouth and licked them clean as swift and neat as a cat, then he began again his arrogant whine.

No one had told him in Tripoli that they would take this

route. No one had told him that he must cross first one desert and then another. He had been hired to go with the Reis to Ghadames, but this was not a good route to Ghadames. They should have travelled by the shorter route. As it was they would die in the desert, he, his camels, his wife, his slave, everything that he owned. There was not enough food. There were not enough camels to carry the quantity of water they would require. His camels were worn out already and would die in the desert.

Laing said steadily, 'Yahia Mohammed says there was enough food. He says that you steal corn from me for your own camels and that is why there is not enough. Why should I buy more for you to steal? I am not obliged to feed your camels. It is my camels that go hungry.'

'That is a lie,' Bagoola shouted at him. 'Yahia Mohammed is telling lies.' He had got to his feet in one swift movement and went without another word back to his own tent.

The next day, while Laing lay out the afternoon heat in his tent, he was wakened by cries and a savage thudding. Without thought he was on his feet, running barefoot over the stony ground, gripping his sabre like a short stick, although the metal scabbard was so hot as to burn his hand. Behind the tents he found Bagoola beating without mercy at his slave, who lay on the ground trying to ward the blows from his face with dusty jerking arms. He no longer cried out but muttered in a patient wheedling sing-song his plea for the beating to stop. Laing ran towards them through the thick heat shouting his hatred of Bagoola. He stopped to draw his sabre and ran on, waving it threateningly above his head. Bagoola got in one more cut across the boy's arm before Laing could get to him. Then he turned and strode off, saying viciously to Laing that the boy was his and he would do to him what he chose.

Laing had supposed that the boy would make his escape. But he made no move beyond flattening himself entirely face downward on the ground. Laing squatted awkwardly beside him. 'It's all right,' he said. His voice was shaken and distorted with rage. 'He won't hurt you again.' He lay without any sign of life. His eyes were shut. Jack came up and knelt down beside him, laying his cheek on the dust to stare into the boy's face.

Laing said, 'I think he's killed him.'

182

The Creole began to poke at the boy as a child might poke at a dead thing, with little meaningless bursts of talk, 'Hey there. You there. Come on. Speak to Jack. Jack le Bore. He you friend now.'

'He's killed him,' Laing said again.

'He scared,' Jack said. 'He half scared to death.' He laughed, picked up the boy's limp arm and let it drop again.

'You'll hurt him,' Laing said sharply, but the boy had turned his head a little and opened his eyes.

'You see,' Jack said. 'He not bad hurt. 'He scared.'

The light was fading. He wrote to the Consul:

Do not be surprised if I send Sidi Mohammed Bagoola back to you from Ghadames. No doubt he served the needs of Captain Clapperton admirably, but he is useless and worse than useless to mine. I have treated him as a companion, though with becoming distance; at his request I gave him charge of everything. In return he is sullen and overbearing in his manners, a tyrant to his poor slave and a constant cause of quarrelling and dissension among my people. Even Babani, who is as just a man as one might meet, tells me he cannot abide him and advises me to sent him packing.

As for the rest, they do well enough. Rogers is a good-humoured rough fellow. Harris is a quiet, nobody-disturbing sort of Jack Tar and bears patiently the mild ophthalmia that has recently afflicted him. And as for Jack, he is the same as ever, good, cheerful Jack le Bore, a favourite with everyone except, that is, Bagoola. He wishes me to recommend him to you all: especially 'his excellent Consul-General' and 'Mr Osman Warrington'.

To Emma, as the sun set, he wrote nothing of these troubles lest they alarm her. Instead he reiterated his love for her, his promise to return, his reassurances that he was well and in good spirits and added the little note to the others which he would post from Ghadames.

No Bagoola came to sit by Laing's fire that night. Nor could Laing sufficiently trust his feelings to seek him out. In the morning, as they loaded up the camels, they passed and repassed one another without a single exchange. Neither lowered his eyes nor met the eyes of the other. The slave boy's welts had stiffened in the night so that he could hardly move.

Without a word to his master, Laing ordered Jack to take him on his camel. Bagoola, passing, spat deliberately onto the sand, but otherwise ignored him.

By ten o'clock they had climbed out of the valley of Shati and crossed a narrow ridge of hills. By noon they had come out onto the farther side. Spread below them was a wide expanse of sand whipped by some past wind into steep irregular dunes, their smooth concaves yellow, their outer curves grey and ridged like a petrified sea. It stretched without alteration to the horizon. With no sound other than the clanking of harness and the dreary plodding of the camels, they lowered themselves down into this new element.

He rode then until the halt for prayer at noon. He wound the chronometer. It kept its rate. The thermometer recorded 120°. He wrote it in his notebook. No one spoke when they rode on again. Only rarely now did the camelmen break out in their mournful ditties, only to abandon them a minute later to the silence. He walked. He dragged the bull camel by its rope, which burnt and lacerated his neck and shoulder. Each day, when he stopped at noon to wind the chronometer and write in his notebook, he counted up the days, two, three, four. His watch was clogged with dust and useless to him. He thought the chronometer's rate had changed, but he could not be sure of this. On the fifth day, when he took out his thermometers at noon, he found their ivory mounts had warped in the heat and the glass tubes snapped. The quicksilver ran into the palm of his hand. He stood there stupidly, tipping it this way and that, watching its uncanny movement.

They travelled northwards now. The sun was on his right cheek in the morning. At noon he wound the chronometer, but no longer wrote in his notebook. The sun burnt on his left cheek. Then it faded. Time no longer passed in a succession of days, but in the endless repetition of a single one. He had lost count.

Babani ordered the halt. The word was shouted hoarsely up the straggling line. He sat by Babani's fire; there was fuel enough for the one only. They burnt dung collected during the day in baskets hung under the camels' tails and a dried root that spread out under the ground from a single withered blade. All day as he walked he looked for these so that he would have something to bring to the fire. They had dragged the luggage together to form a barrier against the wind. He leant his back against it. He heard the canvas wrappings rattle in the wind. He thought of nothing but the taste of sweetened tea that would soon be in his mouth. It was the best time of the day, when nothing more was wanted of him.

The camels were hobbled and set loose. They sat in a circle, shoulder to shoulder, watching Babani strike together his flint and steel. Jack crouched beside him with a little scrap of cloth cupped in his hands, holding it out to catch the spark, then close to his lips, breathing on it. He laid it on the sand and quickly piled the dried roots over it, then the small pellets of dung, quickly with his fingers. He laid his cheek on the sand and puffed at it through big cracked lips. They all leant forward watching intently for the thread of smoke, the first bright movement of the flame.

No one spoke. Babani measured the tea from a pouch into a tin teapot. Then he crumbled in a portion of sugar and set it to boil in the smouldering dung. The smell of the burning dung clung in his rigid throat. When it was his turn to drink, it took him all his concentration to raise the little cup to his lips. His hands shook with exhaustion and anxiety lest he spill it. Only when the hot liquid lay on his tongue did any sort of life return to him.

They sat in silence, too absorbed in sipping at the rim of the little cups to think of forming speech. Laing forced himself to drink it slowly, sip by sip. He could not eat. He would eat when it was morning. Jack lay by the fire and slept. Harris came to him and held up his head blindly while Laing smeared zinc ointment onto his swollen lids. He and Rogers lay each night together now under a single torn blanket, clinging like lovers, but too exhausted now to derive anything but a modicum of warmth from the embrace. It was cold at night. Laing let them be.

It was dark now. The little pellets of dung glowed on the sand. He would sleep soon, but sat for the present in silence hunched inside his cloak, shivering with cold. Yahia Mohammed said to him, 'He takes the food for his camels. See, his camels are fat and strong and yours, *Reis*, die for want of food. There is no more food after tomorrow.'

'How many days?' He formed the words but did not speak

them, knowing their futility. He could retain no sense of the days past nor conceive the days to come. One moment he sat upright. The next he was compelled to lie on the ground and within seconds slept.

He could hear Babani's thin chant, 'Come to prayer. Come to prayer. Prayer is better than sleep.' He was awake, clutching the cloak against his mouth. He shook with cold. No, no, no, like a cry in the head. His legs still tingled with exhaustion. He was stiffened with cold, yet almost at once he dragged himself upright and, going a few paces from the pile of luggage, squatted, as they did, to urinate. Jack and Bagoola's slave moved about in front of him bent double gathering the black pellets of dung the camels had dropped in the night. He hawked up foul-tasting spittle from his throat and spat it onto the sand.

Jack blew up the charred roots from the last night's fire, and the boy squatted beside him, laying the pellets of fresh dung into the heart of the low flames. Babani measured out the tea. They sat in a circle around the fire, their foreheads smeared with pale dust from their prayers, waiting for the sun's warmth to touch and enliven them.

The camels never strayed far from the camp now. They were held and tormented by the odour of water. At night they stumbled in among the sleepers, nuzzling and biting at the full skins, until they were driven off. In the morning they could be found quickly. The men moved about like ghosts in the disturbed dust, dragging down the grumbling beasts, avoiding their snapping lips, tying on the luggage, every day the same. Harris passed him. Laing caught at his chin and turned his face to the light to see his infected eyes. 'Have you washed them?'

'There's no water,' the man said. 'They won't let me use it.'

He let him go but later, when Harris sat on his crouching camel, Laing wrapped his own handkerchief gently over his eyes and tied it into the dusty stubble of his hair.

First they walked. Then they rode. In the heat of the day they walked again to spare the camels. Towards evening they rode. Only Harris rode all day. The slave boy never rode, but trotted uncomplainingly, barefoot in the burning sand. At night by the fire Laing could hear him cry and whimper. 'Why does he cry?' he asked Yahia Mohammed. 'Is he still in pain?'

'He is tired,' the man said indifferently.

'He should ride like the others,' Laing said.

'He must learn.'

They made their way, dragging the camels obliquely up the impacted outer curves of the dunes. Then they followed the crests so long as they led northwards. All the time they must pull and strain on the ropes lest the camels flounder and fall into the deep soft sand of the dunes' inner curves. Then, when the ridges of the dunes altered course, they unloaded the camels and on hands and knees scraped paths through the hot sand and dragged the camels down them. Sand poured in and out of his broken shoes and pressed and burnt into the naked arches of his feet. In the least declivity the entire world was lost. He could not recall how it had been.

When the ground levelled they rode. Legs might cease to move. Shoulder was free of its rope, feet of the tormenting sand. They dangled in their broken shoes against the soft corrugations of the camel's neck like things he had cast off from him. He was lifted up; the great waste of sand stretched out all around him. The mound he had toiled over shrank to insignificance at this jolting height. He might think that he would reach Ghadames. Then the great weight of tedium would bear down upon him. For there were hours yet to be endured before they halted, trapped at the centre of an unchanging disc with nothing on which the eye might fasten. The suffocating wind blew without remission. He watched the vast indifference of the place, the surface nature of it. All was volatile; subject to no permanent form, tormenting the mind with its old certainties, for here it seemed creation was ground down so finely that all distinction had been lost. And what if this great disintegration were universal now? The variety of matter become as uniform and unrelated as grains of sand, and all the bright remembered world to have existence only in the minds of these few dying men?

Bagoola said to him, 'Give me sugar, *Reis*.'

'No.'

'Oh why? Give me sugar.'

Laing said, 'Where is the corn for the camels? Why do your camels eat corn when mine do not?'

'There is no more corn.'

'You have taken the corn from my camels and fed it to your own. Yahia Mohammed has told me this.'

He shrugged with contempt and moved away from Laing to the other side of the fire. There was silence except for the rattle of the wind in the loose canvas of the luggage. The slave boy came and sat by Laing in the space that Bagoola had left. Presently he curled up on the ground beside him and wept himself rhythmically to sleep. Later Laing, too, stretched out and covered the boy with a portion of his cloak. He slept instantly. When he woke the boy was gone. He saw him grubbing with Jack in the sand behind the crouching camels for the shining pellets of dung dropped in the night.

Ahead they had halted. He knew it was too early in the day, but a great joy filled him that he might stop. The taste of tea haunted his dry mouth. He would stop now where he was and sleep later, when the sun had set, drag himself over to where the others camped and drink the tea. Still, as he thought this he managed to keep riding forward. On the ground behind the long legs of the camels one of the mules had fallen and lay stretched on the sand. They were dragging its load free and shouting to one another. He no longer made the effort to understand what they said. Its haunch poked sharply up, lifting the dusty skin. Yahia Mohammed kicked it on the shoulder. Its legs jerked but it made no effort to rise. They were silent. How solemnly they stood about it, looking down. Laing wondered why it did not shut its eyes. They hauled down the camels and distributed the mule's load among them. Every rope must be untied and tied again. They worked without hurry. Laing had time to unpack and wind the chronometer. He found he had no recollection of having wound it the day before, but when he laid his ear against it it still ticked.

The mule had not moved. Yahia Mohammed stabbed it in the base of the throat. The jet of blood gushed upwards, a thing of wonder in its force and colour. The mule coughed oddly when it died because the sound came out not through its mouth but through its severed throat. They moved on. Later he tried to remember what was in the load the mule had carried, but found he could not.

And Emma suddenly with total clarity faced him, so that he

thought her ghost had come to tell him of her death. He saw the tight damp curls at her neck, the sweat beaded on her short upper lip, the watchful alarm in her eyes. Well, I am changed, he thought, she cannot but find me changed. Her lips moved eagerly. He saw her teeth. Yet it was all inaudible. And she was gone. He asked, What have I done? What have I let them do to me?

And now he saw the old king, Assana Yeera, stare at him and ask again, 'Is he a man? Is he a man?' and he remembered how the old man had reached out and rubbed his hand in wonder against Laing's hair and touched his cheek, quickly drawing back his finger lest the skin's pale sickliness transfer itself. And, 'Allah, Allah, Allah,' when Laing took off his gloves. 'Look how he pulls the skin from his hands and still there is no blood. Has he bones?' Now he stood before him on the sand and asked again, 'Has he bones?' He laughed and shook his head, saying, 'No, he cannot be a man.'

He slept by the fire with the slave boy wrapped inside his cloak for warmth. There was no food now, but he was not hungry. Something fell onto him. He would cling to sleep and drag this thing down with him into his dream and make it the crack of the tawse across his hand. Shouts then and staves that beat about his head so that he cried out, 'No, no. I did not. Truly I did not.' He woke to shouts and legs that trampled past him in the dust. A camel was beaten away from him with sticks, and beside his head was his rifle with the butt snapped in two where the beast had trodden on it.

He held the portions of wood in his hand and swore slowly and deliberately in his native tongue while they stood and stared at him. Always they surrounded him. He would leap up and flap his arms to drive them from him like a flock of crows but continued sitting there, his mouth filled with the thick obscenities, carefully fitting together the two segments of the stock. See how exactly they fitted together and only the faintest hair-crack to show. 'But it's useless,' he shouted to no one. 'It's useless.' He felt it bitterly.

Babani sat beside him making little sounds of sympathy with his tongue. 'Here,' he said, reaching out for the rifle. 'Give it here.' But Laing would not, knowing that the moment he released the pressure of his hands the broken pieces would

189

gape apart again. Babani slowly unwound his turban and tore a long narrow strip from the edge. 'Give it here,' he said again. Laing let him have it. Babani held the stock clamped between his knees and bound the strip of cloth tightly about it. Then he tied it with one end of cloth held between his teeth. Laing watched him with the fixed attention of a child, knowing it would not hold, but calmed instantly by this show of kindness.

Babani mimed that he should lift it to his shoulder and gave it back to him, saying, 'There is a man in Ghadames who will mend it for you.' But Laing would not raise it, knowing that his hands shook.

The Sheikh rose and touched him swiftly on the shoulder. He wept perhaps. His face was burnt stiff. He did not know whether he shed tears or not. He raised his hands to touch his eyes but the lids were as dry as paper. He could feel that the skin had cracked all along the ridge of his nose. He felt the two stiffened lips of skin and the thin line of smarting flesh between. He thought, I am become a thing of horror to myself. He laid down the gun and went silently about the business of loading up the camels. Before they left that place he found the piece of mirror in his luggage and, going aside as if to urinate, buried it in the sand.

'Praise be to God, the Lord of all creatures; the most merciful, the king of the day of judgement. Thee do we worship, and of thee do we beg assistance. Direct us in the right way, in the way of those to whom thou hast been gracious; not of those against whom thou art incensed, nor those who go astray.'

The air burnt his lungs. Each breath pained him. His throat was parched and stiffened so that it might snap, he thought, if he were suddenly to bow his head. When they looked at him they clacked their fingers together and sucked in their breath as if to be near him scorched them. They jostled him when he staggered with fatigue. Even Jack laughed at him, with his easy black laughter, openly, without respect or malice. He would smile to show he took it in good part. His teeth were so coated with dust that he must force his lips to move. He thought constantly of the taste of the sweet tea. He thought his eyeballs might dry, the lid no longer slide to cover them and he be condemned to an eternity of sleeplessness; a prisoner in the outer world, excluded from the safety of his own recesses. He wrapped the cloth about his face and bit it with his teeth to stop himself crying out in terror. The visions came and went like sad familiars, so seemingly real he wondered if they might be part of the mirage so that the others might see them too. Yet he was ashamed to ask them, lest they think him mad. Now he saw the old man at Falaba again, Assana Yeera, staring up at him and saying, 'My son, I see your heart is fixed upon the water.'

At noon, when they stopped for prayer, he took out the chronometer and wound it. He walked. The Consul sat by a well with his back to Laing, yet surely it was he. There was the gold fringe of his epaulettes and the oak-leaves stitched in gold thread on the rim of his cap. He continued staring down into the well and saying with great distinctness 'I wish Alexander would return to me. I wish he were here. She frets for him grievously. I should not have sent him off so.' Something failed, then. He was gone. Emma sat staring at him without expression.

He had heard the call to halt. He might press his painful shoulder into the warm sand and sleep, but immediately he began to search about the sand for the single blade of grass that would reveal the root that would light the fire.

He sat by the fire, struggling to swallow the tea. Jack crouched beside him, moaning softly to ease an inner suffering, not asking a response. Jack, poor Jack, where have I brought you? If he had spoken the words aloud Jack did not answer him. Only four skins of water remained to be shared between them all. Two of Babani's men had ridden ahead on the maherries for food and water.

They must all walk now. The camels were too weak to bear them. Even without the extra burden they stumbled frequently and fell, casting their loads. Each time they were kicked and coaxed upright and reloaded. He led Harris, whose eyes were no better and still kept bandaged. The good Babani brought him a rope and tied it to his waist. He knotted a loop for Harris' hand. How gently and kindly he tied the rope, as if he suffered with them the aching eyes and ulcerated skin. They prayed.

As soon as he began to walk his mind fastened on the moment when he might stop. He walked ahead and seemed to hear repeatedly the voice calling him to halt. Each time he turned to see the tottering approach of the slow beasts through the dust and turned, holding the rope away from his waist to ease the galling of the sores, he set himself to count a hundred paces, but his mind was dulled with heat. He lost count at thirty and began again, but the effort to recall the sequence of the numbers was too great.

He had slept and surely now he was awake again. His feet moved through the sand. He pulled on the rope. The beggar of God, he counted his sores, but these sensations though they had not lessened had lost their power to bind him to Body. Body, self, Laing; he watched from his great height toiling in solitude across the sand, with the sun his powerful adversary. Where are the others? he thought, and might have cried out, 'Ah, poor Jack, what is to become of you?' A voice which had been speaking just out of earshot could be heard to say, 'Well, he was unworthy of it. Since his childhood there have been flaws there of wilfulness and egotism. In a man of genius it would be forgiven, but he has always fallen somewhat short of that. Something in him fails. It always has. People,' the voice said, 'do not like him. Oh, women perhaps, and a few old men make use of him, but his contemporaries steer clear of him. Do you notice how he has no friends?'

It spoke, Laing realised, of the poor toiling creature below, so that Laing thought with infinite weariness, I must get back to him or he will fall, but found that he could not. What now? he asked himself. He will surely fall.

The voice continued, 'Oh, let him be. We have no need of men such as he, whose sole concern is themselves, who must always put themselves in positions of singularity. The others do not like him, and of course the claims he makes for his achievements are quite preposterous. One might pity him if one cared to.'

I must get to him, Laing thought. Yet he was loath, for all his pity, to be seen associating with that poor wretch.

The men who spoke these words appeared out of the dust and then dissolved again into its particles. They were there. Yet he had seen too many phantoms not to be distrustful of these towering shapes of men on camels whose flanks were swollen out with skins of grain and water.

Nine men. Each in turn greeted Babani, again and again, with quick dry embraces, all done quietly and solemnly, as people meet at a wake mindful of what has been suffered. They greeted Laing, too, with the same sad deference. but he stood apart from them and kept the filthy cloth drawn across his face. He stared above it at the whiteness of their garments, which seemed the very same that they had worn in Assana Yeera's compound. He stared at the sleek flanks of the camels and their bright proliferation of bells and tassels.

They had brought skins of fresh water. He drank and drank, hopeless of slaking his thirst. The water filled his mouth with sweetness. 'I had not known that water could taste so. It must come from a miraculous well, or I have never known thirst before.' He was speaking aloud. The man to whom he spoke laughed kindly at him. He touched Laing pleasantly on the arm and said, 'It is true, *Reis*. A man only comes to know the true nature of water in the desert.'

They were speaking to one another in the Bambera tongue. The words, wakened by the touch of the water, came to his lips from that more deeply planted language.

He said to the man, 'You have been to Bambera?'

'Many times, *Reis*, with the dates.'

'I too,' Laing told him. 'I have visited Assana Yeera at Falaba.'

'You, *Reis*, have visited Assana Yeera? At Falaba? *Wa lahi!*' He told them all of it in Arabic and each must give and receive the Bambera greeting before Laing could ask of them 'Is Assana Yeera dead?'

They consulted and vigorously shook their heads. It was several years, the man said since he had been to Bambera but he would have heard if Assana Yeera were dead.

They had brought fresh bread and dates and melons. As he brought the slice of melon to his face he felt with joy the cool exhalation against his stiffened lips and cheeks. Its sweet flesh clung to the roof of his mouth. He kept it in his mouth as long as he was able without swallowing it.

When night came they built a fire out of the brushwood the men had carried with them. How beautiful was the bright clear flame. They had brought a sheep and slaughtered it. The smell of roasting meat hung in the air. Yet he found he could eat very little of it. Silence fell, but now the moaning of the wind was powerless against their safety and well-being. The great stars hung and glided overhead. The distance might exist again. It contained the place these men had come from.

He had drawn back from the rim of madness to know them as they were, friends of the Sheikh Babani who, out of their respect and love, had left their homes in Ghadames to come to greet him in the desert. His nephew Alkadir was one, and Hadji Hassan, who had been to Falaba, another. The rest were still unknown to him by name.

Their faces hung about the fire, snatched at one by one by the glaring flames. He stared at them through air so shaken by the fire's heat that it seemed the inner passions played across the still features.

There was faithful Jack le Bore, who carried in his head dark images of the burning sugar fields of San Domingo; of Buonaparte gesturing among his officers. There was Rogers, and the stupid, patient Harris blinking his swollen eyelids, and the slave boy smiling sleepily, lifted out of woe. There was good Babani, the cause of this munificence. He leant over and, rolling a ball of greasy rice between his fingers, offered it to Laing, saying kindly, 'Eat, eat.' His benefactor. And there was evil Bagoola, the slave's tormentor, who had loved Clapperton, who mocked Laing, who stole his corn. He watched him in the quivering light tear the sinews from a sheep bone with his teeth, and suck at it avidly with the molten fat gleaming on his chin.

He cried out suddenly, 'We should have taken the other route,' as if all that must be lived through again. Yet he scarcely knew what words he spoke and had said them perhaps in English. There was silence then. He thought they stared at him.

The young man, Alkadir, said, 'You were in great danger, *Reis*. They said you travelled with much gold in many boxes.'

'But I have nothing,' he told them, spreading out his hands. He thought they did not believe him.

The young man said, 'Indeed, the Christian has everything but God.'

Then Hadji Hassan, who had sold his dates at Falaba, said 'Indeed, *Reis*, it is true. The man had no cause to lie. They let you pass at Wadi Echmed lest the Bashaw's men should pursue them. They moved on ahead of you, thinking that you would take the shorter route. They lay in wait for you at the well of Duish, two miles out of Ghadames. Had you taken that road they would have killed you.' They had been directed in the right way. In the way of those to whom God was gracious.

The good Babani smiled at him across the fire. 'God is merciful,' he said. 'We have arrived.'

I have been mad, Laing thought. God is merciful. My sanity is restored to me.

In the morning they travelled forward until they came to a well. The servants and camelmen drew water continuously for six hours for the parched beasts. Laing was too weak to help them, but could not bring himself to leave the well. He squatted by the wooden troughs set beside it and watched the shouldering camels toss their great necks and fling gleaming drops of water from their loose hairy lips. The constant sound of pouring, the sucking and slobbering of the camels filled him with delight.

They stayed for the next two days by that well, too exhausted and too plagued by the constant purging of its brackish waters to move on. Laing slept inside his tent. He woke to drag himself a little way from the encampment to relieve his bowels. Then, worn out by this effort, returned and slept again. He could eat no more than a handful of bazeen. At noon, when he opened the chronometer's box, he found the hands fixed at a little past four-thirty. He laid his ear against it, imagining that he heard its beat, but realised he listened to some fugitive pulse inside himself caused by the pressure of the glass against his ear. The chronometer itself had stopped. He made no attempt to wind it, but quickly shut the box with a curious relief, as if a great burden had been lifted off him. His mind was as clear and still as water.

They broke camp at dawn. Laing asked Alkadir what day it was. It was Sunday. How many such had passed without his noticing he did not know. He told his people that he would say Matins at the noonday halt. They might stay dressed as they were. They must keep their European clothes unsullied for their entry into Ghadames.

Part IV: Ghadames

For the next two days, weak as they still were, Babani kept the koffle on the move for fourteen hours before he called the halt. On the third day they would reach Ghadames. That night around the fires the servants and the camelmen shaved one another's heads and picked vermin from each other's clothes. Laing had Jack shake and brush his European clothes, but they were sadly crushed and soiled.

Before dawn Babani called them, 'Come to prayer. Come to prayer. Prayer is better than sleep.' In the dark he fumbled with narrow unfamiliar clothes. He was forced to tie the trousers painfully tight against his raw and shrunken waist. His jacket hung about him like another man's and the military cap fitted low over his shaven head. He tied a handkerchief across his mouth and the open split on his nose.

He rode. Something flickered before his eyes, an ash, a scrap of paper. He reached out for it but it eluded him. He thought it was some failure in his sight, the effect of weakness. It played about the camel's head. He kept his eyes fixed on it as the light increased and saw with wonder that it was a butterfly. 'Look, look,' he cried out to Jack, and thought with the same child's wonder how by nightfall he would hold Emma's letters open in his hand and stare as he read them at her portrait.

More men had ridden out to meet them. It was Babani they welcomed, not himself. As each dismounted, embraced him, exchanged greetings, the good Sheikh accepted their homage with a sober modesty that well became him. Then they mounted again, vaulting in the air as the camels rose to meet them. They wheeled, hauling round the camels' necks and pulling back on the reins with movements of angelic grace, their great white sleeves billowing.

*   *   *

Laing rode among them, a man in a dream, watching the distant town reveal itself; the dark heads of the palms, the white spires of the mosques, the castellated walls. They moved steadily forward over an infinite complexity of camel tracks twisted like serpents; the termination of other men's travel overlaid by their own. And still the town withheld itself. No hour of the journey passed more slowly than this last, when the great joy of his delivery propelled Mind forward towards its goal, while Body was forced to drag forward at the pace of the poor exhausted beasts.

He stood in a dusty open space in front of the town walls. He was made stupid by the crowds of people, the white-robed Ghadamese and, here and there among them the dark-robed desert tribesmen, the Tuareg, leaning on their tall spears. A crowd of youths stood in a rough circle, their heads hung to one side, their eyes screwed up, their mouths twisted open in speculation. Jack had been sent ahead into the town to collect the letters. Bagoola had turned on his heel and gone off without a word. Laing stood in the sun alone. His baggage lay scattered about him.

They mocked him. 'Kaffir, Christian, take the cloth from your face and show us what a Kaffir looks like.' He lowered the cloth slowly and turned to each of them in turn the altered face he had not seen himself. 'Oo! Aeii! Yeii!' They sucked in their breath at that charred relic. Some of them ran off. Some moved in closer. He could not judge what degree of malice lay in their taunting. 'Kaffir, Kaffir. The Kaffir has no God. Say this, Kaffir: "There is no God but Allah." Say this, that Mohammed is his prophet.'

Babani came then, moving over the dust, followed by his attendants. Their full white robes dazzled the eye. With a word, with a gesture he scattered Laing's tormentors.

He led him by the arm through the town gates into an area where narrow alleys ran between garden walls and houses. Through one of their obscure doorways he ushered Laing into a dusty courtyard.

'This is a good house,' Babani was saying. 'There is room for all your people here.' The rhythms of joy were strong in his voice. 'I am fortunate to own so good a house as well as the one in which I am living.'

In the courtyard two white goats nibbled at a pile of green stuff. A thin child squatted in the sun, drubbing a cloth up and down in a bowl of water. 'Yimpsi,' Babani shouted at her. 'Yimpsi.' But before the words were spoken she had let out a cry and run from them, leaving the cloth in the dust. A woman appeared in the doorway, bowed and retreated again.

Babani led him into a dark room that opened off the courtyard. The walls were close, the air between them still. The room was without any aperture other than the door they had entered by.

'This is a good room,' Babani was telling him. 'It is the best room in all the house. When I lived in this house this was the room I chose to sit in.' Laing could just make out a number of small alcoves set into the wall and a sleeping mat laid out on the floor. No more. It was sufficient; it offered privacy.

'It is a good room,' he repeated to Babani, 'a very good room. I am grateful for it.'

He was alone in the empty room, trembling with the cool and the sudden solitude. He closed the door that led into the courtyard. The room became entirely dark. He opened it again. He lay down on the mat, but the pressure of the impacted floor was intolerable against his body. He sat in the patch of sunlight that fell through the open door and took his silent watch out of the inner pocket of his jacket. He prised open the back with his thumb-nail, which he now noticed had grown long and hard like a part of someone else's hand. He blew the dust out of the mechanism with slow repeated breaths. Then, with it still open in his hand he wound it and watched the little parts jerk into life again and continue independently of him. He squinted through the open doorway upward at the sun and set the watch at noon. Tomorrow he would adjust it accurately.

Outside there was a mounting din of voices. Jack stood in the doorway, black against the glaring light, grinning and swaying like a drunken man, saying, 'This fit day to sing psalms and pray, Capitaine.' He was holding out to him the prayer book.

'The letters,' Laing said. 'Where are the letters?'

'There are no letters, Capitaine. But they bring food all the time. Give it to us.'

'What do you mean, no letters?' Laing said. 'That is

impossible.' He stared sternly at Jack, who was not himself but laughed an alien laughter and held out the Prayer Book as he said again, 'They say no letters, Capitaine. No messenger. No one comes from Tripoli. He come any day now. When the moon full he come quick then. He ride day and night. He get here safe then.'

The courtyard behind had filled with people carrying baggage and others who had come to crowd and stare past le Bore at the white man in the darkened room. 'Go back,' Laing shouted at him. 'Go back and ask again.'

He went out into the courtyard and ordered that the bundles of gifts be stored against the walls of his room where they would be safe from theft. He had no wish to rest. The longer he might keep awake, the longer sleep would stay with him when it came. Then, when he woke, the letters would be there. It was three weeks until the moon was full again. There could be no truth in what they said. There had been some error. He sent a servant to enquire of Babani, but the man came back with the same answer, that no messenger had come from Tripoli for the last two months.

'Why?' Laing asked him. 'Why has no one come?'

'There is war between the Bashaw and the Halifa, *Reis*. It is not safe to come.'

'Where is the guide, Hateeta?' Laing asked him. 'He was sent money to meet me here.'

'He is here, *Reis*. He will come.'

'And the Consul's courier, Sala?'

'He is coming, *Reis*.'

He dragged the sleeping mat into the light by the door. He had Jack unpack his portfolio and fill his inkwell. He wrote at length to the Consul, to Sabine, to Bandinel. His mind was very clear and very active. He wrote with that unguarded eagerness with which he would have spoken had they been there in the room. Quotations flashed into mind. He wrote them down in his exuberance, marvelling that he still carried such a wealth inside his head.

I would have drunk of the gilded puddle, he wrote to the Consul, and was reminded then of Antony who bestrode two continents like a colossus, who came back smiling from the world's great snare uncaught. *Emma, my most beloved*, he wrote, *I am alive still and will return to you.* He wrote again to the Consul about Bagoola's ill-treatment of his slave, his theft of the corn, his neglect of Laing on their arrival. He wrote of Body's suffering with the brisk vigour of one who has ceased to suffer. He spoke again of Bagoola, the iniquity of his behaviour, whom Clapperton had recommended. Now that he was restored to himself he might wonder that he had tolerated such a man. *He left me in the square outside the town*, he wrote, *without a word. And went off with his own two camels. which creatures are the only two things in this world he has any feeling for.*

To Bandinel he wrote, *There is nothing here to interest or detain me. In five days, once my poor camels and my people are restored to health, I shall set out again for that great desideratum on the shores of the Niger.*

A man stood in the open doorway, smiling and bowing: Sala, whom he had last seen at the Garden. 'Where is Hate-eta?' he asked him. 'Why is he not with you?'

'One has been sent to look for him.'

'Will you take letters for me? It is most important that you take my letters to the Consul. When I leave Ghadames.'

'Yes, Reis.'

'How many days? How many days through the mountains to Tripoli?'

'Eight days.'

'And you could return?'

'Within sixteen days, Reis.'

'How is it possible?' he said. 'How is it possible that there are no letters from the Consul if you may come and go as you please?'

'God knows. I do not know.'

'We leave here in five days' time,' Laing told him. 'You are to come on that day and take my papers to the Consul.'

He must hurry to complete his letters. He wrote on to Bandinel, *I mean to upset all the theories that have as yet sprung up from hypothetical imaginings, first by my own theories and afterwards by practical solutions. As for Clapperton and his aspirations, I laugh him to scorn. He may try to pluck a feather from Caesar's wing but what will it gain him?*

A shift of light upon the page made him glance up and start with terror. A figure of nightmare, swathed and masked in black. The angel of death. Douce, douce. His hand, perhaps his features, had jerked, had shown fear. Hateeta then, at last. The tall Tuareg who had appeared as suddenly to Clapperton. He held up his hand in greeting. The dark garment fell back to show his hand and arm strangely dyed with indigo.

'Salaam aleikum.'

He held his spear upright in his other hand. His broadsword was slung across his back. The bogleman, Laing thought. The bogleman approached as silently. His shadow fell across Laing's writing on the page.

'Will you sit with me?' Laing asked him. He drew the mat a little way inside the room. The Tuareg followed, lowering his spear, easing the great sword through the doorway. He squatted down, facing Laing in a profound silence. Laing waited, staring at the eyes above the leather veil that masked his features.

At last Hateeta said, 'How is my friend the English Consul?'

'He is well,' Laing told him. 'He sends you his greetings.'

'Praise be to God.'

'Are you well?'

'Praise be to God, I am well.'

There was silence until Laing said, 'Tell me, is there danger on the road from Ghadames to Tuat?'

'God, God,' Hateeta said 'death is but once. The people are evil. The Shabah fill the road with evil between Ghadames and Tuat.'

'And the road to Timbuctoo?'

'Death is but once. There are many evil people. Between Tuat and Timbuctoo the Uilid d'Ulim fill the road with evil.'

'They are your people?'

'No, Reis. They are the enemies of the Tuareg. The Tuareg are my people. They will not kill you.'

'Is it true what they say, that if a Christian travels with Hateeta, no one will dare to, kill him?'

'It is true, Reis.'

'Will you come with me, then? In five days' time?'

Silence.

'I will give you money,' Laing told him.

'I have no need for money, Reis. What I do I do for my friend the English Consul.'

'Very well then, will you come with me to Timbuctoo out of friendship?'

The Tuareg was silent again. Laing kept very still. At last he said. 'Perhaps I will come. Perhaps I will take you safely through Tuat and go afterwards to Tripoli to see my friend the English Consul and receive the robe that he has promised me by his courier.'

Laing said quickly, 'The Consul has sent the robe with me. If you will return when I have unpacked my luggage I will give it to you with other gifts that I have brought myself.'

Hateeta rose and left as swiftly and silently as he had come, but Laing had no doubt he would return by nightfall. He called for Jack to unfasten those bundles containing the gifts intended for the greater chiefs along the Niger.

There was little time to accomplish all he must before he left. Five days were all that he might spare.

He had a servant take his rifle and saddle-bags, with a request that the Sheikh should arrange to have them quickly mended. He had Jack drag out the box of instruments. He squatted in the open doorway and examined them one by one. The thermometers were gone, the hydrometers useless to him. When he held the sextant to the light he found that sand had penetrated the oiled canvas in which he had wrapped it and scoured and obscured the surface of the artificial horizon. He would not let this daunt him. He had Jack take it and the chronometer up onto the roof and erect an awning over them, as they had in the Garden.

He meanwhile took out his almanac to find if there were some conjunction of the planets within the next few days that would enable him to ascertain the exact time at Greenwich. To do so he put on his spectacles and found the lenses too were so excoriated by the sand that they reduced the small columns of print to a grey blur. Only by holding the pages at an angle and looking askance through the clear portion by the rim could he make out the tiny print.

It was afternoon. More and more people had crowded into the courtyard and squatted in the dust to stare at him, some out of idle curiosity, some he recognised as the ubiquitous tribe of the sick. But the letters must come first. He kept himself sequestered in the room, watching through the half-open door as the rest of the luggage was brought in, shouting instructions as to where it should go.

205

He wrote to the Consul, *It is the height of the date harvest The flies are very bad. Tell my favourite Ossy that his frogs might feast on them.*

Sala had returned with a servant. They carried a metal box. 'That's not mine,' he called out to them. 'There's been some error. Take it away. It must be the Sheikh's.'

'It is Tyrwhitt's box, *Reis*,' Sala told him. They had carried it to the threshold of the room. Laing stood up and backed a little away from it, a plain boy's trunk. He had seen a dozen such stacked in the attics at Edinburgh, lining the passages on the night before the summer holidays. His mind was very clear now. He saw the peril that it put him in. For what if it held papers? What if Tyrwhitt had received information concerning the termination of the Niger before he died and could lay claim to it? What if he had come by Park's papers? What if they contained evidence in Park's own hand about the river's lower course? Might it not be said of Laing that he had been given these papers in good faith in Ghadames and claimed the information as his, incorporating dead men's findings in his own reports?

'What's in it?' he said to Sala.

Sala said, 'They say in the town, *Reis*, that there is six hundred pounds of the Consul's gold in that box.'

'And is there?'

The courier smiled. 'It is very light to carry, *Reis*.'

But Laing saw the danger in this too. 'Send for the Sheikh,' he said to Jack; to Sala, 'Fetch back Hateeta here.' He went to the door and called out at random to several of the loungers in the courtyard that they too should come and witness the opening of Tyrwhitt's box. They pushed past one another into the room and squatted down, shifting on their haunches, pressing their backs against the wall in a silent row. The strident buzzing of the flies throve on their solemnity. It irked Laing to be kept waiting for the others. He drummed his fingers on the lid of the metal box to disguise their tendency to shake. When at last all were assembled, he lifted the padlock on his finger and let it clank against the side of the trunk. 'See,' he said to them, 'I have not touched the lock. It is just as it was when Tyrwhitt locked it last. Do you agree to that?'

There was a murmur of assent. The room was hushed with the morbid awe which might attend upon an exhumation. He

206

took the key from the thong around his neck, hiding as best he could the other key that hung there, and released the padlock. Then he lifted the lid as upon some profound privacy. Inside there were two tin boxes of cocoa and two packets of sugar. He was nothing to me, he told himself. I cannot grieve for him. But his hands were trembling violently as he set them one by one on the ground. Then he lifted up the empty box, displaying it with ceremony to all the corners of the room, saying to them, 'Look, look, there is nothing here.'

It was evening. 'Stay,' he said to Babani. 'Won't you stay?' He did not wish to be alone. He ordered tea to be prepared in the courtyard. He urged Hateeta to stay, too. With Babani watching he presented the Tuareg with the splendid robe that had been intended for the Sheikh of Timbuctoo, saying it was from the Consul, while from himself he gave him the pair of silver-mounted pistols. Hateeta bowed and pressed these gifts repeatedly to his heart. It seemed to Laing that at last he had found the true measure of liberality. 'Will you come with me, then?' he asked him. 'In five days' time?' He turned to Babani. 'In five days' time?'

'If God so wills it,' the Sheikh told him.

When they had gone he shut himself into the room and stretched out on the straw mat. He had thought that he would sleep immediately but for a while he did not. The room's emptiness oppressed him. He could not rid himself of the fancy that it was the room where poor Tyrwhitt had died although that, he knew, was many hundred miles from here. He thought of Tyrwhitt hoarding up his only treasure, the last of his cocoa and sugar, against the time that never came when Clapperton should return to share them with him. Then, with his head clutched in his arms, he wept without sound or shame and woke to find the sun blazing in the open doorway, flies crawling on his face, the room half-filled with squatting figures staring at him and a sense that Emma had lain beside him in his dream, already just beyond his grasp. It was Wednesday the fourteenth of September.

Later on that same day, Emma sat in the salon. Ossy leant against her leg. Her mother said of something, 'Is that true? Is it really so? I must tell Gerda. Really, I cannot believe it.'

She spoke to Tom Wood, who had returned that day from Leghorn and come at once to spend the evening with them. All the time that he had been away she had scarcely thought of him. How brisk he was about the business of being agreeable to each of them. He stood by the piano humming and rocking on his polished shoes, turning the pages for Jenny, who laughed and tossed her head about as if her hair were in her eyes. He took Louisa's chin, as once he would have done Emma's, between his thumb and fingers and turned it to the light, crying out, as if she had cheated him, 'Oh, you have grown up since I was away.'

When Ossy was sent to bed and the dogs dragged out to the kennels, he came and sat by Emma He smelt of cigars and some other pleasant scent. He was not entirely English. It pleased her to despise him slightly on that one count. It meant she might be very free with him and speak whatever words came into her head.

He said in a low hurried voice, 'I heard nothing of all of this until yesterday. I do not know what to say to you.'

'You are to say you are very happy for me. You are, are you not?' She was very bright with him. Some kindness in him made her fear that she might cry.

'I have not kissed the bride,' he said. His eyes were quick and dark when he mocked. She had forgotten him. He rose and then stooped forward and kissed her on the lips as slowly and as delicately as he might have kissed a child.

August was drawing to a close. The packet with the mail from London was overdue. The letters, the accounts of grain returns, must be ready to send off within the week. Tom Wood had no other occupation now other than to help the Consul. He came almost daily to the Garden and stayed there often to entertain them in the evening.

The others were riding. Emma's health would still not permit her to go with them. She sat with Tom Wood on the verandah, waiting for their return. He had drawn up his chair and sat with his shoulders hunched and his arms thrust down between his knees. turning his head from side to side as if in search of something to divert him. She could not. It was many weeks since she had left the house. She had no gossip for him and was shamed to have so little power over his attention. Then, when some slight movement made her fear he was about to go, she said suddenly, 'My throat is sore.' She was clasping her hands about her neck as a child might to feel the vibrations of her speech. 'It has never ceased to hurt since I was ill. He put something down to rid me of the poison. Did they tell you that? I do not like to say so when he has been so kind. Doctor Dickson. But I think that he has injured me. It does not heal.'

She had begun to cry shamelessly in front of him. She heard him say, 'My poor Emma. It should not be like this for you.'

He had come to sit beside her on the sofa. She talked in a low rapid voice, sniffing and swallowing as she spoke. wiping her tears to the edge of her face, permitting herself this ugliness. She was telling how Herr Knutson had delayed over the portrait. How the packet she had wrapped it in still lay with her letters on the Consul's desk.

'He's waiting for the bag to come from London,' Wood told her. 'He'll send it all together.' But the answer could not quiet her. The words of her grievance unfolded out of one another without any effort on her part.

'He promised that he would go to Laing at Beni Ulid and he did not. I cannot make out the significance of that.'

'Perhaps there was none,' Tom Wood said.

'Oh, but there was. I am sure of that.' In her sad agitation she had taken up his hand in hers as if she would draw him into agreement.

'That was months ago,' he said. 'You must put it out of your mind.'

'But I cannot.' She told him how they had said Laing would be at Ghadames in thirty days. How she had tried to count. How since her illness she could keep nothing in her mind, but weeks and weeks had passed.

She was no longer crying. She heard herself speaking with the angry disappointment of a child to whom a promise has been broken.

'Can't you get news of him?' she said. 'They never speak of him. He never says his name. Oh, I am sure there are things he does not tell me.'

He released his hand slowly from hers and as he rose said, 'This is hard on you. I think of that, believe me.'

That evening he sat across the room laughing and talking with her sister, caring as little as the rest of them, but as he was going he came and sat for a moment beside her, saying as if there had been no interruption in their speech, 'You must not think of this. You must put it from your mind. You must think of his return. Of the triumph you will share with him. Of the life you will live together away from here.'

She said, 'I cannot think of these things. Don't you understand that? It's all to be undergone. None of it's completed yet. Oh, if I should be responsible for harm coming to him.'

'But that's absurd,' he said. 'How could you be?'

What had she been saying to him? When he had gone she could scarcely think what had been the substance of her flow of words. How light she felt without them! He must find me tedious, she thought, but it scarcely mattered. Tomorrow she would find something to say that would divert him. She would ask him . . . she scarcely knew what. None of her thoughts would hold their course. They slid from one person to another. Now she thought, It cannot be that another day will come and go and there is no word of him. She tried again to calculate the days but was too ignorant of the calendar. She would think to ask Tom Wood when he came again how many days had passed. She had neglected to write Laing that day. On the following afternoon she sat in the kiosk with the pen in her hand, but was too distracted to find the words. At last she wrote, *Laing, I am sick with worry for you – sick with love.*

In the days that followed Laing kept much to his room. The day of his intended departure came and went. He had been mistaken to suppose that the decision of when the koffle should leave Ghadames rested with him or even with the Sheikh Babani himself.

The town lay isolated in a sea of sand. The merchants who resided there lived in constant fear of the desert marauders who preyed upon their caravans. No one carrying anything of value ventured forth alone. At this season they congregated inside the town, waiting to set out in bands of twenty and thirty when the dates were harvested, north to Tripoli, west to Ghat and south through Tuat to Timbuctoo. The men who would travel with them met each day in the Sheikh Babani's house to discuss and argue their departure by the hour. So

Laing had seen starlings impelled to one particular tree where they would chatter all together for a time. Then, as night fell, they would disperse again only to return on the next evening and the next, until without warning some common instinct drove them suddenly in a great cloud southward. Nothing he might say or do would hurry that event.

For two weeks he had lived in the house Babani had put at his disposal. Laing's camels grazed in the Sheikh's date plantation. Daily the Sheikh sent food sufficient for them all. But they were scattered now. Bagoola slept elsewhere in the town. So now did Rogers and Harris in circumstances of which Laing preferred to stay ignorant. Only Jack and Yahia Mohammed stayed with him.

Still no word had come from Tripoli. He kept Sala with him to take back his official despatches when he left, but he sent Jack each morning to the market place to find a messenger willing to take his private correspondence through the Garian mountains to Tripoli. None was forthcoming. Nevertheless he continued to write at length to the Consul and brief daily messages to Emma. These he kept neatly stacked and waiting in an alcove in his room.

There was much to do. He had yet to complete and copy his *Cursory Notes on the Termination of the Niger*. They too must go to Tripoli with Sala if they were to reach London before the first of Clapperton's despatches from Benin.

He wrote in the early mornings before the sun was at its height. His eyes pained him. He could not read or write for long without intolerable strain. He was forced to leave his door ajar to have sufficient light to see by. Flies clung to his salty lip and settled on the open split along his nose. They rode insolently on his right hand as it moved across the page. He wrote without spectacles, with his head bent like a labouring schoolboy's so close to the page that it rested on his arm.

He wrote to the Consul, *I have always held Babani in the highest esteem as regards his personal qualities, but little realised his consequence among his own people. Now I find he is the very governor of Ghadames and thank my good fortune that I am under his protection. He shows a father's liberality in providing for myself, my people and even my poor camels, while we stay here.*

211

He paused then to rest his eyes. Much that had come easily was an effort to him now. He had failed to recommence his journal since leaving Berged. In a fresh notebook he wrote the date following his last entry and underlined it. He made out from his almanac that they had been nine days in Ghadames, but found his memory unable to distinguish one day from another. This confusion made him fearful of filling in the empty days, however briefly, lest he commit some error in which a future traveller might find him out. As for these recent days of waiting to depart, they were too tedious to record. For as he raised his pen to write, he heard the English voices: 'Why should Laing suppose we are interested to know that he breaks his fast at dawn in the courtyard? That his sores are healing? That the old men beg love philtres of him? That he has sent his saddle-bags to the town to be repaired?' Yet this gap spoiled the continuity of things. It grew with each successive day. He could not put a stop to it.

That other voice spoke then, the voice that meant him well. 'Apply yourself, Alexander. Apply yourself. You cannot hope to learn your lesson if you do not apply yourself.' He titled the initial page of another of the untouched notebooks *Notes on Ghadames*.

He forced himself to make his way into the town and to record what he saw there, not day by day, for the sequence of these static days was meaningless, but under headings: the town, the climate, the inhabitants, and the antiquities. He must go at once in order to be back for the noontime observations. He would visit the cistern in the centre of the town. To reach that he must pass under an archway and into a maze of dark alleys, so narrow and so solidly roofed over that they formed tunnels. He was forced to grope along them with either hand until his eyes adjusted from the brilliant sunlight to the gloom, only to be blinded again when he came out suddenly into an open square, where the sun seemed to pour down as to a catacomb from the upper world. There, outside a mosque, the marabouts sat by the hour on mud benches built against the wall, expounding their narrow tenets. They cried out, 'Kaffir, Kaffir,' to ward him from their sacred spot.

Once a flock of crones all swathed in black, like bats released from Erebus, ran at him over the dust chanting, 'Kaffir, Kaffir,' but he cared nothing for them. He wrapped his cloth about his face and walked on, looking neither to the right nor to the left. He recorded the dimensions of the cistern in his notebook lest he forget them by the time he had returned to his house. He wrote furtively, fearing that they would find some evil magic in his writing down of their water supply.

A little boy no more than six years old squatted like a toad against a wall. Even as Laing smiled at him he called out, 'Kaffir, Kaffir,' and running forward stood in Laing's path and spat at him, striking him expertly in the corner of the eye. He felt the crawl of the child's spittle down the side of his face but controlled himself and walked on as if he had not noticed. Only when the child had fled into an alleyway did he raise his arm to wipe the stuff away and then rub his shirt-cuff repeatedly against his trouser-leg. A few streets further on he heard children's voices pitched together in furtive excitement and, as he passed, felt a hail of date stones patter against his arm and leg. But he was proof against them now. He walked past them without turning and heard them run, jabbering like apes, into the darkened alleyway.

In the intense still of mid-day, when he had taken the meridian, he stood on the roof of Sheikh Babani's house and stared across the shifting palms to the great glistening ring of sand towards Tripoli.

When he was in the room again he wrote to Emma: *I have described a mighty circle in the sand since last I held you in my arms. In eight or nine days' time I could complete it now with less than half the toil I have expended to fetch up here. Would to God, my dear, I could.*

Under a new heading of religion he wrote in his notebook. *I care nothing for their bigotry. There are mad old women in every faith and clime who dress in black and sup on spleen and vent it where they safely can.*

He took his tables and his notebooks to the open doorway and peered at the figures askance through the clouded lenses of his spectacles. Then he checked and rechecked his calculations. gripped with anxiety lest he had mistaken a figure. For his results differed widely from Lyon's, printed by the Admiralty. Yet he, it was well known, was a careless ignorant fellow who had made errors in the places he had visited and merely surmised the longitude of Ghadames from what he had been told in Murzuk. Laing knew himself the better man, but what insidious errors of fractions of seconds might have crept into his calculations, through the obscuring of the artificial horizon, or his own faulty eyesight? Now that the chronometer no longer held its capsule of pure untainted time, might it not bear the taint of Laing? Some error invisible to him because it was of him might swell with each successive observation. He must not think so. His figures had never failed him. He wrote them down. He wrote to Sabine and to the Consul the mean of eleven separate observations, pointing out the margin of Lyon's error.

His eyes were dazzled by the light and pained him severely. He lay on the mat in the room. The heat was intense. He could not sleep.

Beyond the door he heard Jack le Bore tell his stories to the crowd of eager listeners. He heard the broken phrases of Mandingo; the rush and tension of the voice, now whispering, now shouting out: the deep indrawn breaths of the hearers, their muted cries of terror and astonishment. They scattered towards dusk back to their masters' houses, their heads confused with wonders. The house was very quiet then. Yahia Mohammed chanted his prayers in a corner of the courtyard. Laing ate alone outside the doorway to his room. 'You are to come back,' he called after Jack.

'Oui, mon Capitaine.' But he spoke over his shoulder and was gone to some dark act in the recesses of the town denied to Laing.

At this hour Laing felt his solitude most keenly. In the desert his sufferings had been endured amongst a group of men. Now all were scattered, as if they shrank from recollection of their closeness and extremity; the Sheikh and Bagoola to their houses in the town, Rogers and Harris to some unseemly lodgings in the quarter inhabited by slaves. Even Jack had withdrawn from him, and Emma who had come so readily to his imaginary sight during those long hours of pain and tedium was now entirely lost.

Is it not strange? he wrote to her. *I can conjure up the faces of twenty men who are nothing to me, but the one dear face I would keep hourly before me eludes me quite and, I fear, shall, until I hold your portrait in my hand and can imprint once and for all its dear features on my mind.*

214

Now he ate the rice and sweet fatty chunks of camel meat that Babani had sent him. He kneaded the food in his fingers and tucked it carefully into the corner of his mouth, fearful of spilling it, or seeming clumsy, for though he ate alone he thought Babani's servants, who ran the house, watched him from the darkened doorways.

He stood on the roof waiting for Jack to return and for the moon to rise. From somewhere inside the town there came a barely distinguishable throb of drumming, a single steady beat that presently doubled and redoubled its pace until the heart was hurried and oppressed by it. The sky was a mass of stationary and moving lights, the earth entirely darkened. Occasionally a solitary lamp would make its way between one house and another along the dark streets below him. Presently he heard a slight sound on the stairs and Jack appeared, carrying a lantern. He said sharply, 'You are late,' but immediately, without another word, they took up their old positions waiting for the moon to rise. He was happiest hearing Jack call out the familiar exchanges, 'Coming, coming, coming! Up!'

The strange occulted light was soothing to his aching eyes and held the town's hostility in thrall. He might move with his old certainty about the unaltered patterns in the sky. The stars still kept their assignments at the appointed hours. On each occasion he found it necessary to make only the slightest adjustment to the hands and now felt reasonably confident that the chronometer's accuracy had been restored.

Lately he had made it his habit to pay his respects to the Sheikh in the afternoons, rather than wander aimlessly about the inhospitable town. He wrapped the cloth about his face and made his way through the dark maze to Babani's house. There, in a cool vaulted room off a courtyard, the Sheikh held a daily divan among the worthies of the town. Like Laing's room, it had no other source of light than the open door, but its furnishings reflected something of the Sheikh's position here. Faded pier-glasses were set into the plastered walls and little clay ornaments stood in alcoves. Laing noted it all in his journal. On these occasions there was a constant coming and going of the Sheikh's faction. Petitioners, merchants, debtors, clients, relatives, swiftly squatted down or rose from the circle of men gathered round a tray of tea things. Laing sat among them. Their dark eyes regarded him. Their faces were expressionless.

Here he met again Babani's nephew Alkadir, and learnt that the young man intended to travel with them to Tuat. Hadji Hassan, the merchant who had been to Falaba, was always present and on one occasion, to his surprise, Babani's principal wife joined the company. Although she kept her cloth across her face, she entered the room without embarrassment, exchanging greetings and reaching down to shake the hands of one or two men of her acquaintance as she passed. Babani led her over to Laing. He felt the soft light touch of her hand. She was young, he thought. She was shy with him and kept her eyes averted. 'Women are very curious,' Babani said to him and smiled. 'She has heard about you and wishes to see for herself.'

The season was on the turn; the dates nearly harvested. Rumours came into town about the movements of the tribesmen in the desert and were discussed at length. The caravans were on the move again. A band of Tuareg led in fifteen camels loaded with senna from the south. They brought news that the Shabah had left their summer encampment and attacked a group of Ghadames merchants returning home from Ghat with thirty loaded camels. Only two slaves had escaped into the desert with a single skin of water. Some Tuareg had found them at the point of death and taken them back to Ghat. An old man, they said, had been disembowelled and left to die. A child of three had been stabbed to death in his mother's arms.

Such tales were circulated daily at Babani's gatherings. Laing stayed listening until the light began to fade. At the first cry of the muezzin the company slipped out one by one into the courtyard to pray. He left them then. For an hour the streets would be quiet and he might make his way unmolested. He passed a lighted mosque. Through the open doorway he could smell the pleasant odour of the fresh straw matting that lined the floor. A row of men knelt and stood together in the bare interior.

He sat in his own courtyard and wrote in his notebook under the heading of Religion: *Is it not the same God? The one God? The father? And is it not a curious anomaly that the meek, the true instructor and mediator, the cleanser of the temple who was born amidst that very odour of straw, must be worshipped in blackened reeking churches littered with the battle trophies and gaudy memorials of the rich?*

He saw Jack move like a shadow across the far side of the courtyard and out to some assignation in the town.

'You must be back,' he called out to him, 'before the moon rises,' but Jack had gone without a word. A servant brought his food. He had little appetite. Although his sores were healing he gained no weight. The flesh had vanished from him. When he woke in the mornings he would stare down at his bony feet and think they were no part of him. He must force himself to eat.

When he next looked up three Tuareg had made their silent entry and stood close to him. One of them he recognised by his height and general stance to be Hateeta. They held their palms raised towards him in greeting, or to ward off evil. They sat with spears stuck upright in the dust in front of them, staring at him in silence as he ate.

Then, 'Give me paper to write charms, *Reis*.'

'No.'

'Why?'

'Because I need it.'

Hateeta sat apart, contemptuous of this. It was only him Laing cared for. He said, 'No,' again.

'Give me powder, then?'

'Why do you want powder? Is it to kill me in the desert?'

'No, *Reis*, it is to show our people when we go home again.'

'No.'

'Why?'

'Because I need it.'

'You have much and I have nothing.'

'No.'

'Let us see the rifle that fires without a flint.' For its fame had spread about the town, so that Laing might speculate about its sojourn at the menders. How many hands had held it? How many dark eyes had peered into the mysteries of the breech? How many of the random shots that rang out continually over the town had come from its barrel? He kept it constantly by him now and slept with it pressed against the side of his body.

217

He longed for them to go and leave him in peace but patiently he opened the breech and showed them. Hateeta came forward and peered with the others. Their stained hands fluttered over his. They snatched at the barrel. When he made to set it to one side they clamoured to see more. He showed it to them again. He feared constantly lest he antagonise these men at whose mercy he would be once he left the shelter of the town. Finally he took the gun into his room and found them each a piece of sugar. They took it gravely without thanks. Each tucked his swiftly into the leather pouch about his neck. They rose and bowed and left as silently as they had come. All except Hateeta, the lover of the English.

'I will take you through Tuat for five hundred dollars. You will be safe with me.'

'For five hundred dollars you should take me to Timbuctoo.'

'No.'

'Five hundred to Tuat is too much.'

'Abdullah did not say so.'

'I am not Abdullah.'

'Besides, I do not care for money.'

'Well, then.'

'If I return to Tripoli from Tuat and take the *Reis*' letters to my friend the English Consul will he give me the sword he promised me?'

'Most certainly, if he promised it.'

'Then what need have I for money?'

'Indeed.'

'Other than twenty dollars to buy presents with.'

Laing bade him good night. They would speak again. The moon would not rise for another hour. He lay on the mat in his darkened room. He had been there twenty days and still no word had come from Tripoli.

Evil thoughts assailed him; that the road through the Garian mountains was not closed, had never been. It was a ruse to keep him from her. She was dead. Her spirit and health had broken under all that she had suffered. They did not tell him lest he should turn back. How else might their silence be accounted for?

When he heard Jack's voice across the courtyard he

opened the door of the room and shouted at him, 'Why did you go without speaking to me?'

'I'm here now,' le Bore said sullenly.

'It's too late now.' For the moon had already risen and gleamed in Jack's eyes as he stared at him. Laing told him angrily, 'There will not be time to do what I must do before we go.'

'You go, Capitaine. I stay in Ghadames and eat dates.'

Laing could not judge whether he spoke from jest or insolence. 'Are you afraid?' he asked him coldly.

'They will kill you and make Jack le Bore a slave again.'

'Who has told you that?'

'They tell me that.'

'Who are they?'

Le Bore was silent, looking away.

'You listen to the talk of slaves,' Laing told him. 'You talk to ignorant men.' He went inside his room and shut the door.

One afternoon when he arrived at Babani's house the servant at the gate told him that the Sheikh was away from home. At the same moment an old woman appeared on an upper balcony in the courtyard and beckoned fiercely to him.

'Is it allowed,' he asked the servant. The man nodded and ushered Laing to a stairway leading to the upper storey of the house. He found the old duenna peering down the well to watch for him.

'Is it allowed,' he asked again of her, 'when the Sheikh is away from home?'

She nodded as ferociously as before and dragged him forward by the arm into a room lit only by a skylight. In the very centre of it Babani's wife sat cross-legged on a little dais. She was heavily veiled and decked out in far more jewellery than she had worn on her visit to the downstairs chamber. Laing could see nothing of her but her eyes and her little hennaed hand gesturing him to sit.

She clapped her hands. A servant brought cups of sherbet. She was very shy after her initial boldness of inviting him in. She kept her head bowed but by the quick dark movement of her eyes he knew she watched him covertly. He was distracted by the heavy odour of musk and the constant rattling of her ornaments. Shyness afflicted him, too. He could think of no single word he might address to her. Then, as he raised the little spoonful of sherbet to his lips, the loose sleeve of his shirt fell back and she cried out with a shrill voice to the old woman, 'God, God, how beautiful he is. Look, his arm is whiter than the moon. God, God,' she said to him with coquetry, questioning him urgently as a child might, 'are all Christians as beautiful as you?'

'In my country I am indifferent plain,' he told her gravely, 'but you, lady, would outshine our proudest beauties.'

'Is that true?' she asked him excitedly. 'Does he mock me?' she asked the old woman. 'Have you a wife?' she asked Laing.

'Yes,' he told her.

She was quiet and lowered her eyes. Presently, without raising them, she asked, 'Am I as beautiful as she?'

'Alas, I cannot see,' he told her. 'But could I, I think that I should find you as beautiful even as she.'

She tittered then, tugging at the edges of her veil. He was very curious to see her and watched her closely for any revelation of her face.

'How many children have you?' she asked him now.

'No children.'

'God, God, how can that be? He has no children,' she repeated to the old woman. 'Will you take another wife?' she asked Laing.

'In my country we do not.' Then he said quickly, 'I married her the day before I came away.'

She was much relieved at that. She told it all again to the old woman as if she alone were capable of hearing it direct from Laing.

The old woman nudged her elbow into his and said roguishly, 'Perhaps when you return there will be a son to greet you.'

'Perhaps,' Laing said. He was anxious to be gone before Babani might return. 'I must go now,' he told her.

'You will come back?'

'I should be honoured.' He smiled and took her hand.

She said, all in a rush before he must go, 'Why do you wear those clothes, *Reis*? Where are the clothes they have told me of, with gold coins sewed to them? Where is the clothing you take on and off your hands like skin?'

After that on all his visits to the Sheikh he was requested

quite openly to climb the stairs and pay his respects to Babani's wife. He wore his waistcoat with the brass buttons for her. He took his gloves on and off repeatedly at her request. She snatched them from him and groped excitedly inside, staining them with henna, but he had not the heart to deny her. He took to bringing little diversions to amuse her, his last lodestone, his matches. though he was very short of these. He spoke to her as he might have spoken to a child, save that there was a quality of amusement in this talk from the shared knowledge that neither was a child.

One day as he entered the room he saw her hastily hand the servant a small musical instrument. So welcome was he, so bold now in the assurance of this, that he reached forward and intercepted it. Then, pretending to ignore the lady, he held it under the skylight to examine it. It was a single-stringed violin. 'Do you play this?' he asked her.

She ducked her head away.

'I think you do' he said very gravely, sitting down and holding the little fiddle out to her. 'Please,' he said, when she would not take it from him. 'Please. Think how long it is since I have heard a woman sing – how long it must be before I may hear such a sound again.'

'Are you going then? God, God, my husband made no mention that you were going.'

'It is the will of God,' he told her archly, 'whether I go tomorrow or in ten days' time, or never.'

'I shall play to you,' she said. She took the instrument and, settling it across her lap, began to draw the bow rapidly back and forth across it. He was free to watch her reservedly. All her confusion was gone in her absorbed effort to perform her task. When she sang her voice was slight and plaintive, but charmingly melodious. He was sorry when she had done.

'Thank you,' he said, 'thank you,' and smiled without averting his eyes from hers, for he thought his pleasure might be taken to lie in the song and so cause no offence. 'Will you sing to me again?'

'Another day,' she told him. 'When you come next.'

But it was accepted between them now that he came every day. He was happy in the hours that he spent with her. He forgot entirely what lay outside that upper room. Only occasionally the sense of his outer existence in hostile streets and the anxious tedium of his lonely room would be recalled to him like an evil dream.

The following day Babani's wife asked him, 'Shall I sing you the same song or a different one?'

'Oh, the same,' he said, 'and then a different one. Today you will sing me two. Oh, please don't deny me that.'

Her eyes showed him that she smiled. She sang first a more playful ditty, then without intermission the plaintive song that had first come to her mind. 'Which do you like most?' she asked him.

'The second one,' he told her.

'Why?'

He said, 'Because I heard you sing it first. Because I think it is the one that you prefer.'

One day, while she was singing, the door opened without warning and the Sheikh himself came into the room. The lady broke off abruptly and made to hide her fiddle behind the cushion that she leant against. Laing too felt an odd alarm and reminded himself that he attended the lady at the Sheikh's request. He watched Babani acutely. He merely urged his wife to continue, and, smiling with pride and pleasure at her performance, sat down familiarly at Laing's side. When she had finished Laing rose to go. The Sheikh urged him to stay longer with all his usual openness and benignity. In the street outside Laing considered his momentary alarm and his absurdity in supposing such a man petty enough for misunderstanding or offence in such a matter.

A change had come over the weather. Laing woke on the following morning to a sense of strangeness in his stifling room. When he opened the door the brilliant light of morning had failed. Hot air seemed to crowd out past him into an altered world. As he stood there rain began to fall in heavy drops that felt warm to his skin. They fell onto the ground at his feet in large separated discs that vanished instantly, but not before they had released a disturbing smell of quickened dust that haunted the back of his nose and throat. Within an hour the sun was as powerful as it had been but something in it had suffered a defeat. By his third week in Ghadames the air in the mornings and evenings was noticeably cooler.

His spirits lifted. His sores were healed over, as was the split on his nose. The elasticity of his movements was restored to him. He slept less during the day and more profoundly at night. The great plague of flies attendant on the date harvest had lessened too. He might keep the door of his room permanently open during the day now. The number of sufferers from ophthalmia waiting his ministrations in the courtyard was greatly reduced and the discomfort in his own eyes alleviated. But different ailments plagued the people. He heard coughing as they passed him in the street. Babani's wife was indisposed and sent word that he should not attend upon her. It surprised Laing how long the day seemed without that diversion.

By evening he grew restless and wandered into the moonlit town. It was cool enough for him to be glad of the warmth of his military cloak. He wrapped it close, with the hem of one corner tossed over the opposite shoulder, and felt as shrouded and obscure as the figures who sidled past him in the narrow alleys. He was drawn to the street of the slaves, where the drumming had its source intensified and where those unfortunate souls sang and danced into the night as if they had not a care in the world.

When on the next afternoon he called on Babani he was told that the lady was still indisposed. It occurred to him then that she might have been forbidden to see him. When the Sheikh drew him to one side and requested a word in private, Laing found himself again assailed by a formless guilt. But Babani too seemed ill at ease. He spoke distractedly of the change of weather and the colder nights. At last he said, 'It is necessary to buy more firewood *Reis*.'

'Well?' Laing asked him.

'I need money, *Reis*, with which to buy it.'

'Very well,' Laing said. Relief had made him hasty. He checked himself and said, 'I had supposed the servants gathered it.' He was confused as to who had paid for the wood until now. Had it been a gift which Babani had now withdrawn? He thought not. The Sheikh was saying, 'There is no wood in Ghadames, *Reis*. Men must go into the desert and search for it. They must be paid for carrying it back to the town on their camels.'

It was a small sum, though large enough, Laing judged, to

pay for all the firewood burnt since his arrival. He was unwilling to take issue on the matter and paid the money then and there, but it puzzled him that Babani had asked for it when he had not repaid the four hundred dollars he had borrowed at Beni Ulid. Laing had resolved out of delicacy not to press him on the matter. Now he told himself he must bring it up at the earliest opportunity.

At noon on the following day, as he was taking his reading on the roof, he heard a hubbub in the street below. When he had done he looked out over the parapet and saw a string of laden camels issuing out of the northern gate of the town. He shouted down into the courtyard, 'Where are the camels going?' No one had seen them. No one knew. 'Go after them,' he shouted. He ran down the stairs. At their foot he found Jack grinning widely, saying, 'They go to Tripoli, Capitaine. They have heard that the caravan from Tripoli is coming here. One day only. Two days now. So they know it's safe to go.'

'Why was I not told?' Laing said. It angered him that it could leave so suddenly and so casually, as if the route had not been closed at all. 'Well, go,' he said to Jack. 'Go after it.'

'It's gone too far now,' Jack said.

'Go,' Laing shouted at him. He ran into the room. His hands were shaking with agitation. He gathered up the packages of his personal correspondence and the completed journal and stuffed them together into his saddle-bags. Then he ran out into the road. Jack was dragging his horse through the gate of Babani's garden. Laing saw him off and ran up the stairs again. He stood by the parapet, watching the rider in his cloud of dust move across the plain until he merged with the koffle and then broke free again. Immediately he was filled with anxiety that he had surrendered the precious letters too rashly into unknown hands.

By evening he sat in the courtyard, too agitated by the thought of the caravan's approach from Tripoli to apply his mind to any task.

When Yahia Mohammed had finished with his prayers he came over to Laing and said. 'You should not have let Babani take the camels.'

'Why not?' Laing said. 'He provides their feed. It is generous of him.'

'He has deceived you, *Reis*. He hires out the camels to the men who gather wood in the desert and sell it in the town. It is more profitable for him to feed them a little and hire them for much. I have seen them, *Reis*. They are thin and tired from the work.'

'That is impossible,' Laing said, and immediately wished that he had not, for he could not now without show of inconsistency ask, How long has he been doing this? Who has told you?

He was disinclined to believe Yahia Mohammed. The more so that, if what he said was true, Babani had cheated him twice over. The voice in his head said. 'It is cowardice, Alexander, that makes you too nice to vex him for the money owing you. Cowardice and shame.'

The next day when he attended at Babani's all the talk was of the imminent arrival of the caravan from Tripoli. He excused himself early and as soon as he had reached the house climbed up to the roof and stood staring northward across the plain. His eyes ached and watered in the glare of the late sun. His vision blurred and was confused by flashing colours. Still he could not bring himself to go inside, until he thought he had made out a more substantial form in the cloud of reddish dust that lay along the horizon. Then, fearful of disappointment, he groped his way half-blinded back down the stairway to his room. There he sat on his trunk and pressed his fingers against his aching eyes. He opened and shut them repeatedly, tormented now that in the very hour that Emma's features were restored to him his sight might fail and she be lost for ever.

An hour and another hour passed before there was a pounding on the door and a messenger thrust into his hand a small carefully wrapped parcel. He was trembling violently at the suddenness of access to the thing that had been so long withheld from him. He closed the door and leant against it, feeling with his fingers around the little oval shape of Emma's portrait. It was dark in the room but only here could he be sure that no one watched him. He found one of his last remaining candles. His hand was shaking so that he struck again and again before it took light.

He set the candle in its holder on the floor beside his mat and, kneeling down, took out his knife and cut clumsily through the string. He undid the outer layer of canvas, then the inner wrapping of paper, and the soft white silk. The chain slipped into his hand. She had told him of the little golden eagle surmounting the frame. For a moment he closed his hand about the portrait before he looked at it. Then he held it close to the flame, and stared at the minute face trapped under its oval disc of glass. Its pallor seemed released like an evil exhalation in the room. He was staring at a dead thing. He could not take his eyes from it.

He took it to the door and, opening it a crack, stood peering with the portrait held up close to his face. He crouched again by the candle, staring at it. For surely he could not have failed to see this thing in her, had it been there. And she had turned to him. The shadow of that movement had stayed in his mind. Her face had been flushed, and her lips when he first saw her had seemed swollen and suffused with blood, as if she bit at them. And when he had dropped Ossy and made her angry, the blood had stood in her cheeks in two red patches. He strained to recall how she had looked then, but he could not. The dead white thing with staring eyes had erased that other; had robbed him of it. An evil trick was perpetrated on him. He thrust it into his inner pocket and lay down trembling on the mat, too fearful of the darkness now to blow out the candle. Like a man who wakes abruptly and seems for an instant to see his life on the far side of sleep lit with a total clarity, he thought, I should not have left her so.

Presently there came a second pounding on the door and Jack's voice called out, 'They have come, Capitaine. The letters have come.' He went to the door and reached through it to take the letters without looking at le Bore. There was a thick bundle of newspapers and a packet of folded letters tied together with string. He cut the string and kneeling down, spread the letters slowly out on the mat and separated out the different hands he knew, Emma's, the Consul's, one from Bandinel, one from Whitehall.

He glanced up and saw Jack watching him through the door. Douce, douce, he told himself. He said, 'Why did you not bring them with the package?'

'Two men brought them.' le Bore said. 'One brought the package. Then another brought the letters.'

'Very well then,' he said. 'Go.'

He let his hand move over the letters but he was fearful of the loss they might inflict on him. Emma's he took up and quickly put inside his shirt with the locket. He would read the Consul's first, to learn the truth about her health. But now that he had the letters he saw that they were meaningless. If she were dead, her letters would still have been sent on to him. If she were ill, she might have died while the messenger made his way across the mountains. He took up his knife to open the seal of the Consul's letter and began to read in such agitation that he could scarcely make out the words. Yet within the minute he seemed to hear the Consul's voice as clearly as if he had been in the room, cutting across the train of Laing's own thoughts, sweeping all before him. He did not mention Emma but spoke instead at length of the severe reprimand that he had received from the Colonial Office for the debt he had incurred on Laing's behalf. They had accused him of extravagance and irresponsibility in the most ungenerous terms. They had refused to honour the gift of two thousand dollars to the Bashaw.

But it was Laing that they accused. It was the ruin of his hopes.

The candlelight moved on the folded surface of the official despatch from Whitehall until it seemed a living and malignant thing. He would not open it, knowing what it must say. He would not let their scorn take on the form of words that must etch themselves in bitterness upon the very substance of his heart. The edges of the room were dark. He was ringed by isolation, his voice pent up inside him for want of anyone to hear.

And they had said to one another, 'If it comes to it we can cut him loose. There would be no questions asked over such a man as he.'

And they had done a crueller thing; had cut Laing from Laing. Had, by so discrediting him, cut him loose from his own fame. That they could split a man so, with pen and paper, filled him with terror.

He was shaking violently. He told himself the fever had returned. He took out the packet of Emma's letters. On the outside of each folded sheet she had written his name and the date. He selected the most recent as the one most truthful of her present health. His hands were so unsteady that he was forced to spread the paper on the ground to read it.

My beloved husband, Angelo Heri said when he was here *that you were ill with fever. Laing, Laing, my heart misgives me lest you are lying untended when I am not with you to care for you. How can I endure the thought that you are alone? I have had no letter from you since and, though Papa exhorts me to keep up my spirits, until I see in my own dear husband's hand that he is well and as happy as either of us can expect to be, I shall not rest. I fear constantly that he keeps something from me.*

He could read no more of it. He blew out the candle. The air was filled with the odour of spent flame. He groped about in the darkness until he found his jacket. He put it on and wrapped his cloak over that. Then he lay down on the mat and gave way to shivering. His teeth chattered in his head. He felt cold beyond redemption.

By morning the shaking had ceased. He was free of fever, but the fearful sensation of cold persisted. The sun had risen. Jack watched him through the partially open door. He said, 'You sick, Capitaine?'

'No,' Laing told him, but when he tried to rise he was stiff and weak. The Creole took his arm and hauled him upright.

'I'll manage,' Laing told him.

Jack squatted in a corner of the room. He watched Laing moving about like an old man. 'You sick,' he said again.

'No,' Laing said. 'Chilled. Not sick.'

'I bring you medicine?'

'No.'

He had no need to dress. He had slept as he was. He moved slowly out into the courtyard and lowered himself against the wall with his legs and the strange white emaciated feet stuck straight in front of him on the ground. He sat with his head against the wall, his eyes shut, his face held up to the sun, waiting for it to warm him. He could hear Jack moving about inside the room and presently called out to him, 'Bring me my writing things.'

'You have the blue devil,' the Creole said when he had handed Laing the portfolio. 'I see that. You have the blue devil.'

But Laing ignored him. *It cuts me to the heart,* he was writing to the Consul, *that they should use you so, and if you,*

228

who are an old and trusted servant of the Crown are used so, what abuse must lie in store for me?

The letter from Whitehall lay untouched inside the room. He would not open it. Sunlight glared on the paper. His eyes pained him and watered so that he could not clearly read the words he had written.

He took the portfolio back into his room, shutting the door behind him. The room went dark. He went cold again with the fear of it. He opened the door by a crack. The pale dim walls emerged around him. He sat on his mat and began to write again with his face bent over his hand: . . . *and what now is the purpose of continuing if I return and find my Emma dead? I am a dead man then myself. Nothing could restore to me the thing I have cast away. I have sacrificed my happiness with Emma, my health, my promotion . . .*

The words would not form. He was overcome with an intolerable restless drowsiness. He lay down on the mat again, retracing in his mind the route to that point where Laing had split from Laing. And slept perhaps, for he started up again and wrote, *I should have abandoned the mission at that first interview with the Bashaw.* Up until then he had been entire and had owed nothing. He had felt sullied to accept their paltry guinea a day for his services. He would make a note of the day, the twenty-seventh of September. From this day he would accept no more from them. He was Laing again, free to come or go as he pleased. He had drawn up at the brink of a great error.

He dipped his pen in the ink and wrote again to the Consul, *Very Private. Forgive my broaching so delicate a subject, but I am half, nay far more than half resolved to abandon an attempt that has caused much suffering and met with very little interest (except from you, my dear Consul). I allude of course to my promise that I would not make the sacred claims of husband upon wife until my return. Should I return, but not from Timbuctoo, would you find it in your heart still to hold me to that promise? For it preys upon my mind that Doctor Dickson and his wife were united by no stronger bond. Now, my dear Consul, unless I have some assurance from you I must return by Tunis or Morocco rather than endure another day in her presence knowing I cannot claim her as my own.*

He watched the words proceed across the page. His hand

229

was neat and perfectly formed. Watching it, he feared that there was something in him indestructible; that even the final power over his own life might be denied to him. His rifle leant in the corner of the room just beyond the faint reach of the daylight. He need not turn his head. He knew exactly where it stood. Anderson at Freetown had done so. He had knelt, they said, and rested his chin upon the barrel of his rifle and pressed the trigger with his thumb. no pain beyond the instant's shattering. All done then, so that were he to hear that she was dead he need not survive her by one instant. He dipped his pen again and continued to write. *My heart throbs with sad pulsations on account of my dearest, most beloved Emma. You say that she is well and happy but I fear that she is not. Good God, where is the colour of her lovely cheek, where the vermilion of her dear lip? Tell me, has Mr Knutson, or has he not, made a faithful likeness? If he has, my Emma is ill, is melancholy, is unhappy. Her sunken eye, her pale cheek and colourless lip haunt my imagination, and adieu to resolution. Was I within a day's march of Timbuctoo and to hear my Emma was ill, I would turn about and retrace my footsteps to Tripoli. What is Timbuctoo? What is Niger? What the world without my Emma? Should anything befall my Emma, which God forbid, I no more wish to see the face of man; my course will be run. A few short days of misery and I shall follow her to the grave.*

I am agitated. You will bear with me, I hope. Never since this terrestrial ball was formed was there a man situated as I am – never never never, and may no man ever be so placed again. It requires more than the fortitude which falls to the general lot of mortals to bear it – I must again entreat you that you will 'Bear with my weakness, my brain is troubled' – I must lay down my pen awhile.

He slept then. When he woke and went to the door cold moonlight lit the courtyard distinctly. His mind had stilled. He had resolved to go back. He might do it now. Call Jack. Say, pack this, pack that, release the horses and the mule from Babani's garden. Mount them by moonlight. Ride by night as well as day. 'Jack,' he called, 'Jack,' for he would order up those actions which would make the thing irrevocable. There was no answer, no sound at all in the house outside this room. He hesitated then and thought, I will not go without the money that Babani owes me. He stood up and wrapped his cloak around him. He would go now, but immediately he shook so violently that he could scarcely stand. I am ill, he thought. I can do nothing. He lay down on the mat again, shivering and aching with fever.

Once he woke to find the moonlight on his face and roused himself sufficiently to drag the mat further into the shadow. Once he heard the English voices in the courtyard as clearly as if the speakers lounged against the wall outside his door. They spoke negligently; their minds drifted between the words to other more important matters.

'Did I not always say you could not trust him?'

'He looks well enough,' the other said dismissively. 'Gives a good enough account of himself.'

'Believes it all, I dare say. They often do.'

'Turner spotted it at once though, that, bring him to the test, he fails to stand his ground. He sensed it without even meeting him, but then the others had told him.'

'Did he not turn back a day's march from the Niger's source at Falaba?'

'He claimed that McCarthy could trust no one but himself with the despatches, but of course his health was broken. Real combat often does that to them. He denies it all now, of course, and poor McCarthy's not alive to give his version of it.'

'And now this affair.'

'It was the desert crossing. It proved too much for him.'

'Well, it's always so. When the time of test comes he cuts and runs for it.'

He sat up and shook his head between his hands to rid himself of this. Then he lay back and slept again.

There was sunlight in the room. Jack brought him water and held his shoulders while he drank. At noon the fever broke and with Jack to support him he managed to climb onto the roof and wind the chronometer. Then he dragged his mat into the sunlight and lay there shivering. When Jack brought him water, he said, 'You must not go out tonight.'

Jack said, 'I go. I come back.'

'You are not to go. Why do you go when I am ill?'

'It is the night of the slaves tonight, Capitaine.'

231

'Jack le Bore's a free man,' he told him. 'Why do you go among slaves?'

'I go. I come back,' Jack said.

He slept. It was night. He could hear drumming in the distant centre of the town. He was damp and chilled with his own sweat. His head was clear. His weakness had passed. The fit of shivering and aching had left him as suddenly as it had come. He climbed the stairs onto the roof and, turning to the south, directed his gaze across the throbbing labyrinth of the town to the cool simplified wastes beyond, in which the great river lay concealed and waiting for him. As for Clapperton, his journey up river from the Bight was all in vain. For had not Laing's Mind reached out ahead and bent the mighty river westward from its supposed course? And were Laing mistaken, were Clapperton already set upon the bosom of the Niger? Well, Clapperton was doomed then. For it was well known that an Angel with a flaming sword guarded the mouths of all those rivers and would smite him down.

'Remember, remember the Bight of Benin.
One comes out of the nine that went in.'

One was Laing. Therefore Clapperton must die.

He stood gazing across the moonlit expanses. So Caesar on the eve of his crossing left the others revelling and went forth alone. The entire passage lay stored in Mind since he had first read it as a boy. How he had stood gazing long at the fateful river and the land beyond it. So he had thought of the suffering that crossing would bring. Then he had thought of the fame of the story of his exploits which he would give by way of recompense to all posterity. Laing too would choose that twice abstracted thing, whatever fleshy joys or tribulations he must sacrifice or endure.

He went below into his room and, feeling in the alcove where he had set the letter from Whitehall, took it out into the moonlight and broke the seal. What they said was a matter of indifference now. Still, he strained to read the black words in the unfamiliar light. There was no reprimand, no summons back to England, no refusal to honour sums drawn already on the Treasury, no hint of blame or even of displeasure. They wished him well; they expected confidently that he would be in Timbuctoo by Christmas Day.

He stood staring down at the moonlit words, scarcely able to believe in them. He pressed the little pendant inside his shirt and now it seemed that all his fears for Emma must too have arisen from some trick of light and mood. Although he kept his hand upon it he did not draw the portrait forth. His mind was still at last. He went inside and, stretching out again upon the mat, fell into a profound sleep.

He was woken by sunlight falling through the open door. The fever had left him. Jack brought him tea and told him that the Sheikh Babani had called the night before and left a message that sufficient merchants were ready now to form a caravan. They would set out for Timbuctoo in eight days' time.

All was haste then. As always after long periods of waiting, it seemed that nothing had been accomplished in the interval. Now on the advice both of Babani and Hateeta he began to reduce his party to a minimum.

He sent for Bagoola whom he had not seen for several weeks. The man came and stood squinting in the sunlight of the courtyard. Laing sat on the domed lid of his trunk just inside the line of shadow in the room. He thought Bagoola shrunk in stature from the man that he remembered. The sullen expression was replaced by something cautious and obsequious. Word had reached him, perhaps, of Laing's intention. When he heard of his dismissal he hung his head and, twisting his locked fingers back and forth, began on a long lament. Had he not given satisfaction? Had he not fulfilled his contract? Had he not suffered side by side with Laing in the desert outside Ghadames? Abdullah had found no fault with him. What was he to say to the Consul when he was asked why the Reis had dismissed him?

Can I have hated him? Laing thought. He tried to recall the sources of his rage but they, like much else that had happened along the route to Ghadames, had grown indistinct. A scrupulous fear now overcame him that when Bagoola returned to Tripoli with his own version of events the Consul might think that Laing had been unfair to him, and in doing so had betrayed his own weakness in command. He would be

233

seen to be entirely fair. He purchased a maherry for Bagoola's return to Tripoli, as he was bound to do by the conditions of their contract. In addition. he gave him a handsome dagger as a token that they had parted on friendly terms. Finally Laing offered to purchase from him the slave boy who had travelled with them in the desert. Bagoola readily agreed.

He gave the boy, whose name he now knew to be Mohamet, the choice of staying in Ghadames, but he chose unhesitatingly to continue with Laing.

This new addition to his party enabled him to send back Yahia Mohammed's three assistants with their camels. To each he gave eight dollars and a burnous. When he had completed these arrangements his supply of dollars had dwindled to the last three hundred. He resolved to go that very morning to the Sheikh and ask him to repay the money that he owed him. He sent word to the town that Rogers and Harris should return to his compound to be in readiness for the departure.

The Sheikh welcomed Laing in the courtyard as if he had expected him and, taking a key from inside his robe, unlocked the door to a store-room. The gifts for the chieftains of Tuat were laid out around the walls of the room as if they were on display. The Sheikh pointed from one to the next, saying in a low voice, 'Look at this, Reis. Is it not fine?'

'Why do you show me these?' Laing asked impatiently. 'Should they not be packed?' But he was checked by his own discourtesy and submitted to being shown the various items one by one. He fingered a stiffly sequined robe and agreed that it was very fine.

'Do you like these things?' Babani persisted.

'Yes,' Laing said curtly. 'Very much.'

'They are yours, then.'

'No,' Laing said. He thought, What is this? What is it now? 'They are not for me.'

'For you,' Babani said urgently. 'All are for you.'

'Will you not sell them, 'Laing said, 'and pay me the money that you owe me?'

But Babani had failed to understand. 'You are my friend,' he told Laing now. 'If you will not accept these things as gifts you will give me money for them.'

234

'No,' Laing said. 'I have bought all the gifts I need in Tripoli.'

Babani did not move but stayed staring down at the ornate robe. At last he said in a low voice, 'Then you will lend me the money, Reis, and keep the gifts as surety.'

'I do not understand,' Laing said. 'Why should I lend you money?'

'To buy food. Reis, for the journey.'

'But you were given money,' Laing said angrily. 'I gave Giovanelli a thousand dollars at Tajura. You cannot have spent it all.'

Babani gestured at the array of gifts.

Laing said stubbornly, 'The money cannot all have been spent on gifts.'

'These things are not gifts,' Babani said. He spoke as if a great misunderstanding had been finally cleared away.

'But you said they were gifts for the people along the road through Tuat.'

'We shall go by a different road, Reis. In that way we shall avoid paying the tribute. Then we shall sell these things in Timbuctoo, so that I can repay the money you will lend me now for the food.'

'But I have lent you money already,' Laing said. 'At Beni Ulid I lent you money. You were to repay me here. You were to sell your goods and repay me here.'

'It would be foolish to do that, Reis. It would be foolish to carry so many dollars, when everything is known in the desert. In Timbuctoo the price will be better. If you will buy these things from me now I will buy fresh camels for the journey, and the corn.'

Laing said again, 'I do not understand where the money has gone.' It occurred to him that he should demand that Babani bring what dollars he had left and count them over, but he could sense that the interview had been distasteful to the Sheikh's pride and was loath to humiliate him further. He told himself that Babani had merely committed too much of the cash to the purchase of goods.

'How much do you need?' he asked him.

'Two hundred dollars for the hire of the camels and thirty for the corn.' He met Laing's eye as innocently as a child. yet Laing could see it shamed him to ask.

'And if I refuse?'

'Then we must wait, *Reis*. I must sell these things here. But they will fetch a very poor price, *Reis*. It will take time.'

'Very well,' Laing told him.

There was need to practise economy now. He had already decided to part with the horses and travel by camel from now on. To show he bore Babani no ill-will he gave him the Consul's bay. It was a generous gift. The Sheikh showed a simple delight in it which pleased Laing deeply. The best mule he gave to Hateeta. The grey and the remaining mule he arranged for Sala to take back to Tripoli. The little horse which Jack had ridden he sold for a pittance in the market, but every penny he could add to his dwindling exchequer he was grateful for. Of his baggage, Tyrwhitt's box could be returned with Sala. The broken instruments might remain in Ghadames until Hateeta returned from Tuat.

He would take with him only his rifle, the sextant, the watch and the chronometer. Of personal possessions he had nothing but his writing things, a few warm clothes purchased in Ghadames, his useless spectacles, and Emma's miniature. *I have shed much*, he wrote to the Consul. *Like my great namesake, I set out only with my hopes.*

The main body of the koffle would consist of twelve merchants and their thirty camels. Laing's own party was reduced now to Babani and Alkadir. their two servants, his own people, Yahia Mohammed, Bagoola's former slave Mohamet and Hateeta. All of these men he felt were bound to him now by his generosity and shared experience. He was eager to be gone. There was nothing to keep him here but the hope that another messenger might arrive from Tripoli before he set out.

Two days were left. Nothing remained for him to do but say his farewells to Babani's wife.

She received him as she had before her illness, seated on the dais in her finery. He showed her the little portrait of Emma, explaining carefully, 'This is a picture of my wife. It is dear to me. See, I wear it against my heart,' lest she think he intended it as a gift for her.

She held the oval frame cupped tightly in her hand. With the other hand she rubbed over the glass and fingered the little bird. Almost immediately he could see her interest in it

236

was exhausted. She said in a whisper to the duenna, 'Why does he say it is his wife?' He wanted it back but did not know how to ask for it.

Then suddenly she cried out, 'God, God, these are eyes.' She held it out to the old woman, prodding her two fingers against the glass and saying, 'Look, look, these are eyes. And a mouth. That is the hair. What is it? What is it? Is it alive?' It frightened her. She wanted him to take it from her, but immediately he had it in his hand she snatched it back again. She held it too close to her eyes to see, then sniffed at it and set her little teeth against the rim. In spite of himself he said sharply, 'Be careful.'

But she was too excited to take offence. 'Where is she?' she asked him wildly. 'Where is she? Can she see me? Why is she so little? Is she a spirit? Is she a child? A child not born?' she asked in a whisper to the old woman, who looked at it in open terror and rubbed repeatedly at the silver medallion hanging from her neck which would protect her from the evil eye.

Laing had brought his pencils and his small portfolio. He asked the lady now if he might draw her. She agreed and sat intently still, staring directly at him. He worked quickly, but veiled as she was he thought he had caught something of her.

'You must give it to your husband,' he told her. 'Then, when he is away, he will remember you.' But he did not think that she would ever part from it. She sat exclaiming over the eyes. 'Look, look,' she told the old woman, 'these are my eyes.' She touched them on the paper. She laid her fingers across her closed lids. She begged to look at Emma's portrait once more, and for some minutes looked repeatedly from one to the other. Then she said, sadly he thought, 'Her eyes are my eyes, but her skin is as white as the moon. She is as beautiful as you are, *Reis*.'

The little portrait, when he took it back, was warm from her hand and smelt of musk. It had no terrors for him now. He gave her his gloves and the buttons from his waistcoat and took his leave of her.

He spent his last day in Ghadames finishing his correspondence. When he had written his final note to Emma he sent for Sala and entrusted the letters to him, with the copied notes on Ghadames and the Niger's termination. In the morning Yahia Mohammed and Mohamet left early with the luggage.

Laing despatched Jack into the town to accompany Rogers and Harris to the southern gate. Then, without regret, he left that house and made his way there himself.

It was cold. The sky was overcast. He found the open space inside the gate already filled with the merchants and their well-wishers. The camels sat folded patiently amidst the piles of baggage and the din and movement of the servants loading them. Babani and the merchants sipped coffee under an awning. Laing joined them. The talking seemed interminable. It was decided that the koffle should move off in two parties. The merchants first, then later Laing's party.

'Why?' Laing asked.

'Together we should drink the wells dry, *Reis*. With half a day between us the water will flow back again.'

He settled down to wait under the awning. Then, seeing Sala in the crowd, he had Jack unpack his writing things and wrote a final letter to the Consul. Beyond the awning Jack's following, with Rogers and Harris among them, danced and sang and beat their drums.

At last at a little after ten, the merchants rose and came out among the crowd, embracing their friends and embracing them again. They prayed together briefly. Then suddenly they mounted and the whole koffle rose with one swift united movement and began to file through the gate. Their friends ran after them calling and reaching upwards as the travellers leant down for one final touch of the hand. Laing continued with his writing. He was jostled and frequently interrupted by men stooping to touch his hand and give out their good wishes. Some he knew by sight. Some he had never seen before.

By mid-afternoon the others were deemed to have had a sufficient advance. The prayer was spoken. Babani's friends pressed around, touching the Sheikh's hand and resting their cheeks against his. They were all mounted. The great beasts heaved and stumbled upward. Jack blew his trumpet. The koffle jolted forward and through the gateway while the crowd crushed around them. Outside the town boys raced ahead on the wide beaten road and turned back their heads over their shoulders to shout encouragement. Babani's friends on their horses rode sometimes abreast of the camels, sometimes galloped ahead, wheeled and turned back. One by

238

one the boys grew weary and halted where they were, with their hands shielding their eyes, and watched the slow swaying movements of the receding camels. Then the horsemen fired their rifles, shouted their good wishes and turned back together.

They moved slowly on across the grey sands that had seemed for so many weeks to throw an impenetrable barrier around the town. Laing rode at the head of the little koffle. Their travelling companions had vanished already over the rim of the horizon. Nothing marred the beautiful simplicity of the empty land ahead. He never once looked back to the town, but rode forward, without regret, without alternative, across his arid Rubicon.

Part V: Timbuctoo

In November the palace at Tripoli assumed the passive chill of climates intended to be warm. For some weeks past Mohammed d'Ghies had ordered a brazier of coals to be lighted in his room at dawn. On the morning of the fifteenth he sat beside it, drinking the first cup of coffee of the day with Hassuna. Within the hour he must bid his son farewell on his journey through the Garian mountains to Ghadames. There he had given him instructions to stay as long as was required so that he might intercept and read all Laing's despatches as they came through the town. His private correspondence, too, should be scanned for any information it might contain. The old man clasped his beloved son to him as he prepared to go. All travel was perilous. All partings had an air of finality, now that he was old. It was known only to God how long his son must be gone. He rallied himself at the thought and sent a messenger to the Baron Rousseau informing him of Hassuna's departure.

In the dark room off the inner courtyard the Bet-el-Mel drew in the first warm breath of his pipe. His shivering ceased. The blood stirred again in his extremities. He cast his mind back over recent developments with his usual serenity. The British Consul's recent need to ask back the two thousand dollars given to the Bashaw had been met with instantly, with all the courtesy due to one who must endure so bitter a humiliation. Signor Giovanelli had produced the silver upon demand. It was well known that the English traveller had taken with him a sum of money that must far exceed anything that he could possibly spend upon his way. When he returned, arrangements for the payment of this new debt could be made to everyone's advantage. Meanwhile gratitude had been incurred which might at a later date prove of some value.

The chill had struck the English Garden too. It aggravated Emma's cough, so that frequently her sisters complained that she wakened them at night. The little irritating sound – which they were all convinced she could quite well control if she had a mind to – persisted during the day. She had taken to wearing a light woollen scarf about her neck. The gesture of clasping her throat and rocking her head slowly to and fro had become habitual, and was surely an affectation. She seemed neither well nor ill. The air was cold and dusty. The verandah and the kiosk had been abandoned for the salon. Too often the entire day was lived out in each other's company, with the windows shut and an evil-smelling fire of dried dung sending more smoke than warmth into the room.

Only the Consul seemed unaffected by the change in season. He kept to his habit of walking at dawn through his fresh plantation. His spaniels ran on ahead, their docked tails jerking, their noses sweeping busy arcs across the dust as they trotted forward in eager expectation of some odour entirely new among the familiar tracks. Their optimism was unchecked. His own, the Consul was bound to acknowledge, lagged far behind.

In a life marked out by its vicissitudes the past few months stood out as being especially trying. Poor Tyrwhitt's death had been a sad blow to him. There had been the grim task of writing to his father; the absence of any reply other than a demand, forwarded through the Colonial Office, for the five hundred pounds still owing to him. There had been the unlooked-for upheaval in his domestic affairs caused by Laing's brief sojourn among them. Like a shadow behind his concern for Laing's safety came a less reputable anxiety over his safe return. If he came back with an account of Timbuctoo and of the lower course of the Niger, well and good. Fame and fortune worthy of the Consul's daughter would be his. If he died in the attempt it was not beyond the Consul's unflinching nature to accept that no harm had been done to Emma's future marriage prospects. But say he should return with his mission for whatever reason unaccomplished, what then?

Then, as thanks for all his pains, the reprimand had come from Whitehall. That letter had cut him to the quick. They cared not a straw what it had cost him to go cap in hand to the Bashaw and ask for the money back again. He strode out briskly to work up a heat and dispel the early morning chill.

'And who else?' he said to a spaniel who had doubled back impulsively to nuzzle at his hand. 'Who else but Hanmer Warrington could have brought that one off? Could have said to the Bashaw, "It is not I, but government. Were the money mine, pride would forbid me to make such a request, but your old friend must humble himself before you in the name of government." '

And the old reprobate and murderer had answered handsomely, 'The friendship between ourselves must not be damaged by the actions that our high positions force upon us.' They had parted most amicably. Shortly after nightfall, to the Consul's great relief and not inconsiderable surprise, the two thousand dollars had been returned discreetly to the Consulate.

But not the same two thousand. He was not fool enough to suppose that that had not been spent long since. Where in his thirsty realm had he come so quickly on this sum? From Giovanelli? A further debt? And where might that be made up? Not his concern. He put it from his mind.

He had come to the end of his domain and to the very spot where Laing had set up his tent. For six months the dust had sifted to and fro across the ground, erasing any trace of that encampment, so that the Consul might allow himself to think, He might never have been here. He turned back and whistled to his dogs, who bounded on ahead of him again and thought of nothing but their breakfasts.

But the Consul, as his house appeared serene and permanent in the early sunlight, reflected on a time when his worst foreboding had been that he would be forgotten in this place and not recalled within a year or two to England. Now he felt the goading of a new alarm. What if, for all the severity of their reprimand, their lordships had withheld their full wrath in the expectation that Laing would, after all, succeed? And if he failed? Might not he, after all his years of service, simply be dismissed without the offer of a further posting? What then?

As always in these fearful instances, the Consul felt the stirring of excitement. For these, he had come to know, were the great moments in life, when all is at stake, when life itself becomes the wager. The doors are locked, the windows shuttered. The heat of candles is felt against the face. Light wavers on the cards, showing this pattern or that pattern. That's when a man's alive, he told himself. That's when he knows what he is, whichever way it goes. All or nothing. All within the minute.

But this affair of Laing was a long drawn-out thing, harder for him to bear. Laing had intended to leave Ghadames in late September. Now November was half spent and though they had received news of his arrival there, no word had reached them yet of his departure for the South. Then he thought, Laing will get there. He's no fool. 'Hanmer Warrington backed him from the start. Married him to his daughter. He took a fearful risk in that. He won through, though.' This spoken in some crowded gracious room with England outside the curtains.

The dogs had nearly reached the house and set up a furious barking which a moment later ceased. The Consul could see a man on the verandah waiting for him; someone they knew. He quickened his step and a moment later recognised his courier Sala.

He spoke briefly with the man, enquiring after his health and his journey through the mountains.

'And the *Reis*?'

'He is well.'

'He has left Ghadames?'

'I saw him with these eyes fourteen days ago.'

The Consul instructed him to wait on the verandah for further orders. He went into his office and quickly sorted out the letters on the table: those to himself, the package for Emma, the sealed letters directed to Whitehall, and a bulky foolscap package which must be Laing's journal. He was immensely pleased. The November packet would be despatched to Whitehall within a fortnight's time and could now contain tangible proof of the mission's worth. He set it to one side and began upon his letters. To his embarrassment, he found himself reading the rash outpourings of Laing's pen. *Never since this terrestrial ball was formed*, he read, *was there a man*

246

situated as I am, never never never ... Poor Laing, he thought, he can't be well.

He went to the door. Sala scrambled to his feet. 'And the *Reis*?' he asked again. 'You say his health was good in Ghadames.'

'Very good, Eccellenza.'

The Consul went back to his desk and continued to read with mounting alarm. He recalled the wild enthusiasm of Laing's passion, the sickly look of him. He could not recollect exactly what he had written about his own treatment at the hands of Whitehall, but he was sure he had never felt so keenly for himself as Laing did, apparently, for him. Poor fellow, he thought. I should not have mentioned it.

He glanced with some anxiety at the letters addressed to Whitehall, for if Laing wrote so unguardedly to him, what might he have said in his mistaken zeal to them? Poor fellow, he thought again, for the generosity of Laing's anger had touched him. He's all alone. No one to talk to. He had often felt the same himself, but had not allowed events to overset him so. He began to write to Laing, choosing his words with care, although there was little likelihood now that Laing would read them until he called in at Sierra Leone on his homeward journey.

Your fine feelings and generous disposition, he wrote, *I am fully aware of and had I conceived you have, on my rebuke, carried it so far as to make you unhappy I should never have communicated it; as in your passage over dreary Deserts, unknown Regions, and not a Companion to speak to I ought to have been particularly careful not to Introduce a Subject which in some measure would annoy.*

The writing had the same invigorating effect on his own spirits as it would on Laing's. It gave the Consul the courage to set his pen aside for the moment and read further: ... *and what now is the purpose of continuing if I return and find my Emma dead?*

He realised then that it was Emma at the root of this. Her letters, not his, had done the mischief. That Laing could have allowed a lovesick fancy to unnerve him, to make him consider even returning to Tripoli before the mission was accomplished, shocked the Consul. The final letters and Sala's report assured him that Laing was on his way south again, but still the horrid possibility remained that he might have returned to claim Emma as his wife – might at the drop of a hat do so yet – with nothing accomplished, his reputation at risk, open to accusations of cowardice and the misuse of public funds.

The position in which such an action would place the Consul was unpleasant to think upon. Yet he was bound to think of the contempt of the Bashaw, the ridicule of Rousseau, the fury of Whitehall. It would ruin him. He tore at the paper wrapping of Laing's folded notes to Emma and had spilled them out onto the table before his conscience overcame him. He went to the door then and, opening it, was violently startled to see Emma standing there.

'What are you doing?' he said.' The suspicion that she spied on him was overwhelming, although he had gone to the door expressly to call her.

'Sala is here. I have come for my letters.'

He thought her pert. 'Come in,' he said ungraciously.

He sat down at his desk and took up his pen again. *We must recollect*, he wrote, *that Lord Bathurst is responsible to Parliament and to the Country for all expenditures and altho' the observations were galling, still we must acquit him of any ungenerous or Illiberal feeling towards you or I – I have now been under His Lordship for twelve Years and have invariably experienced everything that was kind, Liberal and Handsome. Pray my good Sir, consider the affair as never to have existed and do not give yourself any uneasiness about it.*

When he looked up he was surprised to see that she looked not at him but fixedly at the surface of the desk where the letters lay scattered.

'I wish to speak to you,' he said. 'Your letters have upset him.' He spoke deliberately but not, he thought, unkindly. Immediately, as if he had struck her, tears spilled from her eyes. He said impatiently, 'You achieve nothing by this crying.'

She wiped at her eyes with her fingers and pressed them against her upper lip to stop the tears. She had no handkerchief. He saw her rub at her skirt with her hands and then reach quickly forward as he gathered up the folded notes.

He would not give them to her yet, but tapped their edges together on the surface of the desk as if they were a pack of cards. Then he set them down in front of him again. 'What have you said to him?'

'Nothing,' she said. 'Nothing to upset him. Nothing that a wife may not say.'

'A wife?' the Consul said. 'Do you forget you are a daughter, Miss? Have you complained to him? Of your treatment here? By myself? By your mother? By any of us?'

She shook her head. 'What has he said to you?'

'Only that he was half distracted with worry for you. That on your account he nearly turned back. What would they have said to that, knowing you to be my daughter, who had tempted him to so great a dereliction of his duty?'

'Give me the letters,' she said.

He thought she had paid insufficient heed to the wicked thing she had done. 'Not yet,' he told her. 'Not so quick. I've a task for you. You're to take a copy of this letter for me when it's done.' He returned to his writing. *Your wife dear Emma you may believe me is well and happy as it is her duty to be so I am sure you will wish her to be so and that you do not suppose she loves you the less because she is so. I have impressed upon her as much as possible and cautioned her against representations which cause you to entertain a different belief. It is very natural she should wish to see you and it is very probable she might resort to every argument to induce you to return, but for Heaven's sake do not let your powerful feelings operate on you so as to adopt a proceeding which you would for ever repent.*

'Here,' he said to Emma. 'You're to make a copy of it now.' With his finger he knocked the quills in their jar towards her and pushed the finished letter across the desk. 'Sit down.' he told her.

She sat in the chair opposite him and began to write. Her hands, he noticed, as she gripped the pen, were disproportionately large and that displeased him. The sharp disturbing odour of her sweat cut through the mellow atmosphere of the room. He sensed her misery and was sorry then that he had withheld Laing's letters from her. When she had finished and pushed the paper towards him he read it frowning. It surprised him to find her hand so formed when she had so few occasions to employ it. He handed her Laing's letters which she took without a word. 'That's well done,' he told her when her hand was on the door. He saw her flush. He must suppose with pleasure at his praise.

Emma walked quickly through the blazing Garden to the deserted kiosk. There she spread open the letters one by one and read them in great agitation. They spoke of Laing's love for her. They told her where he was and that he thought constantly of her. Again and again they assured her that he was in good health; that he would soon return to her. They begged her for assurance that she was well.

Your little portrait, he wrote, is at every private moment the sole study of my eyes. How dear it is to me, next only to the dear original. Only were I the artist I should have done more justice to the lovely flush of those cheeks and lips that haunt my sleeping and my waking dreams.

At first, when she had read his letters, she had heard the very intonations of his voice, Now she could not capture them. Still, as she read his words again and again, she was comforted. He was not unhappy except in that he was absent from her. There was no lessening of his love.

Then it occurred to her that he had perhaps written quite differently to her father; that there were matters between them of which she knew nothing; that he was ill; that he had been wounded, and they to spare her would not tell her. All in an instant in the wavering light of the little room she bathed the heavy white flesh of his lacerated arm. He lay against her heavy and inert. His feverish head burnt against her breast. She turned to face his enemies and they desisted. None of this was true. There was no one of whom she might ask what the truth might be.

In the morning, when the Consul went into his office, he was surprised to find Emma sitting where she had sat the day before, at the opposite side of his desk.

'How long have you been here?' he asked. He glanced at the surface of his desk but nothing there had been disturbed.

'I have come to write for you,' she said. 'I'll copy out your letters.'

'That will not be necessary,' he said quickly, but even as he said it he admitted to himself that the task of copying was infinitely tedious. He had taken up his stance by the window and stared out into the Garden. Now he glanced quickly to see if she had moved, but she sat there with her hands waiting in her lap as if he had not spoken. He sat down at the desk then and began to write the despatches for London, and she, as he finished each page, took it from him and slowly and carefully copied it.

For a fortnight after leaving Ghadames the koffle proceeded by regular and easy stages. Between dawn and dusk they rode in a straight line towards a bare horizon. There was no shortage of water. Each night they camped beside a well where the advance party had drawn water the night before. There they found the embers of fires already whitened and made indistinct by the drifting of the sand. Hateeta pointed to footprints which Laing could not see.

From the day that they had left Ghadames he had begun again on his journal. For this, for all its monotony and desolation, was country unperceived by any European eye. All day as he rode he scanned the bleak terrain for its minutest details. At the noontide halt he rehearsed them in his mind. As dusk approached he listened eagerly for the signal to halt, gauging by the alteration of the light the time left for him in which to write. He kept his notebook by him when he slept so that on first waking he could resume his task in the short interval before riding on. For what he did was nothing unless he wrote it down, and in that vast featureless landscape nothing might assure him that he journeyed forward other than the steady advance of his line of words across the page. He counted the days in reverse now. Thirty-eight days until Laing arrived at Timbuctoo. Thirty-seven. Thirty-six. The great distance diminished. Only the mounting pile of written pages might convince him that it was so.

Every delay was irksome to him. He would have ridden out the heat of the day but Babani insisted they should rest. They crouched on the bare burning plain in the shadow of the kneeling camels. Laing sat apart, with only his cloak to protect him from the relentless pressure of the sun. Then he was beset with thoughts of Clapperton daily propelled up river by other men's exertions. Were he to reach Youri, should the Benin prove to be the lower waters of the Niger, he would devour as he went Laing's journey's other end. In the sullen monotony of these wasted hours he drew up his cloak to cover

251

his head and face entirely. He breathed the sour odour of his own sweat and brooded on these things.

He quarrelled in Mind with Babani, whom he no longer trusted. Where was the money he had given Giovanelli at Tajura? He added up again and again the sums that had been spent: four hundred dollars at the most. He had lent him that at Beni Ulid and a hundred more at Ghadames. Yet beyond the purchase of the camels and the corn, what expenses had there been? They had eaten frugally; paid tribute to no one. He has cheated me, Laing thought. From the start he has cheated me and held me in contempt.

Then at night he watched Babani measure out the tea leaves with slow deliberation and sprinkle them into the teapot. The firelight shone on his smooth broad face; nothing stirred beneath its placid surface. Yet, Laing thought, words form incessantly there and tell their separate story of what happens. He watches me as I watch him. Babani poured the tea. Laing took the cup from his hands and breathed the fragrant steam before he drank it. His heart misgave him then. He remembered Babani's kindness to him in his need.

He was at peace. No sensible world existed beyond the close limits of the firelight. Within it the ring of faces was lurid and immediate, but should one of them rise and walk away silently in the sand he was lost in an instant, as if he had never been. His return was as sudden and complete. Only the camels kept up a partial reality beyond the light, where they could be heard stumbling in their hobbles. The rest was void; without fear, because it harboured nothing. Forest terror, dungeon terror, the terrors of the crowded European dark could not exist. He was tired and lay down with his feet to the fire and his head pillowed on his rifle butt. He slept instantly.

In the morning he woke stiff and sluggish with the cold. In the dark Babani chanted his prayers. The servants blew at the embers of the fire and heaped the remaining brushwood into a blaze to warm their naked feet and legs. Laing ate a few dates and passed them among his people. Slowly sufficient strength came to load the camels.

He rode ahead with his cloak wrapped round him and the cloth tied about his head. Only a slit was left open for him to scan the land they crossed. By mid-day his eyes ached with the glare. He put on his obscuring spectacles. The world grew blurred and colourless. His mind journeyed in other places. At noon he sat hunched in the darkness of his cloak and thought, The goods cannot be worth the money he has had of me. He cheated me at Ghadames over the matter of the firewood. At a little distance he heard the rapid mutter of their voices. They were sullen with him. They conspired together as to how to cheat him of his money.

They moved on. They camped by the half-buried fires of the other koffle. In the morning they reloaded the camels and set out. Hateeta rode far in advance, following the invisible traces of the advance party but never once catching sight of them.

On the morning of November the sixteenth Laing watched him ride off, dwindle to a dark speck on the dingy horizon and disappear beyond it. An hour later he heard the slight flat sound of a single rifle shot. Immediately Alkadir rode past him, jogging his bare heels furiously against the camel's neck to urge him to a gallop.

'What is it?' Laing called after him. He shouted something unintelligible. Laing at once rode after him. Presently he made out both men halted on the skyline gesturing urgently to the west. He looked back and saw that Babani had wheeled the koffle abruptly on the open plain and headed in the way they pointed, at right angles almost to their original course. He rode on towards Hateeta. As he came closer he called out, 'What has happened? Are we lost?' Already he was filled with anger at the carelessness and delay.

The two men had dismounted and stood staring at the ground. Hateeta knelt down. They ignored Laing as he rode up to them. Stretched face downward on the sand was the body of a man. Laing, too, dismounted and stood beside them. Sand had gathered in the folds of his clothing. His hair and outstretched arms were pale with dust. 'Who is he?' Laing asked.

Hateeta turned the dead man by his shoulder. His head dropped back. His throat had been cut through. Laing turned away. One of them laughed quietly and harshly. Laing asked 'Who is he?'

Alkadir said, 'It is Hadji Hassan's agent.'

'Who has done this?' Laing asked.

All around them the wide plain glittered and revealed

253

nothing. Hateeta had risen and vaulted to the saddle as his camel rose. Alkadir was already mounted.

'The Shabah, *Reis*,' he called back. 'They have attacked the caravan.' He was urging the camel forward.

'How do you know?' Laing shouted.

He gestured behind him. A few bales of goods lay slashed and ransacked with the sand already drifting over them.

They set off at a swift trot westward to where their own koffle could be seen strung out across the plain. The riding camels were well in advance. The baggage train already lagged behind.

'And the others?' Laing shouted after Alkadir.

'That is the will of God, *Reis*. They too must be dead.'

They rejoined Babani and rode forward at a fast pace, heedless of the growing gap between them and the baggage. That day they took no rest at noon but journeyed on directly towards the setting sun until nightfall. Babani forbade the lighting of a fire. They chewed dried dates, sitting out of habit in a circle in the dust. The silence that fell between them was profound.

In the dark he could not see Babani's face. All day no sound or sign of grief had escaped him although, if what they said was true, among the dead must be many of the men who had come daily to his house in Ghadames. Laing tried to recall their faces, what this one had said, what that one had told him of his journey, but already they were gone. He said to Babani, 'We should have ridden on to see if there were any left alive.'

'Death is but once,' Babani told him. His voice was mild and steady in the dark. 'It is a pity, but it is the business of God.'

At midnight they heard the sound of camels and subdued voices. Laing's hand was on his rifle when the Sheikh called out. It was the baggage train with Mohamet, Yahia Mohammed and Babani's servants. At dawn they rode forward. Again the baggage train fell behind. Again they did not pause to wait for it. At dusk they came suddenly to a well set in so deep a cleft that the heads of the date palms that grew beside it barely showed above the desert floor. The old man who tended the dates assured them that they were now outside the territory of the Shabah and might rest there a day or two.

Laing asked, 'Where then?'

'To In Salah, *Reis*. We cannot journey on alone. The danger is too great. There we can join the caravan heading for Timbuctoo.'

Laing said again, 'We should have gone on after the others.'

Babani said simply, 'They would have killed us too.'

Fuel was plentiful here. That night they built three separate fires. By one Babani, Hateeta and Alkadir sat and talked quietly with the man who tended the dates. Laing and his people sat by another, the camel drivers and servants by theirs. By day Laing sat in his tent and wrote. The delay and the change of route were irksome. The desperate energy of hindered flight vibrated through him. Each day that he stood still Clapperton was propelled forward. On the second night Hateeta crossed from his fire to Laing's. He planted his spear in the sand and lowered himself beside it.

'I will go back now,' he said to Laing.

Laing said sharply, 'You said that you would come to Timbuctoo.'

'My home is to the East,' Hateeta told him. 'This is not the land of my people but of the Uilid d'Ulim, who are my enemies. I shall go back to my home in Ghat.'

'You promised you would come,' Laing said. 'That you would protect me on the road.'

'That was a different road, *Reis*. My camel is lame or I would turn back now. In In Salah you must buy me a new camel.'

At dawn before they moved on Laing wrote to the Consul, *I am fortunate that Hateeta is willing to return and can be relied upon to take my letters. I had not hoped to address you again with any confidence until I had reached the coast.*

But in his dark noontide mood he thought that Hateeta all along had trifled with him. Like all men who bore the taint of Clapperton he had not been what he had seemed. He thought of the faith that he had placed in the man; the gifts that he had lavished on him in Ghadames. And now, because the route was changed, Hateeta would abandon him. He is afraid, he thought. Like the men who turned back at Serked. He knows what lies ahead and I do not. One by one they all abandon me.

'It's all a ruse. Humbug and trickery,' the Consul said and smiled at him with narrowed eyes. For even though he had seen the man's head gape back from his severed throat, what proof was that? He thought, There has been no attack. The greater caravan pursued its way across the empty desert unmolested, approaching steadily to Timbuctoo without him, while Clapperton moved implacably towards it from the south. They had conspired at it, Babani, Hateeta and Alkadir. To keep it from him.

For might not the murdered man have died in a servants' brawl over the fallen goods; or be a solitary traveller set upon and robbed, whom Alkadir for his own purposes had pretended to know? He saw again the two men standing by the body, their heads inclined, speaking to one another beyond his hearing. All along they had intended to delay and lure him from the right way. Finding the body in the sand they had whispered together and seized upon their chance.

Then the voice that meant him well spoke in his head: 'Fool, fool, Alexander, and a coward too. For a brave man and a Christian would have ridden on. You have followed in the way of those who have gone astray, against whom God is incensed.'

At night in the firelight he watched Babani and could see no evil in him. Placid, without grief for those who might have died, he kneaded the bazeen between his fingers and extended it unsmilingly to Laing, who took and ate it like a child.

For two more weeks they followed a steady course to the south-west. On November the twenty-fifth Laing made an observation of the moon's eclipse and found that his watch kept Greenwich time with reasonable accuracy. He placed no faith in the chronometer now. For local time he used his eye and could calculate the gradations of light to the nearest half-hour. By this uncertain method he took a meridian and a longitudinal reading at Wadi Thakkouset and recorded his findings in a letter to the Consul. He begged him not to forward his findings to the Colonial Office lest they were mistaken, nevertheless it served as a rough indication that they were now nearly due south of Morocco.

Shortly after noon on the third of December Laing saw two black specks moving at a distance. He told no one, lest he was deluded. He shut his eyes and counted until he lost the sequence of the numbers. The black specks remained rising and sinking at a short distance from the ground. After a time he could distinguish them as a pair of vultures perched on the naked rib-cage of a bullock. As the koffle approached they heaved upward from their feast and flapped off slowly. One for sorrow, Mind said. Two for joy.

They rode past the bare ribs arching from the ground, the leg-bones picked clean, stretched out where it had lain to die. The startled head was toppled on one horn, intact but for the hollow sockets. It was indeed a joyful sight, Mind told him. They were approaching again the settlements of the living.

Outside the high mud walls of In Salah a great crowd had gathered. From their midst came the sound of drumming, women's excited trilling and the high-pitched blaring of a horn. As they rode slowly closer the whole mass began to dance and jog towards them.

'Nasra, Nasra, Christian,' they shouted.

'Nasra, Nasra, Nasra.'

His fame had spread across the desert: the Christian taller than the Tuareg; whose hair was coloured like the fire; whose skin was as white as the moon; whose eyes reflected the light; whose rifles fired without a flint; who measured the sun; who wrote in his book words which even the marabouts could not read. Even though he had not thought to pass this way they had waited for him.

'Nasra,' they shouted in a thousand voices.

He rode among them, high on his camel, wrapped in his dusty cloak with his face and eyes hidden from them. Their pale fluttering hands reached up to him. They clung to the edges of his saddle blanket as they trotted along beside him. They hauled at the lead rope of the camel. So had he entered Falaba, swaying on his mule in the weakness of his fever, while they had laughed and sung and danced with joy that the white stranger had come among them.

'Show us your face, Nasra, for we have never seen a white man.'

'Show us the gun which fires without a flint.'

'Is he white?'

'Has he a beard?'

'Is his hair like a Turk's?'

So that Mind in its joy cried out, It is intended that I come here. I am come into my own.

He was drawn in through the gates, inside the walls, like a trophy, along the dusty alleys of the town, by a spate of jostling, exulting people. In the square outside the mosque they hauled down his camel. An old man, the Sheikh of the place, greeted him, touching his hand, bowing repeatedly, saying in a plaintive breathy voice which Laing must stoop to catch, 'I have long looked for you. I am glad you have come. Here is my house for you. Look upon my country as your own and do in it whatever you wish. There is nothing in it too good for you, so you must ask whatever you desire. Should any person annoy or trouble you, kill him instantly.'

Laing thanked the old man. He thought, I am safe now. There is nothing more to fear. The old Sheikh led him down an alley and through a door into a courtyard. The crowd pressed behind him. He was shown into a room. Behind him the court-yard filled. The open doorway to his room was walled up with people staring at him. Their faces shifted from side to side and up and down to see him the better. 'Where is the gun that fires without a flint?'

Outside, the chanting continued, 'Nasra, Nasra, Nasra.'

He kept the cloak and headcloth wrapped close about him and faced them from his darkened room. The old Sheikh moved in front of him and struck with his stick at the men closest to the door until they cleared a passage for him. Then he urged Laing forward between the walls of shouting, staring men across the courtyard to the steps leading to the roof.

'Come, Reis, come,' the old man called up to him. 'You must show yourself to the people. Take the cloth from your face, for they have never seen a Christian.'

He climbed the stairs. He heard the old man's rapid breathing behind him. He crossed the roof to the parapet over-looking the street. Slowly and stoically he unwrapped the cloth from his face while the old man tugged at his cloak until it fell away from his shoulders.

'Nasra, Nasra, Nasra,' they chanted from the street below. He looked down onto their open gleaming mouths. He turned his face without smiling from side to side so that all might see, little knowing what it was they saw.

258

On the neighbouring roof a great crowd of women were packed together, as in the gallery of a theatre, yipping and trilling. They stretched out their arms to him and gestured obscenely between their legs so that he turned abruptly from them and must ask of Mind whether he endured a triumph or a martyrdom. He pulled the cloak up onto his shoulders and wrapped the cloth about his head and forced his way back to his room.

When it was dark he followed a servant through the narrow streets to the old Sheikh's house, where he had been bidden to take his evening meal. The crowd still pressed behind him, reaching out to touch him and to touch the rifle which he carried slung across his back. He had Jack walk behind him to ward them off but still their quick cool hands reached through to him. When he returned as large a crowd followed him back into the courtyard of the house. When he closed the door of his room and stretched out on the floor to sleep he heard the creak of its hinges and the babble of low voices and knew that they had prised it open to stare in at him as he lay there in the dark. When he woke in the morning the door was open and the space entirely filled with staring faces.

He sent a servant to seek out Babani and Alkadir and request them to call upon him in the evening to discuss their departure. At noon he and Jack forced their way through the crowd in the courtyard to carry the chronometer up to the roof. He had Yahia Mohammed stand at the foot of the narrow stairway and bar it with his rifle, so they might take their readings undisturbed. Then he pushed his way back among the crowd and made his calculations in the darkened room while they shoved and jostled to stare in at him. His patience was exhausted by the unceasing attrition of their eyes and voices. He told Jack to broach the keg of nails designated for the raft on which to navigate the Niger.

Mind said, If you waste the nails now, how will Rogers and Harris build the boat to sail to Youri?

Laing said, Clapperton will be at Youri. Clapperton may be at Timbuctoo. The route is wiped out. I go westward to the source. The nails are useless to me now.

He had Jack force the door closed despite their protests, and while the Creole leant his weight against it Laing hammered home the nails. The room was utterly dark then, but he had found a little oil lamp in an alcove. He lit it and by its low glimmer wrote to the Consul:

You must keep up the spirits of my dearest Emma, and allow nothing to create the smallest alarm. If ever you should be six months after the receipt of this without hearing from me you must always consider me safe, for it is my destiny to be so.

Behind him he could hear Jack breathing where he lay with his back against the wall, waiting for his release. He wrote to Bandinel:

We leave here in a week's time, which means I shall not now reach the great Capital before the end of January, but that signifies little. I scorn to run a race with Captain Clapperton, whose only object seems to be to forestall me in discovery. It is now my intention on arriving at Timbuctoo to proceed westward . . .

To Emma he wrote:

What is Timbuctoo? What Niger? I think of nothing now but my return. I write in haste. Soon all must be sealed and ready for Hateeta's departure.

In the evening he released the door to admit Babani and Alkadir. They sat in a corner of the darkened room with their backs against the walls, dipping their fingers into the circular tray of rice and mutton that the old Sheikh had sent to Laing. Outside the babble of voices never ceased. Inside they ate in silence. At last Laing said, 'We leave in four days from now.'

They did not answer.

'Well,' he said 'is it not true?'

Babani said 'There are many merchants here who wait to form a koffle. Some have waited for as much as ten months.'

'Why is that?'

'The road is very dangerous, Reis.'

He made an impatient sound in his throat. 'The road is always dangerous. Why do they wait?'

'They waited for us, Reis. They had heard that you would come. They thought you would offer them protection.'

Laing said scornfully, 'We could not protect ourselves.' Then he said quickly, 'Tell them I am here and am happy to protect them. Tell them we go in four days' time.'

Babani said, 'Some of the merchants grew impatient waiting

260

and went on ahead. Now they wait for word from Timbuctoo that they have arrived safely.'

Laign said, 'We go in four days' time, whether the rest of them care to come or not.' But even as he spoke the words he knew them to be entirely idle.

As at Ghadames he found there was a daily assemblage of the waiting merchants in the house of Babani's host. They were a different breed from the simple people of the town who still clapped their hands and cavorted about him as he made his way through the streets. These were transients: Arabs from the North, delayed in their passage to Timbuctoo, Moslems, bigots. He sensed their sullen pride and hostility towards him. When he entered the crowded room they fell silent. Babani, since he kept their company, was strange with him. Nevertherless he continued to introduce himself daily to their gathering.

He entered their circle and they shifted sideways to make room for him. He asked if they had heard of a white man travelling on the Great River. They turned from side to side among themselves and shook their heads. He questioned them about the route ahead. Always the answers were the same.

'It is very dangerous, Reis, so long as we are in the territory of the Uilid d'Ulim.'

'Who are the Uilid d'Ulim?'

'They are a tribe of evil men, Reis, who live by plunder in the desert.'

'Where does their territory end?'

'It ends at the well at Timissao, Reis.'

'How many days must we travel to reach the well at Timissao?'

'Ten days.'

'What then?'

'The well at Timissao is under the protection of the Ahaggar Tuareg.'

'And they will protect travellers?'

'If they are paid to do so, Reis.'

He said loudly to them all, 'There are many of us and few of them. We have only to travel ten days to reach the well at Timissao. When will it be safer than it is now?'

They were silent then. Babani's host said sullenly, 'In the hot weather it will be safer.'

'You have waited ten months already,' Laing told them. 'You were as afraid in the hot weather as in the cold.'

They watched him with their still dark eyes. He thought that he had moved them; that suddenly they would give assent and rise and go with him.

He left them quickly. Tomorrow he would return and press his case again. It was the tenth of December. The days remaining in his almanac were running low. In five days' time, he told himself, he would move on, whether they came or no. He would celebrate Christmas day at the well of Timissao. Tomorrow he would deliver his final terms to them.

Shortly after dawn on the following day he heard a commotion in the courtyard and going to the door found four dark-robed Tuareg leaning on their tall spears. Together they raised their hands in greeting. Laing did the same. One of them addressed him in Arabic. It was known that the *Reis* was skilled in medicine. Would he come with them?

'Where?' Laing asked them.

'To a house not far from here.'

He went with them through the streets, Jack behind him balancing the box of medicines on his head. The people who pressed after him were silent with expectancy. They entered a doorway into a courtyard. A cluster of people sat in the shade, one woman with her head thrown back, her elbows on her knees, her bared arms held up in silent lamentation. He was ushered into a darkened room. He could see nothing but heard the drone of flies and smelt the sweetish odour of stale blood. His eyes adjusted. A woman leant against the far wall slowly waving a palm branch to and fro. In front of her, stretched out on the floor, three men lay motionless.

'Are they dead?' he asked the woman. He could not speak above a whisper.

'They are hurt, *Reis*.'

He squatted down by one of them, lowering his head sideways to look into the wounded man's face. He lay on his side, curled slightly inward, with his head on his arm as still as if he slept. But his eyes were open and listless with pain.

'Can they be moved?' he asked the woman. She went heavily to the door and called out. Two men came and without hesitation lifted one of the men by his shoulders and his legs, so that he let out a moan of pain. They trotted with him out into

262

the courtyard and laid him in the shade. The others were brought out and laid beside him.

Their wounds were recent and severe. All had received sword cuts about the head; one had an ear severed, another a dreadful gash on the forearm where he had fended off a blow. Another had the nerves and sinews of his right hand severed as if, to protect himself, he had seized at a naked blade. There was little he could do for them. They would survive: the wounds were clean and had begun to heal. But Laing was sickened by the savagery of their infliction.

The Tuareg had gone. He asked one of the men in the court-yard, 'Who are these people?'

'They were among the merchants who did not wait for you, Reis.'

'And the others?' Laing asked.

'All dead.'

'The Uilid d'Ulim killed them?'

'All of them, Reis. These were spared only because they pretended to be dead. The Tuareg found them and brought them here.'

By the afternoon, when he paid his visit to Babani, news of this attack had circulated in the town. All that his oratory might have gained him yesterday was lost. It was useless to persist.

The days were expended, the seventeenth, the eighteenth, the nineteenth. Clapperton, had he reached Youri when he expected, would have had time to travel on to Sokoto and return to the Niger. Laing attended daily to the wounded men, questioning them on the exact position of the attack and the number of attackers. None of them had any clear impression of what had befallen them. They had come sud-denly. At mid-day. There was a great noise and shouting. There were many of them. Everyone was dead. All they possessed was taken.

'How will you live?' Laing asked them.

'That is the business of God,' the man with the crippled hand told him.

He pencilled through in the almanac the twenty-second, the twenty-third, the twenty-fourth, while Clapperton might make his way steadily up river towards Timbuctoo. On the morning of the twenty-fifth he called Jack to him and by the oil lamp read out the collect for Christmas Day. He left Rogers and Harris to their own devices now. Nor did he attempt to detain Jack longer than the brief service required. When he had gone Laing hammered the door shut again.

By the dim light he wrote at length to the Consul and to Bandinel, only to keep the sound of other voices in the silent room. But after all the only voice was his own which, as every hour passed, he grew more weary and fearful of hearing. The light flickered. The oil was spent. Still he would keep apart, where he was, and continued to sit in darkness with the door nailed shut, although it seemed, as the day consumed itself, that the walls of the room and the ribs of his breast caved inward on his loneliness. He thought of Clapperton carousing with his companions in some riverine settlement, perhaps in the fabled city itself.

On New Year's Eve he put the spent almanac in the skin containing his completed notebooks. The store of days allotted to him had run out. He could endure no more of this. His plans were laid. He confided them to Jack alone. Roger and Harris could be sent back to Ghadames. He had abandoned the scheme of building a boat. He and Jack would proceed from Timbuctoo by foot if need be, or in a native craft. The ship-building gear and all the useless merchandise could be dispensed with. Yahia Mohammed could be sent back, too. He would sell all but four maherries: three for himself, Jack and the boy Mohamet. The fourth he would burden lightly with his papers and what remained of his medicines, his cash and his instruments.

At noon, when the town was still, he set out in the heat to the house where Babani lodged. At the gate a servant dozed with his head between his knees. Laing roused him and demanded to be taken directly to the Sheikh. The servant led him to a room off the central courtyard. After the brilliance of the sun he could see nothing, but heard the rhythmic breathing of a sleeper. Then, as his sight adjusted to the dark, he made out the pale garments of a man hunched against a curtain at the far side of the room. It was not Babani but the young man Alkadir.

Laing said, 'I have disturbed you, but I must speak with your uncle while the others are not here.'

'Sit,' the young man said, as he was bound to do. Laing lowered himself slowly, so that they sat half-facing one another on either side of the angle of the walls.

'Where is the Sheikh?' Laing asked him.

Alkadir indicated the far side of the room where Laing now saw a man lying prone on the floor, with his face turned towards the wall. 'Shall I wake him?'

Laing said quickly, 'Will we disturb him if we talk?'

'He will not wake.'

Laing lowered his voice. 'Why does he hold me here? Why does he delay?'

Alkadir said, without concealing his irritation, 'You know why he delays. He is fearful of the harm that will come to you along the road. He waits until the road is safe.'

'The road will never be safe.' Laing said. There was no answer. He said again, 'Why does he not hire an armed escort to take us through? He could have done at Ghadames. He could do here.'

Alkadir said bitterly, 'What would you have of him, *Reis*? Has he not spent enough already on your behalf?'

'What's this? What's this?' Laing said to him. Anger at such insolence welled like the slow blood to a wound. 'He has spent nothing. I have given him sufficient money to buy a hundred guards. If he has told otherwise he has lied to you.'

'It is you, *Reis*, who are lying,' the young man said excitedly. The movement of his eyes and teeth were startling in their whiteness. 'It is well known among us that you give my uncle nothing; that you grudge him even the price of firewood while he has had to pay out constantly for the things you are lacking.'

'What is it that you are saying?' Laing asked him. Still the prohibition of the sleeping man kept their voices low; their anger pent up inside them.

Alkadir said sullenly, 'I say only what everyone says.'

'Does everyone suppose he does what he does for me out of charity?'

'He does it for the Bashaw.' the young man said but he hesitated now in the face of Laing's unflinching right-eousness.

'And do you suppose the Bashaw has not rewarded him?'

Alkadir said promptly, 'He has given him a garden in Ghadames, but no money.'

'I sent him a thousand dollars from Tajura,' Laing said, 'by Giovanelli.'

'I know nothing of this. Nothing of this man.'

'He is the merchant from Tripoli who gave your uncle the merchandise he carries.'

'No, no,' the young man said with a vigorous certainty. 'Everything he carries belongs to Hadji Hassan in Ghadames.'

They were staring at each other in confusion now, each aware that if the other spoke the truth everything must be reversed. Mind would not compass it.

Laing repeated, 'I sent him a thousand dollars from Tajura. I lent him another four hundred at Beni Ulid. And a hundred more at Ghadames.'

'Is this true, Reis?'

'Wake him. He will tell you it is true.

The young man said with a rush of feeling, 'If you tell the truth, Reis, we have wronged you all this time. My uncle has told no one of this money. He has told me that he left Tripoli with only fifty dollars. That you are constantly asking for expenses which he must pay or anger the Bashaw.'

'Wake him' Laing said. 'Wake him and ask him this.'

The young man called across the room. Babani shifted his position. Then he sat upright and, rising all in one movement, went to the door, cleared his throat and spat out into the courtyard. As he came back he saw Laing and greeted him with his same grave smile before he settled himself against the wall beyond Alkadir.

Laing broke out passionately: 'You have told lies of me. You have said that my government has paid you nothing; that you have been forced to pay my expenses. That the contract we signed before the Bashaw does not exist. Alkadir has told me this. Tell him now when I can hear you that these are lies.'

For a time there was no answer. Then Babani said, 'It is true, Reis. All that I have said is true.'

'It is lies, damned lies. I sent you money from Tajura.'

'That is not so, Reis.

'Did Giovanelli or did he not give you a thousand dollars in silver coin before you left Tripoli?'

'No, Reis. He never gave me money.'

266

'Where in God's name is it, then? I gave it him.'

'God knows. I do not know.'

'That is impossible,' Laing told him. 'Do you deny that I gave you four hundred dollars at Beni Ulid?'

'No, Reis. You loaned me the money and I wrote down the account of it.'

'And the hundred at Ghadames?'

'That, too. You have the goods as surety.'

'Well?' Laing shouted at him. 'Well?'

'It has all been spent, Reis. On gifts. On food. On the camels at Malrhail . . .'

'And what of the three thousand waiting for you at Tripoli?'

Babani's face set still. It comprehended nothing.

Alkadir said to Babani in a high angry voice, 'If this is true, if he believed the money had been given you, we have all wronged him in our hearts.'

Babani made no movement. Laing could just make out that he sat with his head turned against the wall in an attitude of exhaustion. At last he said quietly, 'You have been misled, Reis. The contract that you signed meant nothing. I have no money. The goods I have were lent to me by Hadji Hassan out of pity, that I might attempt to sell them in Timbuctoo and recover some of the losses I had incurred in caring for you.'

Laing said in scarcely more than a whisper, 'Then I am very sorry for it.' A moment later he broke out again in disbelief, 'And the Bashaw gave you nothing?'

'He gave me a date garden at Ghadames.'

'How much was it worth?'

'The dates are good,' Babani said. 'The garden is near the wells. Two thousand dollars?'

'And that is all he gave you?'

'I swear that is all.'

'No money?'

'I have had no money, Reis, beyond what you have loaned me.'

Laing said, 'I cannot take this in.'

Alkadir said again, 'We have wronged you, Reis.'

'And I you,' he said to Babani. 'If what you say is true I have wronged you. I am confused. I cannot remember how but I have wronged you in my mind.' After a time he asked 'What is left?'

'Two hundred dollars.'

Laing reckoned that he had the same.

'There is a fine of twenty dollars for every loaded camel that enters Timbuctoo.'

'That's it, then,' Laing said with a little laugh. Other men than he had begged and lived.

They sat in silence then, each struggling to alter in his mind what had seemed the truth. Slowly and exhaustedly the journey must be taken back to the point where falsehood had misled them. Laing thought, I am too tired to go back. It is too late to mend. He forgave Babani. There was nothing now to forgive. He felt as he had felt in the desert when the chronometer had stopped; nothing but relief. And Mind cried out, At last it is simple enough to comprehend. He said quietly, 'I leave here in five days' time, whether you care to come with me or no.'

Babani gave no answer.

Laing said 'If you choose not to come, I will absolve you of it. I think you have been as ill-used as I. The Consul will see you right in Tripoli.'

Babani said in a low voice, 'I must go with you. If you go I must go.'

'You must do as you please,' Laing told him. He rose and went to the door. When he had opened it and filled the room with light he turned to look back at Babani, who sat as he had with his head tipped back against the wall as if the will to move had gone from him.

All afternoon Laing worked at copying out his journal. In the morning he had Jack and Mohamet drag all the luggage into the courtyard and divide it into what he would take with him and what send back to Ghadames. He worked with joy, casting aside the useless articles they had loaded and unloaded in their extremity, as if life itself depended on them; the keg of nails, the shipwrights' tools, the bales of cloth, the yards of gold lace. The weight of all of it was lifted from him.

In the afternoon he wrote to the Consul explaining his decision to go on alone if need be. He recommended what he pay Babani into his hand, being two thirds of the sum promised less the loans he had had of Laing. The date garden at Ghadames must make up the rest. He would attach no blame to Babani's treatment of him until the Consul had cleared up the matter of the contract with the Bashaw in Tripoli. A portion of the merchandise he would return to Babani as a reward for certain past kindnesses.

At dusk Babani and a deputation of merchants called upon him. Laing sent for tea. They crowded into his room and sat leaning against the walls. Then, one after the other, they pleaded with him not to go.

Laing listened with complete detachment. Nothing would divert him now. His trust, he told them, was in God and his own destiny. Not their concern for him nor the ferocity of the Uilid d'Ulim could dissuade him.

'Consider, Reis,' they said to him. 'Consider what was the fate of those men who would not wait.'

'My fate is known,' Laing said. 'Nothing will alter it. Tomorrow I finish my preparations. The next day I go.'

'You will be killed, Reis.'

'I have nothing to lose,' he told them. 'Nothing to fear.'

They muttered in a ragged unison, 'Death is but once.'

Babani's host said, 'If we go with you, Reis, will you lead us? Will you protect us with your guns and your men?'

Laing said, 'If you choose to come, my guns and men are at your service, but I will not delay for you. I leave at dawn on the day after tomorrow whether you come or whether you do not.'

'We will come with you, Reis.' They were all agreed. One day to make ready. The next to set out.

'How many will come?' Laing asked.

'One hundred men.'

'And each has a musket?'

They assured him it was so.

'What have we to fear, then?' he asked them.

'He speaks the truth,' they said together. 'Indeed the Reis speaks wisely.'

Babani said nothing. Laing watched him where he sat against the wall with his face obscured by shadow. When the others rose he did not move. When Alkadir stooped and spoke to him he did not answer.

Laing, left alone with him, sat across the room in silence. At last he said, 'Are you glad that we are going?' When Babani gave no answer he said in an odd tone, both bitter and wheedling, 'You will be glad that you are done with me, I think – if it has cost you so much, if you have come all along

269

against your will. You know I would gladly have released you from your obligation and gone on alone.'

Babani said, 'I beg of you not to go.'

Laing said, 'There is nothing for me but to go.'

'So be it,' he said. He did not speak again, but sat against the wall as if he must summon strength to go. Presently he rose without a word. Laing rose too and went before him to hold open the door. Babani bowed and murmured the formalities of farewell. When he raised his head his face was as void of passion as it had ever been, but his eyes were filled with the tears of an inexplicable sorrow.

'I am sorry,' Laing said again. 'I have wronged you.'

'I, too, Reis, have wronged you. May God forgive me.'

For twenty-four hours he toiled ceaselessly at his correspondence. There was no time to make up a fair copy of his journal. That must wait for Timbuctoo. He sent for Hateeta, gave him the money for the purchase of his camel and entrusted the letters to him. From the roof of his house he watched him ride out northward from the town until he could see him no longer.

The next day the caravan assembled on the open ground outside the town. Of the hundred men promised, forty-five presented themselves. Nevertheless with their own party, the camelmen and the servants, they made up a sizeable band. Laing fired a single rifle shot. Jack blew the advance. Rogers and Harris fired their rifles in the air. With one swift successive movement the camels rose and trotted forward. The drums rattled, the women ululated. The crowd ran with them, singing and dancing with as much jubilation as they had shown on Laing's arrival.

By nightfall they were camped around their myriad fires, talking and breaking into song. Relief after the long delay, the heroism of their departure, fear itself, kept them all in a state of rare elation.

They travelled for two days without any lessening of spirits. At dawn a scout was sent ahead and returned at noon with reassurance that the road ahead was clear. On the third Laing was the first to dismount at a well where a man and a boy watered a camel. The man told Laing that a party of the Uilid d'Ulim had passed the well two nights before and stolen a sheep from him.

'I am sorry to hear it,' Laing told him.

'God is merciful,' the man said. 'We are fortunate to be alive.'

The boy showed him a bruise on the arm where he had been struck with a stick. Laing gave the man a coin.

'For the sheep,' he said. Then, when the man had dipped his head and thanked him repeatedly, he said, 'Go now, when the camel has drunk. Do not tell the others this.'

By nightfall news of the Uilid d'Ulim had spread throughout the caravan. There was doubt whether they should light fires. Laing judged that as there was little chance that their progress was unnoticed their best tactic was to put on a brave showing. He gave permission for the fires but took care to organise a guard composed mainly of his own people. He sent an order around the camp that no rifle should be fired except in the event of an attack.

During the course of that evening several of the merchants came to Laing's fire and berated him soundly for having led them out so rashly.

'You came of your own free will,' he told them. 'I did not beg you to come.'

He had Jack signal the next morning's departure with his trumpet, but when the jarring notes had died away the march was silent and oppressive. The scout went on ahead and returned at noon, having seen nothing to alarm them. They rode all day without halting.

That evening around the fire he asked Babani, 'How many days before we reach the well at Timissao?'

'Two days? Three days?'

'We shall be safe then? We shall be out of the territory of the Uilid d'Ulim?'

'It has always been said that their territory ends there.'

'We shall be safe then,' Laing repeated.

'In two days . . .' The voice broke off. There was a sudden intense silence in which the soughing of the wind grew loud. Across the flames and the column of whirling sparks he saw their still faces; their staring eyes fixed above and beyond him. There was a shifting to the left. A gap was made in the circle. Without a sound, out of the blackness beyond the fire's reach, four masked Tuareg had appeared.

They raised their hands before their faces in salute. No one returned it. No one spoke. One by one they stepped over the rim of the firelight and striking their spears in the sand before them sank swiftly down. The broadswords hung across their backs clanked one against the other. Firelight gleamed dully on the long shafts of their spears and caught the quick movement of their eyes.

'Offer them tea,' Laing said in a low voice to Jack. But the Creole sat huddled where he was. 'What is the matter with you?' Laing said, the more harshly that he himself had been violently startled. He forced himself to stand and pour the tea, which he offered in silence. With the slightest nod of their heads they accepted. Laing returned to his place. No one else moved or spoke.

In time, when they had sipped slowly at the little cups, one of them began to speak at length in a loud heroic tone, staring fixedly into the flames, gesturing occasionally into the outer blackness, addressing no one. The others joined in from time to time with low murmurs of assent. They spoke in their own tongue but there was no mistaking that this was the story of a battle. When they fell silent one of the merchants said, 'They are of the Ahaggar Tuareg, *Reis*. He says the Uilid d'Ulim attacked a koffle out of In Salah a month ago and planned to lie in wait for us on the route to the well at Timissao. He says that he and his brothers fell upon them ten days ago and killed eight of them and took away their camels and the booty they had taken from the koffle. He says that he and his brothers have come to offer us protection to the well at Timissao.'

'Thank him,' Laing said. 'Tell him that he and his men are welcome.' The merchants smiled now. They talked again, softly at first, then in louder more animated voices. They called out their good wishes to the Tuareg, who sat like dark effigies among them, too proud and separate to smile. That night the Tuareg kept the watch. When Laing stretched out to sleep he felt the absence of a fear he had not acknowledged to himself.

In the morning, when they rode out, two of the Tuareg went on ahead and two guarded their rear. During the morning eighteen more of their tribesmen appeared singly and in small groups. They saluted Laing in silence and took up their positions as outriders to the caravan.

At the noon halt they gathered around Laing, begging to see

his gun. He broke it open, removed the cartridges and handed it to them. They examined the breech minutely, snatching it from one another, bending their dark turbans in a mass above it. Laing in his turn inspected their muskets. All had been kept immaculate and were well oiled but were without exception too antiquated to be relied upon. Two of them jammed repeatedly. Babani suggested they exchange them with Rogers' and Harris's for the next two days. 'Ask them if they will,' he said to Jack.

All that day no living thing appeared on the wide glittering plain. At night Laing and his people slept again while the Tuareg kept guard. Towards noon on the following day a shout went up but it was only an ostrich running in frightened zig-zags across the sand. It pleased Laing that, though none of them had eaten fresh meat since they left In Salah, discipline held and not one shot was fired at it.

By evening several of the merchants felt secure enough to come to Laing, complaining that the Tuareg would charge them heavily for their protection and that he should have negotiated the fee with them before accepting their offer.

'How much?' he said to Alkadir who sat with him.

'They will tell us when we reach the well at Timissao.'

The others left. Alkadir rose with them, but lingered behind. 'I have come to say goodbye, *Reis*.'

'You are leaving me?' Laing asked. 'You are turning back?'

'No, *Reis*. I go ahead to Timbuctoo.'

'Alone?'

'Death is but once,' the young man said and smiled at Laing, as if he were his friend.

'Why?'

'My uncle wishes it.'

'But why?'

'He wishes me to go on ahead with some of the merchandise to raise money for him. I shall ride back and meet you outside the city.'

'It is too dangerous,' Laing told him. 'Let me speak to him.'

The young man said, 'He has been a father to me. I am happy to do this.' When he took Laing's hand to say farewell he said, 'When I complained of you in my heart it was undeserved. You are a brave man, *Reis*. You were right to lead us out of In Salah.'

In the morning, when they had loaded up the camels and prayed, Laing clasped Alkadir by the hand a final time. They mounted together but the young man rode on ahead with one of the Tuareg. By mid-morning they had disappeared from sight. By noon the Tuareg returned alone and reported that they had reached the well of Timissao unmolested. They continued without halting. By three o'clock they reached the well and set up camp beside it within sight of a lake and a thin plantation of palms.

It was the twenty-seventh of January. In the late afternoon he walked with Babani towards the lake. They were in the territory of the Ahaggar Tuareg now, where the Uilid d'Ulim would never dare to follow them. In the morning their escort would demand its due and leave them. Babani reminded him that Alkadir would meet them outside Timbuctoo with sufficient money to pay the necessary fines for entering the city. They would meet at the camp of Sidi Mohtar, who was a friend of Babani's.

'In how many days?' Laing asked him.

'In twenty days.' He ran forward suddenly, turning back to Laing and pointing. An ostrich ran directly ahead of them in an ungainly lope, twisting its long neck from side to side.

'Shoot,' Babani called to him. The first shot missed. The bird began to run in panic-stricken circles. Quickly he reloaded and fired again. Its legs disappeared as if they had been struck from under it. It settled abruptly into a mound of feathers.

Laing reloaded. Babani ran forward, retrieved the bird and hauled it back by the legs. When he reached Laing its neck still jerked on the sand. Out of sudden pity for it Laing shot off its head. He reached automatically for a cartridge to reload once more, but Babani laid his hand upon Laing's arm and said with his gentle smile, 'No need, my friend. We are past the danger now.'

On the twenty-ninth of March the Consul rose as usual at dawn and made his morning tour of his estate. As he returned to the house the spaniels, who had raced along ahead, stopped in their tracks by the verandah outside his office and set up a furious barking. A man, clearly a stranger to them, was squatting on the steps awaiting his return. The Consul called the dogs to heel and, shouting for the syce, had them led away. The man rose then, touched his hand and greeted him.

'What is it?' the Consul asked him in English. 'What do you want?'

The man began to speak in rapid Arabic. The Consul raised a hand to silence him, saying clearly and rather loudly, 'I do not understand you.'

Immediately he reached inside his clothing and drew out a wrapped packet of letters. The Consul snatched them from him. It was the month in which Laing expected to reach the Guinea coast, yet no word had reached the Consul of his whereabouts since Sala had brought the despatches from Ghadames. There was the neat clerk's hand. He began to tear the paper, clumsy with excitement. It was just conceivable that he held in his hand the historic first despatch from Timbuctoo. At the same time he called Vincenzio to rouse Fred and have him come at once.

He went into his study, beckoning the messenger to follow him, and spread the letters out on the desk: Emma's packet, several addressed to the Colonial Office and to the few friends he wrote to in England. His own he tore open and saw at once to his bitter disappointment that the inscription was In Salah. He opened five separate letters, all from In Salah, and arranged them in order on the desk. The latest was dated the thirteenth of January. He read, *I send this by Hateeta on the eve of my departure from In Salah.*

'You are not Hateeta, are you?' he said to the messenger, who was clearly no Tuareg. He provoked a flow of words the only one of which he recognised with any certainty being Hateeta's name, which was repeated several times. Fred appeared unshaven at the door. The Consul said all at once, 'Ask him who he is? Where did he get these? Where is Hateeta? Why is he not here?'

Hateeta was in Ghat. Yes. He had come there from the Reis.

'Where?' the Consul demanded. 'Ask him where he left the Reis.'

He had left the Reis at In Salah. All the time Fred questioned him, the Consul scanned the letter. Hateeta was to bring this. Why did he not come?

'He says Hateeta waits in Ghat for further news of the Reis.'

'Humbug,' the Consul said. 'He lives there. It suits him to stay.'

'He says there is a letter from Hateeta.'

'Is there, then?' The man was fumbling inside his clothes. He handed Fred a letter written in the Arabic script. The Consul watched his son unfold and read it with what seemed a maddening slowness. Then he saw the blood rise suddenly in the boy's face. 'Well,' he said. 'What does he say?'

The boy did not look up at him but read aloud hesitantly from the letter:

To the head of his people, the respected and honoured by the children of his nation, the English Consul resident at Tripoli, from Hateeta of Ghat, the friend of his people. Praise be to God and blessings and peace be unto the Apostle of God. Word has reached me at my home in Ghat that the English traveller has been attacked and wounded in the desert before Timbuctoo. I am sorry for it but it is the business of God.

The Consul's immediate concerns were to check the accuracy of this report and to protect Emma from the knowledge of it. Throughout the winter her health had given them constant anxiety and at all costs no extra burden of anxiety must be placed upon it. He would not trust himself to appear before her with the fresh imprint of this disastrous news upon him, but sent for his horse and rode directly into town, taking the messenger and Fred to act as his interpreter. As soon as he reached the consulate he sent a servant to the palace with a note urgently requesting the Bashaw to grant him an audience regarding Major Laing's mission to the interior. By the same hand he sent Hateeta's letter and a bottle of his finest brandy, wrapped in sufficient cloth to disguise its shape. His request was granted by return and within the hour he was sitting side by side with the Bashaw on a carpet in a private chamber of the palace. Something of their old intimacy was restored as they talked, although the brandy was not broached, as once it would have been. The Bashaw assured the Consul, with his hand pressed to his heart, that no word had reached him of any such attack. Indeed, such occurrences were all too frequent, but any harm befalling a Christian would have been reported to him directly from In Salah. Mohammed d'Ghies had been sent to and while the Consul sat there a message was delivered from him saying that none of his informants had made any mention of an attack. He added that all the Saharan towns were rife with such rumours; that the slightest incident could be distorted out of all proportion.

The Consul rode back to his garden at dusk with all his fears dispelled. He had paid the messenger generously and made him swear on the Koran in the Bashaw's presence that he would not repeat this rumour. For his own part he had no longer any doubt that the message was some ruse of Hateeta's to excuse his absence from Tripoli without putting in jeopardy any future gifts he might receive for his services. He had debated with himself whether he would be justified in reading through the packet of letters addressed to Emma, but was relieved now to find that unnecessary. Instead, fearing that the excitement might rob her of a night's sleep, he set the letters aside and made no mention of them until the morning.

Since Laing's departure Emma had not been well. Her throat still pained her and she was troubled with an incessant cough. Then, at the end of January, she had been taken ill. There had been days and nights of feverish restlessness which, even when she slept, persisted in her dreams. Dickson had warned the Consul of the danger that she might fall into a consumption. He walked with him briefly on the verandah and said, 'She should be got to Europe.'

'When Laing returns,' the Consul said.

'They'll take care of her at the Lazaretto in Leghorn. Have him take her there.' He touched the Consul's arm, as if to emphasise the gravity of what he said. Then he went back up the stairs to Emma and gave her a phial of tablets, two of which painfully she swallowed.

'There's only one cure for you,' he said, touching her cheek. 'My medicine is wasted on you.'

Nevertheless within a day or two the cough had been soothed and the discomfort in her throat dulled at last. Only the dreams remained, recurring almost nightly, so that she woke chilled and damp in the disordered sheets, convinced that solemn processions had marched all night around her bed outside the muslin curtain; that if the mourners had once turned their heads all of them would have been familiar to her. All the next day she was oppressed by the belief that they had mourned for Laing. His name was seldom mentioned in

277

the Garden and she was shy of speaking it in front of them. She thought, He is dead. They are afraid to tell me. Immediately she coughed and felt again the pain in her throat. She begged her mother to crush the tablets in a little wine for her.

She was better then. She told herself that the lassitude of mind and body that persisted since her illness was caused by idleness as much as weakness. In the mornings, when the others went out riding, she rose from the sofa where they had left her and walked restlessly to and fro along the verandah until her legs were tired and she felt a chill sweat cover her face. Then, until dinner, she sat in her father's office and took copies of the letters he would send to London.

The Consul had grown accustomed to finding her there on his return. At first he had resented her presence in the room. Then, when she had been ill, the burden of the copying had fallen heavily upon him. On the morning when she was judged strong enough to undertake her duties once again, he had been touched to see her look of anxious expectation while he checked through her work for errors. He had smelt with pleasure the familiar odour of rose water as he bent over her shoulder to indicate the closing of a sentence.

On the day after the messenger had come from Ghat he laid the packet of Laing's letters suddenly in front of her. She looked at it for a moment, as if she could not bring herself to touch it, then raised her eyes slowly to his. They were without enquiry but awaited a response.

'Well,' he said, 'will you not read them?'

'Not here, Papa?'

'Yes,' he said. 'Yes, here. I will not disturb you.' As if to demonstrate this he moved to the far end of the desk and began to sort through the papers lying stacked and waiting for the return packet to London.

All the time Emma read she could hear the shuffle of papers and occasionally the tap of his ring against the table top. She sensed that he watched her but would not look up lest if she met his eyes Laing's words would be in some way betrayed to him. She turned each page in fear of what the words might say, but there was nothing to alarm her. He was well. He longed to be with her. He loved her. She raised her eyes to find her father watching her intently. 'Is he well?' he asked.

'Yes,' she said, 'he is well. He says he'll be in Timbuctoo in twenty days.'

In May, on her birthday, Tom Wood gave her a copy of de Gotha's almanac. He sat beside her on the sofa and guided her hand down its pages. When he had gone she found the thirteenth of January, the date of Laing's last letter, but she must turn the pages for February, March, April before she came to the page that held her birthday. In all that time they had heard nothing.

She kept the almanac by her constantly and studied it whenever she was left alone. The year had come around. The anniversary passed of the day when the guns had sounded across the bay and the Consul had ridden into town; of the day when Laing had set up his tent at the end of the Garden and she, under the pretence of fetching Ossy, had spied upon him. Then one by one she identified those anniversaries known only to herself and Laing. With the almanac open as evidence that it was true, she told herself the story of these events again and again, but as the weeks went by it seemed these memories were worn down as one might obliterate a path by crossing and recrossing it. The little gift, so kindly intended to give her mastery over the days, now only increased her fears. Too many days had passed. More than ever before she felt inside herself the emptiness and silence of the desert beyond the garden walls.

Tomorrow was to be the anniversary of her marriage. Although everyone had commented on the improvement in Emma's health over the past few months the Consul still made his anxiety for her his excuse not to attend the Bastille Day celebrations at the French Consulate. Tom Wood was required to represent him. The Consul had sent for him to the Garden, to instruct him to listen out for any rumour of Laing's whereabouts that might have reached the town through Rousseau's agents.

Afterwards he went out to the verandah to pay his respects to Mrs Warrington. As he was leaving he went over to Emma's sofa and, taking her by the hand, said in a voice too low for the others to hear, 'Timoleon will be sad you do not come. I know that he had hoped to see you.'

He thought her very pale. The sweat stood on her lip in

separate beads. She gripped his hand, as if she would raise herself by it, and whispered, 'Ask him if he has heard anything. Oh, beg him for our old friendship's sake if he has heard – if his father has heard anything of Laing. He would not be so cruel as to withhold it from me. If I offended him I could not help myself.'

Two weeks had passed. No word had come from any source. A full moon had enabled the Dicksons and the Knutsons to ride out to the Garden. With Fred and Jenny two sets might be got up for whist. Tom Wood sat by Emma and told her the gossip of the town.

Madame Rossini's son had asked for Amy Coxe's hand in marriage and had been refused.

'Has not Timoleon?' she asked him. 'I thought when he could not have me he might have her.'

'He is faithful, Emma.' He put on a solemn voice when he spoke of his friend who, they said, would die.

'Poor man, then,' she said lightly.

She rose abruptly and went out onto the verandah. Her mother's voice, like some faint echo she had set in motion, called after her, 'Should you not wear a shawl, Emma?'

She thought that Wood would bring it out to her but he did not. She went inside and said as she passed him, 'I wish to speak with you.'

When he came again to sit by her, she said in the same low rapid voice, 'Does he read my letters – the letters that I write to Laing?'

'I am sure that he does not.' He shook his head to and fro as if what she had said displeased him, but his bright dark eyes watched her.

'But he has,' she said, 'in the past. He took them all and burnt them. Timoleon's. You have reminded me. Oh, he should not have done that.'

'No indeed.' How prim and pursed he made his mouth. He would not yield to her.

'And Timoleon knew nothing?'

'Nothing, as I told you.'

'How was he?' For she had not asked before.

'Better, they say.'

'Is he in love again?'

'Shall I tell him you asked?'

'No,' she said. She laughed. Something inside her had quickened. 'No, you shall not. I only asked because you were annoyed with me.'

'What, I?' he asked, widening his eyes in mock astonishment.

'Because you would not say whether he reads my letters.'

'I am sure that he does not.'

A year ago today, she wrote to Laing, *we were clasped in one another's arms. Had I known then how many days must pass I do not think I could have borne it.*

She folded up the note and kept it in her box. She would not entrust it to her father until the very moment that the packet was sealed. She might never send it. Indeed she scarcely knew to whom she had written it other than to herself.

It was late in July. The family rode before breakfast now so as to have their exercise before the worst of the heat. Emma, although her health was much improved, was forbidden to risk overtaxing it by riding with them. She waited on the verandah while the still heat gathered beyond the vine. Madame de Breughel had called early. Through the open windows of the drawing room she could be heard translating aloud from the French papers to Mama. The day stretched ahead without limit or promise.

There was an uproar of barking at the front of the house. Madame called out, 'Ah, they are back so soon.' She heard her father's voice shouting at the dogs to be silent; then Ossy's heavy precipitate step in the passage. He came through the door and ran up close to her. He was panting. His face worked with the importance of his message: 'The feather man has come.'

For a moment the words meant nothing. Then she remembered that a year ago, scarcely more, before Laing came, an ostrich hunter had come in from the desert and sold his feathers to her father.

'But he was here a little time ago,' her mother came on to the verandah to say. 'Has a year gone past? And the Colonel bought all the feathers that the poor man had.' Jane and Louisa had come onto the verandah too, tossing their hats and veils and gloves carelessly onto the table. They began to drag the wicker chairs to the edge of the porch. 'Come and sit here, Mama,' Jane told her loudly. 'Fred is bringing the ostrich hunter.'

As soon as she saw the man Emma remembered him exactly: a slight wizened man. He wore his shirt hitched up between his naked legs and his bow and arrows slung across his back. He stood in the garden as he had before, grinning and ducking his head as they settled themselves in the row of chairs like an audience arriving in a theatre. Fred, Harry and Ossy sat at their feet on the top step. On the bottom one the ostrich hunter slowly unrolled a strip of dusty cloth to reveal the precious feathers one by one. He lifted each in turn, stroked it against his cheek and reached it up to the ladies on the porch. They lay in Emma's lap, alive and not alive. She felt their weightless warmth through the thin stuff of her dress and watched the hunter enact for them how he had crept to stalk the ostrich across the sand. How it had run from him, first this way and then that. She laughed when he jerked his head up and down like the poor ostrich. He fell then suddenly and lay dead and sprang up when they all applauded him. Her mother was saying in a tone of scandalised contentment, 'When you think what the price would be in London.'

The Consul, who stood behind his wife's chair, said suddenly to Fred, 'Ask him where he is from.'

From Ghat, the hunter told them.

The Consul pushed his way between the women's chairs, and stepped down over the feathers into the garden. He took the hunter by the arm and led him out of earshot. Fred followed him. The women were left watching, idly waving their feathers. Then for no reason they were standing, each with her feather in her hand as if about to take part in a procession. It seemed to Emma that she felt tears on her cheeks before she saw Fred break away from the little group of men and come running towards her. He was shouting, 'He's there. He's there.'

She was weeping with joy, running with her skirt bunched up in one hand and the feather gripped in the other, down the steps across the dust, regardless of the burning air.

Now the Consul called out, 'He's there. He's done it.'

They were waving their caps, her father, Fred, Ossy. Harry shouted. 'Hip, hip, hip.' They all cried. 'Hoorah.' She clung to

Fred, repeating, 'What does he say? What does he say?'

'That they say in the market at Ghat that the English *Reis* has arrived in Timbuctoo.'

'When? Ask him when,' the Consul said.

But the ostrich hunter shook his head. He knew nothing more than he had already told them.

'Is he well?' Emma asked him. 'Did they say that he was in good health?'

But they had said nothing except that an Englishman whom they called *Reis* had arrived in Timbuctoo.

'He's there. Laing's there,' Ossy shouted. He ran back to where his mother and Madame de Breughel stood on the steps leaning forward with their arms about each other's waists, calling out, 'Is it true? Is it true?'

'To think,' Madame de Breughel said as she hugged her friend to her, 'that I should be here when the historic announcement arrived.'

The Consul took the ostrich hunter to his office. He kept a volume of the Koran there for the purpose of taking oaths. He made the man swear on it that he had heard the report and repeated it in good faith. He had Fred ask him, 'Did you hear anything of any attack?' No. There was no attack that he had heard of. The Consul purchased his entire stock of feathers and dismissed him. Immediately he wrote messages to the Bashaw, to Mohammed d'Ghies, and to Baron Rousseau repeating this report with more caution about its accuracy than he could bring himself to feel.

At dinner they toasted Major Laing of Timbuctoo. The words echoed around the table like a magic charm. The thing was accomplished. The waiting all but over. For they assured Emma that in the time it had taken the ostrich hunter to come with his news Laing might well have completed his stay in Timbuctoo and have set out on his return journey by land or by sea. They spoke Laing's name again and again. They smiled at Emma and touched her lightly on the arm, as if they were in awe of her. She sat among them, very pale and very straight. Her dark eyes were enlarged with excitement. There seemed to hang about her the golden aura of that distant city which through her they could lay claim to. They toasted 'Mrs Laing,' as if suddenly, on that very day, she had made her appearance among them. 'Mrs Laing and her good health.' Her head was confused with wine. She tried to imagine the greater happiness that would be hers on Laing's arrival but found she could not.

In the morning it was found that the excitement and the talk had irritated her throat. By evening she was coughing and a little feverish. The doctor was called and suggested an increase of medicine. In a day or two the coughing eased, the stiffness in her throat relaxed.

It was the end of the month. The July packet had arrived from London. She worked for several hours every day at the creaking table in her father's study, making copies of the despatches he would send to London. They were to be kept back until the last possible moment in the hopes that Laing's despatches from Timbuctoo might be added to them. A servant was posted on the roof during the daylight hours to give warning of the approach of any messenger. Another was sent to keep watch outside the palace. The Consul was in constant touch with the man he paid in Rousseau's household. No word came. He was bound to seal the packet and send Sala with it to the harbour, knowing that if the despatch arrived tomorrow another month must pass before he could convey the confirmation of Laing's triumph to London.

'You'll see,' he said to Emma. 'The moment it is gone, we'll hear.'

But they heard nothing. The stifling days of August had numbered themselves out. At first it had seemed to Emma, every time there were horses in the yard, or the dogs barked or a servant appeared at the door to summon her father, that Laing had come. She told herself that he would not send despatches; that he would come himself. One day as now, when her head was bent over her work, she would look up. And there. Some part of her would be returned with him that would know what to say, what to do, what to feel.

She was troubled at this time by a recurring dream that seemed to take up large portions of the night and leave her in the morning exhausted and oppressed, as if she had not slept at all. She walked through a luminous expanse of landscape. At first she was filled with a sense of peace and reassurance, for even if some menacing thing were to appear on the horizon an age must pass before it reached her, while there before her lay an infinity of paths by which she might escape it. When she sensed that something moved behind her she was untroubled. She began to run. A great exaltation carried her faster and faster into that shining fearless space. Then the path she had taken began to rise ahead of her like a giant causeway. It stretched on and on ahead as far as she could see. Then, without warning, in the very pride of her flight it was no longer there.

The dream was inescapable. No exertion of her mind could alter it or let her free by waking. With a slow reluctance she forced herself to look down at her running feet. The sudden corner of the wall came towards her so rapidly that she must leap sideways and run at right angles to her former path, faster now lest she teeter and fall, and turn again and run on because she knew without looking back that the wall consumed itself behind her. Exposed there in the relentless light, unable to hide, unable to pause, unable to deviate either to the left or to the right, she ran now to meet the thing she fled from.

In the morning it would seem that she had dreamt of Laing and the unknown places that had denied him shelter.

The August packet came with the news that Clapperton had reached Kano, but no single word of Laing. Again the Consul was obliged to seal his answers and send them off without being able to include the triumphant despatch he was still in perfect confidence of receiving.

Then, in the second week of September, as they sat to dinner, the servant crossed the room with a message on a tray and, going to Emma's place, handed it past her shoulder. She took it automatically, staring without recognition at the hand in which her name, Emma Gordon Laing, was clumsily written.

She heard her father say, 'What is it? Bring it here.'

'It is for me, Papa.' She had begun hurriedly to open it. Her hands shook. She spread it on the table, but the words blurred and she had difficulty in reading them. How had it come so simply? It seemed that Laing might be in the house and have sent the little message to prepare her, so that frequently, as she tried to read the few lines written there, she looked up towards the door.

Her father was standing, leaning impatiently forward, saying 'Is it from Laing?'

My dearest Emma, she read.

'Well,' he said, 'well, what does he say?'

'He has hurt his hand.'

'Where is it from? Does he say anything of Timbuctoo?'

She could not see the word.

The Consul shouted for the servant. Who had brought this? Where was he now? A man had brought it. He had gone.

She began mechanically to read aloud, *I write with only a thumb and finger having a very severe cut on my forefinger.*

'For God's sake.' the Consul said, 'has he dated it?'

There was no date.

'Oh well,' he said, 'that's no use, then. It's some old letter delayed along the route or he'd have said.'

But Emma could not free herself from a sense that this last message had somehow superseded the news of Laing's arrival in Timbuctoo. In the days that followed she fretted ceaselessly about this injury, which was all her sense of misery might fasten on to. She was beset by fears that her father and Wood had information they would not reveal to her. Fear of dreaming made her reluctant to sleep. That in turn made sleeplessness a habit. Frequently she was irritable, even with Tom Wood, whose company once had diverted her.

He had some papers in his hand. Without even greeting him she said, 'What have you brought? Are there letters? Is there news?'

'Nothing,' he told her. 'I had thought you might like my company.' He sat sideways at a distance at which it was uncomfortable to talk. Sometimes he effected this melancholy air so that they might coax him from it. She was impatient with him and sighed.

'You should go riding with the others,' he told her. 'You are quite strong enough now. The weather's cooler.'

But more than ever she felt the need to keep to the house, to keep still, scarcely to disturb the air in the room, as if by doing so she might prevent anything befalling him until his safe return. How could she tell Wood that? She said, 'I hardly care to.'

'Then you should make yourself. This is unkind of you.'

'How unkind?' She sensed that he had spoken the word at random and cast about now for something that would justify it.

286

'Well, to Jenny. She has no companion now.'

'She has Louisa.'

'Louisa is a child.'

'Has she said this to you?'

'We talk sometimes.' He watched her with no expression on her face.

'Then she has you.'

He sighed then and got to his feet. 'I think you do not want me here.'

'Oh,' she said. 'I am worried half to death.'

He turned back but would not sit again. 'His hand will have healed by now. It was a month ago. Two months ago. We are all different now to what we were then.'

'You were kinder to me then.'

'It is not for long,' he said in an irritable tone that mimicked patience. 'Believe me, it cannot be for long. He has been in Timbuctoo for two months now. You can be sure of that, believe me.' He left, only just touching her hand.

It was the twenty-seventh of September. A wind had blown since dawn. She was more agitated than she could remember being. By nightfall her fever had risen again. The wind persisted and penetrated the rooms, although windows and shutters had been fastened against it. She lay in the dark hearing it try the flimsy house, which had not been built for such extremes of weather; listening to her sisters' breathing and watching the ghostly movement of the muslin curtains; wishing to be free of the wretched weight of consciousness; fearful of sleeping.

Throughout this trying time the Consul had managed to preserve his buoyant mood. Although he was careful to hide any mention of the fact from Emma, the news of Laing's hurt fingers had dispelled his last remnants of anxiety. Clearly this wound confirmed the rumour of an attack and as clearly it established that, whatever the circumstances, Laing had escaped with only trivial injury. For the first time in months the Consul might contemplate a future that veered closer to the course on which his life had originally been set.

It was many years since Colonel Warrington had received any encouragement from his royal patrons. At the lowest ebb of his fortunes they had perhaps been powerless to help him further than the consulate. The exile entailed he had accepted with good grace as temporary. Then, in 1820, hearing that the old King's health had entered its final decline, he had taken the opportunity of sending several columns from the ruins at Leptis Magna as gifts to the Prince Regent. By the time the necessary arrangements had been made he was able to accompany these antiquities with a letter recommending himself to his old friend and new monarch. The answer had been a note of formal thanks from an equerry.

Now it occurred to him that this might be the time to make overtures once more; to remind his former patrons, before the news of Laing's triumph was made public, of the part his long devoted service had played in these proceedings. In the past months he had made several visits with Fred to the nomadic encampments south of Tripoli. These in the past had provided him with news from the desert towns. Now he learnt nothing concerning Laing, but had in the course of his enquiries been shown two particularly fine Arab mares. He could not let such an opportunity slip and resolved to send both to Gibraltar as gifts for the Duke of Kent.

Again a loan must be negotiated with Giovanelli, and arrangements be made for transportation. On the night of November the third the Consul had Vincenzio bring his brandy to his office, where he planned to spend an hour composing the letter that would accompany the mares. He sat at his desk with head thrown back and eyes closed, pondering the exact choice of words and might briefly have dozed. A sound of knocking startled him unduly.

'Come in,' he said, looking towards the door. The sound came again from behind him. Someone must stand on the verandah seeking entrance, as Laing had done on the night he came to ask for Emma's hand in marriage.

'Who's there?' he said. He could make out a blur of pale clothing by the window. 'Laing?' He crossed the room quickly and opened the door.

An Arab stood close by it, his face obscured by shadow. 'Laing,' he said again, although he sensed it was not he. Still he looked past this visitant in the hopes that Laing might be there, holding back out of sight to lessen the shock of so sudden and so late an arrival. No one else was there. 'Do you want me?' he said.

The man began to speak in a low rapid voice which the Consul failed entirely to comprehend.

'Come into the light,' he said. Then, 'But I know you.'

'I am Yahia Mohammed.'

'Good God,' the Consul said. 'Where's Laing?'

Yahia Mohammed stood staring about him and was silent. The light, the unfamiliar room had confused him perhaps. The Consul strode across to the opposite door and said to Vincenzio who waited there, 'Fetch Signor Wood from the drawing room. Tell him to come at once. But quietly. Let no one hear you.'

'The *Reis*?' he said turning back to Yahia Mohammed. 'Where's the *Reis*?'

The camel driver reached inside his clothing and drew out a letter. As he did so his sleeve fell back. The Consul snatched at his wrist and drew his arm into the lamplight. It bore the scar of a sword cut so recently healed that the lips of the wound were still stiff and swollen.

'What's this?' the Consul said.

The camel driver bowed his head before him. There on the back of his neck was such another, more superficial and better healed.

'Where is the *Reis*?' the Consul said again, more loudly. He fumbled with the letter, which was unsealed, and read:

Azoad, July 1st 1826. My dear Consul, With a mind sadly depressed with sickness, sorrow and disappointment I lift an unwilling pen to acquaint you that I am no further on my journey than when I last addressed you . . .

Wood knocked on the door and came directly in. 'There's something up,' the Consul said. 'He's been hurt. For God's sake ask him what's become of Laing.' He continued to read the letter over the quick exchange of their voices but was too agitated to absorb the words.

'He's alive,' Wood told him. Thank God. he thought. 'He's hurt, but he's alive.'

The camelman continued in a rapid monotone some tale of grief, chopping repeatedly with his hands, letting out little cries of pain.

'And Babani?'

'Dead.'

'And the others?'

'All dead – all save Laing himself.'

289

'Where, man? Where?'

'He left him in an Arab camp five days out of Timbuctoo.'

'When was that?'

'In July.'

'He's there, then,' the Consul said. 'He's there in Timbuctoo. There's no question of it. Tell him that we have heard that the *Reis* has reached Timbuctoo in safety.'

But the news meant little to the camel driver. He hung his head, oppressed by grief or exhaustion or some permanent confusion of the mind. All he would say was, 'God knows, I do not know.'

'Who did this thing,' the Consul asked him.

He was silent for a while, as if he struggled to remember. Then he said, 'The Tuareg did this thing.'

The Consul was determined that Yahia Mohammed should not leave his sight, lest word of the attack be spread among his household. He told Vincenzio to bring food and water to his office and, while the camel driver squatted down to eat in the corner of the room, he read and reread Laing's letters.

When I see you, he read, *I shall a tale of treachery unfold* ... He said aloud to Wood, 'He's within a week of Timbuctoo. It was written in July. He plans to come back the way he came and reach Ghadames early in November.'

'He may be there now,' Wood said.

There was a list of things he hoped to find on his arrival there, news of the family, the European papers, a little tea and sugar, half a dozen pairs of stockings, and, as he appeared to be entirely out of funds, four hundred dollars.

All that night the Consul questioned Yahia Mohammed through Wood, who wrote down his deposition in Arabic. At dawn the Consul escorted him to the edge of the desert and sent him on his way, well rewarded for his sufferings and bound to solemn secrecy.

For two days he spoke of these events to no one other than Wood, continuing to believe that Laing's despatches must come from Timbuctoo too to soften the blow of his misfortunes and give more exactly the date of his arrival in Ghadames. As much as he was able he put from his mind the full extent of Laing's suffering. One cannot suffer for another man. Time had passed. As much as would ever heal would be healed by now. But the simplicity of Laing's list of wants preyed on his mind. He could not bear the thought of his arriving in such extremity at Ghadames to find nothing.

The next day, when the family gathered for breakfast, he announced simply that a messenger had brought a letter from Laing written on the eve of his arrival in Timbuctoo saying that he hoped to be in Ghadames early in November.

'He may be there now,' he said. 'I shall send Sala to him in the morning.' He watched his daughter as he spoke. For a moment her face was as still and indifferent as the dead, then a look of astonished pleasure violently altered it. She cried out. The others rose and went to her. The room was filled with the shrill primitive sounds of women.

He was glad then for the little list which he had had the foresight to make a copy of. He presented it now to his wife with instructions that all the items should be ready packed this evening so that Sala's departure would not be delayed in any way.

Immediately they were quieted and absorbed in the series of problems the little paper posed. Madame de Breughel was sent to at once and begged to sacrifice even the most recent French papers. Vincenzio was freed from his other duties and sent into the town to purchase the stockings. A pair of the Consul's was sent with him to measure by, as Mrs Warrington remembered distinctly that Laing had been quite as tall as the Colonel. She and Emma crossed the yard to the kitchen compound and had the cook pack up a quantity of loaf sugar and a generous amount of the best tea.

By evening everything was collected in the drawing room and Emma herself was allowed the special pleasure of fitting and refitting these items into the box in which they were to travel. At the last moment the Consul thought to have Vincenzio bring a dozen bottles of wine to add to Laing's comforts. All must be taken out another time and rearranged. No one thought to question him as to when the letter had been sent or who had brought it. The lamplight concentrated on Emma's absorbed face as she bent over the box. Two red spots of colour stood out in her cheeks as they had not for many months. They had not passed so lively an evening since news of Laing's arrival in Timbuctoo reached them in the summer.

Shortly afterwards the Consul withdrew to his office where

Wood had worked on the translation and copying of Yahia Mohammed's deposition. The Consul sent for brandy and sat drinking and watching him complete the task. The sound of laughter and singing came from the neighbouring room. Wood raised his head and said quietly, 'You must tell her the truth of it. He might appear at any minute.'

He pushed the paper across the desk to the Consul, who read the English rendering of the words that Yahia Mohammed had spoken.

We were attacked sixteen days after leaving Tuat, about three o'clock in the morning.

Five days before twenty Tuareg on maherries joined the koffle and continued with them. At the time mentioned these twenty suddenly fell upon the rest of the koffle consisting of forty-five persons. The twenty Taureg had guns, swords, spears and daggers. They attacked Major Laing and his part of the koffle, and never molested Babani or anyone else. They surrounded Laing's tents and baggage and without saying a word fired into them, one ball striking Laing when asleep in the side but with little injury. They then rushed on the tents, cutting the canvas and cords. I raised myself. I received a sabre wound on my head which brought me to the ground. They entered Laing's tent and before he could arm himself he was cut down by a sword on the thigh. He again jumped up and received one cut on the cheek and the ear and the other on the right arm above the wrist which broke the arm. He then fell on the ground where he received seven cuts, the last being on his neck.

In the morning the family assembled on the verandah to see Sala mount and ride away to Ghadames with two mules to carry the money and supplies. Seeing Emma at the breakfast table so happy and animated, hearing her mother order an old trunk of warmer clothes to be brought down and inspected in the parlour to see if anything would be of service for Emma's wedding trip to Europe, the Consul reasoned that another happy day would both strengthen her and lessen the sum of days before Laing himself would come to reassure her.

But the duty that was shirked today must be taken up tomorrow. The morning after Sala's departure he sent early to his daughters' room to tell Emma to come to his office. She felt unwell. The night had been restless and broken with dreams. She had been feverish, perhaps, for the sheets had been damp with her sweat. She sent for water and carefully washed herself. When she worked for her father she wore a little muslin scarf pinned about her neck to cover her. She arranged it modestly. She splashed rose water on her wrists and behind her neck and shivered at its evanescent chill. She combed it through her hair. She was ready. She knocked on the office door and when there was no answer went in. The room was empty. There was fresh paper stacked on her table. Directly she saw it she wished to write to Laing, although the letters had gone yesterday and he would surely be here before another post was sent. Nevertheless she felt the need to write and tell him this before she might believe it entirely to be true. She dipped the pen and wrote, *Yesterday, my beloved Laing, I had the pleasure of closing my letters and delivering them to Sala who is now on the road to meet my adored husband.*

She heard her father's approach across the bare planking of the verandah and quickly folded the letter and hid it in the pocket that she wore around her waist. He came into the room and, without a word, unlocked the drawer of his desk and drew out a letter. 'I want a fair copy of this,' he said. Then he turned his back on the room and seemed to stare through a gap in the shutter at something that had caught his eye. He was in no hurry. She settled herself and took fresh paper. 'It is to Laing,' she said, surprised, for she had never seen any of the correspondence between them. Without turning around the Consul said, 'It is the draft of one I sent him yesterday. I need a second copy.'

She began to write: *I need not tell you of the grave alarm with which the camelman's news of your misfortune has been received here. My heart misgives me at the position you are now placed in as much as at the extreme severity of your wounds . . .*

She watched her hand form these words as if they were something of her own devising. 'What is this?' she said to him. She had dropped the pen and held the letter up close to her face, scarcely able to make out the words in her distress.

'He has been wounded,' the Consul told her firmly, 'but he has recovered and arrived at Timbuctoo and set out again for

Ghadames. Sala will meet him with our letters and will accompany him back to Tripoli.'

But Emma seemed not to hear him. She had risen uncertainly. The Consul moved quickly to the door and sent the servant for his wife. He turned back to see his daughter transformed into something grey, squat, inert. As if her meagre body had grown too heavy to be carried upright, she had fallen not forward but down into herself. When he caught her up there was no response in her, only the great weight of her unwillingness to hear what she had heard. He shook with outrage at the refusal of the bones to stay upright; of the world to keep to its appointed place.

She was put to bed and the doctor sent for. Although within a minute or two she had regained her senses, she lay without speaking or crying or perhaps comprehending what had happened. At last she slept. Her mother sat all night beside her bed, but she dozed off in time. She was wakened by the sound of Emma's sobbing. Dawn had broken. Her child was crouched by the open window holding in her hand the little miniature of Laing which now bore no resemblance to him, and weeping over it most bitterly.

Laing himself could remember nothing of the attack. He had been in pain which seemed to intensify and fade with the brilliance of the stars, for they had laid him on the open ground. He was at peace. Something had passed by that would not return. He was astonished at the beauty of the stars and would have been content to lie there for a long time looking at them. From time to time faces peered closely down at him. He recognised Mohamet and Yahia Mohammed. They have been hurt, he thought. Who can have done that? Other faces were strange to him. They sat around him as they had at Falaba, waiting for him to die.

They were mistaken. He would not die, but lacked the strength to tell them so.

'Jack,' he cried out, 'Jack,' but must have made no sound for Jack did not come. He heard them say that he would be dead by dawn, but the sky paled and filled with light and colour as it would not have done had he been dead. They waited. At a distance he could hear the sounds of the camels being loaded. They will go and leave me, he thought.

294

He was tormented by thirst, but could not free his tongue from the roof of his mouth to beg for water. Nor, he discovered, could he move his hands. A man he thought to be Babani stared down at him, but turned his head away without a word, so that Laing thought, It cannot be he. Babani too must be dead. For a time a little boy he had never seen before squatted down staring, it seemed, without blinking. The sun stung and stiffened on his face. He thought, They will grow tired of waiting. At any minute now they will rise and ride away and leave me here. He forced his entire being into one great cry. It tore his throat. There was blood in his mouth. Still, it seemed a feeble bleating thing when it came forth. Mohamet's face stared in terror into his. Then he spilt water slowly from the edge of his hand into Laing's mouth. He swallowed then and opened his lips for more and more again.

'Jack,' he cried. 'Where is Jack?' But he had spoken in a whisper which Mohamet must bend close to his lips to hear. No one answered, as if they judged him already beyond hearing.

Then, when he was still alive and they could wait no longer, they lifted him on a litter and tied him to the camel, talking all the time, though not to him. 'Here. Put it here. Aie. Aie,' as if they felt the pain. 'Aie, not so tight. Cover his face.' Their voices were childish with awe at what had happened to him.

The hours of his torment were beyond counting. They had stretched a cloth canopy above his head. The sun blazed through it in a single point. A voice close to his ear moaned and pleaded with them to stop. Sometimes he knew that it was his. At other times he thought it was the voice of the strange child who rode sideways in the bend of the camel's neck and sometimes sang and sometimes wept.

The camel lurched forward and back and was still. They gave him water. He begged with them to leave him where he was but almost at once they urged the camel on and he was caught up again in the incessant jarring of his pain.

Then all was still. He lay on the ground with his face uncovered. There were stars. One by one the faces stared down at him, Mohamet, Babani, Yahia Mohammed, crying out in astonishment that he was still alive. Jack knelt beside him, weeping, saying, 'Vous devez être mort, Capitaine.'

Laing said, 'I thought you were dead.'

He slept. Everything was still. He could see nothing. He thought, They have left me here to die. Then he heard Jack's breathing close to his ear and was comforted.

It was light. He was consumed with thirst. Jack put water in his mouth and washed the blood from his face with a great strong hand that seemed larger than his aching head. Then for an instant he was a child; a big face staring down at him. He could hear the shouting of the men and the grumbling of the camels. They would go on. The fear that they would leave him was greater than the fear of being moved.

He lay under the awning that lurched in time to his pain. He was shut in with the sound of his own voice moaning and cursing them. From outside Mohamet called up to him, 'Not yet, Reis. Not yet, Reis. They have gone ahead of us.'

They stopped. Jack fed him water. But no sooner had the pain and nausea subsided than they moved on again. The voice and the pain were indistinguishable. One by one the faces peered down at him. Poor old McCarthy, whose head they had successfully severed. The Consul squinting quizzically down, as if to say, 'What's this?' Emma then, fleet as a shadow, for he would close his mind against her. Then the unknown child, squatting by his head, staring intently, as if at any moment Laing might spring away from him. It was dark. Now the lamenting voice pleaded that they stop. But they did not. Nothing then. Their voices assuring one another that he was alive. The steady stars were above his face. His head was in Jack's lap. The water in his mouth tasted of blood.

'What has happened to me?' he said to Jack.

'You are hurt, Capitaine.'

'Who hurt me?'

'The Tuareg.'

But his mind would not turn back to comprehend it.

Light then, and the flattened faces hanging over him. Later he said to Jack, 'I thought I saw Babani, but he is dead.'

'No, Capitaine. Babani is not hurt. Harry is hurt. Rogers is dead. Yahia Mohammed is hurt. Mohamet is cut on the head.'

'No one else?'

'No one, Capitaine. Only the Christians.'

'And the child?' Laing asked. 'How did he escape?' Jack did not answer and Laing knew not to ask again.

They rested by a well. For two days he might lie still and not

296

be moved. Jack soaked the filthy clothing from him and washed him, singing grimly as he worked. His left arm was broken. He fainted when the camel driver set the bone. Jack bound it to his scabbard. His right hand was nearly severed above the wrist. It lay on his thigh, throbbing and inert. Before Jack bandaged it he saw the bone, but did not feel that it was part of him. He was helpless. When the call of nature came, he cried out to Jack, 'I can do nothing. You must help me.' Then, when it was done, 'I have no choice. I have no choice.'

After two days by that well they rode on again. He lay on the jolting litter and watched the sun burn its course through the thin stuff of the canopy. The faces came and went. The voices moaned and babbled in his ear. He lay by the fire with his head in Jack's lap while gruel was spooned into his mouth. He slept in the tent and woke and called out. Jack roused himself and brought water. Then nearby in the dark he talked aloud of Falaba. He told Laing how he would settle there when this was done and grow yams and take his place in the council hut among the wise men of the village and take three or maybe four young wives.

'How will you afford them?' Laing asked him. 'I cannot pay you.'

'With the gold from Timbuctoo, Capitaine. Jack le Bore will be a rich man.' He would buy a she-goat and keep her tethered by the hut and feed her on cassava roots.

When it was light Jack bathed his head and picked from its wounds fragments of shattered bone which he showed to Laing. He was stronger and might sit up, and even walk a little way, for he carried the worst wounds on his head and arms. The fingers of his left hand had begun to heal. He could feed himself and feel out cautiously the nature of his various wounds, so that now he recognised their separate voices as they cried out to him during the incessant hours of the day. He felt the great gash where they had tried to cut off his head and called out to Jack, 'I wore a chain around my neck and there was a key on a string.' Jack handed him the key on its severed thong and a little leather pouch.

He said, 'The glass was broken, Capitaine.'

Laing took it in his hand. For all the time it took them to load up the camels he sat feeling around the edges of the oval shape with his painful fingers. He did not open it. Nor did any image of what it contained come to mind other than that of the little golden bird with outstretched wings. He could just make out the shape of it through the leather. When it was time for them to lift him on the camel he put the key inside the bag and hid them both inside his shirt.

They must ride on. He could feel the strength was failing in him. The days passed more quickly now and grew confused and indistinguishable from one another. Frequently, when they halted, they found that he had fainted. On the last he was too exhausted to swallow more than a little water.

Then, while the sun still burnt through the canopy, it was still. They had come to a settlement. Dogs barked. He heard the women shrilling. He was lifted from the camel. New faces peered at him. He heard the intake of their breath and their little awestruck cries at the thing he had become. An old man came and squatted by him and touched his face lightly with a shaking hand, saying repeatedly, 'How can it be that he is alive?'

They carried him inside a tent. He slept and woke in dread that he must move again. He could smell meat. There was a fire. He could see the bright motion of the flames through the dark stuff of the tent and hear their eager voices interrupting one another. They feasted in honour of his arrival. He slept. When he woke again the fire was dead; the voices gone.

He cried out for Jack who had abandoned him. Then Jack's blurred voice said beside him in the dark, 'Taisez-vous, Capitaine. Dormez encore.'

When next he woke sun sparked through the rough weave of the tent. Jack lifted him and gave him milk to drink. He knew he need not move but might lie there night and day without disturbance. Sometimes he woke and it was light. Sometimes it was dark. He lay awake until he slept again. He kept his own time.

He woke. Inside the dark wool tent the light was dim but outside the opening it blazed and flashed. Jack sat cross-legged, polishing his trumpet. Yahia Mohammed lay stretched asleep on the farther side of the tent. Between them the box of instruments, the medicine chest, the portfolio, the skin of papers and the camel saddles were neatly stacked. He lay and recognised these things one by one. He knew what was inside them. He called to Jack to raise him and help him from the tent. He had one of the saddles dragged outside the tent so that he might sit upright against it. Then he had Jack bring his portfolio and dip his pen and hold his left hand steady by the wrist while he wrote to Emma, *I write with only a thumb and finger, having a very severe cut on my fore-finger.*

Yahia Mohammed had come from the tent. He spat onto the sand and came and squatted down by Laing, watching him write. 'Let me take the letter to Tripoli,' he said.

'Later,' Laing said. 'Later.' His head and arm ached with the effort of what he had done. He had Jack help him back into the tent. He lay down then with a great burden lifted from his mind. He had put her fears to rest. She would ask no more of him. He might sleep again.

There were days when his head ached so severely that he must lie blinded and nauseated inside the tent. Then, when the pain was most intense, he found the power to rise above it and look down. He saw the back of his head then. He bent over it, studying the gash; the pale gaping lips, the line of white. It was the wounded man at Shati who had followed him to the edge of the desert. It was the men in the darkened room at In Salah, the wounds of all four bodies inflicted into one. And it was himself. Though who Laing now was he could not have said. Once there had been such a man over whom, in the night, he sometimes wept and grieved.

Then whole days would pass when he might sit upright, walk out unaided from the tent, feed himself with the thumb and little finger of his left hand. In the late afternoon he came out and sat before his tent. It was set in a slight declivity so that the horizon clung closely to it and Mohtar's camp was hidden from his view. He was glad of the seclusion and without curiosity as to how they lived. The few figures that walked across the dingy blur of the skyline seemed to move without discernible purpose and quickly disappeared. Nor in that windy evening hour did the dunes themselves keep any final form but smoked and whirled like heaps of smouldering ash. Sometimes, as he sat watching, it seemed the low sun created there phantoms of an outer world, great forests, cities, armies that marched and wheeled. But none of these he would let speak to him. He was without memory or ambition. As he had learned to move Body only within the limits prescribed by pain, so Mind preserved its cautious stillness. He waited without impatience for the time when they would tell him that he must move on.

Towards nightfall food was brought to him over the rim of sand by a bent wizened servant of Mohtar's, who lit a fire for him and reached his crooked hands right into the flames to rearrange the branches of brushwood. Sometimes Sidi Mohtar accompanied him. He spoke with great kindness to Laing, praising him for his endurance, and urging him to drink camel's milk from a roughly carved wooden bowl. He was a holy man. He sat stroking his white beard and gazing at Laing in wonder. Sometimes he broke out in an extempore prayer to the effect that Laing's survival was a miracle of God. 'God is favourable to you,' he told him, 'even though you know him not.'

He begged paper and ink from Laing and wrote out a text from the Koran which he instructed Laing to steep in water so that he might drink the solution of the holy word and hasten his recovery.

'Later,' Laing assured him. 'Later.' He was moved by the old man's kindness to him. When he had gone he found that he could no more throw the little scrap of paper on the fire than if he had believed the old man's superstitions. He rolled it tightly and put it in the leather pocket with the portrait and the key.

Babani came and sat by him, clicking his tongue and shaking his head in dismay at Laing's condition. He told Laing that the rest of the koffle had continued on its way to Timbuctoo six days after their arrival; that when Laing was strong enough the Sheikh Mohtar would provide them with protection to Timbuctoo. He said little else. Laing thought him altered and perhaps unwell. Shortly afterwards he left, making his way across the sand with an old man's heavy step.

When it grew dark he went inside the tent and waited for sleep. In the dark he read with his left fingers the strange terrain that now was Laing. Mind formed its inventory. He would tell it to the Consul.

300

Item: Five sabre cuts on the crown of the head and three on the left temple, all fractures from which much bone has come away.

Item: A ditto on the left cheek which has fractured the jaw-bone and divided the left ear. A most disfiguring wound. A ditto on the right temple.

Item: A dreadful gash on the back of the neck which slightly scratched the windpipe.

Item: A musket ball in the hip which made its way through the back, slightly grazing the back-bone.

Item: Five sabre cuts on my right arm and hand, three of the fingers broken, the hand cut three-fourths across and the wrist-bones cut through.

Item: Three cuts on the left arm, the bone of which has been broken, but is again uniting and a cut across the fingers of my left hand.

Item: One slight wound on the right leg and two ditto with a dreadful gash on the left.

Twenty-four in all, of which eighteen are exceedingly severe.

Mind, in the dark, read the writing of their swords, which told the story of a man who lay asleep and his enemies came by night and stood in a circle around his tent and fired with their muskets into it. How he was struck in the leg so that when he tried to rise he fell onto his left side. How they stood around him, slashing at him without mercy with their swords, until the right arm with which he tried to shield his head fell useless. How then they struck their final blow across the neck and left him for dead. Though it was the story of himself he could remember none of it. Nor, for all its itemising, could it form a picture of the thing their swords had carved anew; the thing that stood between him and the outside world. So that he called out to Jack in the night, 'You must not leave me, or who will vouch for me that I am Laing?'

Later he took the bag from his neck and felt with his fingers until he found the little golden bird. In the dark he prised free the oval thing it held and going out into the night buried it and smoothed the sand over the place where he had dug.

*   *   *

In the morning Yahia Mohammed sat by the opening of the tent, stitching at a saddle-bag. Laing watched him drag and cut the twine with his teeth. He said to him, 'When the Tuareg attacked us, why did no one fire back?'

'Jack ran away, *Reis*.'

'But Harris? Rogers?'

'They did not have their guns.'

'Why was that?'

'Sheikh Babani told them to give their guns to the Tuareg, *Reis*, so that they could protect us.'

'And you?'

'My leg was broken, *Reis*. I crawled to Babani's tent.'

'What did Babani do?'

'He did nothing, *Reis*. I never saw him. His servant took me in.'

'The rifle,' he called out suddenly to Jack. 'Where is my rifle?'

Jack raised himself in his corner of the tent and said, 'The Sheikh Babani took it when you were ill, Capitaine.'

'Why ?' he shouted angrily. Pain seized him at the back of the skull, so that he must cover his eyes with his hand.

'He has sent it to be sold in Timbuctoo.'

'Why was this done without my knowledge?'

Jack said, 'We thought that you would die, Capitaine.'

'Fetch Babani here,' Laing told him.

He watched Jack trudge across the dunes but the light was intense and pained his eyes. He withdrew into the darkness of his tent. All the old grievances which he had forgotten returned to pace around and around in his aching head. How Babani had not repaid the four hundred dollars Laing had lent him at Beni Ulid, nor the hundred at Ghadames. How he had tricked him over the matter of the firewood.

Jack returned to say that Babani was ill and could not come to him.

'I shall go to him then.'

But he knew that he could not make his way there in the blinding light. He lay in the corner of the tent. His head ached cruelly. Babani sat inside his tent. Outside there was musket fire and shouting. He made no move. The black man came crawling and dragging his wounded leg, crying out for help. He sat inside his tent with his broad placid stare and made no

302

move. Babani laid his hand upon Laing's arm and said, 'No need, my son, the danger is past.'

By afternoon, when Babani's servant came to him and begged him to bring his medicine and help his master, Laing was too weak and agitated to move. Towards evening, when the pain had lessened and he was calmer, he sent Jack ahead into the camp to warn them of his coming. He had Mohamet carry the box of medicines and Yahia Mohammed support him, but as he left the tent Jack appeared over the crest of the surrounding sand calling out to him that Babani was dead.

'It is judgement on him,' Yahia Mohammed said. 'He cheated you, Reis. He conspired with the Tuareg to have you killed.'

He would be just. He would not accuse the dead, but he could feel no grief at Babani's death, though once he thought he had loved him.

In the morning he sent Jack to the tent of Sidi Mohtar, requesting that he might leave for Timbuctoo at once. That evening the old Sheikh came to him and explained that he had no way of knowing which of the goods in his safe-keeping were Babani's and which were Laing's. He told Laing that he had sent for Alkadir from Timbuctoo to act as arbitrator. Once the matter was settled he promised Laing that his son and an escort of tribesmen would see him safely to Timbuctoo.

'When will that be?' Laing asked him.

'Soon, Reis, soon. The messenger has been sent.'

It was afternoon. He sat outside the tent. A man came over the rim of the sand. He saw his head first. Then his white robes blown to one side by the wind. Only when he came up to Laing and spoke his name did he realise that Alkadir had come more quickly than he had thought possible.

The young man wept. His hands which he had extended to Laing, hung uselessly before him. Repeatedly he shook his head and cried out, 'Walahi. Walahi. How is it that you are alive?'

'It is hard on you,' Laing told him. 'I have grown accustomed to it, but it is hard on you.'

They sat in silence until Laing said, 'Babani is dead, then. I am sorry for it.'

'It is the will of God, Reis. His fate had come to him.'

'Some say his sickness was a visitation on him; that God was incensed with him because he betrayed me to the Tuareg.'

'God knows,' the young man said, shaking his head to and fro in his distress. 'I do not know.'

They said nothing for a time, but the sight of Alkadir had wakened Laing's mind from its long torpor. Presently he asked, 'Is Abdullah in Timbuctoo?'

'No, *Reis*. It is said that the white man came by the river to Youri and from there to Sultan Bello at Sokoto. Nothing has been heard of him since.'

'How many days will it take us to ride to Timbuctoo?'

'Five days, *Reis*.'

All this unmeasured space of time he had lived without curiosity, so close to his goal. He said to Alkadir, 'When can we leave?'

'When I have sworn before the Sheikh which goods are mine and which are yours.'

When Babani died Laing had murmured in his heart, 'God has struck down the man with whom he was incensed, who had strayed from the right way.' Yet within days of Alkadir's arrival the same sickness had spread throughout the encampment and struck down the good old Sheikh who had taken Laing under his protection and succoured him. Laing, who had not until now ventured into the vicinity of the camp, went to Mohtar's tent and treated him as he would for yellow fever, which the symptoms resembled. But Mohtar was old beyond the reckoning of anyone else still living in the camp. Within two days of the onset of the illness he was dead, and Laing himself lay in his tent racked by the same symptoms.

For two days and two nights Jack nursed him and brought him water, and sprang up quickly in the night when Laing called out to him, and sang and talked till he was still again. On the third night Laing woke and heard moaning and retching on the far side of the tent. 'Jack,' he called out, 'Jack.'

When there was no answer he found himself too weak to rise and go to him.

'Ah Jack, poor Jack,' he cried out. 'Where have I brought you?'

Later, when Jack cried out, Laing said in his confusion, 'Are

304

you hurt, too? They told me you were not. Surely they would not try to kill you, too.'

Jack babbled in delirium of yams and brandy and names and places that were strange to Laing. Towards dawn he soiled himself so that the tent reeked with it and Laing called out wearily, 'You must see to yourself. I can do nothing for you.'

For the next two days Harris and Mohamet tended them as best they could. At night they both raved in their delirium so that the old man who continued to bring their food and firewood reported that the tent of the Christians was possessed by demons. On the third morning Jack was silent. Harris came and turned him over and told Laing that he was dead. Mohamet and Harris dragged his body a little distance from the tent and buried it.

They carried Laing to the graveside. He and Harris spoke the Lord's Prayer from memory. Then the three of them repeated the Adun, the prayer of departure. By nightfall Harris had collapsed from these exertions. Three days later he was dead of the same fever.

Still Laing survived. As the days went by something of Mind and Body were returned to him. He had strength enough to make the five-day crossing to Timbuctoo. Nothing more was required of him.

The month of Ramadan had fallen in the hottest season of the year. By day an exhausted stillness hung about the camp. Laing waited for nightfall in the empty tent. He spent the last hour of the day watching the light wane in the confined area of dust around his tent. He knew now the vast indifference of this place; the surface nature of it.

All that was available to the eye or understanding was volatile, illusory, subject to no permanent shape. He was familiar with the cold playfulness of the thing that worked it.

At night he lay alone in the tent, turning his throbbing head from side to side in the soft sand. Around and around the people paced. Emma, at a distance, dressed in white and shrunken to a child, came down among the little trees searching for her brother, but came no nearer. Ossy rode on Jack's shoulder looking imperiously about him, pointing to something on the ground. Once the Consul looked at him and turned away. Babani and the old Sheikh Mohtar came and sat by him so vividly that he must remind himself that they were dead.

A small koffle had come from Timbuctoo and rested in the encampment overnight before moving on to the North. Yahia Mohammed came to him, begging that he might be allowed to travel with them and take his letters to the Consul. When Laing questioned him he shed tears and said he did not wish to travel on with him and be mistaken for a Christian and be killed. Laing swore at him steadily and bitterly; that he should desert him now, when Jack was gone, when he was the last of that brave troop that had ridden with him out of Tripoli. The pain sprang in his head. He struck out a useless blow which wrenched his arm and was easily evaded.

Some moments later, when he had recovered himself, he sent Mohamet after the camel driver to tell him that he scorned to keep any man in his service against his will and would have the letters ready for him to take by nightfall. He took out his portfolio and undid the skin in which his completed notebooks were sewn. He turned the pages written in his erstwhile hand, the story of his life as Laing. For the final entry on the thirtieth of January he had written, *Have reached the well at Timissao in the safekeeping of our escort . . .*

He questioned Mohamet as to how many days had passed since then and sent again to Yahia Mohammed to confirm this. They both agreed that after the attack they had travelled three days, then rested two days, then travelled twenty days; that four months had passed since they had come to Mohtar's camp. As near as he could reckon it was the first of July. He wrote it at the top of the page. *My dear Consul*, he wrote. It was many weeks since he had spoken his own language. After Jack's burial it had died finally on his lips. Now, like some forgotten childhood tongue, it was restored to him, rich in memory and allusion. All that he had heard and surmised about the attack, all that he remembered and had puzzled over since came crowding into Mind at a speed that the clumsy labouring of his left hand across the page could never hope to match.

I have suffered much, he wrote, *but the detail must be reserved until another period, when I shall 'a tale unfold' of base treachery and war that will suprise you . . .*

He gave instead the catalogue of his wounds which must tell their own story and finished with scrupulous instructions about the just payment due to the camelman. He gave Yahia Mohammed the camel that Jack had ridden and sufficient money to buy food as far as Tripoli. The Consul would pay the wages owing him at an increased rate from the day that he was wounded in Laing's service. Then he thanked Yahia Mohammed curtly for his former loyalty and turned away from him.

The sudden vigour of mind that had been awakened by the writing of the letter deserted him now. He lay in the tent brooding over how one by one they had betrayed and abandoned him. Jack, even Jack, had left him in his hour of greatest need.

At nightfall, out of very loneliness, he was drawn to join the circle of men who broke their fast outside Mohtar's tent. He would avoid their eyes and the reflection in them of his disfigurement. In his modesty he sat back from the line where the flapping firelight gave way to sudden dark. There he kept company with Mohtar's gaunt brindled herd dogs whose outstretched paws touched exactly on this line, whose bodies lay tense and watchful in the dark beside him.

Food was brought him in a wooden bowl, but he had no appetite and was reluctant to eat before them with his left hand, lest he bring their contempt upon him. In the shadows he pinched up portions of bazeen and mutton between his fingers and fed them to the dogs, half-fearful of their teeth. But they took these morsels delicately between their narrow jaws without touching his hand or betraying him by a sound.

They sat in silence. Only the great hemisphere of stars suggested there was anything beyond the circle of unfamiliar faces. Occasionally a servant pushed his way between them and tossed an armful of brushwood on the fire, so that it blazed and sent large sparks spiralling upward. The faces altered then, so that sometimes he saw Babani and sometimes Alkadir, who he knew had returned to Timbuctoo. Has he come back, he thought, to travel with me? Once Bagoola leered at him. Once he saw the wounded man from Shati and wondered, Did he die then? There was a child who moved outside the circle of seated men. Sometimes, when the fire flared, Laing saw his face staring intently at him from under an outstretched arm or over a shoulder. Once he made out his slight shape leaning in perfect confidence against one of the dogs with his arm thrown about its neck. Is he the same, Laing thought? Was he real? After a time he rose silently and withdrew. Behind him their voices rose as if his going had released them.

He sat outside his tent. Young Mohtar came striding over the ridge of sand, thrusting his long stick ahead of him. He greeted Laing and squatted down by him. He told Laing that he must travel to In Salah.

Laing said, 'You have promised to take me to Timbuctoo.'

'I have no choice, *Reis*,' the young man told him. 'I must negotiate with the Tuareg on the safe conduct of the caravans in the cool weather.'

'Who will take me, then? You have given your word.'

'My kinsmen will take you – but, *Reis*, I have come to beg you to travel with me to In Salah.'

He said softly to Mohtar, 'I cannot go back.'

'*Reis*, I beg this of you. You will be killed. The tribesmen outside Timbuctoo know of your survival. They are incensed against all Jews and Christians.'

In the slow cautious speech that now was his, Laing told him, 'It is my destiny not to die until I have seen the great river. Look how I have been struck down by misfortune beyond the strength of mortal man and still I am here, my wounds heal. Look how the sickness passes over me. You must trust me to my fate.'

It was agreed then that Laing would remain in the camp until the feast of Birain was celebrated. Then Mohtar would have his kinsmen escort Laing to Timbuctoo and there introduce him to men powerful enough to give him protection.

Laing took the key from the pouch and, opening the box of silent instruments, drew out the last two remaining bags of silver. One only he withdrew for himself and returned to the pouch, the rest he gave to Mohtar. He took pen and paper and wrote consigning all the merchandise to him. He was free now of everything that might provoke their envy.

When Mohtar left him he went inside the tent and set about writing the letter that he would take on the first stage of its passage to Tripoli.

I have now obtained permission to proceed to Timbuctoo, he wrote, *but it is at the expense of everything that I have got. I have no alternative, and I consented because I am well aware that if I do not visit it, the World will ever remain in ignorance of the place, as I make no vainglorious assertion when I say that it will never be visited by Christian man after me.*

He watched the words come haltingly onto the page.

With Timbuctoo my research must for the present cease, as I have no funds to carry me further: it is therefore my intention, as soon as I possess myself of such information as I desire, to mount a fleet maherry and return to Tripoli. I shall be in Ghadames, please God, early in November, where I expect to be greeted by a courier from Tripoli.

The taste of tea came into his mouth as he wrote. Could the Consul send him tea and sugar? And a little tin teapot to brew it in? He remembered Ghadames and the chill descent of winter in September and October. In November it would be colder still. He wore sandals now or went about with naked feet. He asked for stockings. He could write no more. His left arm ached, his eyes watered so that he could scarcely see the page, yet he forced himself to continue.

I dare not yet trust myself with my feelings; for which reason I have not attempted a line to my dearest Emma. I shall make trial at Timbuctoo and in the meantime remember me with kindest love and beg her to think nothing of my misfortunes for all may yet be well.

He dipped the pen and placing it in the crippled fingers of his right hand gripped the damaged wrist with his left and forced it painfully across the page until his name was written, Laing. The illusory sense of other voices in the tent, his power to assume his former self as he spoke to them, deserted him when he stopped writing. He lay back, sick and sweating with the effort. In the morning Yahia Mohammed and young Mohtar rode out of the encampment to the North. Except for his servant Mohamet he was left finally and bitterly alone.

It was only a matter of days now until he set out on the final short lap of his journey. On the night of the feast of Birain he sat among Mohtar's kinsmen by the fire. Through the wavering air above the flames he saw again the child squatting on his hunkers watching him. He smiled, though what if any alteration to his face that painful movement made he did not know. It surprised him when the child smiled back,

309

with a shy sideways lowering of the head. On the following night he was there again on the far side of the fire staring steadily at him. Laing beckoned him with a movement of the head. Immediately the child got to his feet. Laing watched him trot behind the lighted circle of men, who ignored him entirely. He sat down a little way from Laing, then slowly propelled himself closer by digging his heels ahead of him in the sand and dragging himself after them. Presently he rested his shaven head against Laing's arm. 'Are you not frightened of me?' Laing asked him.

'No, Reis. I am not frightened.'

Laing gripped his wounded wrist and with a great effort reached forward and pinched up a portion of bazeen and mutton in the fingers of his right hand. The child took it and poked it carefully into the corner of his mouth.

He is merely begging, Laing told himself.

When he felt the child's slight weight against his shoulder again, he said, 'Do you want me to give you more to eat?'

'No,' the child said. 'Not now.'

Laing saw him clench and unclench his fists at his side. He was half asleep with warmth and pleasure. 'What is your name?' Laing asked him.

The child smiled at him.

For three days the feasting continued by moonlight; the smell of roasting meat and singeing hair hung about the camp. On the fourth morning Laing rode out of the camp of Sidi Mohtar. The boy Mohamet led his camel. Although he now had the strength to sit upright on it, he was lashed as before with rope to the saddle to prevent strain on his wounded arms. Behind him a single sumpter-camel was loaded with the box of useless instruments, Jack's trumpet in its case, the empty medicine chest, the portfolio and the skin of completed notebooks. Around his neck hung the red leather pouch with the key to the chest, the golden bird, his last remaining dollar and the old Sheikh's text. Fifteen of Mohtar's kinsmen travelled with him, accompanied by servants and camel drivers. By nightfall he sat among them at the fire in great pain and fatigue. But he was content. One day less lay between him and his goal. In the morning they moved on. On some days he caught glimpses of the child running over the pacing shadows of the camels, beating the dust from their flanks with a stick raised above his head. On other days he caught no sight of him. On the seventh day after their departure from the camp they arrived at Timbuctoo.

His arrival caused no stir in the city. He was as gaunt and brown as his companions and dressed now entirely as they did. Nothing but the odd shapes of his baggage and his wounded state might distinguish him from them, and as for Timbuctoo it was just another desert town like In Salah, like Ghadames.

He entered it without elation. Mohtar's men took him to a house which had been put at his disposal. In the evening the leading merchants of the town, among them Alkadir, came to pay him their respects. He had grown accustomed to the awe his misfortunes evoked in them. They bore him no hostility. One after the other they undertook to guarantee his safety in the town, for a month. Beyond that they could promise nothing and urged him to return with Mohtar's kinsmen to In Salah.

But though he nodded and thanked them, he knew that he could not go back; nor Mind, nor Body could endure it. The way he had come was sealed off from him as surely as if it had been erased from the surface of the earth.

'Could I not go westward by the river?' he asked Alkadir. 'By Jenne and Sansanding and then to the French factories on the Senegal?'

'That would be most dangerous of all, *Reis*.' The young man told him how Seku Hameda, the governor of Messina, to the west, was known to have sworn an oath never to let the Christians enter his country by the great river. 'He has had word from Sultan Bello of Abdullah's return, *Reis*. The Sultan Bello has told him of the Christians; how their visits will be mischievous and the cause of perpetual war. He would never let you pass through his land alive.'

On the following day he showed him a copy of a letter sent to the Governor of Timbuctoo by that same Seku Hameda.

To give you to know, Laing read, *that having heard that a Christian traveller desires to visit our country, but not knowing whether or not he is arrived at Timbuctoo, you are to endeavour to prevent his entry, if he is not already come, and if he is come, endeavour to send him away and take from him all hope of returning into our dominions.*

'Will I be safe here as they promised?' he asked Alkadir.

'As they promised, you will be safe for one month if you remain within the confines of the city. Then you must return with Mohtar's men.'

The time allowed him was very short for all he must do. The more so that everything was an effort to him now. He limped still but had not the strength in either arm to support himself by a stick. Nevertheless each day he made his painful progress through the town. The people watched him pass without molesting him. If sometimes little troops of children followed him it was silently and at a distance. He was even permitted to enter the great mosque and question the kadis about the history of the city. He went into the market place and questioned the traders there about the routes they travelled and especially about the course of the great river beyond the city. He asked repeatedly for news of Abdullah, but beyond the fact that he had reached Youri and then gone inland to Sokoto he could learn nothing of him. He sat in the doorway of his room in the late afternoon, when the light was less painful to his eyes, and recorded all this information slowly and painfully in his notebook. In the evening Mohamet brought him his supper of rice and meat, the gift of one or other of the merchants who had befriended him. Sometimes they came to share his meal and to question him, as they had at Ghadames, about the world beyond the sea. But the writing made his head ache acutely at times. They saw he was in pain and, murmuring and bowing, they withdrew. By showing them the letter of credit from Mohammed d'Ghies he managed to raise a little money for his return journey. He sensed behind their generosity and courtesy a mounting desire for him to be gone before Seku Hameda used his presence in the town as an excuse to attack it.

But he would not go yet. He reckoned that the darkest night would be in five days' time. With some of the money he had raised he had Mohamet hire a horse, giving out that he did so for his own use. On the day itself he told the servants in the house that he was unwell and would see no one. He kept to his room, sleeping and resting throughout the day. When night fell he waited for the town to grow quiet. Then, wrapped in a dark burnous, he rode through the deserted streets alone, and on beyond the town for five miles to the south where he reached the town of Kabara. He rode on for a further two

312

miles and there saw spread before him the great still expanse of
the Niger.

He dismounted and stood for a long time, staring in simple
wonder that at last his eye might contain the thing it had craved
for so long. On its still dark surface the starry concave of the sky
was perfectly reflected, so that he seemed to see the universe
complete, its two halves sealed about by the dimly shining river.
It was accomplished. I required no more of him. But something
remained that all this time had been denied to him, the river's
source. He knew then that he could never have intended to turn
eastward and follow the river's course to Youri and the sea:
Clapperton's route, if he, poor man, were alive to lay claim to it.
Nor for all their persuasion was the route back across the desert open to him. All along, it seemed, he was destined to turn
west and follow the river until he reached Mount Soma and the
very spot where the spring gushed out between the rocks.

He would cross the mountains until he met his old route in the
wooded foothills of Mount Soma and travel along it to enter
Falaba from the east.

And the Jelleman would say:

'Come out from your sorrowful hut, Assana Yeera. Your
white stranger is returned to you.'

And the Jelleman's wives would sing:

'Who is this who has come from the mountains when we had
all supposed him dead?'

And the Jelleman would answer them:

'Look. It is your son. Arise, Assana Yeera. Come to the door of
your hut. It is your son who stands here. No obstacle has stood in
his way. He has jumped across the source of the great river
where it is small and weak and see, the gree-gree has attempted
to wrench his right arm from his body and failed, and the gree-
gree has tried to strike off his head from his body and failed.
Arise, Assana Yeera, and see for yourself how your dream has
misled you.'

Mind was resolved: The night was passing. He must return
before dawn broke. He mounted and turned his horse's head
back towards the city.

On the following evening he told Alkadir that he intended to
follow the river to Falaba.

'It is impossible, *Reis*.'

313

'You must trust me to my fate,' Laing told him. 'A way will be found.'

He set about his final preparations. He visited one by one the merchants who had promised to lend him money. With his right hand he signed as firmly as he could the promissory notes to be taken northward with the caravan to Ghadames in November. Each of them pleaded sternly with him to return across the desert under Mohtar's protection. To each he repeated simply, 'You must trust me to my fate.'

One of their number, Ahmadu Labeida, came to him after nightfall and told him of a caravan of merchants leaving in three days' time for Morocco. 'If you leave with them, *Reis*,' he told Laing, 'Mohtar's men and Alkadir will not oppose you. After three days I will ride after you and meet you at the well at Sahab and guide you back to the river far to the west of Messina. In that way we will avoid Seku Hameda and you can travel to the coast in safety.'

It was agreed. Laing had known that it would be so. In the morning he sent for Mohtar's cousin to explain that he would travel northward to Morocco and impose no further on his hospitality. He asked for no return on the silver and goods he had given Mohtar in the camp: merely for the gift of the three fresh camels they had provided for the journey into Timbuctoo. To this Mohtar's cousin readily agreed. Nor did Alkadir set up any opposition to this plan. They were anxious to be rid of him. Yet they had kept faith with him. He gave Alkadir his scarlet regimental jacket and his sword. For neither had he any further use. Jack's trumpet he sent back as a final gift to Mohtar.

He was prepared to go. There was nothing now to pack. The medicine chest and the box of instruments had not been opened. These he entrusted to Alkadir to distribute among the townsmen who had shown him kindness. What clothes he still possessed he wore. All that remained was to write to the Consul the despatch announcing his arrival in Timbuctoo, which only now it occurred to him that he had neglected to do.

My dear Consul, he wrote. *A very short epistle must serve to apprise you, as well as my dearest Emma, of my arrival at and departure from the Great Capital of Central Africa.*

He outlined his projected route as far as Seku, where he would rejoin the Niger.

Again, he ended, *may God bless you all. My dear Emma must excuse my not writing. I have begun a hundred letters to her, but have been unable to get through one; she is ever uppermost in my thoughts and I look forward with delight to the hour of our meeting, which, please God, is now at no great distance.*

It was done. He gave the letter to Alkadir, who would carry, it northward when the caravan left for Ghadames in November. He had Mohamet sew his journals and remaining papers into a waterskin. In the morning he said his farewells where the caravan had assembled in an open space on the northern edge of the city.

Together they prayed: 'Praise be to God. the Lord of all creatures, the most merciful, the king of the day of judgement. Thee do we worship, and of thee do we beg assistance. Direct us in the right way, in the way of those to whom thou hast been gracious: not of those against whom thou hast been incensed, nor those who go astray.'

Then, with the same rush of movement which always stirred him to hope and excitement, the camels rose and trotted forward. The people ran with them a little way for friendship's sake and then turned back.

That night by the fire he saw without surprise that the child who would not reveal his name had followed him here, too. He asked no one who he was. When the child sat beside him at the fire he shared his food with him as he had before. It was September. The nights were cold. When he lay back to sleep, the child crept close to him. Laing threw the hem of his burnous across him.

In the morning the sun burnt on his right cheek. He rode towards the North. He was pleased with this new beginning. It seemed that never before had he set out so hopefully with such freedom of spirit; such lack of earthly encumbrance. Those things he had carried with him in the past he could not clearly recall, but they had oppressed him and now he was relieved of them.

He rode. Mohamet walked beside him. Sometimes the child rode lightly in the bend of the camel's neck, singing or talking to Laing in a childish rigmarole that he could scarcely comprehend. Laing spoke, too, when some thought occurred to

315

him. He spoke his own language, letting his tongue find pleasure in the broad dialect of his boyhood, which he had learned
to curb among the English officers. So Alexander, when
moved to wrath, had spoken in the Macedonian tongue. But
there was no anger now nor frustration. He could never
remember a greater sense of peace and happiness.

When, on the third day, they reached the well at Sahab and
found no sign of Ahmadu Labeida, he felt no anxiety. He sent
Mohamet to the reis of the caravan to say that his master was
tired and would rest a little longer by the well. Only when the
koffle had moved on did he notice that the child had stayed
behind. His heart misgave him then that he was unarmed and
powerless to protect him, but the child had chosen freely.

He slept sitting upright, with his back leaning against a
tree. He was wakened by Mohamet's frightened voice saying,
'Look, Reis.' Riding toward them at a furious pace was a small
troop of men on camels.

Laing stood to watch their approach, but the glare reduced
them to shadows. He shut his eyes then. They would come in
due course whether he watched them or no. He leant back
against the tree. Then he heard Mohamet call out, 'It is nothing, Reis. It is only Ahmadu Labeida.'

'Best get across the river,' he told the child. He saw him run
down to the river bank and squat down to watch the rush of
water which Laing could hear now, clear and incessant,
between the rocks. Then he stood and reached out tentatively
with his bare foot, as if he would attempt to jump onto the first
stone.

'Not yet,' Laing called out to him. 'You can step across it at
the source.' He was in great pain but might detach himself
from that. The odour of the water, its cool breath, played
upon his face.

'Go on,' he said now to the boy. He was tensed; bent forward slightly with his fists clenched at his sides, willing himself to jump.

'Jump,' Laing called after him. 'It's the next one's difficult.'
For the first rock was flat and raised above the water, but the
second, which demanded a longer jump, was covered in a
brown slippery growth and gave no secure footing. The child
was shivering slightly, staring down at the white swirling
water. 'Jump now,' Laing told him. The more one hesitated the

316

harder it became. 'Look at the rock. Don't look at the water.'

There. He had jumped and crouched unsteadily, gripping with his bare feet on the slippery stone. There was, he remembered now, the small ledge on the left and the slight declivity on the right.

'That was well done,' he called after him.

The last three stones were flat and close together. The boy went leaping across them with his arms outstretched, without any hesitation. Laing watched him climb the far bank and run between the reddish peeling trunks of the pines until he was hidden in the dark areas between. 'He's safe,' Laing thought, and turned back again to where he lay looking upward against the light.

Part VI: Passage to Leghorn

Towards evening on July the fourteenth, 1827, a small caval-
cade could be seen to make its way through the alleys of the
Menchia and out across the plain before the town. Two outriders, their sashes and turbans trimmed with scarlet and
gold, came first, with the consular flag flicking at the head of
their upright spears. Behind them rode Colonel Warrington in
his blue dress coat and cocked hat, the fresh ostrich plumes
tumbling in the breeze. He was escorted by his Vice-consul,
Thomas Wood and followed by his two elder sons. Then came
the carriage in which his wife and daughters sat and jolted
through a haze of dust. The heavy hot mantillas were thrown
back from their faces. A bottle of rose water circulated
among them, to moisten the handkerchiefs they pressed
repeatedly to their lips and temples with stiff gloved fingers.
The mother's turban rested on her knee. It, too, sported a
number of new feathers which made it too lofty for the
cramped interior of the carriage. Jane and Louisa wore
white. Emma, on this second anniversary of her marriage,
wore her wedding muslin, lined with a becoming shade of
apricot, a colour of the Consul's own choosing. Behind them
so enveloped in dust as to appear as shadows, rode two more
outriders and the Consul's *chouish*.

They were bound for the Bastille Day celebrations at the
French Consulate, which for many years Colonel Warrington
had so skilfully avoided. In March the Bashaw had sent for
him and told him of an unsubstantiated report that Laing was
dead. He assured the Consul that he himself did not believe it,
and when no other news came it seemed that the great
silence off the desert quite outweighed that one unlikely
rumour. Still, the Consul deemed it necessary to put in an
appearance that would demonstrate to the small community

his unshaken conviction that Laing was still alive. For that reason, although Emma's health was certainly no better than when he had last made it his excuse, he insisted that she attend, decked in some colour that bore no association with mourning.

At the town gates they all dismounted. The livery stable provided a palm canopy where Jane might settle her mother's turban and tweak a few curls into sight from under its brim. She and her sisters adjusted one another's mantillas, so that every trace of their fair skin was hidden. Then, at a word, the little troop reformed. The *chouish* went first, beating off impertinent starers with his stick. Behind him came Mrs Warrington and her daughters, pressed together two by two and making what head-way their narrow skirts would permit, while the Consul and his sons and outriders surrounded them with their hands resting on the pommels of their swords.

When they reached the French Consulate, the ladies withdrew to remove their mantillas and refresh themselves. The Consul waited with his sons and Wood among the fragrant shrubs in the courtyard until they reappeared. Ahead of them a flight of stairs led to the open door of Rousseau's reception room, which had been tastelessly draped with a *tricolore* bunting. It seemed to the Consul that, as he waited, the din of voices from inside became more subdued. Word of his arrival would have sped before him. Now, undoubtedly, they waited for that moment when he must finally present himself as Rousseau's guest at a celebration of those principles he most abhorred. As he approached the steps with his wife he recalled his true motive in coming.

'You will excuse me,' he told her and, transferring her to Fred's arm, placed Emma on his own and led her briskly forward so that the two of them entered the room slightly ahead of the rest of the party. He had timed his arrival with care. The rest of the diplomatic community were already assembled.

There was a noticeable hush. People turned from one another to face the door. There stood the Consul with his great gloved hand pressing on his daughter's narrow shoulder. There was no one in the room who did not know the full poignancy of her story: that she was a bride and not a bride. (I was wrong in that, the Consul thought afterwards; I should have had her wear white.) No one could fail to imagine the suffering she had endured on his behalf; no one had not heard the rumour of his death. But many of the people there had not set eyes upon Emma since her marriage. It astonished them to see her become the very thing which they would have her be. There had always been, they remembered, something startled, something spiritual, about the girl's appearance, but in the past it had seemed an ephemeral thing, a residue of childhood innocence that would at any moment glow, substantiate itself and thicken into something ordinary. Now it seemed that all that was untouched and expectant in her had taken on profound and permanent significance; that she had been lifted out of the normal processes of time and caught, poised between the inception and completion of an act. In the two years since they had seen her her eyes seemed enlarged in her narrow face. As befitted her married state she had grown her hair and wore it twisted up in a Grecian knot at the back of her head. But it had altered her hardly at all. The line of her chin and the set of her small ears were as clear and defenceless as when she had worn her hair cropped. The colour of her simple dress set off her lovely pallor to perfection. The only ornament she wore beside her wedding band was a gold chain about her neck on which hung Herr Knutson's portrait of her husband. As her father propelled her forward, it seemed to the de Breughels, the Knutsons, the Rossinis, even to the crude Coxes, that all those sensibilities which the world's demands had forced them to cast aside might be preserved for ever in Emma's slight form. A way was made for her and from the edges of the room a discreet patter of gloved hands was just audible.

Baron Rousseau greeted her with a charming deference. His stout outlandish wife, who had never been seen to take any active part in these functions in the past, now came forward and kissed Emma and led her by both hands to a dais at the side of the room. There Timoleon reclined on a chaiselongue, protesting and apologising that the doctor would only allow him to attend at all on condition that he stayed in this ridiculous position.

Attention was quite diverted from the meeting between Rousseau and the Consul. This, which might have taken a variety of forms, became a simple handshake and a particularly intimate exchange of glance between two fathers who must watch their children suffer.

For the next hour the two young people sat side by side upon their platform. At first it was observed that they were shy with one another. Then perhaps the sentiment rising from the crowded room encouraged Emma, for she was seen to lean forward with some comment and he, poor young man, to laugh, until, presently, they both were laughing and talking with the freedom of old friends.

No one intruded on this delicate and interesting reunion, although nearly everyone came close enough at one time or another to smile and dip their heads to one side with a look of sympathetic understanding. For it was clear to all but those closest to Emma how tragically they mirrored one another's condition.

The Consul was aware only of their regal attitude upon the dais, and the instinctive homage paid to it. He was profoundly moved. In all humility he might claim a divine hand had led him to enthrone all the old and sacred values, innocence, fidelity, sacrifice, in the very midst of the devil's own junketings. With perfect timing he withdrew his party early in the evening, before the effect of it might fade. They spent that night at their own consulate and early in the morning returned to their retired life of waiting in the Garden.

It was many months before Emma was to appear again in public. The summer passed and the restless irritable months of winter returned again, when the desert wind rattled the windows of the country house and made everything gritty and unpleasant to the touch. Then an excuse to visit town was as eagerly awaited as was the chance to escape from it in the summer. On three occasions that winter the candles blazed in the British Consulate and the doors of the *skiffir* were opened to the diplomatic community. On each occasion a British man-of-war had come into the harbour and the Consul's daughters rode in from the country to entertain the young officers to cards and dancing; that is, Jane, who was always a great favourite with them, and Louisa who, some said, had grown to be the prettiest of the three. Emma never accompanied them. When discreet enquiries were made of those intimate with the Consul's family the answers were always the same. Frau

Knutson would sigh and say simply, 'She is an angel', but with such a look and such an emphasis as to imply a world of physical and mental anguish. Madame de Breughel, appealed to more subtly as to whether Mrs Laing wore mourning yet, replied with quelling dignity, 'Whom should she mourn? Poor child, she is as yet neither wife nor widow.'

No news of Laing had come. The social pleasures of the frigates' stay in port concealed from no one the nature of their presence. Three times the Consul had requested from the governor of Malta that they be sent to lend support to his demands that the Bashaw mount a search in the desert for Laing. As each was sighted entering the bay the Consul demanded an audience from the Bet-el-Mel. Three times the Bashaw promised to hasten the departure of one of Babani's kinsmen on that quest. Three times assurances came from Ghadames that his departure was imminent. But it did not take place. Excuses arrived which were less and less convincing.

My camel is grazing in the desert seven miles from here, he wrote on one occasion to the Consul, and on another, *Your Excellency knows well that the ship of the desert is the camel, and the sails of that ship are made with silver.*

The Consul was determined to read nothing into this beyond the normal evidence of humbug and trickery. He was convinced that Laing might yet be alive. It seemed probable that he was wary of entrusting his despatches to his French hosts along the Senegal. Who could blame him? But it is well known of the desert that nothing ever disappears in it. Everything is accounted for. Nothing stays hidden. He was comforted by the assurance that he had done everything in his power for Laing. He was sustained, too, by the extraordinary composure of his daughter Emma. At some point during that year, the few people who still saw her regularly agreed that a new strength had entered her, making her impervious to the shifts of hope and despair she might well have succumbed to.

The Consul was inclined to attribute this change to her triumph at the Bastille Day reception. Certainly for a day or two afterwards she seemed to have regained the old animation, that made them exclaim, 'There is the real Emma.' She had been able to join in her sisters' talk of who had danced with whom and bring the authority of long absence to a discussion on Amy Coxe's loss of looks. Even when the talk of the day passed onto other topics, of which she had no knowledge, there was still something in her bearing that made them feel some permanent change had taken place.

Never since those terrible hours when she had learned of the attack on Laing, and life had seemed suspended in her, had she given way to grief or shown the slightest wavering in her intention to be ready for her husband's return and to accompany him in whatever state he was back to Europe. The trunk which had been brought out, when it appeared that Laing's return was imminent, remained beside her bed in the crowded room. She continued to lie down at night and sleep and wake again and rise; to speak in short distracted sentences to her sisters and to move among them remarkably free, it seemed, from any interest in happiness or sorrow.

She understood the little they required of her. She must remain exactly as she was. Not grow strong; her delicacy was the thing they most approved in her. Not succumb completely, for that would show defeat. Not grieve openly, for all grief expends itself. Then a new beginning must be made and that was not to be.

So she continued to move in the old diurnal round about the house. In winter she read for an hour in the salon with Ossy and Louisa, as her father had wanted Laing to do. She set them little tasks to write. Sometimes, in a fit of spirits, they would recruit the others to take part and act out some scene from their father's Shakespeare, or one of the wild tales of love and death she had learnt as a child from their mother's maid. Whenever the weather permitted them to go out on their morning ride and she was alone, she left the sofa and began to walk rapidly around and around the verandah until the chilling sweat broke out inside her clothes and she was forced to hold onto the railings to steady herself in her fatigue. Always when they returned she was sitting where they had left her. In the afternoons in the salon, or as the weather grew milder on the verandah, she continued to sew intently at the clothes that she would wear in her new life in Europe. After dinner she withdrew to her bedroom where her sisters, peering through the crack in the door, might see her kneeling and sorting without haste through the contents of her trunk, or writing with her box upon her knee so rapidly

326

that sometimes she gripped the wrist of her right hand with her left, as if to urge it across the page towards the completion of some task.

It was to Laing she wrote, although for many months she had not troubled to take these missives to her father's office. The store of words remained inaudible until she was alone. Then she discovered them posed already in her mind; demanding to be written. She wrote more freely now than when she had been certain he would read them.

Laing, Laing, it is he himself who did you wrong. Why did you permit it? You taught me to believe in destiny and I have always known it was my destiny to leave this place. My trunk is waiting. I have begun upon my journey. Nothing, nothing that he can do will now prevent me.

She was almost fearful of the speed with which her pen was drawn across the vacant page, trailing words she hardly recognised as hers.

He will never let me marry. He sent you to your death rather than you should have me. Just as he sent Walter Tyrwhitt. Just as he would condemn poor, poor Timoleon.

She folded these messages swiftly without reading through them and kept them in the box.

There were other notes. Since the Bastille Day reception she had openly resumed her correspondence with Timoleon Rousseau. She did not ask her father's permission to do so, nor did she attempt to conceal from him what she did. Twice or thrice a week the little messages would come; not the passionate outpourings of the past, but snatches of gossip, extracts from the book he read. Always enquired after her health, never mentioning his own. Pity for him, gratitude for his kindness, made her answer in the same playful plaintive tone. She took care always to write in French; anxious lest in her own language she assume the tone of wild intimacy that had lately overtaken her pen.

One day in early March, when the wind off the desert was unseasonably sultry, she snatched away the little woollen scarf to ease her throat against her hands, and they noticed that she no longer wore the chain and pendant with Laing's portrait. No one summoned courage to mention it or wished to think what significance, if any, this might have. They were all aware now that the silence off the desert, which once had seemed a reassuring thing, had extended itself too long.

It was shortly after that that Baron Rousseau rode over to the British Garden from his country house further along the coast at Sukkara, and begged a second time that Emma might marry his son. Recently Dickson had warned him that the young man had only a year to live. With Emma beside him, it might pass in tranquillity and even joy; without her in a feverish anguish.

He placed on the Consul's desk a report in a recent French newspaper that an English traveller had been murdered outside Timbuctoo. He begged him to accept the fact and allow the two young people some happiness at least after all the suffering they had endured.

The Consul gave way to an outburst of ungovernable rage. Laing was alive. Emma was married to him. The report was a wicked lie, emanating, he was suddenly convinced, from Rousseau himself. Or, if it were true, why was Rousseau privy to facts that he knew nothing of, unless he had had some direct part in them? The Baron was seen to leave the house with his face grey and his hands shaking so with grief or rage that he had to be helped to mount his horse and take firm hold of the reins.

The Consul did not deign to tell his family of this interview, but he had been heard throughout the hushed passages and rooms to shout that the request was an insult to his daughter's honour, which he would defend with his life.

The following day was still and cool; the pleasantest to dawn for some time. The riding party set out early to take full advantage of it. Emma sat in the empty salon, fanning herself, by habit rather than necessity, with a letter she had written to Timoleon. In it she had made no reference to the distressing scene of yesterday. To do so could only give him pain. She said instead that she feared her father might intercept her messages again, and that therefore in future she would coax Tom Wood to act as emissary between them.

Will not this secrecy give zest to our innocent pleasures? she had written. *Is it not just that we defy the prejudices of our parents, as in the past we failed to do?*

She was waiting for Tom Wood now, listening to the indolent slip-slap movements of the servants in the passage until his polished shoes should ring busily among them. Presently she heard them, but even so it seemed she was ill-prepared for his presence in the room. He had taken her hands. He had kissed her cheek. She seemed scarcely to feel it.

He drew a chair up close to hers and reached out to take the little note, saying in a low conspirator's voice, 'Have you spoken of marriage to him? Have you given him any hope?'

But she would not yet relinquish it. She continued to rattle the folded paper impatiently before her face. Something in the air between them must be dispersed. 'Oh, I cannot,' she said.

'Why, Emma?'

'I'll write again. You'll come tomorrow?'

They went silent then, as if each had lost track of what the other said. She rose suddenly and went to stand by the window. Behind her Wood said softly. 'He's dying, Emma. What harm?'

What good? she might have said. What good is there in a dead man? She was breathless, and leant her head against the cool glass, thinking, He is repelled by me. I cannot feel. I cannot pity.

Behind her his voice continued, 'Don't you see how he is placed? He has nothing to offer you, but you could transform his last days on earth. Are you listening to me? Do you hear what I say?'

She rocked her head from side to side against the glass by way of answer.

'You know that he would marry you if you were free.'

'But I am not,' she said in a loud startled voice.

He sat where he was, watching in torment the narrow rigour of her shoulders, hearing the pain of which he was the cause. She had come to sit opposite him again, turning towards him a face that was grey and flattened with misery. Tears spilt intolerably down her cheeks without altering in any way its bleak expression.

'What is it?' he asked sharply. 'Is there something you have heard?'

'No. Have you?'

'Nothing . . . What is it, then?'

'Well,' she said with a long intake of breath. 'It is Laing. Oh,

329

how can it be? It is me. It is me.' She was sitting very upright on the edge of the sofa with her hands pinched between her knees, her thin arms tensed so that the elbows butted together, her whole being concentrated there in intense thought that utterly excluded him. 'I have not the strength to endure it.'

He was stunned by her unhappiness and his quick instinct for its true source. No words came to him, he could make no move towards her, but sat wretchedly watching her, across a great distance, rigid with denial. From the yard outside came the muffled clatter of the returning riders. There was no time. Now they leant towards one another, speaking quietly and urgently:

'If I say that he is dead you will tell me he is not.'

'I can tell you nothing. I know nothing.'

'I know he is dead. I have known it a long time. And don't you see, I am bound to live. I cannot help myself.'

And the door was flung open; the dogs running into the room, the people behind them talking across their shoulders in their loud outdoor voices, noticing nothing of what they had broken in upon.

As soon as the weather grew warmer, Emma took one of the servants down to the kiosk and had it swept free of the reddish dust that had accumulated there over the winter. The dust and exertion left her coughing and feverish and she was obliged to spend the next day in bed. But on the day following she was seen to walk down between the trees, carefully carrying the wooden box in which she kept Laing's letters and his portrait. After that, even when the days grew intolerably sultry, she made her regular habit to retire to the kiosk after dinner, returning only at nightfall. No one followed her. They were fearful that if they made their way along the cluttered path and pushed aside the vine they might surprise her in some wild abandonment of grief – for grief there must be, although no member of her family had ever seen it.

Only Ossy was sometimes drawn to the end of the Garden to kick his shoes idly through the dust in the spot where he thought he could just remember Laing's camp to have stood. No trace of it remained. Sometimes he crouched down to watch the frogs again describe their shallow graceful arcs

330

between the bushes by the well, but the chase could not absorb his interest as once it had. One afternoon, as he squatted in the still heat, he was startled to hear Emma's laugh nearby. On his next visit, hearing the unexpected sound again, he had ventured towards the kiosk. There was another voice, a man's. A moment later he recognised it as Tom Wood's. Something in it made him hesitate and then turn back towards the house. He avoided the spot after that. He told his father he was grown too old to take lessons from his sister. More and more he spent his time in the stables chattering in Arabic to the syces, following Harry with an exaggerated stride and pestering Fred to take him with him on his rides to the encampments at the edges of the desert.

But neither Fred's enquiries nor the Consul's frequent calls at the palace yielded any news of Laing. He reckoned now that any word direct from Laing himself must come by sea, perhaps from London, but May passed and June and July and still the mails brought nothing. Each day followed, with only the minutest variation, the pattern of the one before. Only Emma could have marked out the day in early spring when they had sat on the verandah before dinner, Jane and Louisa sketching one another; her mother sewing; Tom Wood reading his book. He had lowered it upon his knees and leant back in his chair with his polished boot resting on his knee. The backward angle of his head caused him to look at her from under lowered lids. He fixed his stare upon her and did not move it. It was she who looked away, aware that throughout the afternoon she had harboured a strange sensation which presently she identified as happiness.

Only she knew of the day soon after that when, as he sat beside her in the kiosk, she found she had reached out, as often in the past weeks it had occurred to her to do, and drawn her hand lightly down the stubble on his cheek. He had laughed comfortably then, laying his hand, which she could feel to tremble slightly, across her shoulder and pulling her towards him. The airborne smell of jasmine and the closer smell of dust compounded with the myriad deaths of insects were obscured by the odour of his breath which had taken on a profound and interesting sweetness.

And shortly after that he had pushed his way between the leaves of the vine and come without a word to sit beside her and cupped his hand about her breast while she leant back against him, laying her head upon his shoulder, drawing her open mouth slowly across his. 'Emma, Emma,' he was saying. His hand was thrust down upon her naked breast, and she, ah-ah with delight, clasped her hand above the flimsy stuff on his that moved beneath it.

'Good God' he was saying to her. 'Good God.' Then, in the voice of a man gone too far to save himself, 'Ah, Emma, I should not, my dear, really I should not.'

How apparent, how flagrant must be her happiness, and yet, though Gerda Knutson might exclaim how well she looked and the doctor wink and frown and say that he had evidently cured her but was damned if he knew how, and kind Madame de Breughel smile and say, 'My brave, brave Emma,' none, she was sure, guessed at the source of her well-being.

She laughed so when he told his stories about the goings-on of the town, but then he had always made her laugh. If his demeanour towards her had changed at all it was that now he was careful never to let his hand brush against hers, never to vie for her quick look, but to redouble his attentions to her mother and her sisters. And she, watching him eat at table with his neat fussy gestures, watching his small pale hands, would think, Are they the same? Can they be? But it was easier not to attempt to combine the clothed, restless sweating selves of the salon and verandah with the dark swollen landscapes of the touch, or those rapt altered features glimpsed in the underwater light of the kiosk. There he would cry out, 'Oh, oh, oh,' into her very being, and she whimper against him, possessed by joy which an hour later, as he held out her mother's skein of wool, she could not imagine.

Of Laing, and the thin tensile passion that had held her to him, she would not think. When she wrote her short cheering notes to Timoleon, she was careful not to disturb the papers in the box, lest her eye fall on the portrait or the creased and folded messages he sent her from the desert. Only sometimes, when the touch of her deep pleasure flung her this way and that, she would cry out as if a demon left her, shouting of grief and pain in quite another voice to hers. So that Wood must quickly rouse himself to press his mouth on hers, lest the sound travel up the still slope to the silent gathering on the verandah.

Once when he went quiet, he felt and heard that she was weeping. 'There,' he said absently, 'there.' Then, when she could not stop, 'Emma, what is it?'

'Oh, it is Laing,' she said.

He shrank from her then. Their arms and legs were wooden, knocking together as she tried to hold him, saying, 'No, no, it is not that I still want him. It is for what was denied him.'

And even when she had calmed sufficiently to hide her thoughts, she wished there were a grave where she had some assurance that he lay at peace and might not reappear out of the desert, wild-eyed, sunken-cheeked, staring with horror at her feckless pleasure.

In August the Consul was summoned to the palace. The grave deference of the Bet-el-Mel, the look of concern on the Bashaw's dissipated features left him in no doubt of the news they had for him. Standing by the dais in the audience chamber were two young men. The elder, a handsome youth, was introduced to him as Babani's nephew, Alkadir, who, Laing had written, would carry his despatches back to Tripoli; the younger, Mohamet, a servant who had accompanied Laing out of Timbuctoo. He was ordered to give his evidence before the Consul.

The tale was simple. Laing had stayed in Timbuctoo for two months. Of his own free will he had left the city. He did not know exactly where they were going but the sun had been on his right cheek. On the third day his master was attacked and killed. He himself had been wounded in the defence of his master. Slowly he unwound his turban and displayed before them a healed white sword scar across his shaven skull. They had not killed him too, only because they had thought him already dead. The next day a traveller passing by had given him water to drink and helped him to bury Laing. Together they had travelled back to Timbuctoo.

'And the papers?' the Consul asked him.

'I was stunned by the wound and did not think of the papers.'

'But your master had papers with him?'

'Yes, there were papers. He kept them in a skin.'

'What became of them?'

'God knows. I do not know.'

'And the letters?'

'There were no letters.'

But there must have been the letters he would have written nightly to Emma, at the very least. Had he left the journals with Alkadir? He, too, claimed to know nothing of them. The Consul was immediately suspicious. He insisted that the two men accompany him to the Garden, so that Laing's poor widow might put to them what questions she wished about his final days. There, under Fred's questioning, they revealed that they were being fed and clothed by Mohammed d'Ghies and living under his protection while they were in Tripoli.

Yet whatever the significance of that might be of Laing's death there could be no doubt. Nothing, the Consul thought, was more affecting than the sight of his daughter's slight form between these two strange men who must, he supposed, have known her husband more intimately than ever she had. She questioned them in their own tongue. He was touched by the gravity and compassion of their manner towards her, and was assured by her demeanour that they had omitted to tell her the manner of his killing. Repeatedly she asked them if there had been letters addressed to her. But the young Alkadir shook his head. There had been nothing.

This the Consul was unwilling to accept. During the winter news reached the town that a young Frenchman of humble origin and no education had arrived in Toulon with a written account of a journey he claimed to have taken from Port St Louis on the west coast to Timbuctoo and thence across the Sahara to Morocco. Here was the print of the cloven hoof indeed. For it was inconceivable that such a man should perform such a feat.

Not for one instant did the Consul doubt that the details of Timbuctoo on which the authenticity of René Caille's claim was based came from any source other than Laing's missing journals; obtained he knew not how by Rousseau, smuggled across to France and there used to give substance to the fantasies of some half-crazed vagrant. That a man's very life could be so plagiarised appalled the Consul. It seemed his son-in-law's mangled body must bleed afresh at this new violence done him.

The temptation to parade his daughter's mourning figure through the town was powerful, but to be resisted. He let it be known that no member of his family would wear a trace of mourning until the truth were finally known. Until Laing's final resting place was identified, until the lost letters were returned with their seals unbroken, until Laing's journals be delivered into his hand, no ceremony of his would lay Laing's ghost to rest. He struck his flag from the roof of the town consulate and announced his intention of retiring to the country as the only way he could be sure of severing all contact with Baron Rousseau.

In March word spread through the town that the priest had been rowed across the bay to Sukkara to administer the final rites to Timoleon. That evening it was known that the poor young man was dead. Burial follows fast in hot latitudes. At dawn, as the Christian cemetery lay beyond the western walls, and it was forbidden to carry the dead through the town, the cortège set out by barge. In the lead, under an awning of black crêpe, was Timoleon's narrow coffin, draped first in black and then in a gaudy *tricolore*. In a second barge were the Baron and his wife; in a third the consular servants, wailing and ululating. As it crossed the bay other similar craft were unmoored from jetties and took their place in the procession: the Coxes, the de Breughels, Hassuna d'Ghies. Then, surprisingly, as the cortège passed the landing for the English Garden, the consular barge, with its black side curtains lowered, was seen to glide from the jetty and bring up the rear. The line of little boats passed under the palace walls to a solemn cannonade and rounded the cape to the landing for the cemetery. There the coffin was lifted and carried, to where the priest was waiting with the black mourners trailing behind, along the dusty track between the graves. The brief service of committal was spoken; the coffin slowly lowered. There was a moment then to glance, under cover of veiling, and notice who was there and who was not.

The barge from the English Garden had given particular cause for speculation. Now Tom Wood was recognised and had, of course, always been a friend to Timoleon. Of more interest was the woman leaning on his arm. Her face was hidden by her mantilla but she was identified, by her extreme fragility, as Emma Laing. She was dressed entirely in black and carried in one gloved hand a spray of orange blossom as casually as if she had plucked it as she walked down to the jetty. She, poor soul, was unable to keep still in her evident distress, now turning away as if she could not bear to be a witness to this act, now turning back to lean her face against Tom Wood's shoulder while he bent down his head to comfort her. Now he raised her free hand to his lips and chafed it between his own, as if it were intolerably cold.

Only when the family had thrown in handfuls of the dusty earth and turned back towards the quay did she move forward and throw in her flowers. Then she turned, almost running, while Tom Wood caught and steadied her. Some thought her brazen to have come at all and wondered if she had glimpsed, in the course of her pacing to and fro, the wording on the headstone: *Timoleon Rousseau: Mort á Tripoli, victime d'un amour insensé.*

Others, more tolerant, had noticed how little aware she had seemed of herself, and reflected pityingly that this was the only rite of mourning she had been allowed for any of the young men who had loved her.

By the time she returned to the Garden this one show of grief had been concealed. But she had overtaxed herself.

Two days later she noticed she had coughed a speck of blood into her handkerchief. That afternoon, sitting on the verandah, she began to cough again. Her mouth went salt. She pressed her handkerchief to it, thinking she might vomit, and stood up in confusion and embarrassment. She heard Jane let out a small scream. The handkerchief was soaked with blood. She cupped her hands about it to hide it and felt blood trickle in the gaps between her fingers. They made her sit back in the chair and Fred and Wood attempted to carry her indoors in it. They could not manoeuvre it through the door and in the end Fred lifted her and carried her upstairs to her bed. She could see their distress and fear, but could not share in it. The bleeding had ceased. She felt instead a consuming thirst. She asked repeatedly for water, which they assured her they would bring in just a minute. She kept apologising to Fred for the blood on his shirt.

The doctor was sent for and, when he had examined Emma, remained for some time with the Consul in his office. On the following day the Consul sent for Tom Wood and told him with tears in his eyes that Emma's only hope of survival was to receive immediate medical attention of a kind not available in Tripoli. Dickson had told him that both at the quarantine station in Leghorn and later in the more salubrious air of Pisa she would find nuns skilled in the nursing of consumption. He himself could not take her there. Too many debtors awaited him in Europe. He begged Wood, therefore, in the name of their old friendship, in which gratitude must play some part, to marry Emma and take her at once to Leghorn and to Pisa, in both of which cities he knew Wood to have connections. He stressed that all he asked was that Emma should be taken under his protection. It would, of course, be a marriage in name only. He did not say, but by a solemn look conveyed, that the arrangement would not long be binding. Wood acquiesced with a generosity that moved the Consul profoundly.

When next he called he was permitted an hour's conversation alone with Emma in the salon. There they might murmur to one another but dared not embrace, nor laugh, nor weep, lest anyone glance in at the windows or listen at the doors.

'Look what privileges illness brings us,' she whispered to him, indicating by her level gaze that only the immediate future need be spoken of. She told him how she had suffered greatly from thirst. Was that not strange? A terrible sensation, but now it was abated. She held the little basket of fresh figs that he had brought her close to her face, breathing in their odour as if it were entirely new to her, and exclaiming with delight at the cool emanation of the fruit against her flushed cheek. 'And water, too,' she told him, 'has the most delicious scent. I might never have known that had it not been for the thirst.'

Wood ascertained from Rossini that the *Guerriero* was due in Tripoli in two weeks' time, bound thence for Malta and then Leghorn. The marriage was arranged for the early morning of its departure. One last sad task remained. On the eve of the wedding the Consul sent for Emma and told her that he thought it only proper that she should burn Laing's letters to her. Her voice was still weak and he was surprised at the force with which she cried out, 'No.' Then immediately she calmed herself and seemed to reflect.

'Best be done with them,' he told her. 'Make a new start.'

'Very well,' she said.

'Bring them now. Then you need not dwell upon it. I shall burn mine, too. Then, were I to die, they would not fall into the wrong hands.' He could not have worded it more tactfully.

'Yes,' she said. The box of writing things waited in her room beside her trunk. She selected the first letter Laing had written her, proposing that other marriage that had never been. That she wrapped in with the portrait, and, allowing herself to look at neither, returned them to the bottom of the box. The rest she gathered together and took down to her father's office.

He had a servant set a brazier on the ground outside. Into it he heaped the private correspondence between Laing and himself. The servant brought a live coal in a clay pot from the kitchen and dropped it in on top of the paper, which immediately flared up. The Consul stood back to let Emma drop her own offerings one by one into the flames. She watched without expression as they swiftly curled and altered. There was one instant when the paper went black and the ghostly writing stood out white against it, as if in a last attempt to speak out. It crumbled, then. When the fire was spent the Consul stirred about the bottom of the brazier with his stick. The remaining ashes sifted through onto the dust and blew away.

In the morning Emma, dressed in her travelling clothes, was married in the salon for a second time. It was feared that the inevitable memories the ceremony must evoke might upset her, but she maintained her composure. So that her frail strength might not be overstrained, the entire wedding party crossed the bay in barges and Emma was helped directly aboard. Many tears were shed during that short journey, but they did not fall from Emma's eyes; indeed, as the barge approached the brig, it was noticed that the brightness they had once associated with her shone again through her new serenity.

The brig would sail directly. They lingered in the rocking barges, waving and straining to make out Emma's slight figure amidst the agitated motion on the deck.

She was well swathed in shawls and had her husband's arm about her. Still, they were puzzled that she chose to endure so much noise and commotion, when she might have gone below to rest. Nor was it for the sake of one last glimpse of the coast on which most of her short life had been lived, for when at last the anchor was weighed and the sails took the wind, they could still see her on the poop deck, leaning eagerly upon the rail and staring forward at the brilliant expanse of water into which they moved, as if there were not a moment to lose; as if immediately the shadowy coast of Europe might appear before her.

Epilogue: The Well at Sahab

Only the Consul, he might tell himself, had kept faith with Laing. His vigour in pursuit of recognition for his son-in-law was undiminished. Hardly a week went by without some new report or rumour coming to his ears concerning Laing or his papers. Each informant swore on the Koran and did not leave the Consul's presence until he had signed a written version of his evidence. He was then handsomely rewarded, as he had expected to be.

During the course of that summer the Consul was approached by a kinsman of Alkadir who claimed to have travelled the same road as he, when Alkadir came up from that, and slept in the same tent. He was prepared to swear that he had seen in his possession two wrapped parcels of Laing's papers, and could bring witnesses to state that Alkadir had surrendered them to Hassuna before he left Ghadames; that Hassuna, on his return to Tripoli, had sold them to Baron Rousseau for a forty per cent reduction on a debt of six thousand francs. Confronted with such evidence the Bashaw at last agreed to take action. First Hassuna and then Rousseau were forced to flee the country for their lives.

It was a hollow triumph. In October news reached him that his beloved daughter Emma had died, six months after her marriage, among the nuns at Pisa. Thomas Wood returned to Tripoli and before another year was out the Consul consented to his marriage with his eldest daughter Jane.

The years went by. The old men spun their intrigues. Mohammed d'Ghies negotiated for his son's return from exile. The Bet-el-Mel continued to hold office, but conspired secretly with the rebels in the hinterland. In 1835 a Turkish fleet entered the harbour and deposed the Bashaw. The old man lingered on in a squalid dwelling in the back streets of the town, senile and impoverished, at the mercy of three brandy-sodden concubines. The Consul visited him once and found him in rags, babbling incoherently of things which seemed to terrify him. The room stank of incontinence. He never sought him out again.

For longer and longer periods of time Colonel Warrington withdrew to the Menchia, dividing his days between his garden and his dossiers on Laing. He had begun to make his own accurate record of these events. For a man's life, he had discovered, is entirely without substance unless he writes it down.

Late at night, with his mind rinsed clear by brandy, it seemed to the Consul, as he worked at his report, that he had known all along that Laing was doomed, that indeed, for reasons he did not care to contemplate, he had sent him to his death. Then in the morning he would read over what he had written, ponder the exact sequence of events, alter the ordering of this paragraph and that, shuffle through the mounting pile of letters and affidavits on the subject, until quite a different picture would emerge. The mistake was to suppose that there were any empty places in the world. Everywhere men cast nets of intrigue of such subtlety and complexity that brave simple souls like himself and Laing, who tried to follow the straight course of aspiration, were bound to be enmeshed by them. There was no task left to him on earth as important as the restitution of Laing's fame, and that could only be achieved by uncovering the fate of the missing journals. He would not let the matter rest. No bag was despatched to Whitehall without further pleas that the matter be taken up by government.

But the world was a different place. It no longer bred such men as Laing and himself, nor cared much what became of them. His letters on the subject met with polite rebuffs. It was made clear to Colonel Warrington that the Colonial Office considered the case closed and advised him to devote his mind to more accurate assessments of the grain returns and more equitable relations with the consular fraternity than his had lately been.

But this the Consul failed to do. When in 1846, the Neapolitan, old Croutchillo's successor, appeared before him insolently puffing a cigar he raised his cane and struck it from his lips. It was unfortunate that the nose was broken. It had not been his intention. Shortly afterwards a letter came from Whitehall demanding Colonel Warrington's retirement. He left Tripoli at last to live out the one year left to him with his daughter and Tom Wood, who now held the post of Consul at Patras.

Only Laing's murderer lived on to enjoy a serene old age in the country of his birth. He was proud of his act. He had killed a Christian and had been right to do so, for he had averted a great evil from his land. Only towards the end of his life did they begin to come again in twos and threes. The young men then seemed of a different breed to the young men of Labeida's youth. It seemed they were powerless to avert this threat or indifferent to its consequences.

But he, Labeida, had not hesitated. He had ridden in that year into the city with twenty camel loads of caked salt and his three closest kinsmen riding at his side. Then they had heard how the Christian walked openly about the town, writing it down in his book, drawing lines, taking from them the things that were theirs.

At first no one would hear him warn them of the danger. The traveller was in the protection of Mohtar. Besides, although he was a heathen, he had undoubtedly some power over the forces of evil to have endured what he had and still survive. And he was brave. But then, when it was known that he had ridden out by night to view the great river and spoken to no one of his intentions, others had come to realise with Labeida that these intentions must be evil, and agreed that he must die.

For though he was a brave man, there was something lacking in him; some power to reach out to other men and touch their hearts and ask assistance of them. He did not smile nor laugh, nor easily sit to eat with other men. So it was that when his time of trial came, he was alone except for one slave.

Young Mohtar might have saved that traveller, but he had turned his back upon Mohtar and determined to head for the source of the great river. What other purpose might he have had in doing so other than to poison it, or, as some preferred to think, to drink it dry at its weak source? So he, Labeida, had agreed to put him to death.

The traveller rode out alone. Labeida followed him and camped on the first night where he could see his fire but stay unobserved by him. The next night, too. He watched the fire and the two dark figures crouched beside it. The traveller had no tent. He slept on the ground with his slave beside him. In the morning he rode on. Labeida followed. They came, he remembered, to a shallow depression in the land which some call Sahab. He and the kinsmen halted their camels before the rim of it, so that they would not appear to him on the skyline. They lay on the sand and watched him move across the desert with his slave, towards a solitary tree.

There they dismounted. The Christian leant his back against it, as if to rest, and Labeida knew the hour had come. He and the kinsmen mounted and rode forward. They saw the Christian rise, as if alarmed. Then, as they rode closer, he had recognised Labeida and raised his left arm stiffly in salute. He had been a brave man. When Labeida and his kinsmen rode towards him shouting that he must relinquish his fate or die, he had stood his ground without flinching although neither he nor the youth who attended him bore arms. His face, Labeida remembered, had been cruelly disfigured by the swords of the Ahaggar Tuareg, but his final stance as they bore down on him had in its utter fearlessness assumed a beauty that abashed them. For a moment they halted.

Then, remembering rumours of his magic powers, Labeida had called, with all the more ferocity, for his kinsmen to seize the Christian. They had dragged him back against the tree with his arms extended while he, Labeida, ran forward and thrust his spear deep into the Christian's side. Then, remembering other rumours that this man was destined not to die until he had drunk up the source of the great river, Labeida himself had turned the body downward in the sand and struck off the head. Then he had kicked it to one side so that it lay at some distance to the body. The other men had been slashing open the only goods he carried, a waterskin filled with books and papers in the heathen script. They burnt these that night on their fire in fear of the power they might contain.

There was nothing else except a leather bag attached to a thong about his neck which Labeida's sword had severed. He had picked it up and emptied its contents onto the sand: a brass key, a silver coin, a gold bird, a text from the Koran. The presence of this last persuaded him that the other items might too be of a sacred nature. He put them hastily back into the bag and later threaded it onto a fresh thong and wore it around his own neck with a collection of other Koranic texts and amulets. Of all his talismen he attached particular significance to this last. It continued to fret at his mind that there must be a connection between these items which the Christian had had power to perceive but he had not.

Sometimes at night, when he sat with his close kinsmen around the fire, he would spread a smooth space in the sand with the palm of his hand and spill the contents out for them to see. Then they watched with awe while the old man arranged them this way and that. As he grew older he devised long rambling tales of a locked castle in the desert guarded by demons and filled with all the gold and silver that the Christians had stolen from the Mussulmen. Another was of a great bird that issued from the spring of a river and could never be captured; never destroyed. But always it seemed that his imagination had fallen short of some truth. He grew tired and querulous. Although they begged him to continue, he picked up the recalcitrant objects one by one and put them back into their bag until he next would lay them out in a different order and make a new attempt at it.

THE END

Author's Note

This novel is based on the collection of letters between Colonel Warrington and Alexander Laing edited by E. W. Bovill for the Hakluyt Society (*Missions to the Niger I*, Cambridge University Press, 1964). Where possible the actual wording of these letters is used, but in most cases the letters in the novel are invented or altered in part.

Not That Sort of Girl
Mary Wesley

'Rose, don't leave me. Promise never to leave me,' said Ned on their wedding night, revealing an unexpected chink in his perfect armour of wealth, good looks, and country estate. Rose promised.

Before the wedding, Mylo had said, 'In bed, with Ned, you will wonder whether this curious act of sex would not, with Mylo, turn into something sublime – When I send for you urgently to come and meet me – just come.'

For the whole of Rose's respectable married life, she had kept faith with both men. To Ned she was a perfect wife, mother of his son and elegant hostess of Slepe. To Milo, Rose was an impetuous and unconventional mistress, answering his erratic and impassioned calls throughout fifty years of tactful duplicity.

After Ned's funeral Rose looks back on a life of dual constancy, passion, humour, and the ambiguities of love – and chooses her future.

'A WITTY AND CHARMING LOVE STORY AMONG THE MIDDLE CLASSES WITH SURPRISING TWISTS. ONE OF THE THINGS THAT I LOVE ABOUT MARY WESLEY IS THAT SHE HAS REACHED AN AGE WHEN SHE CAN SAY DANGEROUS OR NAUGHTY THINGS WITHOUT SHOCKING.'
PHILIP HOWARD – THE TIMES

0 552 99304 2

BLACK SWAN

A Raging Calm
Stan Barstow

Set in a thriving, recognisable urban city, A RAGING
CALM is a story of conflicting passions, of loyalty and
betrayal, and of the agony of an illicit love affair.

'Stan Barstow is one of the very best of our regional
novelists and A RAGING CALM is a fine example of his
work. It is humane and it is perceptive. It never fakes
feeling in the interests of drama, yet it remains
dramatically alive. Deeply felt and skilfully told, the novel
will certainly enhance Mr. Barstow's already high
reputation'.
EVENING STANDARD

0 552 99193 7

BLACK SWAN

A SELECTED LIST OF
OTHER BLACK SWAN TITLES